LONGLISTED *for the*

Center for Fiction's First Novel Prize

A MOST ANTICIPATED BOOK:

Entertainment Weekly, O, The Oprah Magazine, Time,
Glamour, Vogue, BuzzFeed, ABC News, *Bustle,*
LitHub, Newsday, The Millions, Town & Country,
Refinery29, Shondaland, and *CrimeReads*

"The modern story of clashing cultures and classes
already reads like *Crazy Rich Asians* meets Donna Tartt's
The Secret History meets 'Paul's Case,' Willa Cather's classic story of
a desperate middle-class climb. But *White Ivy*, the propulsive debut
novel by Susie Yang, is more than plot twists and love triangles.
It's also an astute chronicle of cultures, gender dynamics and the
complicated business of self-creation in America."

—SAN FRANCISCO CHRONICLE

"Yang's dark, spellbinding debut gives insight into the immigrant experience and life in the upper class, challenging the stereotypes and perceptions associated with both. The surprising twists, elegant prose, and complex characters in this coming-of-age story make this a captivating read."
—BOOKLIST (starred review)

"Susie Yang delves into class warfare and deceit in the season's biggest debut."
—ENTERTAINMENT WEEKLY

"There's nothing better than a novel with an unpredictable plot. And *White Ivy*, Susie Yang's debut novel…is exactly that."
—USA TODAY (4 out of 4 stars)

"What begins as a story of a young woman's struggles to assimilate quickly becomes a much darker tale of love, lies, and obsession, in which there are no boundaries to finding the fulfillment of one's own dreams. Yang's skill in creating surprising, even shocking plot twists will leave readers breathless."
—LIBRARY JOURNAL (starred review)

"Yang's dark, spellbinding debut gives insight into the immigrant experience and life in the upper class, challenging the stereotypes and perceptions associated with both. The surprising twists, elegant prose, and complex characters in this coming-of-age story make this a captivating read."

—*Booklist* (starred review)

"In Ivy, Yang has created an ambitious and sharp yet believably flawed heroine who will win over any reader, and the accomplished plot is layered and full of revelations. This is a beguiling and shattering coming-of-age story."

—*Publishers Weekly*

"The intelligent, yearning, broken, and deeply insecure Ivy will enthrall readers, and Yang's beautifully written novel ably mines the complexities of class and privilege. A sophisticated and darkly glittering gem of a debut."

—*Kirkus Reviews*

"Electrifying . . . Part immigrant story, part elitist takedown, part contemporary novel of wicked manners, *White Ivy* is an unpredictable spectacle. . . . Ivy Lin proves to be the antihero readers will love to hate in debut novelist Susie Yang's assured, deft, biting novel of (manipulative) manners."

—*Shelf Awareness* (starred review)

"Yang takes a character who is a confessed thief from the first page, and etches her with qualities that turn her into a complex, layered, and unpredictable character."

—*Chicago Review of Books*

"It's a testament to Susie Yang's skill that she can explore and upend our ideas of class, race, family, and identity while moving us through a plot that twists in such wonderful ways. But none of that would matter nearly as much if not for the truly unforgettable narrator, Ivy, who is so hypnotic, the way her voice feels both wild and controlled. She ran right through me."

—Kevin Wilson, *New York Times* bestselling author of *Nothing to See Here*

"*White Ivy* is dark and delicious. Ivy Lin eviscerates the model minority stereotype with a smile on her lips and a boot on your neck. Cancel your weekend plans, because you won't be able to take your eyes off Ivy Lin."

—Lucy Tan, author of *What We Were Promised*

"*White Ivy* is magic and a necessary corrective both to the stereotypes and the pieties that too easily characterize the immigrant experience. Most pleasing of all is the story of Ivy Lin, a daring young woman in search of herself, and not soon to be forgotten."

—Joshua Ferris, prize-winning author of *To Rise Again at a Decent Hour*

"Elegant and terrifying, steely and sparkling, *White Ivy* is a propulsive story told with the satisfying simplicity of a classic."

—Rebecca Dinerstein Knight, author of *Hex*

"Bold, daring, and sexy, *White Ivy* is the immigrant story we've been dying to hear. Rather than submit to love, Ivy seeks it out, sinks her teeth into it, and doesn't let go. A stunning debut."

—Neel Patel, author of *If You See Me, Don't Say Hi*

WHITE IVY

A NOVEL

SUSIE YANG

SIMON & SCHUSTER PAPERBACKS

NEW YORK   LONDON   TORONTO   SYDNEY   NEW DELHI

Simon & Schuster Paperbacks
An Imprint of Simon & Schuster, Inc.
1230 Avenue of the Americas
New York, NY 10020

First Simon & Schuster trade paperback edition July 2021

SIMON & SCHUSTER PAPERBACKS and colophon are registered trademarks of Simon & Schuster, Inc.

For information about special discounts for bulk purchases, please contact Simon & Schuster Special Sales at 1-866-506-1949 or business@simonandschuster.com.

The Simon & Schuster Speakers Bureau can bring authors to your live event. For more information or to book an event contact the Simon & Schuster Speakers Bureau at 1-866-248-3049 or visit our website at www.simonspeakers.com.

Interior design by Carly Loman

Endpaper illustration by Shutterstock

Manufactured in the United States of America

10   9   8   7   6   5   4   3   2   1

Library of Congress Cataloging-in-Publication Data
Names: Yang, Susie, author.
Title: White ivy : a novel / Susie Yang.
Description: First Simon & Schuster hardcover edition. |
New York : Simon & Schuster, 2020. |
Identifiers: LCCN 2020002254 | ISBN 9781982100599 (hardback) |
ISBN 9781982100612 (ebook)
Subjects: GSAFD: Love stories.
Classification: LCC PS3625.A6779 W48 2020 | DDC 813/.6—dc23
LC record available at https://lccn.loc.gov/2020002254

ISBN 978-1-9821-0059-9
ISBN 978-1-9821-0060-5 (pbk)
ISBN 978-1-9821-0061-2 (ebook)

For Alex, in every life

The snow goose need not bathe to make itself white.

CHINESE PROVERB

PART ONE

I

Ivy Lin was a thief but you would never know it to look at her. Maybe that was the problem. No one ever suspected—and that made her reckless. Her features were so average and nondescript that the brain only needed a split second to develop a complete understanding of her: skinny Asian girl, quiet, overly docile around adults in uniforms. She had a way of walking, shoulders forward, chin tucked under, arms barely swinging, that rendered her invisible in the way of pigeons and janitors.

Ivy would have traded her face a thousand times over for a blue-eyed, blond-haired version like the Satterfield twins, or even a red-headed, freckly version like Liza Johnson, instead of her own Chinese one with its too-thin lips, embarrassingly high forehead, two fleshy cheeks like ripe apples before the autumn pickings. Because of those cheeks, at fourteen years old, she was often mistaken for an elementary school student—an unfortunate hindrance in everything except thieving, in which her childlike looks were a useful camouflage.

Ivy's only source of vanity was her eyes. They were pleasingly round, symmetrically situated, cocoa brown in color, with crescent corners dipped in like the ends of a stuffed dumpling. Her grandmother had trimmed her lashes when she was a baby to "stimulate growth," and it seemed to have worked, for now she was blessed with a flurry of thick, black lashes that other girls could only achieve with copious layers of mascara, and not even then. By any standard, she had nice eyes—but especially for a Chinese girl—and they saved her from an otherwise plain face.

So how exactly had this unassuming, big-eyed girl come to thieving? In the same way water trickles into even the tiniest cracks between boulders, her personality had formed into crooked shapes around the hard structure of her Chinese upbringing.

When Ivy was two years old, her parents immigrated to the United States and left her in the care of her maternal grandmother, Meifeng, in their hometown of Chongqing. Of her next three years in China, she remembered very little except one vivid memory of pressing her face into the scratchy fibers of her grandmother's coat, shouting, "You tricked me! You tricked me!" after she realized Meifeng had abandoned her to the care of a neighbor to take an extra clerical shift. Even then, Ivy had none of the undiscerning friendliness of other children; her love was passionate but singular, complete devotion or none at all.

When Ivy turned five, Nan and Shen Lin had finally saved enough money to send for their daughter. "You'll go and live in a wonderful state in America," Meifeng told her, "called *Ma-sa-zhu-sai*." She'd seen the photographs her parents mailed home, pastoral scenes of ponds, square lawns, blue skies, trees that only bloomed vibrant pink and fuchsia flowers, which her pale-cheeked mother, whom she could no longer remember, was always holding by thin branches that resembled the sticks of sugared plums Ivy ate on New Year's. All this caused much excitement for the journey—she adored taking trips with her grandmother—but at the last minute, after handing Ivy off to a smartly dressed flight attendant with fascinating gold buttons on her vest, Meifeng disappeared into the airport crowd.

Ivy threw up on the airplane and cried nearly the entire flight. Upon landing at Logan Airport, she howled as the flight attendant pushed her toward two Asian strangers waiting at the gate with a screaming baby no larger than the daikon radishes she used to help Meifeng pull out of their soil, crusty smears all over his clenched white fists. Ivy dragged her feet, tripped over a shoelace, and landed on her knees.

"Stand up now," said the man, offering his hand. The woman continued to rock the baby. She addressed her husband in a weary tone. "Where are her suitcases?"

Ivy wiped her face and took the man's hand. She had already intuited that tears would have no place with these brick-faced people, so different from the gregarious aunties in China who'd coax her with a fresh box of chalk or White Rabbit taffies should she display the slightest sign of displeasure.

This became Ivy's earliest memory of her family: Shen Lin's hard, calloused fingers over her own, his particular scent of tobacco and minty toothpaste; the clear winter light flitting in through the floor-to-ceiling windows beyond which airplanes were taking off and landing; her brother, Austin, no more than a little sack in smelly diapers in Nan's arms. Walking among them but not one of them, Ivy felt a queer, dissociative sensation, not unlike being submerged in a bathtub, where everything felt both expansive and compressed. In years to come, whenever she felt like crying, she would invoke this feeling of being submerged, and the tears would dissipate across her eyes in a thin glistening film, disappearing into the bathwater.

NAN AND SHEN'S child-rearing discipline was heavy on the corporal punishment but light on the chores. This meant that while Ivy never had to make a bed, she did develop a high tolerance for pain. As with many immigrant parents, the only real wish Nan and Shen had for their daughter was that she become a doctor. All Ivy had to do was claim "I want to be a doctor!" to see her parents' faces light up with approval, which was akin to love, and just as scarce to come by.

Meifeng had been an affectionate if brusque caretaker, but Nan was not this way. The only times Ivy felt the warmth of her mother's arms were when company came over. Usually, it was Nan's younger sister, Ping, and her husband, or one of Shen's Chinese coworkers at the small IT company he worked for. During those festive Saturday afternoons, munching on sunflower seeds and lychees, Nan's down-turned mouth would right itself like a sail catching wind, and she would transform into a kinder, more relaxed mother, one without the little pinch between her brows. Ivy would wait all afternoon for this moment to scoot close to her mother on the sofa . . . closer . . . closer . . . and then, with the barest of movements, she'd slide into Nan's lap.

Sometimes, Nan would put her hands around Ivy's waist. Other times, she'd pet her head in an absent, fitful way, as if she wasn't aware of doing it. Ivy would try to stay as still as possible. It was a frightful, stolen pleasure, but how she craved the touch of a bosom, a fleshy lap to rest on. She'd always thought she was being exceedingly clever, that her mother hadn't a clue what was going on. But when she was six years old, she did the same maneuver, only this time, Nan's body stiffened. "Aren't you a little old for this now?"

Ivy froze. The adults around her chuckled. "Look how *ni-ah* your daughter is," they exclaimed. *Ni-ah* was Sichuan dialect for *clingy*. Ivy forced her eyes open as wide as they would go. It was no use. She could taste the salt on her lips.

"Look at you," Nan chastised. "They're just teasing! I can't believe how thin-skinned you are. You're an older sister now, you should be braver. Now be good and *ting hua*. Go wipe your nose."

To her dying day, Ivy would remember this feeling: shame, con-fusion, hurt, defiance, and a terrible loneliness that turned her per-manently inward, so that when Meifeng later told her she had been a trusting and affectionate baby, she thought her grandmother was confusing her with Austin.

IVY BECAME A secretive child, sharing her inner life with no one, ex-cept on occasion, Austin, whose approval, unlike everyone else's in the family, came unconditionally. Suffice it to say, neither of Ivy's parents provided any resources for her fanciful imagination—what kind of life would she have, what kind of love and excitement awaited her in her future? These finer details Ivy filled in with books.

She learned English easily—indeed, she could not remember a time she had *not* understood English—and became a precocious reader. The tiny, unkempt West Maplebury Library, staffed by a half-deaf librarian, was Nan's version of free babysitting. It was Ivy's favorite place in the whole world. She was drawn to books with bleak circumstances: orphans, star-crossed lovers, captives of lecherous uncles and evil stepmothers, the anorexic cheerleader, the lonely misfit. In every story, she saw herself. All these heroines had one thing in common, which was that they were beautiful. It seemed to Ivy that outward beauty was the fountain from which all other desirable traits sprung: intelligence, courage, willpower, purity of heart.

She cruised through elementary school, neither at the top of her class nor the bottom, neither popular nor unpopular, but it wasn't until she transferred to Grove Preparatory Day School in sixth grade—her father was hired as the computer technician there, which meant her tuition was free—that she found the central object of her aspirational life: a certain type of clean-cut, all-American boy, hitherto unknown to her; the type of boy who attended Sunday school and plucked daisies for his mother on Mother's Day. His name was Gideon Speyer.

Ivy soon grasped the colossal miracle it would take for a boy like Gideon to notice her. He was friendly toward her, they'd even exchanged phone numbers once, for a project in American Lit, but the other Grove girls who swarmed around Gideon wore brown penny loafers with white cotton knee socks while Ivy was clothed in old-fashioned black stockings and Nan's clunky rubber-soled lace-ups. She tried to emulate her classmates' dress and behaviors as best she could with her limited resources: she pulled her hair back with a headband sewn from an old silk scarf, tossed green pennies onto the ivy-covered statue of St. Mark in the courtyard, ate her low-fat yogurt and Skittles under the poplar trees in the springtime—still she could not fit in.

How could she ever get what she wanted from life when she was shy, poor, and homely?

Her parents' mantra: The harder you work, the luckier you are.

Her teachers' mantra: Treat others the way you want to be treated.

The only person who taught her any practical skills was Meifeng. Ivy's beloved grandmother finally received her US green card when Ivy turned seven. Two years of childhood is a decade of adulthood. Ivy still loved Meifeng, but the love had become the abstract kind, born of nostalgic memories, tear-soaked pillows, and yearning. Ivy found this flesh-and-blood Meifeng intimidating, brisk, and loud, too loud. Having forgotten much of her Chinese vocabulary, Ivy was slow and fumbling when answering her grandmother's incessant questions; when she wasn't at the library, she was curled up on the couch like a snail, reading cross-eyed.

Meifeng saw that she had no time to lose. She felt it her duty to instill in her granddaughter the two qualities necessary for survival: self-reliance and opportunism.

Back in China, this had meant fixing the books at her job as a clerk for a well-to-do merchant who sold leather gloves and shoes. The merchant swindled his customers by upcharging every item, even the fake leather products; his customers made up the difference with counterfeit money and sleight of hand. Even the merchant's wife pilfered money from his cash register to give to her own parents and siblings. And it was Meifeng who jotted down all these numbers, adding four-digit figures in her head as quick as any calculator, a penny or two going into her own paycheck with each transaction.

Once in Massachusetts, unable to find work yet stewing with enterprising restlessness, Meifeng applied the same skills she had previously used as a clerk toward saving money. She began shoplifting, price swapping, and requesting discounts on items for self-inflicted defects. She would hide multiple items in a single package and only pay for one.

The first time Meifeng recruited Ivy for one of these tasks was at the local Goodwill, the cheapest discount store in town. Ivy had been combing through a wooden chest of costume jewelry and flower brooches when her grandmother called her over using her pet name, Baobao, and handed her a wool sweater that smelled of mothballs. "Help me get this sticker off," said Meifeng. "Don't rip it now." She gave Ivy a look that said, *You'd better do it properly or else.*

Ivy stuck her nail under the corner of the white $2.99 sticker. She pushed the label up with minuscule movements until she had enough of an edge to grab between her thumb and index finger. Then, ever so slowly, she peeled off the sticker, careful not to leave any leftover gunk on the label. After Ivy handed the sticker over, Meifeng stuck it on an ugly yellow T-shirt. Ivy repeated the same process for the $0.25 sticker on the T-shirt label. She placed this new sticker onto the price tag for the sweater, smoothing the corners down flat and clean.

Meifeng was pleased. Ivy knew because her grandmother's face was pulled back in a half grimace, the only smile she ever wore. "I'll buy you a donut on the way home," said Meifeng.

Ivy whooped and began spinning in circles in celebration. In her excitement, she knocked over a stand of scarves. Quick as lightning, Meifeng grabbed one of the scarves and stuffed it up her left sleeve. "Hide one in your jacket—any one. Quickly!"

Ivy snatched up a rose-patterned scarf (the same one she would cut up and sew into a headband years later) and bunched it into a ball inside her pocket. "Is this for me?"

"Keep it out of sight," said Meifeng, towing Ivy by the arm toward the register, a shiny quarter ready, to pay for the woolen sweater. "Let this be your first lesson: give with one hand and take with the other. No one will be watching both."

THE GOODWILL CLOSED down a year later, but by then, Meifeng had discovered something even better than Goodwill—an event Americans called a yard sale, which Meifeng came to recognize by the hand-painted cardboard signs attached to the neighborhood trees. Each weekend, Meifeng scoured the sidewalks for these hand-painted signs, dragging her grandchildren to white-picket-fenced homes with American flags fluttering from the windows and lawns lined with crabapple trees. Meifeng bargained in broken English, holding up arthritic fingers to display numbers, all the while loudly protesting "Cheaper, cheaper," until the owners, too discomfited to argue, nodded their agreement. Then she'd reach into her pants and pull out coins and crumpled bills from a cloth pouch, attached by a cord to her underwear.

Other yard sale items, more valuable than the rest, Meifeng simply handed to Ivy to hide in her pink nylon backpack. Silverware. Belts. A Timex watch that still ticked. No one paid any attention to the children running around the yard, and if after they left the owner discovered that one or two items had gone unaccounted for, he simply attributed it to his worsening memory.

Walking home by the creek after one of these excursions, Meifeng informed Ivy that Americans were all stupid. "They're too lazy to even keep track of their own belongings. They don't *ai shi* their things. Nothing is valuable to them." She placed a hand on Ivy's head. "Remember this, Baobao: when winds of change blow, some build walls. Others build windmills."

Ivy repeated the phrase. *I'm a windmill*, she thought, picturing herself swinging through open skies, a balmy breeze over her gleaming mechanical arms.

Austin nosed his way between the two women. "Can I have some candy?"

"What'd you do with that lollipop your sister gave you?" Meifeng barked. "Dropped it again?"

And Austin, remembering his loss, scrunched up his face and cried.

IVY KNEW HER brother hated these weekends with their grandmother. At five years old, Austin had none of the astute restraint his sister had had at his age. He would howl at the top of his lungs and bang his

chubby fists on the ground until Meifeng placated him with promises to buy a toy—"a *dollar* toy?"—or a trip to McDonald's, something
typically reserved for special occasions. Meifeng would never have
tolerated such a display from Ivy, but everyone in the Lin household
indulged Austin, the younger child, and a boy at that. Ivy wished she
had been born a boy. Never did she wish this more fervently than
at twelve years old, the morning she awoke to find her underwear
streaked with a matte, rust-like color. Womanhood was every bit as
inconvenient as she'd feared. Nan did not own makeup or skincare
products. She cut her own hair and washed her face every morning
with water and a plain washcloth. One week a month, she wore a
cloth pad—reinforced with paper towels on the days her flow was
heaviest—which she rinsed each night in the sink and hung out to dry
on the balcony. But American women had different needs: disposable
pads, tampons, bras, razors, tweezers. It was unthinkable for Ivy to
ask for these things. The idea of removing one's leg or underarm hair
for aesthetic reasons would have instilled in her mother a horror akin
to slicing one's skin open. In this respect, Nan and Meifeng were of
one mind. Ivy knew she could only rely on herself to obtain these
items. That was when she graduated from yard sales to the two big-
box stores in town: Kmart and T.J.Maxx.

Her first conquests: tampons, lip gloss, a box of Valentine's Day
cards, a bag of disposable razors. Later, when she became bolder: rubber sandals, a sports bra, mascara, an aquamarine mood ring, and her
most prized theft yet—a leather-bound diary with a gold clasp lock.
These contrabands she hid in the nooks and crannies of her dresser,
away from puritan eyes. At night, Ivy would sneak out her diary and
copy beautiful phrases from her novels—*For things seen pass away, but
the things that are unseen are eternal*—and throughout those last two
years of middle school, she wrote love letters to Gideon Speyer: *I had
a vivid dream this morning, it was so passionate I woke up with an ache . . .
I held your face in my hands and trembled . . . if only I wasn't so scared of
getting close to you . . . if only you weren't so perfect in every way . . .*

And so Ivy grew like a wayward branch. Planted to the same root as her family but reaching for something beyond their grasp. Years of reconciling her grandmother's teachings with her American values had somehow culminated in a confused but firm belief that in order to become the "good," *ting hua* girl everyone asked of her, she had to use "smart" methods. But she never admitted how much she enjoyed these methods. She never got too greedy. She never got sloppy. And most important, she never got caught. It comforted her to think that even if she were accused of wrongdoing someday, it would be her accuser's word against hers—and if there was anything she prided herself on other than being a thief, it was being a first-rate liar.

2

Outside of Meifeng, only the neighborhood boy, Roux Roman, knew about Ivy's thieving. He was seventeen years old and built like a telephone pole, with black hair and gray-blue eyes always narrowed in contempt at all the idiots around him: the noisy Hispanic boys loitering on the stoops (fart-knockers), the disabled folks collecting food stamps (lazy leeches), his useless teachers at school who taught that the world was a just meritocracy, and most of all, his own husbandless mother, who was widely known by everyone to be a whore, though no one dared use this word within Roux's earshot.

They had met four years earlier, when Ivy had caught him breaking into Ernesto Moretti's backyard shed. The Morettis vacationed every summer by the Cape, an event Ernesto bragged about for months beforehand, and the Morettis' shiny red sedan was already gone from the driveway when Ivy came across Roux unscrewing the nails from the corners of the heavy black padlock on the wooden door. Instead of minding her own business as Meifeng had always instructed her to do (*the straightest tree is the first to be cut down*), she'd called out, "What are you doing?"

Roux cursed when he saw her, but he didn't deny that he'd been caught red-handed. She immediately liked that about him. She had long been fascinated by Roux Roman, having sensed a kindred enterprising spirit beneath his rough exterior. He was always going around the block trying to earn dimes and quarters for bringing up your groceries or shoveling your car out of the snow—though he never attempted to shovel the Lins' old Ford, having enough sense to recognize a lost cause. Indeed, his eyes turned defiant and he even smirked a little as if to say, *What does it look like I'm doing?*

Ivy considered tossing the word *police* around but no one in Fox Hill, the Lins included, trusted the authorities to solve their problems. "I can keep a lookout for you," she said.

Roux's black eyebrows rose to his hairline. "Who are you again?"

She told him her name. "We're neighbors," she added.

"Stand over there and let me know if any cars come."

Ivy sat in the grass and pretended to work on her Baby-Sitters Club scrapbook she'd brought with her, having planned to go "camping" that afternoon in the dense woods behind the Morettis' house. Her eyes diligently scanned the winding street for cars that never appeared. Five minutes later, Roux emerged from the shed hauling the wheels of Ernesto's bike—"for revenge," he said, but when she asked him what Ernesto had done to him, Roux wouldn't tell her. She watched as he reinstalled the padlock, wiped away his fingerprints (she'd been impressed by this detail—he appeared quite the deft criminal), and then, before she could react, he snatched her scrapbook from her hands and flipped through the worn pages. He looked at her with ridicule and a little pity. "Gee, you sure are a creepy kid." In between all the glossy magazine cutout girls, labeled with the names of the Baby-Sitters Club: Kristy, Stacey, Mary Anne, Dawn, Mallory—Ivy had replaced the only Asian character, a Japanese girl named Claudia Kishi, with a photo of herself in her favorite blue dress with the lacy sleeves and sash as wide as her palms.

"It's a joke," she said.

"Sure," said Roux. "And I'm Santa Claus."

Ivy never got around to "camping" that day. She and Roux spent the rest of the afternoon at the dilapidated Fox Hill playground with its plastic slide and rusty swing set, feeding her picnic lunch of baloney in potato bread to the pigeons. Through an unspoken agreement, they met every day for the rest of the summer. The park. The library. 7-Eleven. The creek. The Fox Hill playground where they spent many torpid hours gorging on blackberries straight from the bushes that toppled over the chain-link fence. One afternoon, Roux showed her his shabby spiral-bound notebook of ink drawings of houses with propellers, bicycles floating on soap bubbles, cars growing enormous black wings, like those of a bat. It was his way of opening up to her, Ivy knew. In return, she lent him her favorite library books and even copied a Sylvia Plath poem she liked on pink stationery paper she found tucked in one of her neighbor's magazines, presenting it to him with a magnanimous air. Give with one hand and take with the other. But of her mother's moods, of her family's Chinese ways, of her shop-lifting, she kept quiet for now. Knowledge, like money, was foolish to give away for free. You could never get it back.

THE FOLLOWING SUMMER, Ivy discovered another one of Roux's secrets. While she was purchasing her usual five pounds of baloney at the Morettis' deli for her and Austin's school lunches, she accidentally dropped a quarter in the soda aisle and followed it down the hallway to a lacquered red door, slightly ajar, with a brass handle. There were people inside. She heard urgent whispers followed by a gasp, then a man's low growl. Mistaking the sounds for ones of pain, she peeked through the crack. In front of a heavy black desk, she saw Roux's mother kneeling in front of Ernesto's father. Mrs. Roman's bony arms were wrapped around his portly midsection, her cheek pressed against his thigh.

Ivy thought they were engaged in a struggle at first—they were rearing and gripping and grunting the way she'd once seen two Chinese oxen butt horns over a brittle shrub—but then she realized the sounds were of rapture. Mr. Moretti's belly was tan and curved, there was a line of black hair running down the brown skin, like a path of trees on a mountain, and when he writhed, the trees all waved in the gentle breeze. She must have watched them for minutes, beset with a mix of fear and furtive curiosity that kept her rooted in place. Mrs. Roman finished whatever she was doing. Mr. Moretti made a low groan. He looked up and stared straight at Ivy. Slowly, without moving his head, he reached down and tapped Roux's mother on her cheek, almost a slap, but Ivy didn't see what happened next because she had turned and fled.

Outside, Roux was smoking a cigarette, still wearing his swim trunks from where they'd spent an afternoon by the creek. He'd refused to go inside the deli with her, claiming it was filled with vipers. When she burst through the door, wild with agitation, she grabbed his arm and tried to tow him away with cries of "Let's go! Come on!" but it was too late. Seconds later, Mrs. Roman came hurrying out the door, smoothing down her dark hair. Two deep slashes gathered around the inner edges of her eyes, creasing away from the nose in an expression of perpetual exhaustion. She said something in rapid Romanian. Roux looked at his mother. He looked at Ivy. He threw his cigarette on the pavement and squashed it with his heel. "Let's go." His tone was flat, his face impassive. Mrs. Roman continued to shout at Roux even after they'd turned the corner. Ivy thought how strange it was that even though Mrs. Roman spoke Romanian and Nan Chinese, how similar they sounded when shouting, like a flock of angry ravens, the consonants clipped and hardened by anger. Maybe anger was the only universal language.

On the walk back to Fox Hill, Roux was utterly silent. Ivy felt dirtied by what she'd seen but a part of her was also slightly thrilled, it stirred something in her stomach, like a soft sigh. She looked down at her hand, still clutching the plastic bottle dripping with cold condensation. "Oh! I forgot to pay for my Mountain Dew!"

"*That's* what you're worried about?" said Roux finally, in disgust.

Ivy opened her mouth to say—what? That she felt his shame as her own? That their mothers sounded like angry ravens? Instead, she found herself telling him about the thieving.

Roux's reaction was one of delight. "I *knew* you were hiding something. I *knew* I was right about you."

"Okay but—"

"And your *grandmother*?"

"She only—"

"But *which* houses?"

Ivy tried to explain that it wasn't truly stealing, they were only taking small objects Americans themselves didn't value. Roux didn't care. He was already looking at her with a new respect in his eyes—and something else, insistent and hungry. She noted the dimple on his right cheek, like a comma on an unmarked page, and she wondered why he didn't spend any effort to clean himself up. Certainly, he could be cute if he tried even a little. Wear the right clothes, get a haircut, smile at a few girls, and *bam*—transformation. It would be so easy for him to disguise himself as any other all-American boy, and yet he made no effort to do so, whereas she, who took such pains with her clothes and mannerisms, would always have yellow skin and black hair and a squat nose, her exterior self hiding the truth that she was American! American! American!—the injustice of it stung deeply.

"THAT RUSSIAN BOY is no good," Nan said one day, out of the blue.

Ivy knew immediately who Nan was referring to. "He's Romanian," she said.

"That boy is stupid. How can he be anything else without a father? And what does his mother do for him? Nothing. I see her coming home in the mornings with her hair pulled up in that ridiculous way. Where does she go all night long, leaving her son alone at home? There are only two types of people who stay out all night: burglars and bad women. You stay away from him, you hear me?"

Ivy jabbed at her rice.

"And they're poor," Nan added in afterthought. "They live here."

"So do we."

"We're different," Nan said sharply. "Baba has a master's degree."

Ivy pointed out that Roux's father could have a PhD for all they knew.

"Stop talking nonsense. Go help Grandma with dinner. I have to study." Every hour Nan wasn't bagging groceries at the Hong Kong grocery store on Route 9, she was poring over her tiny blue Chinese-English dictionary in a self-organized curriculum only she understood. Ivy once remarked facetiously at dinner that if Nan bagged groceries at an American supermarket, maybe she would learn English faster. It was the first and only time her father slapped her—on the back of the head, without a word, forceful enough to make Ivy's ears ache for hours afterward.

That fall, Shen started his new job as the computer technician at Grove Preparatory Academy and Ivy was transferred to her new school. Her parents did not say it was because of Roux, but of course, Ivy knew it was.

"What are you *wearing*?" Roux crowed the first time he saw her in her uniform, so fresh out of the shrink wrap everything still smelled of plastic. "Is that a clip-on tie?" He reached for her neck—he was always snatching whatever he wanted from her—and Ivy couldn't jerk away fast enough to avoid his greasy fingers, which had been shoveling down a slice of Giovanni's pizza moments ago, from soiling her pristine white collar.

"Look what you did!" she yelled, but he only sneered in his usual condescending way. She licked her thumb and dabbed at the stain. "It's Grove Academy's uniform," she snapped, knowing instinctively this would hurt him. "I go there now. Over in Andover."

"Your family win the lottery?"

"I tested in," she lied, "on scholarship." She'd read plenty of novels about scholarship students at fancy boarding schools conquering the social chasm through a mixture of grit, charm, and beauty (most of all beauty), to find love among the heather and horse stables. Up to then, she had been perfectly content imagining herself at the local public school, like every other kid in Fox Hill. Now it was beneath her.

She tried her best to avoid Roux after that, sensing the growing divide between them, but he who was so astute at sniffing out her embarrassment was surprisingly dense when it came to her intentions toward him, mistaking her reticence for timidity. He didn't get the point until the day he'd asked her, for the fifth time, to hang out with his "boys"—the same boys he'd once called fart-knockers—and Ivy finally exploded.

"I would never hang out with *those people*."

"Aw, they're not that scary."

"They're poor trash." Nan's words. How far Ivy had already come.

All color drained from Roux's face except for the ears, which turned a scalded pink. She could see the film of sweat over his upper lip where the faint shadow of a mustache was starting to grow.

"When'd you become such a stuck-up bitch?"

"When'd you become a total loser?"

He raised one hand—Ivy instinctively shielded herself—but he was only reaching into his back pocket. He threw something at her, yellow and small, it hit her squarely on the chest and bounced to her feet. She picked it up. It was an old photo of herself in a threadbare blue dress, clearly one of Meifeng's yard sale finds, with a cheap costume-like sheen over the balloon skirt. She couldn't fathom where Roux had gotten the photo until she turned it around and saw the dry patches of glue—and then she remembered her old scrapbook, the magazine cutouts, the first time she'd discovered the empty gap between Stacey and Kristy, where she assumed her own picture had somehow come loose and was lost.

WITHOUT ROUX, IVY had no friends whatsoever. She was lonely but what she craved wasn't friendship. Girls and boys "hung out" at school but real progress was made outside of school, at parties, and Ivy was never invited to any parties. She'd learned (in theory) the mechanics of popular games like suck and blow, spin the bottle, seven minutes in heaven, apple biting, wink, the classic truth or dare, and other acts that were not games but real life. In the girls' locker room, she heard Liza Johnson tell the story of when Tom Cross had unzipped his fly and guided her hand to his crotch—"while my dad was driving in the *front seat*," Liza said with fake horror. Ivy wondered if Gideon did such things as well. He and Tom were best friends; they did everything together. Ivy wondered what she would do if Gideon were to grab her hand and guide it to the mysterious, slightly grotesque manhood underneath his shorts, or lean over and kiss her with tongue the way Henry Fitzgerald kissed Nikki Satterfield in her cheerleader uniform at the last pep rally, one pom-pom dangling from Nikki's hand like a shower of blue-and-white confetti. But Ivy had never even held a guy's hand, let alone kissed one, and the only time she ever felt desirable was when she looked at the photo of herself in her childish blue-sheen dress (why had Roux kept it all this time?) and then a restless longing would throb throughout her entire body, keeping her tossing into the night, waking with bruised tender eyes, so that Meifeng would feel her forehead in the morning for fever.

Then one morning, two weeks into summer break, Gideon Speyer telephoned and invited her to a small gathering to celebrate his fourteenth birthday—"just a sleepover with friends"—and amidst all of Ivy's stammers and high-pitched giggling, she somehow managed to choke out that she'd be there. Afterward, she stormed to the bedroom she shared with Meifeng ("Where are you running off to now?") and stuffed her face underneath her pillow until her mouth was full of cotton, muffling the screams of panicked happiness. That night, she wrote in her diary: *Everything will be different now.*

But there was the problem of getting permission from Nan. Ivy told her mother she was invited to spend the night at her classmate Una Kim's house. She even used the line she reserved for emergencies: *If you're not going to let me make friends, then why even send me to this rich-people school?* It was sheer luck that Una lived three blocks down from Gideon in the new homes over in Andover. Nan's expression had been a scowl, she didn't say yes or no—a bad sign as Nan's thoughts typically turned more paranoid over time.

In preparation for the party (Ivy had determined she would sneak out of the house if it came down to it, Meifeng was a sound sleeper), she pierced her ears with a sewing needle, having stolen a pair of dangly heart earrings earlier that week and hidden them underneath the pile of underwear in the bottommost drawer of her dresser. It was hard to get the earring hook exactly straight through her new earhole and she winced with pain as she dug the metal this way and that, trying to find the outlet in her flesh on the other side. When she finally got both earrings on, her earlobes were hot and tender to the touch. She was delighted.

Unfortunately for Ivy, the lock to the bathroom door had come loose that very afternoon and Nan walked into the bathroom in the midst of Ivy's vanities, sewing needle in hand, making a kissing face in the mirror. Nan went berserk. She slapped Ivy across the face, once, twice, then tried to pull the earrings straight out of Ivy's newly pierced earlobes—which then caused Meifeng to come running and start hitting Nan with the fly swatter, screaming: *You'll rip her ears off! You'll rip her ears off!* The fight lasted for what felt like an eternity, a frightened Austin and stoic Shen, used to these displays, taking cover in the bedroom.

Since then, Nan had said no more about the pierced ears and had been, in fact, more lenient toward her daughter in the following four days. That was the Chinese way: corporal punishment followed by an excess of kindness. Nan hit Shen all the time and then made his favorite soup afterward and fussed over his health. When pushed too far, Shen also hit Nan, then promised to quit smoking. Meifeng never hit Ivy but she hit Austin almost every day, telling him it was for his own good, he should be thankful she made the effort to discipline him, her grandson, as those poor American kids with lazy grandparents grew into hooligans, unspanked and unloved. Then she'd bring him to a Mc-

Donald's for a Happy Meal. In the Lin household, you were rewarded for being punished. Thus, Ivy was allowed to attend the sleepover.

SHE WENT TO Kmart to "pick up" a birthday present for Gideon. She would have preferred to go to the big mall in East Maplebury, but that would have required asking Shen to drive her and asking him for money, and then she'd have to explain what she was buying for "Una." Instead, she loitered around the electronics aisle at Kmart, watching the employee behind the counter flip the pages of *People* magazine; five shoppers walked by and the woman didn't look up once. Reassured, Ivy walked over and picked up the pair of marine binoculars she'd been eyeing. The little attached booklet stated that they were waterproof, fog-proof, and shock-protected with rubber armoring; the optics featured multicoated lenses for excellent light transmission. It was the perfect thing for a boy who loved to sail, who kept photos of boats taped in his locker and read *Yachting World* the way other boys read *Playboy*. Just as she made up her mind to stuff them into her backpack, she saw Roux. The surprise and recognition was mutual. They hadn't spoken since the photo incident, almost a year ago. She saw that he was wearing a red employee polo, with a white name tag clipped to his breast pocket, and like all uniforms, it suppressed his individuality while also seeming to reveal his truest, most essential self.

He walked over in a loping, unhurried way. "Whatcha got there?"

"I was trying to see what that woman was reading." Ivy pantomimed holding up the binoculars like a spy, then placed it back onto the shelf with artful indifference.

Roux's face took on a faint, ironic smirk. "I work here now—in case you haven't noticed—so you can't swipe things from here."

"Reeelaaax. I'm just looking." She turned on her heel and walked out of the store, disappointment choking the back of her throat like undercooked rice.

She was back at Kmart again the next morning at nine o'clock sharp.

"Just looking again?"

Ivy jumped. There he was, in the same tacky red polo, like a persistent, noiseless shadow. It was bizarre how quickly he'd located her. The problem was that she'd been caught in the same aisle, holding the same binoculars. Sure enough, a moment later, Roux said, "Why do you want those anyway?"

"Are you following me?"

"Of course I am. You're a shoplifter."

"They're not for me. They're a birthday present for my friend."

Roux took the binoculars and checked the price tag—$38.99. A fortune. He handed them back to her. "Some friend."

Ivy walked in the general direction of the exit, her heart pounding, one hand still casually clasped over the binoculars. Did she have enough nerve to simply walk out and count on Roux's goodwill toward her, or should she put the binoculars down near the magazine stand, as if she'd changed her mind about buying them? She made eye contact with the cashier. "I'm not ready," she said haughtily. The old man shot her a look: *Too expensive, eh.*

A hand reached out past Ivy's shoulders, holding two crumpled twenties. She turned around.

"What is this?"

"Money," Roux said snidely, "for your *friend's* present."

"Is this a loan?" Debt, in the Lin family, was akin to slavery.

Roux's scowl deepened. "You don't have to pay me back."

Ivy was dumbfounded. Outside of Nan, Roux was the cheapest person she knew; she'd seen him forage his own trash can for expired Hot Pockets even Mrs. Roman had deemed inedible, and not a nickel on the sidewalk escaped his sharp eyes.

Roux waved the bills in front of her face. "You going to take it or not?" When she still didn't move, he said, "Jesus, don't take it then—"

Ivy snatched the bills and handed them to the old cashier, who'd seen the entire exchange.

"Girly, it's your lucky day. Or maybe every day is a lucky day for you. Say, how old are you anyhow? You look about the same age as my granddaughter, and she's still learning to multiply."

You little piggish man, Ivy thought, staring steadily into the beady eyes. You've probably lived here your entire life. You'll die here, in your Kmart uniform, and on your gravestone it'll say, *Here lies a lucky man.*

"What's so funny?" said Roux.

Ivy's grin deepened. "I didn't know you could be so nice." Meifeng always said that a tiger doesn't give a rabbit carrots from the goodness of his heart, but as the cashier wrapped up the binoculars, it occurred to Ivy that paying for something in the open with money that wasn't hers was even better than taking something for free in secret—a lesson not even Meifeng would have had the audacity to teach her.

Roux rolled his eyes and said he had to get back to work. But she saw he was pleased by her compliment—the pink of his ears gave him away.

3

SHEN DROPPED HER OFF IN FRONT OF UNA KIM'S HOUSE AND IVY watched until his car had pulled out of the development before she made her way over to Gideon's. The Speyers' house was a handsome glass and stone manor on a wide cul-de-sac, accompanied by the pleasing electric buzzing of cicadas.

Gideon opened the door. Ivy felt an explosion of pleasure like fireworks. He was wearing a maroon-colored T-shirt that hugged actual biceps where four weeks ago there had only been skin and bone. Gone was his neatly clipped crew cut; feathery hair now spilled over his temples, covering the upper curves of his ears.

"Happy birthday," she said, her voice low and breathy.

"You look different."

"Different how?" *Yes! Yes! Yes!*

"I don't think I've ever seen you outside school." Gideon had one tooth a little crooked and higher than the others and when he smiled, it gave him a mischievous air, although he was not a mischievous person. He took the present she thrust at him with sheepish surprise. "You didn't have to bring anything."

Embarrassment crawled up her face like a rash.

Gideon said they were hanging out in the basement and ushered her inside, even offering to carry her backpack, already so cultivated, so *trained*, at fourteen. She took off her shoes—"Keep them on," he said in the same sheepish tone—and then she followed him across a hallway lit with electric torch lamps, the stiff fibers of the leopard-print rug crunching beneath her toes. "What's that room?" She pointed, unable to resist looking this way and that, trying to imprint into her memories all the details of Gideon's house to thumb over later in the privacy of her room.

"That's the study." Seeing her eager gaze, he showed her the study, the living room, the kitchen, the heavy grandfather clock in the family room that looked like a glass eye following their every movement.

Her own apartment in Fox Hill, she'd always thought of as a place where she ate and slept, a place that belonged to no one, not her, not her family. But Gideon clearly did not share this viewpoint of his house. All the rooms, the furniture, the such-and-such knickknacks they'd bought on various vacations, were "mine" or "ours"; he had ownership over everything. Ownership, Ivy noticed, had a very specific sound. You could hear its authoritative quality in a person's voice, in Gideon's evenly paced sentences and clear enunciations. During their poetry recitations last marking period, Mr. Markle, who was also the debate coach, had lavished praises on Gideon for his oratory skills, and Gideon had explained in front of the entire class that he used to stutter and had been enrolled in speech therapy for ten years. "Why, everyone should enroll!" Mr. Markle had joked, and while everyone else had laughed, Ivy had been astounded because she couldn't fathom that something as easy as talking would require effort and diligence on Gideon's part, the same kind of effort Nan exerted into her little blue dictionary. She'd assumed everything about Gideon was innate and effortless. Did that mean that ownership, then, was something that could be learned?

In the foyer, they ran into Gideon's older sister, Sylvia Speyer, a senior at Grove, on her way upstairs, balancing a tray containing a pint of Häagen-Dazs, a Starbucks coffee, and a little tumbler filled with ice and yellowish liquid.

"Where'd you find the cabinet key?" said Gideon.

"In Ted's penholder. Want some?"

"No."

Sylvia caught Ivy staring—Ivy looked away, pretending to examine a photo along the staircase of the siblings in their swimsuits, curled up in lawn chairs, laughing toward a setting sun.

"That's Finn Oaks," said Sylvia, following Ivy's gaze.

"What's that?"

"Our summer cottage in Cattahasset."

Summer cottage, Ivy added to her repertoire.

"Have you been there yet?"

"No," said Ivy. She couldn't look at Sylvia straight on, the loveliness was too blinding.

"Well, Giddy's always bringing his friends in the summers."

This hinted-at invitation, so carelessly tossed, sent Ivy's heart racing with a longing so acute she felt dizzy. "I'm Ivy," she whispered.

"Like the plant," said Sylvia.

"Dad knows about the penholder, Sib," said Gideon, "so you should put it back soon.

Sylvia rolled her eyes. "Puh-leease. He has a six a.m. flight tomorrow. He won't notice a thing." She floated upstairs with soundless footsteps, a pristine maid doll in her pressed black skirt and servant tray. Her perfume lingered in the air: something tangy, like lemons, and the ocean.

No one acknowledged Ivy when she descended into the basement, at least not overtly, only in side glances and cool smiles. This was a sign of welcome. To fuss over her would have been to state that she didn't belong. Gideon showed Ivy the area with the sleeping bags and told her she could leave her things there. Tom Cross snatched the gift bag from Gideon's hands—"What's this?"—and proceeded to read Ivy's card in a long, drawn-out tone—*I hope we have some classes together next year, Gideon* . . . Tom was a performer: chestnut curls, so many freckles he looked as if he had a year-round tan; he always had an audience. When he was done, he tossed the binoculars in the pile of pillows. "Doesn't your dad have something like this?"

"Yeah, but I don't," said Gideon.

"Where's my birthday present?" Tom asked Ivy.

"When's your birthday?"

Tom's eyes widened. "She speaks!"

Only Una Kim looked furious to see Ivy. They had actually been sort-of-friends once: two Asian loners, Ivy the quiet and poor, Una the rich and chubby. Then Una went to Korea the summer before seventh grade and came back fifteen pounds lighter, with permed hair, contacts, and a higher nasal bridge. She had lost no time in casting Ivy away, the feckless barnacle, by tattling to Liza Johnson that Ivy had called her "a dumb cow" (untrue) who "couldn't pronounce words longer than five letters" (true). The most infuriating part of this entire thing was that Ivy had been contemplating casting *Una* off, had even planned where she would sit at lunch instead (at the fountain, reading books with a sophisticated air of mystery), but Una had beaten her to the punch. From this experience Ivy had learned a critical lesson: timing was everything.

Liza and the twins left the boys and came over to Ivy. Una reluctantly followed. They sat in a circle. Violet Satterfield offered to crimp Ivy's hair. Ivy saw that, indeed, the other girls' hair was all in various states of aggressive squiggles, as if they'd been electrocuted. "Okay," she said gamely. Now was surely when Violet would torch her hair on fire, or shear her head bald. She hid the slight trembling in her lips by blowing bubbles with her stale gum.

Violet returned with the crimper. She snapped at Una to scoot over. Una said, "You scoot over," but she did as she was told, angling her body to the left until she was slightly outside the circle. Una, Ivy saw, was not wearing a bra underneath her dress. The imprints of her nipples rose up through the thin cotton fabric, the size of quarters. Henry Fitzgerald and Blake Whitney tried to find out if Una was ticklish and they took turns squeezing her ribs, mesmerized by her voluptuous breasts, bouncing like water balloons.

"What's that monkey called," Liza asked no one in particular. "The one with the pink face?"

"A baboon?" suggested Henry.

"That's the one! Una looks like a great big bouncing baboon." In that moment, with her translucent skin flushed pink with shame, Una really did. That was when Ivy realized why Liza and the twins were being so nice to her: they were punishing Una for her breasts. This discovery filled Ivy with hope. It was the oldest law in physics: the system itself can never change, it can only be rearranged.

AFTER WASHING HER hands with the Speyers' mint-scented hand soap, Ivy took her time tousling her hair, fixing her shirt, squeezing her cheeks so they appeared more flushed. Idly, she opened the mirror cabinet and inspected the contents: Advil, cotton balls, extra hand soap embedded with exfoliating suds. In the back corner, she noticed a half-empty bottle of a French perfume. She spritzed some on her neck, her wrists. Deeper in the cabinet, she pushed aside a box of Band-Aids to discover an old hair tie, threads of silvery gold hair knotted around the black elastic. Ivy slid it over her wrist. "Hey, Gideon," she whispered, attempting Sylvia's ethereal gaze. She closed the cabinet door and went back downstairs.

At nine o'clock, Gideon's parents came down with four boxes of pizza, freshly baked chocolate chip cookies, and two tubs of vanilla ice cream. You can know everything about a person by looking at his family, and Ivy felt as if she had discovered the key to Gideon's makeup: in his youthful mom with her cropped khaki trousers and green sleeveless blouse that revealed two luminous, white arms; his dad, a Massachusetts state senator, who was dignified and trim and knew all of Gideon's friends by name—"I don't think we've met yet," he said, enveloping Ivy's hand in a hearty handshake. At her look of glowing adoration, he added that she was welcome at their house anytime.

Around one o'clock in the morning, Gideon dimmed the lights and put *The Hackridge Murders* on the video player. Ivy waited until he picked his spot on the sofa before hurrying to seat herself next to him. The world outside of that sofa evaporated entirely. She was only conscious of Gideon's breath, the small shifts in his body, the soft kaleidoscope of light flickering over his upturned face. During a particularly gruesome murder scene, she made a show of covering her ears, purposely knocking into his elbow. He said "whoops" and reached his arm over the back edge of the sofa. If she leaned her head back, the hair on his forearm would graze the back of her neck. "Do you like the movie so far?" she whispered, closing the gap between their heads, close enough to smell the popcorn on his breath. "It's kind of predictable," he whispered back.

The movie plodded onward—dark woods, abandoned sheds, blood dripping out of the bathtub. Liza, Una, and the twins took enormous pleasure in clutching at the guys in the room each time the man with the chain saw appeared. Ivy didn't dare clutch at Gideon, but she imperceptibly shifted her weight toward him, until the sides of their knees met. A hot current shot through her entire body. In response, Gideon pressed his leg against hers, warm and heavy, touching thigh to ankle. This was it! The moment she'd been fantasizing about for three years. She kept her eyes glued to the screen, wanting to remain casual and not embarrass him by looking over. Once in a while, she felt his leg twitch slightly and press back into hers, as if reminding her of its presence. She returned the pressure to show she understood. Like this, they remained conjoined for the last hour of the movie.

When the credits rolled onto the screen, Ivy, red-faced, peeked over at Gideon, wondering what she would say. Her jaw dropped. Gideon's head was tilted back on the sofa; his eyes were closed, his mouth slightly open. He was fast asleep.

NAN WAS AN anxious woman. A light sleeper, prone to insomnia. Her two obsessions were money and her family's health. All night, she'd been tormented by fears of Ivy licking germs off dirty chopsticks, fed stomachache-inducing ice cream, shivering with cold under too-thin blankets in an overly air-conditioned house. It would have shocked Ivy to know that she'd inherited her overactive imagination from her mother.

Nan shook her husband awake just as the sun was rising. "I think you should go pick her up early from that Korean girl's house. I bet she didn't sleep at all. We shouldn't have let her go."

She forced Shen to call the Kims' house—they had Mrs. Kim's number from one orchestra concert in seventh grade so they could follow up about buying a violin for Ivy (they never did). On the phone, Shen's face was bewildered at first, then anxious, then grim. When he hung up, he informed Nan that the Korean woman said Ivy hadn't been at her house last night. Una went to a sleepover, probably Ivy was there as well. "She gave me the boy's address," said Shen.

"*A boy?*" Nan's heart went weak with fright. "That dog-shit daughter of yours. Get up! We have to go right now! Get up, you useless bastard. What if something happened to her? What if it's *too late?*"

"Too late for what?" said Shen.

MR. SPEYER WAS ladling pancake batter into the sizzling pan when the doorbell rang. Sitting at the Speyers' sunlit kitchen table, Ivy listened to talk about the next Red Sox game. When Gideon asked if she could make it, her face hurt from smiling so widely. She hadn't stopped smiling all night. She'd probably been grinning like a fool in her sleep. Before she could respond, Sylvia Speyer, who had gone to answer the door, came back to the kitchen and announced in a dubious tone, "These people say they're here looking for their daughter?"

Ivy turned around in her chair. In an instant, she realized it was all over.

Mr. Speyer did a double take. But, like Gideon, gallantry was such an ingrained habit that even caught unawares, he managed a polite hello. As his gaze took in all four Lins—Nan, Shen, Meifeng, Austin—he clucked, "Goodness, are you all here to fetch Ivy?"

Ivy jumped to her feet, every cell in her body exploding in panic. She opened her mouth but caught herself in time. She couldn't speak Chinese in front of so many witnesses.

"Go get your things," said Nan in her native dialect, her eyes rapidly roving over Ivy's bare legs, the thin strap of her pajama top falling off her shoulder, the unkempt hair. Ivy watched, mesmerized, as her mother's nostrils flared out like door flaps each time she inhaled.

"Now!"

In the ensuing silence, Austin said in a tentative tone that he was hungry. It was what he said at home to defuse the anger toward Ivy. "Can I have some pancakes?" he asked, louder this time. Meifeng gripped his hand. Mr. Speyer suggested that they all wait for Ivy in the living room.

Ivy went to the basement, gathered her things, came back upstairs. She heard her classmates whispering about her in the kitchen—*her mom is batshit crazy*—*like, four doses of Prozac*—*old lady smells like onions . . . seen her dad before, he works at our school*—*NO! Yes! So that's how she got in*—*Shhhhh*—*psycho . . .* She heard Gideon's voice among the others: "I kind of feel sorry for her." Then Tom's wild laugh: "That's why she follows you around, Gideon. She thinks you might actually be into her. You're so cuuute and niiiccce . . ."

Ivy backed away. Her heart made queer palpitations. Her mouth was very dry.

In the living room, the baffling nightmare continued. There was Austin sitting cross-legged on the rug, his face pink with joy, eating the pancakes Mr. Speyer had served him on the coffee table. The rest of the Lins were sitting side by side on the cognac leather sofa, their backs as straight as reeds. When they saw her, they stood as one. Shen gripped Ivy by the forearm, leading her to the front door.

"Let's go, Austin," Nan said sharply.

"But I'm not finished eating!"

"One—two—*thr*—"

Austin came running, tears welling.

"Thanks for coming, Ivy," said Gideon, hovering at the door.

"Bye, kiddo," said Mr. Speyer. "Hope we'll see you back here soon."

Ivy couldn't look at either father or son. This isn't real, she thought. I'm in the bathtub world. Indeed, everything about that walk to her father's car had that languorous underwater quality: the sprinkler's metronomic ticks, the bright emerald grass beneath her flip-flops, the smell of honeysuckle that would permeate her dreams for years to come.

The second they arrived home and the front door closed, Meifeng tried to block Nan's arm from its attempt to seize Ivy's ear—"Go. Hurry up. *Go*"—but this method backfired as Nan, unable to reach Ivy directly herself, picked up an orange from the fruit bowl and threw it at her daughter's retreating figure. Ivy turned at the wrong second and the orange smacked her in the middle of the forehead. Something cold trickled down her nose. She thought at first it was blood but when she felt her skin and then looked at her fingers, she saw that the liquid was clear. The orange had split open.

"I'M GOING TO teach you a lesson," said Nan.

Ivy braced herself. She felt a whoosh of air as her mother strode down the hallway to Ivy and Meifeng's room and pushed the door open. In a flash, Ivy understood. "No! Don't!" She ran in front of Nan and attempted to barricade herself in front of her dresser. But Nan pushed her aside and pulled open all the drawers, flinging out clothes in heaping armfuls. She reached her hand and withdrew a black Walkman, the worn headphones still plugged into the jack. She spun around toward Meifeng. "Did you buy her this?"

Loyally, Meifeng hung her head, complicit liar, complicit thief. "Yes."

Nan plunged her hand back in. Her movements quickened. A two-piece bikini. Black pantyhose. Ripped denim shorts. Silver rings. A pencil case filled with smudged, half-used makeup. Three overdue library books. A stack of cassette tapes. The spaghetti strap dress Ivy had been saving for some future school dance caught on the corner of the dresser as it was tossed down, splayed out in midair as if impaled at the heart.

"I always knew you were a sly child," panted Nan, "but I never dreamed you were hiding *this* much—" She broke off, seemingly too overcome to speak. Even Shen, slipping into the room with cautious fortitude, could not stop his wife's possessed plunder. When Nan got to the leather-bound diary, Ivy was jolted out of her mesmerized state by her mother's insect-like fingers scrabbling at the cover.

"Stop it! That's private!" She lunged forward and attempted to swipe the diary away from Nan's hands, feeling the tear of soft flesh underneath her fingernails as she pulled back, empty-handed.

"Look what you've done!" Shen shouted, grabbing Ivy by her upper arm. "You—never—talk—back—to your mother!"

Through the haze of rage, Ivy could barely make out the jagged red line on her mother's skin, like an accusing finger pointed in her direction.

Nan turned and left the room. Moments later, she returned with a large trash bag. Ivy noticed, with both trepidation and relief, that her diary was not inside. Nan paced around the room, picking things up off the floor and bed and placing them into the bag in a methodical and orderly fashion.

"Nan?" Shen said cautiously after a while.

"Don't just stand there, help me. Bring this bag to the dumpster. Take Austin with you."

Shen did as he was told.

"Did any boy—touch you last night?" said Nan.

"No," said Ivy.

"She's a child," said Meifeng.

"She's a harlot," said Nan.

"It was just a party," said Ivy.

"I don't believe that even *you* would buy her all this disgusting junk.

Which means she's been buying this stuff on her own. I *told you* to stop giving her money."

"She'll be in high school," said Meifeng. "She should have her own allowance, learn to budget. It would help her mature."

Nan snorted. *"Mature?* You've raised a girl who's vain and frivolous. She lies to us about everything . . ."

Ivy squeezed her eyes shut and clamped the back of her throat and eardrums to stimulate the sensation of yawning, a trick she used often to tune out Nan's shrill screams. But it was hard to sustain this almost-yawn for long and each time she unclenched her temples, she once again heard Nan's accusations boomerang across the silent room: —*parades around half-naked at that American boy's house, in front of his parents!—She idolizes them—She hates us* . . . Nan finished scraping the last drawer clean, wiped her eyes, walked out into the living room.

Meifeng, never one for letting someone else get the last word, followed after Nan, shouting insults at her back: *Oh, NOW you want to take charge? . . . You were too poor to raise your own children . . . look at you now, so stupid you can't learn English . . . Bah! With what money? . . . It's no wonder she doesn't listen to you, she doesn't respect you . . .*

"I didn't *do* anything," Ivy whispered to an empty room. What sin had she committed that was so deplorable to be deserving of this punishment? Not a single superfluous item had been spared from the monstrous trash bag into which her mother had deposited her entire life. She'd once accused Roux and his friends of being poor trash. See who was the trash now. She had nothing. She *was* nothing. Except—

She did have one thing. One more precious thing.

SHE COULD FEEL the pull of it: destruction. A delightful feeling, like the anticipation before eating a large, delicious meal. She'd thought her crush on Gideon was an absolute secret, but Tom had known. Tom said she followed Gideon around. Did she? Did everyone at Grove see her as the Gideon follower? And Gideon said he felt sorry for her . . .

had he only invited her to his party out of pity? . . . pity, which was a thousand times worse than hate.

Ivy leaned back against the wall. Her head ached from where the orange had hit her. She could hear the angry cawing of Meifeng and Nan in the living room, still fighting over her as if she were a precious carcass only one of them got to eat, a cacophony that would never end, this soundtrack to her life. Then it went quiet. Ivy's mind, too, went quiet. The pain of her injustices evaporated in the stimulating rush of a reckless plan. The world wasn't fair. Punishments rained from nowhere, sins were rewarded. Timing was everything.

She went to the closet and dug out an old baseball cap, tugging it low on her forehead to hide the bruise. Then she went outside to the living room. Nan was scrubbing the burnt parts of the stove. Meifeng was sitting in her chair, knitting a sweater. The air was so dank you could open your mouth and taste its poisonous residue. Ivy asked if she could go to the library.

"Come back before dinner," said Meifeng, her eyes darting toward Nan, waiting to be contradicted. But Nan didn't even look up.

Ivy tied her shoelaces. Still nothing. The silent treatment, then. A new low. Outside, she turned right and headed toward the building at the edge of Fox Hill. The Romans' unit was situated on the ground floor with windows just slightly above eye level. The shutters were closed. She squeezed through the clearing between two bushes and rapped on a dusty pane. No one stirred. She rapped harder. The shutters rose. Roux had apparently been sleeping. He was wearing only his plaid boxers, an imprint of a pillow on one cheek. He pushed up the window and asked in an irritated tone what she wanted.

Ivy studied him with detached curiosity. The deep slashes beneath the seafoam eyes, the dimple, so rarely spotted. He felt her watching him. A flicker of surprise, followed by a twitch along the jaw. A flicker, a twitch. That was all it took for him to grasp the hinted-at intentions of a girl's blazing face.

He stepped aside. "You gonna come in or what?"

* * *

SHE HOISTED HERSELF through the dusty windowsill. There was no-where to sit in the room. All the surfaces were piled either with paper or drawings and pencils. She pushed aside the crumpled gray-colored sheet and sank into the mattress's creaky depths. It smelled earthy and lush, like a jungle, or unwashed hair.

"Is your mom home?" she asked.

"She has an overnight shift." That same ironic smirk. "Why?"

Ivy shrugged. Nan's voice echoed in her mind: *There are only two types of people who stay out all night: burglars and bad women.* She felt the briefest flash of pity for Roux, followed quickly by disgust. Hurriedly, she tried to focus on his nice parts: his eyes, the smooth skin of his hands.

"I got into a fight with my mom," she said. "They found out about the party and towed me away in front of all my . . ." She could not bear to say *friends.* "Anyway, everyone hates me."

"Your mom does not hate you."

"Not her. The others. The people at the party. They were saying things—they . . . I . . ."

Roux got up from the chair and sat down next to her. She felt his hand, tenuous, on her back. "Jesus. Sorry. Who cares what they say anyway? Rich pricks are the nastiest pricks."

Ivy turned and pressed her face somewhere between his shoulder and chest. She hadn't cried in front of her classmates when they were whispering about her family, and she hadn't cried when her parents dragged her from Gideon's house, but it was a relief to cry now in front of Roux, the only person she could go to at a time like this. This thought made her cry harder.

Roux handed her a tissue. She pulled back to wipe her face and blow her nose. His arm was still around her shoulders. She looked up through the haze of wet lashes. The pale blue flecks among the gray of Roux's eyes looked like the scales of a fish. She leaned in abruptly.

"Ow."

"Sorry." She removed her hat. He was the one to lean in this time. Their lips missed. Roux was absolutely still. Embarrassment? Aversion? She almost retreated, unsure. But a moment later, he was guiding her face with one hand until their lips met in earnest. The intimacy was excruciating: the sucking and smacking, the heavy breathing, the tiny beads of sweat clinging to the hairs on Roux's upper lip. His eyes, like hers, were wide open. She was surprised by the look of utter tenderness in them. They broke apart for air.

"You're beautiful," said Roux.

That word cut Ivy's heart into pieces in a way she had never known. "Again," she said.

Roux tilted her chin up . . . again . . . again . . . again . . . Each kiss and caress filled the bucket inside her with little scoops of courage. When the bucket was full, Ivy reached down, hand steady, and loosened the drawstring of her terry-cloth shorts.

THERE WERE FEW things Ivy could imagine more lowly, more *sordid* (her least favorite adjective) than losing your virginity to spite your mother. But then to guard the knowledge afterward from this mother, from everyone, as if guarding your life—what had been the point then? She couldn't explain it herself. It was a private war.

She disliked that it had been Roux, she would have preferred Gideon obviously, but even a stranger would have been a better choice: clean, no awkwardness, a onetime mistake you could erase. But in the end, it didn't matter. All she remembered from the event itself was the intense pressure, as if someone were trying to plug up a hole in her she hadn't known existed, and the feeling of sweaty skin on skin, a sharp whip of pain. The health teacher said that in such moments there might be blood, but she hadn't bled. Even this proof of innocence had been denied her.

Afterward, Roux asked if she'd done this before.

"Yes," she lied.

"With who?"

"Someone from school." Before he could press her, she said, "What about you?"

"You're the proud owner of my V-card."

"Liar."

"Seriously." He pulled out a pack of Camel Blues from his desk drawer and lit up beside the window.

"Can I have one?" she asked.

He handed her the pack without speaking. She pulled out a cigarette, lit it, and held it between her index and middle finger as she'd seen her father do. She inhaled. Almost immediately she was seized with vertigo and had to lean back on Roux's crumpled gray pillows as the room spun and spun . . .

"What happened to your head, anyway?" Roux asked. "It's turning a nasty puke color."

"I walked into a pole."

Their eyes met. His gaze was full of knowing. She hated him in that moment. He looked away. "You hungry? There are Hot Pockets in the fridge. I have vodka, too. I'll mix it with some Tropicana. You'll like it."

That's when Ivy heard it—the unmistakable sound of ownership.

Why was it that in Gideon's voice, it had such an admirable, dignified quality, but in Roux's, it sounded dirty, like something unearned? But this wasn't fair because if anything, it was the opposite: Gideon had been born rich and cared for, he'd done nothing to earn his big house, his private education, his ten years of speech therapy; whereas Roux had a whore for a mother and a father in Romania who may or may not be dead or in jail, and a part-time job at Kmart. Gideon had done nothing to earn her love. Roux had given her forty dollars. That was how much her virginity had been worth. Forty dollars.

Ivy deposited her cigarette butt in a half-empty Dr Pepper can. The impulse for destruction had passed. She had moved on to regret.

"Where you going?" said Roux.

"Home."

"Are you going to come over later?"

"Don't know." She crawled back out the window even though she could have used the front door.

Meifeng was stir-frying meat on the wok when Ivy slipped in, the apartment smoky with the fragrance of garlic and scallions bubbling in oil.

"How was the library?" Meifeng asked.

"Fine," said Ivy. She lingered in the doorway until Meifeng glanced her way. In some perverse, repentant way, she wanted to be caught. She was sure her shrewd grandmother would see through her, she would know that her granddaughter was not the same person as before. But Meifeng only told her to wash up before dinner and to take off that ridiculous hat.

Down the hall, Ivy saw light from underneath Nan and Shen's closed door and heard their low voices but couldn't make out what they were saying over the sound of the exhaust fan. She headed directly to the bathroom.

She took her time examining herself in the mirror, thinking how lovely her lips looked all swollen like that. Then came the disgust. She slapped her reflection to prove how deplorable she felt. But upon meeting her own clear, unflinching eyes in the mirror, the disgust turned into astonishment. Goose bumps rose up her arms. She was further gone than she'd thought.

When she came out from her shower, she heard the sound of a basketball game playing on the television. Her parents had come out of their bedroom. She went to her bedroom and closed the door. Soon, she heard Austin ask Nan if Ivy had come back yet. "Leave your sister be," was Nan's response. "She's unwell."

"She looked fine to me this morning," said Austin.

"She's sick on the inside," said Nan.

Ivy beckoned her brother inside her room, pressing a finger to her lips. "Can you go to Mom's room and find something for me? I don't know where it is so you'll have to look around."

"What is it?"

She described the brown leather binding, the little gold clasp. "You've seen me writing in it—you remember."

Austin said he knew what it looked like and scampered away. Ivy lay back in her bed, waiting. It only took a few minutes. "It was on the side table," he boasted, handing her the diary. "It wasn't even hidden."

She tugged his earlobe in affection and told him to leave before their mother saw him talking to her. Alone, she looked at the diary, once her most prized belonging. Now it was only a liability.

She cut the spine open and splayed out the pages on the carpet. One by one, she shred each page into thin strips, then placed the strips into the large plastic basin Meifeng used to soak her feet in each night. She filled the basin with hot water. The pile of confetti disintegrated into a glob of gray mush, like old mashed potatoes.

She would be reborn. High school was a big place. In September, she would turn up the collar of her shirt, try out for cheerleading or lacrosse, wear her hair in a French braid with a ribbon, crisp and sweet-smelling, like autumn leaves. She would stop stealing. Also— she would never speak to Roux again. Both were not just sources of shame but liabilities, especially the latter. She would purge these memories from her mind, locked behind walls of steel, never to be reexamined. In later years, in high school and even into college, driven by heedless urges into the backseats of middle-class cars, cocooned inside tube slides in playgrounds, fucking soundlessly while her roommates pretended to sleep facing beer-splattered walls, she would tell the opposite lie of the one she'd told Roux: *It's my first time, I'm a virgin, I've never done this before*. Everyone would believe her. She had long ago realized that the truth wasn't important, it was the appearance of things that would serve her.

Muddy water, let stand, becomes clear.

PART TWO

"WE THINK IT WILL BE GOOD FOR YOU TO VISIT YOUR RELATIVES IN Chongqing," Shen said at the dinner table. It was four days after Gideon's birthday party. The bruise on Ivy's forehead had turned a pale mottled green, like a rotting lime. She clipped her bangs to the side and sat opposite her mother. She never smiled. Whenever anyone spoke to her, she would look them squarely in the eye, sit up straight in her chair, and respond in a dignified and cordial manner. She chewed her food thirty times before swallowing.

"Your aunt Hong misses you," Shen continued, "and suggested that you go visit her. You can practice your Chinese and meet your cousins. My cousin Sunrin wants to take you traveling. She's very educated, you'll like her. You can spend the rest of your summer there until school starts."

Ivy paused on bite twenty-three. A shard of panic pierced the fog of stoicism.

"I don't think that's a good idea," she said.

"Your flight's the day after tomorrow," said Nan.

"Am I going?" Austin asked.

"No."

"That's not fair!"

"You're not getting exiled," said Ivy.

"We don't have the money," said Nan.

Ivy remembered very little of her childhood in Chongqing, but from Meifeng's stories over the years, she'd developed a vivid picture of her birth country as a terrible place of Communists, farmers, little mud huts, persecution. It was what her parents always threatened when she and Austin were bad: "We're going to send you back to China," or "You wouldn't last a week in China with real Chinese kids."

On the evening before her exile, Meifeng brought her a hot towel rinsed in a basin of boiling water and dried herbs. Meifeng's solution for everything in life was a hot towel to the face and a hot water bottle to the feet.

"What's wrong with you these days?" she asked, placing the towel over Ivy's forehead.

Ivy remained silent, but she felt a twinge of savage pleasure that her grandmother had noticed something was wrong.

"Good medicine tastes bad. Stop pretending you're some tragic actress in a play. I get tired just looking at you."

Hurt rolled over Ivy in hot waves.

"Do you know how much money your parents spent on your trip? Your mother's been saving up to visit Hong for years, but she's letting you go instead. She loves you so much she'd rather hurt you to make you better, even if it means you'll hate her." Following her granddaughter's brooding gaze toward the dresser where a stack of CDs used to sit, Meifeng added, "You shouldn't have had all that junk anyway."

"It wasn't junk."

"How you got it was wrong."

"*You* do it."

"I'm an old ignorant Chinese woman close to death. What do I have to lose? You're an American citizen."

Ivy let the hot steam from the towel cover her mouth, nose, lids. She pictured the view from her art classroom at Grove, looking out at a courtyard of wheat-colored poplar trees in autumn, the quiet splash of a quarter sinking into St. Mark's fountain under the peaceful expanse of a cool blue sky.

Meifeng sighed, a movement that sent the entire bed creaking. Then she began to talk. Ivy thought it would be another one of her grandmother's nostalgic rants about China, knife fights in damp alleyways, hunger, the mouthwatering taste of a fried egg on New Year's, poverty—and in some ways it was. But it was also a story Meifeng had never before told anyone, the secret she'd kept for three decades.

FORTY-FOUR YEARS EARLIER, Nan Miao was born in the village of Xing Chang in the mountainous basin of Sichuan Province, cut through by three rivers intersecting at the mouth of the Yangtze River. It was a lush and fertile valley, with long, hot summers and damp, temperate winters. The rains began in June and stayed until the following spring, after which the fog would roll in, creating a misty beauty perfectly suited for watercolor landscapes, which many painters have tried to render Due to the high year-round humidity and a diet of mountainous vegetables cooked in vats of bubbling chili oil, the girls grew up with pearly, lustrous skin, not a blemish or dry flake to be seen. Because of this perfect complexion, the beauty of Sichuan women became famous throughout China—they were known collectively as *la mei nü,* or "spicy beauties."

Of all the pretty young creatures in Xing Chang, none could surpass Nan. She was born during a monsoon in July, the second of four daughters. When the midwife pulled her out, Meifeng's face fell with disappointment—the baby was yellow of skin and scrawny of body, none of her later beauty apparent as a child; more tragically, she was a girl. Meifeng and her husband, Yin, named her Nan, the Chinese word for *man,* in the hopes that she could provide for them in the ways a son would.

Yin raised pigs and chickens on a small patch of land; Meifeng was an underpaid clerk. They also owned an outdoor stall—no more than a glass cabinet on wheels—that sold small items like cigarettes and newspapers and packs of gum. A week after giving birth, Meifeng strapped Nan on her back in a straw basket and went back to work. No one even knew there was a baby inside.

Over the years, Meifeng and Yin had two more children, both girls, and they gave up all hope of a boy. Four daughters were more than they could afford. The Miaos lived off what they grew and sold what little remained to buy the essentials they couldn't grow, subsidized by Meifeng's pay. But there was never enough. Some child was always sick. Medicine and hospital visits emptied the stash of cash tucked under a loose bed slat. Nan gave up school to work on the farm alongside her father while her older sister found work in a factory line butchering rabbits. The younger girls were too little to work. Money and food. Food and money. These were the tenets of life.

The first time Shen Lin saw Nan, she was selling vegetables in a basket hooked in the crook of her arm, her two thick black braids swinging down her back. Shen was thirteen years old to her fifteen, and to hear him tell the story, he knew she would be his wife.

Of course, Nan didn't notice Shen at all. He was small, brown, and scrawny—no more than a child. Nan, like all the girls in her village, admired Anming Wu.

Anming was their village's homegrown treasure. His parents were teachers, but it was really Anming's grandfather who brought prominence to the Wu family—he had been a successful tailor, with women from all over Sichuan flocking to him to make their *qipaos* and other year-end celebratory frocks. Unlike the other boys in their drab gray garb, Anming always wore the latest styles copied from Shanghai. If that wasn't enough, he also had exceptional academic and athletic talents: valedictorian of their high school, class president, holder of the four-hundred-meter dash record.

During his last year in high school, he auditioned for the school play and was cast as the hero: a humble farmer who falls in love with the moon goddess, played by Nan. Anming already knew Nan by reputation, but when he saw her beauty up close—the ungodly lashes, the petallike skin with the slight flush around the cheeks—he thought he might be the right man to look after her. During the play, they fell in love, as pure and devoted to each other as the fabled characters they were portraying. Anming courted Nan, though dating between students was strictly frowned upon, and everyone felt it was a satisfactory match.

Everyone except Meifeng.

It was 1967, during Mao's return to power in China on the backs of the persecuted elite of society. With their accumulated wealth from generations of business-savvy ancestors, Anming's family had undeniable bourgeois roots. Meifeng knew that sooner or later, the Red Guards would come for the Wu family. Anming, along with all his siblings and cousins, would be sent to the countryside for years of servitude and hard labor, perhaps even death. His family's money, property, and titles would be stripped away. No matter how smart or handsome Anming was, he was born a Wu. Meifeng would not allow her daughter to be bound to such a fate.

She pulled Nan from the play (the understudy, a plain girl with a beauty mark on her chin in the shape of a star, would go on to become a famous actress) and forbade her from seeing Anming again. To make certain of it, she sent Nan to live with her aunt in the neighboring village of Neijiang. All the love letters, the hairpins, the red cloth pouch with crushed hibiscus, Meifeng found underneath Nan's bed and threw away. She paid a visit to Anming's house, where she had a shouting match with his mother, telling her to keep her no-good son away from Nan. The entire village came to watch this showdown. Anming's mother didn't stand a chance. She was a cultured woman.

Nan didn't get to say goodbye to her love. She arrived in Neijiang with a woven bag containing two cotton shirts and a pair of navy trousers—all the clothes she owned. Her aunt and mother conspired to keep her letters from ever reaching the Wu household. The following month, Anming left for Chongqing, the first person in the village to attend college. But classes never began. Before he had time to unpack his things at the dormitory, Anming was taken by the Red Guards and sent to a labor camp, where he died the following year, beaten to death by another boy for stealing his ration of sweet potato.

Nan fainted when she heard the news. When she had first been sent away to Neijiang by her mother, she bore the suffering, buoyed by the conviction that once Anming finished college, he would come back to the village. In the short time they had been together in the school play, he had promised that he would one day marry her, he could never love anyone else. Their love was just like the love between the farmer and the moon goddess—not even the heavens could keep them apart.

But then Anming had died. Since Nan's love never had time to ripen to maturity, her heart remained unfinished, frozen in time by shock and guilt. She feared Anming might not have known why she had left town so suddenly and cruelly. Probably her mother had made up a convenient lie to convince him she no longer cared, or—worse—was betrothed to another.

Frightened by Nan's rapidly deteriorating health, her aunt sent her back to Meifeng. One look at her daughter was enough to spur Meifeng on the twenty-kilometer hike to Wuling Temple in Mount Jinfo, where an old fortune-teller resided beside the temple in a wooden hut, making a living from pilgrims like Meifeng who came from afar to change their futures. Meifeng asked the fortune-teller to break the string of fate connecting Anming and Nan. Even in death, the Chinese believed, this red string could bind two spirits together. Meifeng came prepared with an old newspaper clipping announcing Anming's acceptance to Chongqing College. The fortune-teller took one look at the faded gray photo and proclaimed that Anming's hold on Nan from the other world was still strong, as Meifeng had feared. But she assured Meifeng she could break this connection once and for all—for an additional five yuan, which Meifeng dutifully pulled out from the hidden stash in her underwear.

The fortune-teller conducted a Ritual of Severing by tying a string to two rocks, one to represent each party, then she held the contraption over a burning candle until the string broke. This lasted all of two minutes—the gods were swift and decisive. Only after seeing the red thread burned all the way through and the tiny wisps of smoke rising over a colorless sky was Meifeng satisfied that her daughter had been saved. She made her way back down to the village with renewed vigor. Then she waited.

Years passed. Yin passed away in his sleep from pneumonia, as unspectacular in death as he was in life. Meifeng kept herself busy with her four daughters' schooling and jobs, all the while shouldering the household chores and what was left of the farmwork. At fifty-three years old, she still carried the eighteen kilos of rice on her shoulders and walked the three kilometers home from the rice paddies, doing the work of a woman half her age. "You'll live to enjoy one hundred," her friends exclaimed in admiration, "because you are so carefree."

What her friends didn't see were the sleepless nights when Meifeng tossed and turned in fear over the fate of her second daughter. Nan had not been accepted to college—she had fainted from anemia and exhaustion during the entrance exams—and had found a job working at a sewing factory. She still lived with Meifeng and cared for her sisters, but anyone could see she was unhappy. She had no friends or suitors, had rejected multiple offers of marriage, and spent her weekends patching old clothes by candlelight. Her beauty had waned over the years: dark circles puffed out her face; she was so thin that her wrist bones poked out like sharp stones. Meifeng cursed the fortune-teller—that old hag, that fraud, preying on the hopes of the poor—and she vowed to hike back up Mount Jinfo to give that shrew a piece of her mind. She planned the trip with the same tenacity she planned everything: she dusted her shoes, packed her lunch, got out her walking stick. But the very next day—a winter's morning, icy downpour, howling winds—a young man showed up at Meifeng's door.

"I've come to ask your permission to marry your daughter." He spoke as if they were old acquaintances.

Meifeng looked at him in confusion. "Ping?" she asked, thinking he meant her flighty third daughter who was always flirting and giggling around men twice her age.

"No—Nan."

Shen Lin, in all this time, had never forgotten about the girl with the basket and the two braids hanging down her back. When Nan had come to Neijiang to stay with her aunt, he had occasionally seen her walking down the street, head heavy with a sadness that belied a depth of character to her effervescent beauty. He followed her in the shadows, watching, longing, all the while listening to the gossip surrounding her heartbreak with a boy from her village. Shen didn't care that Nan's heart had once belonged to another. He only concerned himself with the present reality—namely, that Nan was the most desirable woman he knew and he would do anything to make her marry him.

The Lins were smart and determined in a no-nonsense way, without an ounce of the charm the Wus naturally possessed. Though they exhibited a calm, rational demeanor, a gambling streak ran through their blood. They were prone to sudden fits of irrational acts interspersed with long periods of meticulous routine. Shen had never before taken a risk or said anything superfluous, but now, he gambled his future on obtaining the woman he wanted.

To the chagrin of his parents, who had thought he would attend a large university to study medicine—one of the last prestigious but safe professions in China—Shen instead went to a local college and double-majored in English and Physics. In his last year, he took the TOEFL exam, passed with nearly perfect scores, and applied for graduate school in the United States. He didn't know a single person in America, nor anyone who had applied to school abroad, but he knew he had to be exceptional to win Nan's closed-off heart.

After receiving his acceptance letter from Suffolk University in Massachusetts, he armed himself with his new student visa and showed up that fateful winter morning at Meifeng's doorstep, asking for her second daughter's hand.

Meifeng gave herself over to a relief so strong it made her hand tremble on the wooden door frame. She knew she was a terrible mother for feeling such joy at the hope that someone was going to take Nan off her hands. Her poor, unbending Nan.

"I'm never going to marry anyone," came a quiet voice behind them.

Both she and Shen turned around to see Nan in her pajamas, hair wet from the shower, ghostlike in her paleness. Her daughter's eyes burned with such grief that Meifeng felt a vise grip around her heart she knew would follow her into the next life.

"Go away," Meifeng snapped at Shen, furious at herself for nurturing such a foolish hope. She slammed the door in his face.

He came back to the house later that week when Nan was at the factory.

"I'm going to America," he stated matter-of-factly, without arrogance. "I want to take Nan with me. In exchange, I'll sponsor your other daughters once they finish college and want to come to the US as well."

Meifeng's heart beat in her rib cage like a trapped bird. America! The land of freedom! The land of abundant food and unlimited water and working electricity and great houses with twenty rooms. She never thought her daughters would have the opportunity to see such a place. Anywhere outside of Sichuan was as theoretical to her as heaven.

"Why are you doing this?" she demanded. "You think Nan's an easy target for you? She's the only eligible woman left so she'll accept any scum? Just so you know, I won't have some penniless scoundrel take my daughter away from me."

"I love her," replied Shen, unfazed. "I've always known she would be my wife."

Meifeng scrutinized him for the usual male ploys of dramatizing lustful yearnings under the guise of love and responsibility. What she saw instead was an honest and competent man, coarse around the edges but sincere in his words.

"Nan will never agree to marry you," she said to test his resilience.

"No one is good enough for her. She won't ever love an ugly, poor man like you."

"You'll have to convince her then."

"*I* can't convince her of anything." Meifeng prepared to slam the door in his face again, even as her arms shook with longing to usher him in.

Shen held her gaze with firm insistence. "I think you can," he said.

Tears sprang to Meifeng's eyes. "She hates me," she muttered, unsure why she was spilling her innermost shame to this stranger standing at her door, with his high, knobby forehead and bulbous nose. But what could a mother do? There was no future for Nan in the village. Her older sister had married and gone away to Chongqing with her gambling drunkard of a husband. Nan's younger sisters were in high school, still with the potential to realize their dreams of college; Meifeng spent all of her time squirreling away money for their tuition and pulling favors for their future job placements. Only Nan was stuck in the in-between, unable to move forward and unable to turn back.

Meifeng closed her eyes. "Be good to her. She deserves some happiness."

"I will," said Shen. "Thank you." He had won the gamble. His hands were steady as he pulled out a pack of cigarettes and lit one on Meifeng's stoop, offering it to her. She took the cigarette from his fingers and took a long drag. Like this, they sealed the deal.

"AND SHORTLY AFTER that," Meifeng concluded, "your parents got married."

Ivy balked. "I thought Mama said she wasn't ever going to get married. What changed her mind?"

Meifeng waved her hand. "She came to her senses and realized your father was a good man. She got pregnant with you in China. They saved some money, then sent for you to join them and Austin in Massachusetts. Now your aunt Ping is living in Pennsylvania with her family because of your parents' help. And I got to see America before I died. It's what I've always told you. One successful marriage can feed three generations." Even a tragic love story, filtered through Meifeng's eyes, boiled down to food and money.

Long after her grandmother's snores filled the room, Ivy lay awake in bed haunted by the image of Anming Wu. Beautiful, aristocratic Anming Wu. Beaten to death for stealing a sweet potato. Was there a more sordid way to die?

For the first time, Ivy's soul quivered in fear of the future. Wasn't her mother proof that your first love wasn't frivolous and fleeting, and that the loss of it could destroy you, leaving behind a bitter husk of a woman who resented her husband and children because they were not the family she was supposed to have? Maybe she was destined to share Nan's fate. But didn't the fact that she had sex with Roux and had felt no guilt afterward demonstrate she was tougher than her mother, who would have killed herself, probably, from shame, and that she was in fact an immoral girl capable of great transgression through sheer impulse? Meifeng said Nan was unbending, like a brittle tree toppled over by the first strong gust, but Ivy was a windmill; she might love and lose but she would never settle for a Shen Lin with the knobby forehead and bulbous nose. Not for her an inane existence governed by Meifeng's tenets. Love would exist for its own sake, and not the sake of getting your sister and mother a United States green card.

5

THE FIRST THING THAT HIT IVY WAS THE SMELL: A DANK AIRLESS cocktail of sweat, oil, boiled cabbage, which within seconds, like sawdust, clung to her clothes and hair so that when she lifted her ponytail from the nape of her neck, it seemed the odor was reeking from her own pores. Shen's cousin Sunrin Zhao was supposed to pick her up from baggage claim. It occurred to Ivy she had no idea what Sunrin Zhao looked like. The crowd was one homogenous entity of crow-haired people scurrying like beetles among rope-wrapped suitcases, making it impossible for Ivy to distinguish any one face from another. She looked toward the line of portly men sweating profusely in their black suits, holding white placards with their visitor's name, and scanned for her Chinese name: Lin Jiyuan. Someone called out, "Ivy!"

Ivy turned. Walking toward her was a tall woman in all white: white polo, white khakis, white strappy sandals, and enormous white-framed sunglasses studded with crystals perched on a rather long nose. "You're all grown up now," she said in perfect English through bright red lips, drawn in the shape of a strawberry. With her sleek hair set in waves on the sides of her ears, she looked like one of those old Hollywood starlets Liza Johnson and the twins had taped photos of inside their lockers.

"How'd you know it was me?" Ivy asked.

"Shen sent me your photo. Also—look at you. Even the shopgirls can tell the ABCs from locals. You must be careful because they'll try to take advantage." Sunrin took off her sunglasses. Her eyes crinkled into half-crescents. "You don't look a bit like Shen though. What big eyes you have! You look like your mother when she was young."

She told Ivy to call her Sunrin, asked after Ivy's flight, the Lins' health, apologized for the terrible heat. As she talked, she led Ivy to the parking lot, where a valet pulled up in a gray Mercedes, the car's compact curves resembling a blown-up version of the toy cars Austin used to play with. The valet handed Sunrin the keys, muttering something about imported cars, to which Sunrin replied affably, "German."

Sunrin drove like a man, fast, impatient, squeezing into nonexistent lanes between dusty cars and scooters crammed four to a seat, her manicured hands on the leather steering wheel painted the plump red-orange of a grapefruit. She played a tape of folk music she said she'd bought from a street performer in Dublin during her student days. The lively sounds of the violin and flutes made Ivy think of ruddy-cheeked peasant girls in starched plaid smocks and little brown moccasins, an absurd contrast to the gray smoggy highway around them, as they passed one rickety bus after another, the windows blackened by grime like the face of a woman with mascara streaking down muddy cheeks.

"Oh, before I forget—I have a present for you." Sunrin reached into the backseat and handed Ivy a gift bag, much like the one Ivy had given Gideon on his birthday, from which Ivy pulled out a velvety pink box that felt like the skin of a peach.

"My kids love these," said Sunrin. "They're Japanese chocolates. Try one. If you like them, we can pick up some more in Hong Kong. They don't sell them on the mainland."

Ivy took off the lid. Each piece of chocolate was wrapped in pink tinfoil. She bit into one. Even the filling was pastel pink. For Valentine's Day in the seventh grade, Gideon had brought to class two dozen of Mrs. Speyer's famous strawberries-and-cream cupcakes; when Ivy had eaten hers to the base, she'd discovered a dark-chocolate truffle, warm and molten, nestled in the center. Sunrin's chocolate had the same taste. It tasted like money.

Sunrin lived in a gated neighborhood guarded by two dark-skinned men in camo jackets, polished brown boots, green army caps. As soon as the gates closed, the city's smoggy streets disappeared and silence descended like a thick blanket upon the cobbled streets and terra-cotta homes. Sunrin's husband greeted Ivy at the door with a limpid hand-shake. He was a squat, jolly man with a double chin and thin hair brushed over his forehead. The two children—a boy and a girl, four and two, both of them with Uncle Wang's pudgy limbs and Sunrin's crinkly eyes—were ushered forth to greet their American cousin. The girl hid behind her mother's legs but the boy dashed around swinging a plastic saber. The relentless blade struck the sofa, table, chairs, the plants, ending with an emphatic thrust at a helpless orchid, causing its stem to curve tragically over the rim of the vase like a fallen swan. Ivy trembled with fear for the little boy's retribution. But Sunrin only frowned and called out for the children's *ayi*, an old woman of around Meifeng's age who had just come out of the kitchen carrying a platter of boiled noodles. The *ayi* placed the noodles on the table and hurried over to bring the children upstairs. "Our Lei Lei has too much energy," said Sunrin. "He's worn out his last three nannies. And one of them was only in her forties."

"Now, now," said Uncle Wang fondly. "Don't speak about our little Lei Lei that way."

Sunrin led them to the table. Next to the platter of steaming noo-dles were the condiments: black vinegar, soy sauce, minced garlic, chopped scallion, slivers of ginger, hot pepper oil, peanut sauce, ses-ame oil, and a beige powder Uncle Wang said was MSG. As they ate, Sunrin described the two-week travel itinerary she had planned: after their historical tour of the Forbidden City and Great Wall in Beijing, they'd take it easy in Shanghai. Dine at a famous duck restaurant in Old Town, attend a jazz performance on Hengshan Road Bar Street, take in the waterfront scenery at the Bund; they'd end their trip in the international malls of Hong Kong with their European-crafted clothes and Japanese cosmetics. "Which skincare brand do you use?" Sunrin asked.

Fingering the dry patch on her cheek, Ivy said self-consciously, "I don't really use anything."

Sunrin's eyes went so perfectly circular she looked like one of those Russian nesting dolls. "But you must! A girl's most important beauty area is her skin." She began listing all the different products they would need to buy for Ivy's new skincare regimen. "We'll get the basics first, then go from there. Do you like makeup?"

Did she like makeup! What else was there to say? "I *love* makeup."

Her fairy godmother had finally arrived.

UNCLE WANG ELECTED to stay behind in Chongqing, he was the head of a Korean-Chinese investment company and was organizing a golf tournament with foreign associates. When Ivy thanked her aunt for taking time off work to host her, Sunrin laughed—she seemed to laugh at everything—and said she'd quit her job when Lei Lei had been born. The *ayi* accompanied them on the trip as well. Her job was to keep Sunrin's two children fed and entertained as Ivy and Sunrin strolled ahead down the streets of Beijing, slurping sheep's milk yogurt in glass bottles, or checking into their various historically preserved, five-star hotels. Ivy pretended that Sunrin was her mother, and they were on a mother-daughter bonding vacation, while her father, a business ty-coon, stayed at home to run his company. *Now, now*, she whispered as she brushed out her bangs in front of the vanity mirror. *Don't speak about our little Ivy that way.* She glowed in pleasure when the concierge complimented Sunrin on raising such a pretty daughter.

Sunrin was always very polite to the servicepeople, saying *please* and *thank you*, though it wasn't the normal Chinese custom to use such formalities. Despite her placidity, she managed to convey a sense of authority that made everyone from waiters to bellboys rush around in circles trying to please her. Once, when their taxi driver heard them conversing in English, he claimed his rate was double what they had agreed upon, he wasn't going to drive them to their destination, stuck in traffic no less, for pennies. Sunrin said, "Let us off here at the curb then." When he didn't oblige, mumbling under his breath about getting cheated, she said, "I mean it. Let us off." They were on a two-lane highway, somewhere in Beijing's second ring, on their way to see the Tanzhe Temple. Around them, cars whizzed by irrespective of lanes, going a hundred kilometers an hour, honking at the motorbikes swerving around them as thick as flies.

The driver didn't let them off. First of all, there was nowhere to pull over. Second of all, he wasn't stupid enough to have driven half-way around town and not get paid for it. He was silent for the rest of the drive. When Sunrin handed him the money after they reached their destination, he avoided her eye as he thanked her with an air of embarrassment. After they got out of the car, he leaned his head out the window and called out "Take care," as if he were a distant relative sending them off.

This left a deep impression upon Ivy. She felt that if it were anyone else, they would have either been ripped off by the driver or started a screaming match that would have lasted into the afternoon. But Sunrin had said only a few phrases, and somehow, by the end of the trip, she had humbled the taxi driver, had tamed him with her presence as one tames a sly donkey. Ivy wondered why her father had never before mentioned Sunrin and Uncle Wang, who had both sung Shen's praises. She concluded that perhaps, unlike Nan, her father had too much decorum to brag about wealthy relations. Her respect for him increased ever so slightly.

AND THE SHOPPING! Oh, the wonderful shopping. When Ivy stepped foot inside the cavernous, ten-story-high Malls at Oriental Plaza, she had the dizzying feeling that she was in a glamorous madhouse, filled with skinny housewives, dapper shop clerks, businessmen in suits as straight as rulers, old ladies in pastel-colored pumps, their salon-coiffed hair as high and fluffy as cotton candy. All the boutiques were softly lit, extravagantly perfumed, and staffed with doe-eyed beauties in black skirts, nude stockings, and stiletto heels. The first time Sunrin took Ivy shopping, the polite voice of a shop assistant asked, *Can I help you find something, miss,* and Ivy was seized with an embarrassment that compelled her to stammer out an apology as if to excuse her presence in such a place, while she hurried away into a corner where they would hopefully just let her be.

"Can we try this one, this one . . . this one's rather pretty . . . Your clothes are a bit plain, Ivy, and I think some color would liven you up . . . I want you to look brighter, more energetic . . ." Sunrin glanced around. "Where are you?"

Ivy took the white dress, of a heavy cotton material, to the changing stall. After strapping on the heels, she looked at her reflection, hardly daring to believe she was the girl in the mirror. A sprinkling of fine baby hairs framed a soft oval face, cut by dark brows arched vividly against iridescent skin, a result of all the plumping moisturizers she'd been using the past week. The drape of the dress was severe in its lines, she would never have picked out something like this on her own, and yet the very austerity of the dress made her appear more feminine and youthful by contrast.

She peeked at the price tag. Her chin quivered with despair. She said in a gay voice, "Do you think it makes me look too—old-fashioned?" The four thousand RMB Nan had given her for the summer would barely cover the cost of the shoes.

Not at all, Sunrin and the shopgirl chirped. You look like a bird— an egret!—you look like a dancer; that white is a shade only very beautiful-skinned girls can wear.

"We'll take everything," said Sunrin, pulling out her Amex from a designer Mickey Mouse wallet.

Ivy feebly tried to protest, but Sunrin laughed her wonderful, deep-throated laugh and waved them away.

At first, Ivy tried to abide by her grandmother's teachings (there are no such things as free carrots) by telling herself she was in Sunrin's debt, she couldn't take advantage of her aunt's generosity without wearing out her welcome or causing Sunrin to think Ivy was an ungracious, low-class girl. But as the days slipped by in two-hour tasting menus, private guided tours, mall after mall after mall, Sunrin's Mickey Mouse wallet flashing its cute black ears in and out of her purse, Ivy's vague sense of caution receded as mist in the presence of Sunrin's blinding sun. She still adopted an air of bashful embarrassment at the sight of the gold Amex swiping for her various purchases, but she'd stopped pretending to pull out her own meager four thousand RMB, still untouched, and she'd toned down her effusive thank-yous, not wishing Sunrin to think her insincere or, worse, pitiful in her overwhelming gratitude for something Sunrin considered inconsequential.

"You're family," Sunrin said one day after Ivy once again stammered out her thanks. "How often do you come to China? And besides, what's the purpose of making money if not to spend it?"

Ivy could not deny this logic. For every RMB Sunrin spent on her, she spent an equal amount of money on clothes for her two children, for her husband, for herself. The only person Sunrin never bought any gifts for was the *ayi*. At first, Ivy felt sorry for the hired help, always coaxing or chasing a screaming child, a three-headed shadow trailing after them in beige slacks and white sneakers. But one evening in Hong Kong, Ivy saw Sunrin hand the *ayi* an envelope of cash as her "bonus" for the trip, and Ivy understood: not all forms of money were equal. She thought: I'll always carry my wealth on my body, not in my wallet.

One day she saw a pair of beautiful blue suede sneakers and thought how handsome they would look on Austin. Intercepting Ivy's glance, Sunrin asked for help in picking out souvenirs for the Lins. She said she'd been meaning to choose gifts for them but Ivy would know better what they liked. Ivy picked out cashmere sweaters, summer pajamas, and leather gloves with fur trims for Nan and Meifeng; battery-powered toys, sweets, the blue suede sneakers for Austin; and for Shen, who Sunrin had said was like a brother to her, a mini karaoke system after Ivy said no, her father had no hobbies, and Sunrin said, "Oh, but how he loved to sing as a boy." Ivy took just as much pleasure—if not more pleasure—in selecting these things for her family as she did for herself. Her stammering embarrassment when dealing with suave shop clerks evaporated. Sunrin had bestowed her authority, as if Ivy were a treasurer whose job it was to allocate the queen's funds. She ordered salespeople around with a loftiness she mistook for ownership, and she only colored a little when, on her last evening with Sunrin, she had to ask her aunt for a spare suitcase to hold all of her new purchases. Awash in the rich peripheral glow of her aunt's money, Ivy felt she and Sunrin were alike, with the same tastes, opinions, and expectations, and that Sunrin's generosity was her own, there was hardly any difference between them at all.

On a sweltering Saturday in August, Sunrin drove Ivy to a very different part of Chongqing, full of crumbling gray and brown homes, where laundry fluttered over plastic wash bins on cement balconies. Aunt Hong came out to greet them, a broader, older version of Nan in a floral blouse and checkered slacks. "*Thank you* for taking our Ji-yuan," she said to Sunrin, bowing repeatedly. "I hope she wasn't too much of a bother! Nan says she has a weak stomach, she's *always* been a sickly child . . . and the trouble you've gone through to take her traveling . . ." Aunt Hong went on and on. After two weeks of listening to Sunrin's mellifluous "proper" Mandarin, Aunt Hong's coarse dialect jarred Ivy's ears. Sunrin drove off in her gray German car after one last jaunty wave and throaty laugh, the fairy godmother back to her fairyland, and Ivy abandoned, back to the real world.

Everything about this new neighborhood repulsed her. Old men spitting on the sidewalks, little boys peeing on the street corners, rotting meat hanging from hooks along the stores, the pushing and shoving and random violence that seemed to occur on a regular basis:

fistfights, knife fights, women pulling at each other's hair while a circle of onlookers shouted their allegiances. The noises from the street vendors woke her up every morning, selling freshly butchered meat, farm-picked vegetables, dried herbs, teas, fresh fruit, dried fruit, nuts. It was a cacophony all day long until late evening, when the food vendors went home and then the entertainment vendors set up shop selling pirated American movies, cotton pajamas, plastic house slippers, cheap light-up toys. This was Meifeng's China, the one she had sold her daughter to escape.

Aunt Hong's older daughter, Yingying, was in her late twenties and engaged to a middle-aged man who owned a car repair shop. The younger daughter was named Wang Yan Jiu but everyone called her Jojo. She was only nine months older than Ivy but nevertheless called her *meimei*, an endearment given to younger sisters. Jojo was short and thickset, dressed most of the time in basketball shorts and tight, flashy T-shirts, her hair brushed into a fluffy bob. Her eyes were the same as Ivy's—those beautiful lashes. Jojo always said what she thought, even if it got her in trouble, as it almost always did. Ivy recalled Nan's old stories of Jojo's delinquency: how she flunked all her exams, skipped class, how she got kicked out of school for fighting her classmates, how she smoked and drank and tattooed her bicep at age nine with the Chinese character for *free*, how she never listened to her mother and suffered beatings for her uncontrollable temper. Stories like this always ended with: "Poor Jojo. But then, she never had a father." It wasn't her fault, they said. She'd had no firm hand growing up.

Those first few days at Aunt Hong's, Ivy was quiet, apathetic to all the foods and entertainment her aunt and cousin tried to engage her with; her complexion dulled. At the dinner table, the plastic tablecloth under Ivy's elbows sticky with oil residue, Aunt Hong and Jojo would laugh at the television set as they ate, chewing with their mouths open, lips smacking, and Ivy would wonder in despair how it was possible she was related to these people. At night, she would press herself against the wall so her new pajamas, which still retained the faint perfume of the Oriental Plaza, wouldn't brush against Jojo, who was squeezed beside her on the living room cot. There were still three weeks left in China. Ivy counted down each day until she returned to West Maplebury, to Grove, where, believing herself fundamentally changed through Sunrin's influence, she anticipated her classmates' heads turning as she walked down the hall with her new buttery lamb-leather satchel with the silver buckles, wearing the cognac penny loafers, slim at the toe with a little half-inch wooden heel so that her legs would appear as long and graceful as Violet and Nikki Satterfields'. The experience of wealth, if only secondhand, had left its indelible mark on her heart, so that long after the details of Sunrin's house and car had faded from her mind, she would remember what it felt like when shopgirls swirled around her, their faces gleaming with respect and deference, and herself, fearless in the possession of something no one could take away from her.

Things gradually improved at Aunt Hong's house. Mostly because her cousins and aunt constantly told her what a treasure she was. Her skin was as light and fine as an egg white, her figure was thin and stylish, her inner *qìzhì* was classy and refined, plus she liked to read *books*—"when's the last time *you* read a book?" Aung Hong chastised Jojo. Plus, Ivy was *American*. Ivy had quickly realized that to be an American in China was almost as good as being royalty. She was of a superior nationality, and they all revered her English fluency, which her family made her show off to the neighbors at every occasion.

At first, Ivy treated these lavish praises with skeptical dismissal, priding herself on her indifference to the opinions of these lesser relations, but as these compliments were in line with what she believed about herself—she *was* different, she *did* read more books, her eyes *were* large and dazzling—her heart softened toward her relatives and she even imbued them with qualities like honesty, good sense, humility, so that their opinions would carry more weight and raise her esteem in her own eyes.

It wasn't just her relatives. Waiting in line at the Ferris wheel, the operator whispered: *You have the most beautiful eyes I've ever seen*; after eating at a noodle stall, the cashier asked for payment in the form of her scrunchie; playing DDR at an arcade, she was scouted by a "talent agent" for a hair commercial; on a rowboat in Changshou Lake, the neighboring rowboat full of teenage boys called out to her, "Hey, *mei nü*, over here, come on board!" *Mei nü* literally translated to "beautiful girl."

Of the six boys on the boat in Changshou Lake, Ivy liked the athletic-looking Wuling the most. He didn't speak much but his black eyes were swarthy and intelligent, and there was an elusive quality about him, not unlike Gideon, to which she was immediately attracted.

Jojo said she liked Kai, a small-framed boy with chipmunk-like cheeks and a pouty lower lip. Jojo flirted with him in the typical Chongqing fashion—by making fun of his clothes, telling him how poor he looked, how dirty his hands were, how crude his accent. But then, in a surprise twist, Kai asked *Ivy* to be his girlfriend. He said that all of them had talked it over, and it was decided by the group that he had first right to ask her out because he liked her most. Ivy supposed this was the Communist mentality she'd heard so much about: even the right to ask out a girl had to be approved by the group.

There was Jojo, trying to snicker, her eyes only a little sad. Seeing Ivy's hesitation, she said, "You two are perfect for each other!" She grabbed Ivy's hand and pressed it into Kai's.

Ivy was as indifferent to the person of Kai as she was to an individual leaf of a tree, but she worried that if she refused him, all the boys, including Wuling, would be lost to her. "I'm willing to try it," she said. Kai grinned from ear to ear. That settled, Ivy and Jojo strolled with the boys around the lake until the moon came out.

"You two should hold hands," instructed Jojo. Kai shot her a grateful look. He took Ivy's hand, they intertwined their fingers. She felt a twinge of aversion, but when she saw Jojo's face looking longingly at him, she quickly repressed her own unpleasant feelings. In the middle of their walk, Kai said, "I want to show you something." He led her a few meters away so that they were out of sight from the others. He stopped and, without warning, leaned in and kissed her in an almost frantic motion.

It felt entirely different from kissing Roux. Ivy had, by now, mostly blocked out those memories, which only occasionally resurfaced in dreams, the details vague and muddled. But there was nothing vague about Kai's taste of garlic and scallions from their dinner, and Ivy had to resist the urge to break free from his wet mouth. She guessed this was the price she had to pay for having a boyfriend.

He told her he loved her on a muggy afternoon, one week later, lying next to her in the attic bedroom of one of his friend's houses, a musty, windowless place that reminded Ivy of a horse stable. "Wo ai ni," he whispered, a shy rabbit look on his face that would have melted Jojo's heart but that only induced in Ivy a mild fondness. She said the words back. She felt nothing except a small prick of desolation, more troubling than disappointment because she couldn't understand why the reality of being loved had failed to live up to her expectations. It was Kai, she decided, who must be the cause of this queer flatness. He wasn't the right boy. Almost immediately, her mind began drifting to Wuling, the detached and watchful friend who'd not said more than a dozen words to her, yet whose silences sent more shivers down her spine than all of Kai's forthcoming kisses.

On her last night in Chongqing, she and Jojo went with Kai and Wuling to the Yangtze River to skip rocks under the Dongshuimen Bridge. At the river, Jojo rolled up her pants and walked into the water. The little tides caused by the boats going by lapped at her ankles, then, as she waded in further, at her calves. They called out for Jojo to get out of the river—it was dangerous to go in too far, they cried, it's too dark, you can't see where the water gets too deep. Jojo ignored them. With a tragic tilt of her head, she waded in deeper and deeper until they could barely make out her outline in the darkness. Ivy cried to Kai, hysterical, "Go after her! She's heartbroken because of you."

"What'd I do?"

"Just go! Do you want her to drown herself?"

Confused but obedient, Kai muttered curses underneath his breath as he took off his shoes, rolled up his pants, and went in after Jojo. Ivy saw the two of them a few yards away from shore, Kai's hand on her cousin's wrist. Jojo made a play at shaking him off. It almost looked like they were dancing.

While Kai and Jojo were in the water, Ivy turned to Wuling. Her legs were planted firmly in the sand, shoulders squared. A pose of defiance. He was the first to speak.

"Do you already have a boyfriend in America?"

"No."

"I don't believe you. A girl like you reeks of pampering." Then he crushed his beer can with one hand and flung it into the bushes. His swarthy black eyes came toward her.

They kissed, hidden in the leafy shadows of a banyan tree, his long, rough fingers on the back of her neck, her hand slipping underneath his shirt, feeling his stomach undulate like bricks coming loose. Maybe passion, Ivy thought dreamily, could only bloom in illicit places. Maybe that was why the only ardent encounter she'd ever witnessed had been between Roux's mother and Ernesto's father, and why Nan and Meifeng constantly warned her of dirty bad boys with dirty bad thoughts and intentions. It was implied that all girls were victims of these boys, and to enjoy the company and caresses of one was to be what Nan had accused her of after Gideon's sleepover—a harlot.

Back at Aunt Hong's living room that night, her lips still stinging from Wuling's kisses and her cheeks sticky from Kai's farewell tears, Ivy came upon the four thousand RMB Nan had given her in the back pocket of her shorts. She gave the entire wad to Jojo. "I love you, *meimei*," Jojo squealed, then wept. "You're the only one who's ever taken care of me."

Ivy finished packing and performed her nightly inspection in the bathroom mirror. She thought she looked like a girl who was ready. Her life in America, which had felt so far away the past five weeks, returned so viscerally that the steel bars of Aunt Hong's bathroom window, the hot steam fogging up the glass, the sound of a man hocking outside, now felt like the dream. Her heart beat quickly; she pressed a hand to her eyes. Everything's different now, she consoled herself. Summer was over. She'd slept with a boy, kissed another, said *I love you* to a third and didn't mean it. Still, *still*, the image of a certain blond-haired boy in a navy blazer, his back forever toward her, was the beacon that all her turbulent desires and hopes sailed toward.

Aunt Hong knocked on the door. "It's your mama."

Ivy came out and took the phone.

"Baba will be late to pick you up tomorrow at the airport," Nan said without preamble. "The moving truck is delayed and now they're arriving around the same time as you."

"What moving truck?"

"Aunt Hong didn't tell you?"

"*Tell me what?*"

"We moved to New Jersey."

6

NAN AND SHEN, AFTER REMOVING THEIR DAUGHTER FROM THE country, had taken out their first mortgage to purchase an old two-story colonial in Clarksville, New Jersey. Ivy was appalled. Her life was not her own. She would never see Gideon again! She cried for a week upon her return. Grief soon turned to disgust. The house, which her parents kept praising in smug, insouciant tones, was awful. The furniture slid toward the back wall, the waterlogged window frames were misshapen, the panes grimy, the kitchen and bathroom tiles yellow and grainy with limestone residue. The previous occupants, a Polish couple who'd priced the house below market, had raised their own chickens in the backyard, and every time Meifeng insisted on opening the windows to "air out" the rooms, a blast of dried feces, fetid earth, and rain-logged feathers made eating unbearable. And *this* was the pinnacle of Nan and Shen's dreams! This chicken coop! The only upside was that she and Austin got their own bedrooms for the first time. Meifeng slept in a converted dining room on the first floor.

Nan had chosen Clarksville for its large Chinese population. Her sister, Ping, had recently enrolled her two children in weekend Chinese school. Ping said she'd never seen Feifei and Tong so well-behaved, surrounded and influenced by the exemplary behavior of their Chinese classmates. She said Nan should never have sent Ivy to that religious school with entitled Americans. Nan felt Ping was right—Ivy needed to be with her own kind: Chinese students who valued schoolwork and family duties. "A mother knows her own daughter," Nan told her husband. "Ivy's easily influenced by others. If she's going to become a doctor, she needs to befriend other Chinese kids who have the same goals. They can push her to study more."

Everything about Clarksville fit Nan's criteria. On Ivy's first day of high school, it seemed the entire hallway was a sea of black hair. Back at Grove, she'd tried so hard to fit in with the majority but here in Clarksville, she wanted nothing to do with her Asian classmates and their obsession with grades and AP classes and extra-credit homework, walking around school always in the same cliques, backpacks overflowing with math and science textbooks and impeccably organized pencil cases. In the few times a friendly soul would invite her to sit with them at lunch, Ivy would notice their Tupperwares of cold rice, beef and celery, lo mein with shrimp, the occasional boiled egg or canned sweet congee—variations of her own daily lunches—and she'd wither a little on the inside, thinking that others would look upon their group and see them all as the same. She became reticent, her gaze would drift over to the lacrosse players and their girlfriends laughing in the hallway behind the music rooms; she feared they were laughing at her.

In the second week of school, Ivy befriended the only white girl in her chemistry class, named Sarah Wilson. Sarah's brother, Brett, was on the junior varsity lacrosse team.

By Thanksgiving, Ivy and Brett were fooling around in the back of the music rooms, and Ivy discovered why it was the prime lunch spot in school: you could lock the doors from inside one of the rooms and turn off the lights so no one could see inside the little glass panel. And the walls were soundproof.

By Christmas, the thrill of being a lacrosse player's girlfriend had lost its appeal; Ivy longed for a refined boyfriend, one who spoke French, who'd lived in Europe, who read poetry, or—better yet—who wrote poetry, or composed song lyrics at the very least, one who would reveal beauty in hidden places and show her a new way of being in the world.

In the spring, she became involved with a thin, sensitive boy from the drama club who had memorized entire soliloquies of *Hamlet* and who could, with just one index finger, activate nerve sensors she hadn't known existed. Ivy discovered that fooling around in the dark, dusty wings of the auditorium, the coarse rope from the pulley rubbing against her back, leaving pink tracks down her skin like a burn, was even more scintillating than the soundproof cocoon of the music rooms. Afterward, they'd sneak out the side doors and share a cigarette underneath a brushed-blue sky. While he ranted about his long-term girlfriend—a college freshman in Texas—she'd trace wings on his knee through the ripped hole of his jeans.

Sarah Wilson asked for a new lab partner. Ivy quickly realized it'd been Sarah who'd written their reports, drawn the diagrams, read aloud line-by-line instructions from the confusing manual during class. Ivy finished the year with a C+ in Chemistry. Her grade in Algebra was even worse.

Nan was beside herself. Even Meifeng didn't take her granddaughter's side, saying hypocritically, "Your mother's in charge of your education." There were scoldings, threats, countless trips to the library for additional workbooks. Ivy complied for the most part. She, too, felt despondent over her mediocre grades. She wanted to be the effortlessly intelligent type, like Sunrin, but instead, she found herself at the bottom of the Asian barrel, like Jojo. Nan always told her to work harder but Ivy felt she *was* working hard, or at least she *cared* about working hard, even if the dread of a certain quiz or exam made it hard to focus sometimes. She made the mistake of saying this to Nan one afternoon and her mother's nostrils flared out, her voice rising through the slanted house: "You don't know what hard work is! You American kids have no responsibility. You're lazy! You think you can just live in this house forever."

"I hate this house," said Austin between bites of fried pork steak. "It smells like poop."

"You silly boy," Nan snapped. "You don't have the capability to live on your own. Your grades are worse than your sister's. If you don't get into college, you'll end up on the streets once Mama and Baba are dead." This was always the inevitable end waiting for the Lin children should they fail: homelessness, starvation.

On the first morning of summer break, Nan barged into Ivy's room at half past seven. "Your cousin Feifei has been helping your aunt Ping pay the bills since she was eleven." She dropped a towering stack of mail on the nightstand. "Look through these letters. Your grandmother was right. I need to let you handle more around the house. *You* can manage our money from now on."

Ivy was used to these kinds of bizarre stealth attacks by now, but she still opened the envelopes with an elaborate slowness, fuming. Bank statements, phone bills, gas and electric, car insurance bills. There were many dollar signs and numbers.

"And don't forget these." Nan pointed to the colorful coupon books on the bottom of the stack. "Look for a filter for our refrigerator. You'll also start grocery shopping with me. Then you'll learn how much it costs to feed this family. This here"—she pulled out a thick square envelope—"is your father's paycheck. It comes twice a month. You can keep track of everything in this." She handed Ivy a checkbook, bound in a transparent case, with a little plastic calculator attached to the lining. "Go on," said Nan.

But Ivy did not touch the calculator. How dinky it looked, like a cheap toy even Austin wouldn't want, and how sad the peeling numbers looked on the rubber buttons, the 6 turning into a 0, the 4 missing entirely.

"It's not easy to shoulder responsibility," Nan conceded. "Mathematics is important in all areas of life, not just for school." She gave Ivy a sidelong, insinuating glance before dropping her gaze.

It was the worst summer of Ivy's life. She was forced to accompany Nan to the China Star supermarket, the bank, the gas station, the post office. She reported back on the weekly deals at the butcher's too short counter, phoned telecom providers to complain of an extra dollar charged, asked for refunds at customer service counters, translated Nan's indignant accusations into polite English questions. Each night, under Nan's watchful eye, she collected the day's receipts and recorded them in the ledger. On Saturday mornings, she paid the new bills that'd been arriving all week in the mail. Nan would triple-check Ivy's handwriting, pausing her index finger under each number and letter as if they might, without constant vigilance, magically rearrange themselves.

Fueled by a determination to never again be "taught" by her mother, Ivy kept her grades up during her sophomore year. She studied more than she studied the previous year, but not as much as Nan believed her to be studying, a weakness that Ivy immediately exploited. When she spoke for hours on the phone with her boyfriend, she told her mother it was her study group. Nan didn't know about Brett Wilson or the sensitive drama club boy or the green-eyed class president or any of the rest. She only saw that Ivy was always in her room, reading what Nan assumed were assigned textbooks, scribbling page after page of what Nan assumed to be homework. As Ivy had rightly grasped, Nan had no method, no confidence, to guide her daughter's academics. Meifeng, relegated to another floor, was no longer privy to Ivy's habits. Shen was no help either. He'd been laid off at the insurance company. He spent all day at the library browsing the jobs sections of the newspapers and playing Go on the library's free Internet. Nan had not been able to find work since the move. Meifeng stopped bringing Austin to McDonald's, no matter how much Austin cried about his hateful new school, his lack of friends, the bullies in the neighborhood who'd called him *fatso* and pushed his bike into a dumpster. But now the spokes of the wheel were bent, said Austin, and congealed banana goo had seeped into the rubber, and could he get another bike, please? No, said Nan. Why not? Baba lost his job. "Freddie Abernathy's father got fired," said Austin over dinner, "and *he* found another job in a week."

Shen turned and backhanded Austin across the face. Ivy cried, "Baba!" Meifeng said. "Let the boy eat."

Chin trembling, Austin shoveled spoonful after spoonful of rice into his mouth, and Shen, tight-throated, said, "Look at him. A Chinese boy. Doesn't even know how to use chopsticks."

FOR THE REST of her life, Ivy would never forget that horrible spring of her sophomore year, when her parents grew gray and ragged, when Nan turned off the lights at eight, when Meifeng started filling empty soap bottles and shampoo bottles with water, when the dishes on the table were variations of fried rice, noodles, flour pancakes, the delectable fatty meats and fresh vegetables and occasional gallon of ice cream luxuries Ivy hadn't known she liked until they were gone. She came home one afternoon and announced offhandedly she'd gotten hired to bag groceries at the Price Rite along Route 1. She'd expected warm praise—*What a* ting hua *daughter we have*—but Shen turned to Nan and shouted, "How can you make our kids go work? Have you become so—so"—he struggled to find the word—"so *miserly?*"

"I didn't know about it!" Nan screamed, pinpoint tears quivering in their sockets. She whipped toward Ivy. "If you waste your time at such a filthy place instead of studying, I'll break your legs!"

Meifeng, through her grapevine of Chinese grandmas who stretched together at the neighborhood park, found a job as an *ayi* to a Taiwanese family who'd recently moved to Clarksville. Meifeng was there before the family woke to make them a hot breakfast of congee, stew, steamed eggs. While the two boys, six and ten, were at school, she dusted, mopped, and vacuumed every corner of the four-bedroom house. At four, she began cooking dinner. When the family complained her food was too spicy, too greasy, Meifeng tried to adapt her cooking to their sweeter taste buds, and when that failed, she added brown sugar and ketchup to the dishes and that seemed to work. Shen picked her up at seven. Meifeng was usually so tired by then she had trouble climbing the four steps to the front door without assistance.

Though Ivy rarely spent time alone with Meifeng anymore, she still felt her grandmother's absence keenly. She resented the two boys, whom she imagined as spitting images of Sunrin's children, abusing poor Meifeng, who could do nothing but plead and bribe. Ivy took over the household chores. Nan cooked their meals. Her cooking was much worse than Meifeng's but even Austin didn't dare complain. After washing the dishes, Ivy would sit in her room with the windows flung open so the smell of chicken manure would conceal the fumes from her cigarettes. Through the thin bedroom walls, she heard her parents' never-ending discussions filled with ominous banking terminologies she didn't understand. Even Nan didn't attempt to "teach" her daughter about such things; the pressure was too great. Ivy began to shoplift again but she derived no pleasure from it the way she had when she was young. Stealing, then, had felt like she was getting the better of the system; resourceful and self-reliant, as Meifeng had taught her. But she knew now that resourceful and self-reliant were traits born of need. Meifeng was resourceful and self-reliant. Now Meifeng was an *ayi*. Ivy was the granddaughter of an *ayi*.

Deprivation made Ivy dream of excess. She fantasized about closets as large as her bedroom, gold Amex credit cards, shoes piled ceiling-high, smoking cigarettes from long gold holders, wearing gems on every finger and pearls three loops deep on her neck, ordering a tableful of dishes and only taking one bite from each plate. She longed to become a lady with so much complacent wealth that others would look upon her and think, *What a sheltered girl, that Ivy Lin. She's probably never lifted a finger for anything in all her life.* They say that self-control is a finite resource and it seemed to Ivy that after her sixteenth birthday, she'd already used up her lifetime's worth of moderation and discipline and henceforth could never deny herself a single thing, not even a cup of coffee.

THE HORRIBLE SPRING finally ended. Shen didn't find a job. Instead, Nan discovered a new livelihood—going to flea markets to bring home cheap houseware items to sell on the Internet. One of her old colleagues at the dumpling factory had given her the idea when she'd called to see if Nan had found another job. The woman said her nephew mailed her knockoff designer bags from Hunan, which sold for 500 percent profit. She was branching out to other products now like jewelry and antiques. The woman said you could make money even on cheap items just from shipping charges. Nan made noncommittal comments—she was a proud woman—but in her desperate state, any new idea for making money felt like a golden lottery ticket. And 500 percent profit was a calculation even Nan could do without her little calculator. The irony of Nan now dragging the Lins to estate sales and garage sales and flea markets was not lost on Ivy. Within six months, the Lins were making Shen's old salary. Meifeng quit her job, the limp in her leg now permanent. She massaged her knees every night with Chinese herbal oils, which made the whole house smell of turpentine.

That Christmas, Shen went to Best Buy and returned with a new Dell computer. Ivy and Austin fought over the honor of unboxing it. Meifeng cooked up a Chinese banquet: whole fish stewed in sour pickles, twice-cooked pork, plate after plate of sliced beef, cold noodles, steamed pork ribs with sweet potato, and Ivy's favorite, delectable slices of pork belly braised to a sugary perfection and coated with red bean paste. After dinner, Nan sat on the sofa, head leaned back, both hands in her lap, her face gentle, her lips gathered in an indulgent smile, and the sight was enough to induce everyone in the house into a state of wild euphoria because none of them could remember the last time they saw Nan sitting idly. The Dell box had been filled with foam peanuts and while Shen, six beers in, attempted to install the computer, Ivy and Austin ran around the living room trying to stuff the foam into each other's underwear.

IVY LONGED TO return north, to Massachusetts or Vermont or Maine, places that in her mind were eternally autumn, drenched in smells of chestnuts and rain, the orange and red foliage crackling under her leather soles; or pristine winter, where she pictured log cabins, silky hair tucked under fuzzy white earmuffs, fresh snow shimmering on steeple roofs and stained-glass windows. In all her years in Clarksville, she'd thought of Massachusetts as her real home, and she spoke often of Grove—"a small private school, so stuffy, we had to wear these uncomfortable uniforms . . ."—to her rapt boyfriends with an air of assumed modesty that betrayed her secret pride. "I'm from Massa-chusetts," she'd say. "I still get homesick all the time." Of course, she never once uttered the words *West Maplebury* or *Fox Hill*. In fact, she described so vividly the quiet tree-lined neighborhoods, the dreamy buzzing of cicadas, seaside vacations where frothy white waves licked pebbled beaches, stone-and-glass manors that smelled of honeysuckle, that she really believed this was the world from which she came and the one she longed to return to.

Her grades guaranteed her admission to a state school with a par-tial scholarship. Shen and Nan spoke of this as the best, inevitable option. "A mother knows her own daughter," Nan told her husband. "Ivy's strengths don't lie in studying. She's good at *social* things. Al-ways talking on the phone. So many friends. Ping says social skills are more important than grades in America." By social skills, Nan meant boy skills. She wasn't as blind as Ivy thought. Nan's aspiration for her daughter to become a doctor had long been abandoned. Her new hope was that Ivy marry a doctor. A Chinese doctor who'd earn a six-figure income and provide Ivy with a house, two children, a boy and a girl; they'd settle in New Jersey and keep a spare bedroom for the sets of grandparents, who would alternate years of babysitting.

Ivy had different ideas. She applied and got admitted to a small women's college outside Boston. Like most girls whose lives revolved around boys, she romanticized chastity and often put herself through elaborate rituals of prudishness (or the appearance of it), as she felt martyrdom was the only purifying agent for her heedless choices. Tuition at this private college was exorbitant. From managing Nan's ledger the past two years, Ivy knew her parents couldn't afford it. She took out a loan.

When she broke the news to her family that she would not be living at home to attend state college after all, and, more disastrously, *she had taken on debt*, there ensued the biggest fight yet between mother and daughter. Ivy was too strong now for Nan to physically thrash but her mother threatened everything else under the sun. "I'll kill myself if you don't *ting hua*," Nan shouted at the end, death being her final trump card.

"You're already dead," Ivy screamed back. "You died with that boyfriend of yours back in China. We're just your replacement family."

Nan's face went slack. Her mouth opened, closed, opened. "You think I'm dead? You don't want a mother? Fine. Go. It won't change anything. One day you'll see. It's not me you hate."

"I DIDN'T DO anything wrong," Ivy said to Meifeng, sweat pouring beneath her blue and silver robes at her graduation ceremony, which Nan had elected not to attend. The ceremony had been held in the football stadium, four hours melting in the beating sun. She tried to put her arm around Austin's thick shoulders, then drew back, startled to discover that he was now taller than she was. The siblings winced for Shen's camera.

"Your mother worries that you've ruined your future," Meifeng said for the umpteenth time. "Do you know how much interest these rotten banks charge stupid students like you? Debt is like a pile of rocks on a turtle's—"

"I've *always* been in debt," Ivy snapped, "to *her*. She thinks Austin and I are her slaves just by being born from her womb."

Meifeng sighed. She handed Ivy a card she had purchased from the dollar store. In front of the *Congratulations Class of 2000* she had taped a hundred-dollar bill.

In August, Ivy packed two old suitcases and a few table lamps in the back of her father's car. Austin said a sullen "Bye." Meifeng pressed a small item, wrapped in newspaper, into Ivy's hand. It was a figurine of a little glass dog sitting on its haunches. Ivy had been born in the Year of the Dog. "Remember to call once in a while," Meifeng said gruffly before turning away.

Shen drove Ivy to Boston, seven hours in standstill traffic. Rain poured down around them. Her father deposited her things in a barren dorm room covered with wall-to-wall brown carpet. "I've never given you much guidance," he said as his parting words, "but if there's one piece of advice I want you to remember, it's this: Be humble and grateful for what you have. Don't expect too much from life. If you go looking, you'll always find people who are better than you."

Resentment prickled Ivy's skin. She said placidly: "Yes, Baba."

"And your mother will forgive you," he added. "Don't worry."

But Ivy wasn't worried. She was *free*. Determination, an old ally, sprung forth once more. Her senior year quote had been: *The best is yet to come.* She truly believed it.

PART THREE

7

AT THREE FORTY, TWENTY MINUTES PAST THE PICKUP TIME, SIX-year-old Arabella Whitaker still stood underneath the ivy-covered awning, shredding her crayon drawing of Santa's reindeers.

"Arabella, I'm going to call Leonine."

"Sib's picking me up."

"Who?"

"My cousin."

Ivy checked her phone. There it was—Ellen Whitaker's email that her niece would be picking Arabella up from school today instead of the au pair. She didn't give a reason why but based on Ellen's track record, Ivy was sure that mousy little Leonine had abandoned ship and fled back to France after sticking around long enough to receive her Christmas "gift."

She waited with Arabella for almost twenty minutes before a white sports car pulled up to the curb and a thin blond woman stepped out, the metal tips of her boots gleaming in the snow.

"You're Arabella's cousin?" asked Ivy, straightening up. She'd imagined "Sib" looking like the plump Irishwoman on the package of butter from her favorite co-op.

"That's right," said the woman. "Sylvia Speyer. Ellen said she'd email you?"

The name jolted Ivy's mind, like dust being blown off an old library book. She pretended to scan her phone, all the while taking in the woman's camel coat, the black scarf dangling to her thighs, her molded profile with its pursed mouth and eyes elusively hidden behind aviators. It could be, Ivy thought, heart racing.

"Here it is," she said, looking up. "All good."

"Great." The woman motioned to Arabella to get into the passenger's seat.

"I was just wondering," Ivy called out, "If we've met before?"

An abstract congenial smile slid onto Sylvia's face, a politician's smile, perfected by those used to being recognized. "Were we at Yale together?"

"No," said Ivy. ". . . Are you, by any chance, Gideon Speyer's sister?"

"I am."

"I went to Grove with Gideon!"

"You're Giddy's friend," said Sylvia generously, one foot inside the car. "Turn up the heat, Bella." She turned to Ivy. "I'll let him know I ran into you, Miss . . ."

"Lin. Ivy Lin. But I moved away after eighth grade and lost touch."

"Eighth grade?" Sylvia drummed her fingers against her purse. "Amazing."

Ivy hastily explained she only remembered that far back because she'd had a horribly silly crush on Gideon back then. "I actually met you the time I came over for Gideon's birthday party. There were all those wonderful vacation photos on the wall . . . and your dad! He was so funny. Is he still in office?"

Arabella yelled that she was late to her ballet class.

"Your mommy says you can skip today," Sylvia replied over her shoulder. "We're going to take some pictures together for my friend's magazine. You love modeling, don't you, kitten?" She had placed her foot back onto the curb.

"If you're in a rush . . ." Ivy murmured.

"Not at all." Sylvia removed her aviators. Her eyes were amber colored and beautifully honeycombed in the cold December light. With one hand resting lightly on the roof of the car, she said no, her father was retired now, her parents had moved to Beacon Hill. Gideon had just finished graduate school and was back in Boston working with a health-care company. "Something with thermometers . . . but anyway, you should ask him yourself." She paused smoothly. "Would you like his number?"

"Oh no," Ivy protested, "he probably doesn't remember me."

"He remembers everyone."

Ivy didn't respond.

Sylvia went on absently, as if recalling another memory "It's such a coincidence to run into someone from Grove . . . Did you like it when you were there?"

"Well. . . no."

"I hated it, too," said Sylvia. "It was such a claustrophobic place—like that Radiohead song about the plastic trees. I couldn't wait to leave. I told myself I'd never come back. But here we are, less than an hour away." She emitted a small sigh. "We couldn't escape."

"It's not quite the same thing," said Ivy.

Sylvia looked startled. "No, I guess it's not." The ensuing silence was the first real moment between them, Ivy felt, seeing the little crease between Sylvia's eyes, the bemused frown, knowing that she wore the same expression.

Arabella honked the horn.

"I'd love to—" Ivy began just as Sylvia said, "If you're—" They laughed.

Sylvia rummaged around an overflowing tote and pulled out her cell. "Here, give me your number . . . If you don't have plans yet on the thirty-first, I'm throwing a small New Year's party at my house. I'd love for you to come. Gideon will be there, you two can catch up." Her eyes flicked up. "You're welcome to bring a boyfriend or partner along."

Ivy recited her phone number. In a rueful tone, she said she'd just be a party of one.

"I just texted you my address. Eight thirty. I really hope you can make it." Sylvia leaned forward. Ivy thought Gideon's sister was going for a hug but Sylvia only squeezed her arm in a friendly way. The car door slammed. A fragrance lingered where Sylvia's cashmere-clad figure had lingered moments before: lemons, the ocean.

Tears sprung to Ivy's eyes.

AFTER A LONG bath, Ivy found herself in an excited, uneasy state. Her cheeks were hot from her soak; she'd forgotten to bring her slippers to the bathroom and her wet footprints across the wooden floorboards looked vaguely ominous. She wished violently for someone to talk to but her roommate, Andrea, wasn't home yet from rehearsal. Why do I have no friends? she despaired, drawing up the blinds to catch the last rays of twilight; her quick, rather forced self-pity evaporated with the icy draft leaking in from the windowsill. She'd never craved friendship with other women, and she did not believe platonic friendship could exist with men.

She crawled under the covers and huddled against the tepid radiator. "Gideon Speyer," she whispered into her pillow. She hadn't said the name in over a decade. It brought back all sorts of hopeful sensations she thought she'd never again feel after the breakup with Daniel. Just yesterday, she'd been bedridden with stomach pains from unexpectedly receiving his postcard in the mail—a stock photo of a mountain range; standing on the peak next to a Saint Bernard with his back to the camera was a man wearing flannel and a Russian beaver hat. *Happy Holidays!* he'd written on the front, no return address. Two years of her life and she hadn't even been worthy of a return address.

He'd dumped her a week before Thanksgiving, right before their trip to Vermont. Andrea had been sure he was going to propose. Why else would he have invited her to meet his family around the holidays? "I know you don't care about these things," said Andrea, "but I think the Sullivans are loaded." Ivy winced. Andrea began rattling off indications of what she thought was Daniel's secret wealth—the lakeside cabin, the Florida vacation home, annual hiking trips to Kilimanjaro and Mount Fuji, not to mention the frequent four-day mountaineering escapades to the White Mountains in New Hampshire for which he took time off his job (as VP of finance at his mother's jewelry company) with seemingly no consequences—and Ivy pretended not to have noticed any of it.

But there had been no Vermont, no surprise proposal, no flowers for Mrs. Sullivan. "I just can't see myself marrying you," Daniel said in the suffocating heat of his car, a statement that'd come on the heels of an ordinary dinner followed by an ordinary movie, which made it that much more of a betrayal. "Who says I want to get married," Ivy had replied. Daniel pressed his glasses into his nose and exhaled slowly, making a noise like a teakettle. "See? This is what I'm talking about. You're so guarded. I never know what you're thinking." One thing led to another and before Ivy had grasped what was happening, he was telling her it was over, there was nothing to be done. He held her for two minutes while she cried—"I'm not guarded, I'm *so honest* with you . . . I've never opened up to anyone the way I opened up to you . . ." Later, when she returned home, she writhed in agony to remember how she'd groveled.

After the breakup, to achieve utter renunciation, Ivy slept with seven—or was it eight?—different men in December. She and Andrea frequented a swanky bar on Commonwealth Avenue called Dresdan's. The men there were mostly pharmaceutical reps and finance guys from other M states—Michigan, Maryland, Minnesota—and they wore uniforms of khaki and cornflower blue. Andrea sucked them over with the force of her luscious lips cocooned over the tip of a cocktail straw, while Ivy angled her body away from the table, the modest friend to Andrea's overt appeal, occasionally glancing around the room as if she were restless. Later, when Andrea said "You're so quiet, Ivy! Come over here and join us," Ivy would pretend she'd just noticed the men's presence. "What do you do?" they would ask her. "I'm a first-grade teacher," she would say, "at the Kennedy School." Only a true Bostonian would have heard of it because they'd all gone there, or to its various sister schools, but whether these men knew of the school or not, they'd all smile like jack-o'-lanterns, place one hand on her knee, and say, "You must be good around kids. I *love* kids. My niece . . ." There was always a plethora of nieces and nephews whose pictures the men would pull up on their phones and thrust into her face. Ivy often felt contempt for Andrea, for the open pleasure she took in these tacky seductions, but she felt greater contempt for herself. She played the same games, felt the same cheap thrills of conquest, yet she felt the need to hide her pleasure. What did that say about her sense of propriety? Her sense of shame?

The day after Ivy's run-in with Sylvia Speyer, Nan called to say she'd received Ivy's three-hundred-dollar check—a monthly guilt of-fering Ivy sent in lieu of her own presence—and asked if she was still bringing Daniel to Clarksville for New Year's.

"It didn't work out," Ivy said curtly, having put off this admission for weeks, but which somehow seemed tolerable now that she had the hope of seeing Gideon Speyer again as mental armor against Nan's criticism.

"What happened?"

"His parents are divorced." She thought this was ample reason to evoke her mother's disdain, but Nan made a noncommittal grunt.

"You're almost twenty-seven now. You shouldn't be so picky. Aunt Ping's friend's daughter is your age and she's already pregnant with her second child. I had a hard time conceiving you and you have my genes. Don't think you can just put off having children. You have to start planning. Each year that passes—" Ivy could hear Meifeng's voice in the background agreeing vehemently, asking for the phone.

"I won't be coming home next week either," said Ivy.

"Why?"

"I'm going to a New Year's party. Maybe I'll convince someone there to impregnate me."

SYLVIA'S APARTMENT WAS on a wide, noisy street with an eclectic mix of brownstones, brick walk-ups, hipster boutiques selling handcrafted furniture next to Wisconsin cheese, Irish pubs, and graffitied walls with profound messages about God and guns and ganja. Ivy passed by several old churches and government municipals with beautiful stained-glass doors. She headed up a narrow staircase next to a kosher delicatessen and rang the bell.

Sylvia opened the door in a wraparound black silk shirt, leather miniskirt, bare legs, and purple velvet slippers with gold tassels. Few women could get away with not looking like a hooker in such an outfit, and Sylvia was one of them. Ivy handed her the bottle of red the sommelier at the wine bar down the street had recommended. "Gorgeous apartment," she said, looking around at the dark-paneled room, which appeared, at first, to be unlit, before her eyes adjusted and she realized that floating atop the wall-to-wall bookshelves were hundreds of candlesticks, flickering between various trailing plants whose tendrils pooled on the floor like a carpet of grass. She was the first to arrive. She'd thought Sylvia had said eight, but when she discreetly checked the text again, it said eight thirty, and now she felt foolish for showing up early.

Sylvia made it a point to tell her that Gideon was running late, which irked Ivy in its presumption that she was eagerly awaiting Gideon's arrival, even if it was true. She offered to help in the kitchen but Sylvia said there was nothing to do; she showed Ivy to the bar cart with an assured remark to "help yourself," before disappearing down the hall without explanation.

Ivy passed the time flipping through a photography book on the coffee table. Classical music swelled from an old record player sitting on top of a heavy mahogany desk. The surface was cluttered with an odd assortment of objects: a figure drawing of an old man, dried paintbrushes, half-used oils, an encyclopedic textbook flipped open to a page about rococo art, a brass hand sculpture, stacks of thank-you cards, dried yellow roses in a fat blue vase with carvings of Siamese cats. She took one of the floral-patterned thank-you cards and placed it in the pocket of her coat.

The armchair in the corner had rose-patterned upholstery and looked straight out of an English castle, the small discolorations set just so, the color gradation of wood—from maple to a chestnut grain—impossible to copy. Out of curiosity, she peeked under the drop-leaf corner stand next to the sofa. A paper label attached in the back read: *Style no 35; shade no 14. Bendt Jessen co inc.* She pulled out her phone and typed *Bendt Jessen*. The first result that popped up was a listing for a nondescript wooden chair—$3,950.

"What are you doing?" said Sylvia, reemerging.

"I thought I dropped my earring," said Ivy.

At five to nine, there came a loud knock on the door and Sylvia's voice came calling from the bathroom, where she was applying her makeup, asking Ivy if she could get that.

Ivy smoothed down her hair, fixed a smile on her face, and opened the door with an exuberant *Hello!* A crowd of people streamed past her in a flurry of noise and laughter. A quick sweep revealed Gideon wasn't among them. *Ivy Lin*, she said over and over, squeezing limp fingers, kissing velveteen cheeks. The guests all seemed to know each other in some capacity, although not always by name. Someone changed the classical symphony piece to a rock record. The noise swelled. Sylvia floated out of the kitchen with a platter of olives and cheese. Everyone made the rounds greeting their hostess; Ivy joined in as if she'd also just arrived. A man in a bowler hat handed her a tall-stemmed glass. She gulped the wine thirstily. The arrival of so many people seemed to raise the temperature in the room; sweat sprang along her hairline. She poured herself another glass and squeezed herself down on an empty square of sofa beside a Frenchman named Mathéo. From over Mathéo's shoulder, she had a clear view of the front door. Each time the door swung open, her heart would leap, then sink again, when a stranger entered. She both feared and anticipated Gideon's arrival. Fear and excitement—were they not two sides of the same coin?

When Gideon finally arrived, he let himself in without knocking and headed directly to find Sylvia. Ivy only caught the back of his head as he disappeared into the crowd, but she knew with certainty that she'd just seen Gideon Speyer for the first time in twelve years.

She turned to Mathéo and looked upon him with soft, shimmering eyes. The shift was instantaneous. Mathéo realized that he was talking with a beautiful girl. Ivy shook her head to move the strands of hair curled around her chin and neck; she kept tapping her bottom lip, drawing attention to her carefully outlined Cupid's bow. She spoke quickly with lively gestures, leaning in to form an upside-down V with Mathéo's body. Someone tapped Ivy on the shoulder. She looked up in the middle of a sentence, her lips still formed in a half smile at something Mathéo had said.

"Sorry to interrupt. Do you remember me, Ivy?"

She held the expression for a puzzled second before letting the recognition sweep across her face. "Of course I remember you! You've gotten so tall, Gideon!" She stood up and they exchanged warm hugs. When he pulled back and she looked full into his face, she experienced an almost painful pleasure of seeing how much he was the same, yet *better* than she remembered. The same mischievous smile, the intelligent eyes on a firm, thoughtful face, the straight nose, the slight hollow of his cheekbones. She'd been horribly intimidated by what she imagined to be a successful young man who'd perhaps let his successes go to his head, but this flesh-and-blood version made it impossible for her to think he had turned cold or snobby. If anything, he seemed softer.

She remained standing to talk to him; a disgruntled Mathéo was forced to turn his attention to the couple to the right of him.

"It's been what—since middle school?"

"You're right," said Ivy, steering them toward the corner of the room where they wouldn't be interrupted.

"Sylvia says you're Arabella's teacher?"

"Yes! What a small world!"

She and Gideon quickly established the rest of their mutual acquaintances: Arabella's parents, Gideon's parents, Sylvia, of course

(Ivy recounted the surprising encounter with Sylvia, only she made it seem as if the recognition were mutual), and they reminisced lightly about their Grove days before entering more recent years. Ivy dropped the name of her college and Gideon said in surprise, "You were so close! I was a stone's throw away at Harvard—"

"Really? I can't believe I didn't see you at any house parties—"

"Which ones?"

"Oh—mostly Currier—"

"I was in Eliot—"

"Eliot had terrible parties."

"The *most* terrible—I threw some of them."

"What about you?" she asked after their chuckles died down. "Where have your adventures taken you?"

In an unpretentious tone, Gideon told her he'd spent two years working for the Clinton Health Access Initiative before going back for his master's degree in California; now he was working on creating a smart thermometer to track how diseases spread. Ivy already knew all of this. After running into Sylvia, she'd looked up everything on the Speyers—family trees, graduation photos, wedding invitations, the article about the Whitaker newspaper conglomerate of which Poppy Caroline Whitaker Speyer was a 0.43 percent shareholder, Ted Speyer's retirement from office, and even an invitation for a christening party some distant Speyer had uploaded on a Word document. That's how she knew the details Gideon wasn't supplying—he got his master's at *Stanford*, he'd been named one of Forbes 30 under 30 two years in a row.

"I've always wanted to live in California," she said, careful not to mention Stanford.

"Oh, you should, it's certainly relaxed there." His tone hinted he wasn't necessarily a fan of relaxed. "But I'm glad to be back. The old crowd's mostly stuck around. We're all huge Celtics fans so we catch the home games together whenever we have time."

Ivy thought he would now invite her to hang out with "the old crowd," but instead his eyes flickered across the room and then his hand was on her shoulder; he was excusing himself to go say hello to a friend. She barely had time to call out "Right—see you later" before he was gone, talking to an older-looking brunette in a moss-green dress.

The important thing, Ivy felt, was not to take his departure personally. Unlike Daniel, men like Gideon preferred their women unruffled, mysterious, independent from themselves; he and his girlfriend would be like two planets orbiting around a common sun, which was work. Daniel hadn't been ambitious at all, she reflected.

At dinner, she chose a seat on the opposite end of the table from Gideon. The man in the bowler hat sat beside her. He said his name was Nicolas. He was a photographer. When she asked of what, his sneer was so condescending she wondered how his ego managed to fit inside his hat. "Of life," he said. Then, perhaps realizing they would have to make conversation for the rest of the meal, he softened his tone.

"How do you know Sylvia?" he asked.

"I just met her," said Ivy.

He nodded. "Me too."

The salmon-pink place mats were set, the ivory linen perfectly ironed, the candles lit, the music lowered. The bread basket made its way down the table. Ivy tore into a poppy seed roll. She felt her stomach gurgling as the warm yeast slid down her throat; she realized she was more than halfway to drunk.

Sylvia served a white fish cooked in some lemony sauce with potatoes and tiny sprigs of parsley; the lamb came next, a perfect medium rare, the pink juices seeping into the fluffy couscous. The dinner conversation flowed without direction or context, like a whirlpool into which random stories and name-dropping were tossed and churned and spit out into an altogether different story, the more obscure, the better. Every gathering deals in its own social currency, and in this particular crowd, it was one's capacity to be *interesting*. By the time the chocolate mousse and coffee were served, Ivy was so full she could feel the acid rise up in the back of her throat.

All this time, Gideon didn't look at her.

Just before midnight, they all squeezed onto the balcony. Ivy tried to push toward Gideon, to at least make eye contact, but his back was to her. They counted down to the new year. Booms erupted across the city, a simultaneous explosion of fireworks so bright it lit the night sky a sapphire blue. They passed around a joint, then another. Gideon, Ivy noticed, did not partake.

Back inside, Nicolas began spouting his vehement opinions on the growth of online platforms selling mass-produced art prints (horrible, commerce, demeaning art). Someone lifted their head off the plant tendrils on the floor and said, "Dude. Shut the fuck up." It was the thought that'd been running through Ivy's head all evening and she laughed until her eyes were blurry with tears. She could feel Sylvia's gaze, cool and judgmental, removed from them all in her gorgeous superiority. But when she looked over, Sylvia was gyrating in her arm-chair with her eyes closed, snapping her fingers in double time, seem-ingly immersed in the music. Ivy stood up to go out on the balcony with a small group for a smoke break. She heard Gideon say to the brunette: "I hate the smell of cigarettes." She excused herself to the bathroom.

When she returned to the living room, the gold clock over the mantel read three thirty-five. Sylvia was curled up on the sofa like a sleek golden lynx, enshrined by the light of her blazing candlesticks. Two knitting needles flashed between her hands with incredible speed, like pincers. Whatever Sylvia was making was gray and shapeless. She paused from her knitting to gesture Ivy and Gideon over. "Did you two have a good evening?" she asked, as if they had been the honored guests, the only people whose opinions mattered to her. It would have touched Ivy if she hadn't seen Sylvia speak in the exact same way at some point to everyone else at the dinner.

"It was a lovely dinner," said Ivy.

"And that lamb," said Gideon, squeezing his sister's shoulders. "I never get a home-cooked meal otherwise." He grinned at Ivy as if they shared an inside joke. Then he checked his watch. "I should get going—I have brunch with Tom tomorrow."

"Tommy Tom Tom," said Sylvia idly, pincers flashing. "Is he still dating that girl from Michigan?"

"Yes—Marybeth. I haven't seen them since Thanksgiving." Gideon glanced at his watch again.

His imminent departure melted Ivy's resolve to appear aloof. "Is this Tom from Grove?" she asked. Gideon's childhood best friend, Tom Cross, was the most frequent sighting in Gideon's Facebook photos. She knew it was a stretch that the name *Tom* should make her think of Tom Cross—all the world's Toms probably lived in Boston—but it was late, she was drunk, her inhibitions were precariously close to nil.

"You remember him?" Gideon said in surprise.

"Sure." Ivy picked at the lint on the sofa armrest. "You guys played soccer together. All the girls had huge crushes on him."

"That's the one." Gideon smiled briefly. "Yeah. He hasn't changed much."

It was Sylvia who said, "Oh for goodness sake, Giddy. Must I do everything for you?" She puckered her lips. "Ivy, *please* go to brunch with my brother and Tom tomorrow. He's not stupid, I promise, just slow on the uptake."

"Oh!" said Ivy, heat radiating up her neck. "I didn't mean—"

"If you're free tomorrow," said Gideon pleasantly, not looking at his sister, "you should come for brunch tomorrow."

"I don't want to third-wheel," Ivy said, unable to help her nervous giggle at the end. She felt a visceral sensation of *spilling out* and tried desperately to gather herself in again.

"You're saving *me* from third-wheeling," said Gideon. "Tom's bringing Marybeth."

"Well, if I'm *saving* you . . ." said Ivy.

They exchanged phone numbers; Gideon said he'd come pick her up, waving away her suggestion that she could meet them there.

"It was fun as always, Sib." Gideon kissed his sister on the cheek.

After a slight hesitation, he leaned over and kissed Ivy, too, his lips warm and dry.

Watching the door swing shut, Ivy couldn't help the feline-like smile that turned up the corners of her lips. She noticed Sylvia staring at her with an odd look on her face. Ivy burst out laughing. The sound was artificial even to her own ears. "What are you making?" she asked.

"A sweater. For my boyfriend."

Ivy tried to recall which of the reed-thin, leather-clad men had been at Sylvia's side all night, but she'd been too distracted by Gideon to notice anyone else. "Was he here tonight?"

"He's in Vegas this week. And he hates my dinner parties. It's like dragging a cat into a bathtub. He hates anything civilized, really." Sylvia fretted over losing her stitch count. "Here, can you hold this for me?"

Ivy took the ball of yarn and released the thread inch by inch, mesmerized by the neat rows of delicate stitches . . . Sylvia's silvery voice seemed to blend with the fibers of the yarn into one harmonious gray tapestry . . .

The next thing Ivy knew, she was walking down a narrow staircase, which smelled of cinnamon and five-spice, and then she was on the pavement, her coat draped over one arm, her purse over the other arm, stumbling to the corner deli to buy a pack of cigarettes. It was just past four in the morning. She flagged down a cab and rode the thirty minutes across the city, her foolish smirking face pressed against the streaky car window.

8

Tom Cross was not aging well. Watery rays of sun gleamed off his carefully combed hair and pallid face, bloated from too many happy hours, giving him the appearance of some kind of brown sea anemone in a pink dress shirt and cuffed chinos, boat shoes on his sockless feet. Next to Tom sat Marybeth Hamill, a woman who radiated such vigorous health—the auburn curls bounced out of a half ponytail, a ruddy blush glowed under a deep tan, which hinted at outdoor sports—that Ivy wondered how Tom could ever keep up in bed. Marybeth's hazel eyes flicked over Ivy's frame with a quick snap of estimation, and sensing in her a kindred spirit, an expression of congenial welcome opened on her face like curtains rising in a theater.

Gideon introduced Ivy as an old friend from Grove who had moved away before graduation. Ivy saw that Tom did not remember her at all. Tom, Sylvia—people like that flaunted their inability to recall names and faces. Gideon wasn't like that. He'd come up to her and said, *Do you remember me, Ivy?* As if she'd been the important one.

"Good old Grove," Tom said after the introductions. "Man, those were the days. We just saw a movie—what's it called, sweetheart . . . oh, never mind, you probably fell asleep. Anyway, it's about two cops going undercover at their old high school. Think we could pull it off, Gideon?"

"Not with your hairline, *sweetheart*," said Marybeth. Her voice was low and hoarse, almost as deep as a man's. "Even with a toupee, you'd only be mistaken for the gym teacher." Gideon laughed silently with shoulders quivering.

"I like being an adult better," said Ivy. "More freedom."

"Ah, lucky you then," said Tom. "I have less freedom than ever, what with work and the damn parents badgering me all the time." He splayed out his hands in aggravation. "My mom, you know. She calls me every weekend to play doubles, or to get brunch or follow her around holding her shopping bags."

"What happened to Gwen?" said Gideon.

"Tore her meniscus riding last month. Anyway, she wanted me to go with her yesterday to pick out a new paint color—"

"She's lonely," said Marybeth, "and I don't think—"

"—to pick out a new paint color for their bedroom"—Tom talked over his girlfriend—"but what the hell do I know about paint color? She's already planned this entire Thanksgiving and Christmas holiday. Imagine the horror if Marybeth and I ever want to take a vacation on our own for Christmas. She requires more maintenance than Hunter. Our German shepherd," he added, his eyes flickering toward Ivy, who smiled sympathetically.

"Last Christmas," said Marybeth, "was almost the death of me."

"Marybeth called me a derelict boyfriend that trip," said Tom.

"There's only so much Catholic gore I can stare at before losing my mind," said Marybeth. "*You* know the paintings I'm talking about, Gideon." She began counting on her fingers. "There's Jesus bleeding on the cross. Some saint getting beheaded. Madonna with one breast. A cherub bleeding out in the eyes. A naked woman getting stabbed to death. All of it's hanging in the dining room while we're cutting into our lamb shanks . . . The more blood and gore the more Tom's dad adores it. No wonder Tom grew up morbid."

"Marybeth has a recurring dream," said Tom placidly, "where she shoots me on a safari hunt and then sticks my head on the wall."

"You can become one of those Catholic martyrs," said Marybeth.

"People find Catholicism to escape women," said Tom.

This continued for some time. Tom and Marybeth took turns speaking about each other—he in controlled rhetoric, she in quick derisive gestures. Their eyes slid back and forth between Ivy and Gideon, but never to each other. Was this a form of banter, Ivy wondered, or was it real disdain beneath their sardonic smiles? Perhaps walking the thin line between the two was what made it exciting.

The waiter finally came to take their drink orders: mimosas for the women, a Bloody Mary for Tom, coffee for Gideon.

"I know what you mean," said Ivy, picking up the thread. "Our parents are becoming children, aren't they, with their quirky ideas and tantrums?"

"I think Tom's parents are beyond 'quirky,'" Marybeth said dryly.

"They sound very attached," said Ivy.

"They're monsters," said Tom.

"You're an only child, aren't you?" said Ivy, imitating their droll tones.

Tom hooked his gaze on her. "What's that supposed to mean?"

She laughed but no one followed. Gideon was no longer smiling.

"I'm just teasing," she said. Clearly she'd misread the subtext. Tom and Marybeth hadn't been subversively bragging about Tom's high-maintenance parents. The irritation had been real.

As punishment, Tom began speaking to her in italics.

"Are *you* an only child, Ivy?"

"I have a younger brother."

"And where is your *family* from?"

Ivy paused. "China."

"But you grew up in West Maplebury, no?" Gideon said smoothly.

"*South* of Andover?" said Tom.

"It's an hour west," said Ivy. "*West* Maplebury."

Marybeth snorted.

The waiter returned with their drinks. They fell silent, studying the menu. Ivy was grateful for the reset; had the conversation gone on any longer, her facade of being a good sport would have become visibly forced.

The second Tom finished ordering his entrée, Gideon asked about his and Marybeth's recent vacation to Saint Bart's. Tom appeared to be slightly diminished, slouching back in his seat with an air of distracted nervousness. At Gideon's question, he sat up slowly and crossed his arms.

"Actually, something happened on the trip."

"Uh-oh," said Gideon.

"Well, the thing is—" Tom cleared his throat. "We asked you to brunch to tell you—Marybeth and I are engaged."

Marybeth held up her hand that had been hidden in her lap for the drama of this moment: a fat, cushion-cut emerald sat on her ring finger in a heavy gold claw setting.

"Oh my God," Ivy gasped.

"W-wo-wo-wow!" said Gideon. "Congratulations, you two!" His grin stretched ear to ear, the little crooked tooth flashing jauntily.

Color flooded the back of Tom's neck. With the bombastic swagger Ivy remembered from Grove, he began regaling them with the story of the proposal. It'd happened on their helicopter tour. The pilot flew over the message Tom had written on the beach: *Marry Me?*

"I thought it was meant for someone else," said Marybeth. "I pointed at it and said, 'Look, Tom, someone's proposing.' The next thing I know, he'd unclipped his seat belt and was on one knee. The pilot was shouting, *Get back in your seat!* I've never been so shocked in my life."

Tom raised one brow. "Why? You've been telling me to propose for years."

"I think you're confusing me with your mother," Marybeth shot back.

"Face it, Tom, that's game, set, match," said Gideon, reaching over the little table to clap Tom's shoulder. His generous teasing rounded the line of Marybeth's lips into its usual smirk. His own smile trembled at the edges, as if about to take flight. When the waiter came with their food, Gideon said, "Can we pop open a bottle of champagne, these two just got engaged!" They all seemed to take a collective breath. Ivy felt the limpness of having exerted some vast group effort, the purpose of which eluded her.

The arrival of the champagne signaled permission to transition into their exuberant, sloppy selves, preceding the actual effects of alcohol. Marybeth told a story about Tom's sleep apnea—he snored so hard he woke himself up; she imitated the snort, a loud, piggish sound—and it was a marker of their heady mood that they all fell to pieces at this. Ivy asked to see the ring again. "Appalling, isn't it?" said Marybeth, not bothering to keep her voice down. "But it's been in Tom's family since the ice age, so what can I do?"

By the second hour, they began to express their fondness for one another in sentimental, boisterous bursts. Tom pointed at Gideon, his Boston accent coming out: "I've known this guy since preschool. And now I'm going to be married. I always thought you'd be first."

"I told you I wouldn't be," said Gideon, shaking his head.

"You two are adorable," said Marybeth.

"Bring us another bottle," Tom called out.

The waiter came over and began to recite the selections. "The same one as before," interrupted Tom.

"The Dom Pérignon or the d'Ambonnay, sir?"

"Which one, he asks us," grumbled Tom. "You're the expert, aren't you?"

The waiter disappeared in high color. "What are you laughing about?" Marybeth asked. Ivy said the waiter was going to spit in their food. Marybeth said, "He wouldn't be such a brute," but when desserts came out, Ivy noticed she didn't touch her crème brûlée.

Eschewing the spoon, Tom picked up a lady finger off his tiramisu with his index finger and thumb, licking a trail of cream off his thumb afterward. It was a disgusting gesture, but everything Tom did seemed a deliberate slap to good form, as if he were too well bred for manners. "I want a yacht as my wedding present," he declared to Gideon, crumbs flying.

"Done," said Gideon.

"I'm going to name her *Nuaa Junior*."

"Name her *The Marybeth*," said Gideon.

"I want that!" said Marybeth.

"Time for your toast, Giddy," said Tom. Then, softer: "Practice for your best-man speech."

"Let's toast to . . . happily ever after," said Gideon, raising his glass.

"We have to get going, Tom," said Marybeth after she downed her drink. "We have the baby shower."

"We have to go to the baby shower," repeated Tom.

Gideon asked for the check. He tried to pay for the entire meal but Tom waved him off.

"The yacht," he reminded Gideon. "You gotta save up."

Ivy peeked at the receipt on the tray. Her heart nearly burst from shock. Their cocktails, four bottles of champagne, gelatinous poached eggs sprinkled with truffles and caviar, various cakes and sweets had totaled up to just over two thousand dollars.

"It was wonderful to meet you," Marybeth said to Ivy as their cab pulled up to the curb. "Gideon *must* bring you around more often. Actually"—she whirled around—"I just remembered—we're going skiing on the seventeenth in Mont-Tremblant. Come join!" Ivy laughed, lurching sideways, but Marybeth said, "I'm serious. Come."

"We'll see," said Ivy, flicking her head coyly in Gideon's direction.

Marybeth raised her voice and repeated the suggestion to Gideon, who was patting Tom on the back with final words of congratulations. "What was that?" he said.

"I said—you better bring this one on our ski trip. It's no fun going solo. Canada is so cold without someone to share a bed with."

Gideon placed his arm around Ivy's shoulder and drew her so close she could smell his woody aftershave. "I don't want to freeze," he agreed.

"Bye, lovebirds," Marybeth sang. "See you two on the slopes!" She waved frantically from the window until the taxi turned the corner.

★ ★ ★

PERHAPS GIDEON ALSO felt diving into a sudden overnight trip would be too risky because he called her a few days later and invited her to a Celtics game. Another trial run before the main performance. Ivy assumed Tom and Marybeth or more of the "old crowd" would be present, but when she saw Gideon waiting outside the Garden, he was alone. How stiff and ungainly her arms and legs felt, swinging this way and that, without elegance, while Gideon stood so tall and formal, the heavy drape of his wool coat, the edges of his plaid scarf, his pressed trousers forming a graceful line from head to toe.

Gideon was a season ticket holder with balcony seats. He quickly gathered that Ivy didn't follow basketball and to make the game livelier for her, he pointed out Boston's Big Three and framed their journeys as an exciting comeback story: they'd each been transcendent talents on lottery-bound teams until they joined together to defeat the rival Lakers and win a championship in their first year together, ending a decades-long title drought. "It's the start of a dynasty," he explained. "That's why all the games have been sold out, even in the regular season. Our team's going to win again this year." Ivy nodded and asked questions. She loved listening to Gideon's voice. Its natural ownership quality was still there. Even the Celtics belonged to him.

At halftime, she bought them two hot dogs and chocolate bars. "You said you hadn't eaten dinner yet," she said, noting that the face underneath the green cap seemed pale.

Gideon thanked her. "You're so considerate," he said.

"Just don't take advantage," she said.

He smiled uncertainly—a furrowed, stricken smile—and she hurried to laugh, to say it was a joke, he could take advantage of her as much as he wanted, which then led *him* to laugh and look away.

The Celtics crushed the Nets 118–86. In the post-win euphoria, Ivy had hoped they might hug or Gideon might wrap his arm around her shoulders the way he'd done the other day in front of Tom and Marybeth. Instead, as they gathered their coats and scarves and followed the crowd down the stairs, he turned to her suddenly and asked: "Do you remember the first time we met?"

"You mean, at Grove?"

"Yes."

"Uh . . . I remember we had American Lit together." It surprised her to realize that she didn't actually remember the *exact* first time she saw Gideon, despite her terrible infatuation. He'd not existed for her one day, and the next, he was her whole world.

"I remember it perfectly," said Gideon. "You were the new girl. Mrs. Carver introduced you and asked you to say one unusual fact about yourself. You couldn't think of one, so she asked you what you wanted to be when you grew up." He paused to look down at her with a wry smile. "You said you wanted to get a PhD."

"*I did?*" She felt her sex appeal shrivel up and die. "How did I even *know* what a PhD was back then?"

"I was so impressed. I thought you were one of those child prodigies Dad would read to us about in the newspaper."

"Trust me"—she shook her head—"I had no idea what I was saying. It must have been something my parents planted into my head."

"Then you sat in the desk next to mine and ignored me for the rest of the year. You were so different from all the other girls I'd known . . . I can't tell you how refreshing it was."

She smiled noncommittally. Was "refreshing" one of those adjectives reserved for "considerate" girls?

They'd finally made it out of the stadium. It was a foggy evening of inky black skies, a wispy, almost invisible moon—a shadow moon, as Meifeng had called it once, when things became possible that had not been possible before. Ivy's face stung with the sudden wind.

"Do you think I've changed a lot since then?" she asked.

"Not really. I was just thinking how comfortable I feel with you. As I get older, I think that a shared history counts for a lot more in friendship than quantity of time spent with another person." His eyes roamed over her face in a frank manner. "And you look the same. Haven't aged a day."

"I can't believe I used to have a crush on you."

"Did you?"

The flow of the crowd around them, a sea of green, the celebratory shouts, sounds of beer bottles breaking on cement, gave her a sense of exhilaration, of being anonymous and safe in her anonymity.

"Oh, come on," she said, pulling her coat closer to her body. "You knew."

He didn't refute her.

"Funny how life works," she said quietly. "Here we are."

Gideon's eyes were two gossamer orbs, reflecting her own face back at her. "Here we are," he echoed.

IVY CHARGED THE flight to her credit card. It was $575—an overpriced last-minute flight from Boston to Montreal. And then there were the accessory costs: ski jacket, pants, helmet, goggles, new lingerie, a wax, manicure, pedicure—all necessary expenses, she knew, but frightening when added up. She could not look at her bank account. She opened one of those spam letters advertising the latest credit card and applied for the one with the highest spending limit. A temporary onetime Band-Aid, she promised herself.

All week, through her morning meetings, coffee breaks, Daily 5, through her long, steamy baths after work and the tedious drone of Andrea's one-sided conversations about her weight loss efforts and latest boy troubles, and most of all, at night, when her mind roamed most free and her stream of desire, while always present but subdued during the day, swelled to a rushing river, she would picture herself making love to Gideon. The heavy quilt of a cold mountain lodge. Her nipples as hard as acorns. His hand running up her thigh, the hollow of his temples pressed against her breast, and his lips . . . his lips—! Hours and hours of pleasure later, the sun rising over snow-covered mountains outside their terrace, they would drink their coffee naked underneath their cotton robes; he'd reach over the pastry basket and press her hand to the purple-veined hickey on the side of his neck.

The day before the trip, Ivy sent Sylvia a thank-you card for the New Year's party. Sylvia texted her a few days later: *Thank you for the sweet message. So nice of you to come. Funny thing—I use the same set of thank-you cards. Great taste!* Ivy had a good laugh at that.

Since her flight was separate from the others, she met Gideon and Marybeth at baggage claim. Tom had gone to pick up the rental car, a gleaming white Range Rover that still barely managed to fit all their equipment. They drove to Mont-Tremblant, mostly silent, all of them sleepy. Tom had the radio dialed to some country station, and he spoke to them in a dead-on Southern accent for the rest of the drive. He could be funny sometimes, Ivy noted, softened by the false temporary fondness that follows inclusion.

When they arrived at the lodge, a convenient three-bedroom villa, Ivy suspected, from overhearing Gideon's conversation with the concierge, that he'd changed their housing just for her. She felt a wave of disappointed misery. Gideon probably would have been appalled had she intimated they share a room. The first time they met, Daniel had slept over in her hotel bed—she was at the Twin Harbor Casino for Andrea's birthday party, and this shy, wiry guy who'd been at their blackjack table all evening had brought up a bottle of wine to her room. Men always think they take the initiative but it's women who make the first, often imperceptible move. Gideon was no Daniel, however. What'd worked before wouldn't work now.

No one lingered in the rooms. As soon as they dropped off their suitcases, they geared up for a day of skiing. Thus began for Ivy what felt like a time loop of continuously strapping on skis, flailing, sliding, falling, getting her poles, pushing herself back up, rinse, and repeat. Slide, fall, find poles, get up. Sometimes her skis would fall off altogether and Gideon had to help her get back into them. It began to snow in the early afternoon. Fat snowflakes stung her cheeks, she tasted cold in her mouth. Around her was white, a sea of white, and each skier on the bunny hill was their own island of misery and exhaustion, their only goal to keep out of one another's way.

"You've never played sports, have you?" Tom asked when he and Marybeth stopped by to check up on her and Gideon. Ivy's eyes stung with tears behind her goggles, but she managed a self-deprecating laugh—at least she assumed she was laughing, she could no longer feel her face. By the end of the day, she had soaked through all her layers of clothes, her gloves, even the soft padding of her ski helmet was damp with perspiration. When she took off her socks that night to shower, she saw the purple hue underneath her left toenail where it had already begun to blacken.

After dinner, Gideon fell asleep on the recliner next to the fireplace. Ivy was forced to bear Tom's incessant jabs, for without Gideon to rein him in, even Marybeth's sarcasm couldn't stop his drunken "jokes," always delivered in the same oblique manner so that Ivy had no way to defend herself, because she was never sure what it was he was implying.

"It's too bad we didn't get to ski with Gideon at all," Tom remarked as he stripped off his socks and wiggled his hairy toes toward the fire.

"We could join them tomorrow," Marybeth pointed out.

"And die from some idiot crashing into me on the bunny hill? No thanks." He took a long swig of his brandy. "Are you having fun, Ivy?" he said kindly.

"Oh, yes." She pulled out her lesson planner. "Thank you for inviting me."

"You can thank Gideon for that," said Tom, "with a late-night visit." She smiled humorously.

"I mean it." He leaned forward. "Gideon loves aggressive women."

"*Is* there anything going on between you two?" Marybeth asked, switching allegiances.

"We're just friends," said Ivy.

"So there's no chemistry?"

"Well . . ." Her blushing face reflexively turned toward Gideon. She was struck with the sudden fear that he was awake, listening to their conversation about him, that perhaps he and his friends had even contrived this setup to test her. In a low voice, she said, "We're just getting to know each other."

Marybeth studied her.

"You're going about it all wrong." Tom frowned. "He's your typical shy dude. Loves it when the girls come on to him. The kinkier, the better. He's an animal in bed. What, you don't believe me?"

Ivy looked at Marybeth, but the other woman didn't come to her aid.

"You're joking, right," she said.

"Am I joking . . . am I joking . . ." Tom struck the armrest with his fist. "Are *you* fucking joking?"

Ivy drew back.

Marybeth said, "I think it's bedtime."

Tom blinked. He set his drink on the table and yawned. "Didn't mean to push . . . Please excuse me. I'm going to bed." He looked at Marybeth. Marybeth looked at Gideon. Ivy looked down at her lap. The ink from her lesson plans had bled onto her damp fingers.

THE NEXT MORNING, she convinced Gideon that she wanted time to practice by herself. After making sure she was able to get off the lift on her own, he disappeared to find Tom and Marybeth on the black diamonds. Ivy bore through the pain but on her second run, her legs simply gave out and she tumbled violently down a hill and skidded into the marked-off terrain on the side of the slope. She unstrapped her skis and walked all the way back down. She went to the lodge. The breakfast crowd was still thick at nine in the morning. She purchased coffee, a plate of eggs, ham, beans on toast, and an enormous slice of apple pie, eating everything in great greedy mouthfuls, barely chewing, burning her mouth with a large gulp of coffee. Around her, people clomped around in heavy boots, the snowboarders dressed extravagantly in colorful gear, the skiers sleek and elegant in their fur-lined jackets.

After she finished eating, she relocated to a recently vacated chair by the window. She sat, facing the slopes, and she waited. She'd brought no book or magazine, and her phone had no service. There was nothing to distract her as she waited for the people she'd come with. If they decided to abandon her here, there was nothing she could do. Ridiculous really, how one could attach oneself to strangers and pretend it was normal. *Are you fucking joking?* Joking, always joking . . . Am I a joke to them, she wondered. Were the three of them together now, laughing about her? She looked at the landscape outside. The spots of brown peeking underneath the branches of the trees in the distance sent a shot of loneliness through her.

When Gideon came in for lunch, she waved him over and pretended she'd just come in not too long ago.

"How was it?" Gideon asked, apple-cheeked, exuding vitality.

"Fine," she said with a tight smile. "Fell a few times. I was getting sore so I called it a day. Where are Tom and Marybeth?"

Gideon shrugged. "Not sure . . . I've been on my own all morning. They're probably on the moguls, but these old things can't keep up." He patted his knees.

He'd been on his own all morning . . . ! There was nothing like dissipating paranoia to make a person feel so giddy and gay . . . Ivy wanted to laugh and cheer and say frivolous things. Sensing the change in her, Gideon grinned and said, "I think I'll hang out with you here after lunch."

"Let's get dessert," Ivy said joyfully.

They found two armchairs in the smaller dining room, next to the bar. A band was setting up in the corner. Gideon ordered two hot toddies. "You've never had one of these?" he said in amazement when Ivy asked what it was. "Never," she said. She drank three. It was so delicious she wanted to cry.

That evening, the four of them relaxed in the hot tub on the balcony of their villa. The temperature was a cool fifteen degrees, the black night lit with a million stars. In the distance came the twinkling lights from the little ski village below where they'd had dinner: cheese fondue and poutine. This time, Ivy kept the fact that she'd never tried either to herself.

Tom and Marybeth, having exerted all their aggression skiing, were in an agreeable mood and kissing in the water. The green strap of Marybeth's string bikini was partially untied, trailing behind her back like a blade of grass. On the opposite end of the half circle sat Gideon, the steam rising over his handsome face, his eyes gazing into the distant mountains. Ivy floated over to him.

"Where are you thinking?"

He smiled at her. "There are two places I love most—here and our cottage in Cattahasset. Give me mountains and water and I'm a happy man."

She thanked him for keeping her company today.

"I had a good time." His toe touched hers under the water. Their eyes unwillingly fell on Marybeth and Tom.

"Ivy?"

"Hmm?"

"I'm going to kiss you now." And he did.

How did it feel? It felt as light and buoyant as the stars above, watching over them in their cold, distant glory.

9

THEIR FOURSOME WAS A REGULAR FIXTURE AT BOSTON'S BEST brunch and seafood spots that winter. Platters of oysters doused with sriracha and lemon, creamy clam chowders bubbling in sourdough bread bowls, sweet and tender lobster meat dripping with butter. And how lovely the city looked in winter! The dreamy glitter of fresh snow, the cold noonday sun, the nippy air carrying with it smells of earth, sap, the impending whiff of spring. Never before had Ivy found her students, especially Arabella, so pleasant and endearing, eternal sources of stories for Gideon. They all had their roles in the new group—Gideon, the voice of reason; Marybeth, the instigator; Tom, the talker, the one whose moods they all navigated around; and Ivy, the outsider, someone they showed off for yet took for granted. The temporary distraction.

Only she wasn't. She stuck around.

She waited a month before sleeping with Gideon. It happened on Valentine's Day. After drinks at the Hotel Commonwealth, he took her back to his studio apartment. Exposed brick walls, bay windows, marine-blue bathroom tiles so cool and polished they appeared fluorescent, like being inside an aquarium. "S-sorry for the m-me-me-mess." He glanced around vaguely, lifted a pile of books off the sofa, put them back down again without purpose. Ivy's heart softened. This was the real Gideon, she thought. The one who stuttered when he was nervous. The one who couldn't meet her eye. She was always looking for the real Gideon. She never stopped to wonder what would happen should she find him one day. "It's wonderful," she said before pulling him down on top of her.

Afterward, he wrapped her in her coat, kissed her on the cheek, and put her in a cab home—as neat as wrapping a present. It was raining outside. A foggy, gray sky cast everything in its cold shadow. *What do you see when you look upon the world, Gideon?* She tried to infuse the city's dark alleys with his dignified imperturbability, but she could not. Without his presence, the loiterers on her corner frightened her, the gossamer objects floating in the gust of wind were just plastic bags. That was the thing about getting too much happiness at once. Without time to adjust, the pain of not having it suddenly became unbearable.

A week later, Gideon came over to her old Victorian house for the first time. To prepare for his visit, Ivy scrubbed the toilet, cleaned the fridge of the moldy onions and garlic, vats of gunky yogurt, Andrea's half-eaten yams and empty egg cartons. She washed her bedding, vacuumed the carpet, bought so many long-stemmed irises, their purple and yellow petals iridescent by candlelight, that her walls glowed like a lava lamp. There was nothing she could do about her seedy neighborhood but she even tried to tackle the yard, raking the dead leaves, mostly reduced to brown slime, from the patch of sidewalk in front of the house, and dragging the ugly row of trash bins into the backyard.

Gideon was distracted when he came over. One of the Big Three had injured his knee, he told her, and suddenly the Celtics' championship no longer seemed so certain. Ivy, too, felt despondent. She had cooked spaghetti Bolognese, toasted garlic bread, tossed a salad with stuffed olives, and opened a bottle of Sancerre, but Gideon was barely eating. *He must really be cut up about the basketball thing.* She felt a wave of tenderness toward him then, for his passions and his troubles, which, to her, were the wholesome troubles of a child.

After dinner, they went to Dresdan's for drinks so Gideon could meet Andrea. Ivy had prepared him by explaining Andrea as "my friend who plays violin for the Boston Symphony Orchestra. She's quite a handful, but she's kind," Ivy added, not wanting Gideon to think she was bad-mouthing a friend. "She'd be the first one to have your back in a fight."

"That's all that matters," Gideon agreed.

When they got to the bar, a jazz quartet was just setting up. Already, it was packed with a noisy, buoyant crowd, driven mostly by a group of office workers jostling to buy another round for the birthday boy, whose right forearm was covered in tallies, drawn on with permanent marker, of how many shots he'd had so far. Just as Gideon ordered their drinks, Andrea arrived dressed in skintight faux leather leggings and a shrunken leopard-patterned sweater, her lipstick the deep plum color of sangria. Lips and hips, Andrea's trademark weapons. "Traffic was awful!" she said, somehow managing to hug both Ivy and Gideon simultaneously. Her yam and boiled egg diet had worked. She'd lost fifteen pounds and her face had taken on that taut, dark-eyed look of the hungry. She was very luminous tonight. The undercurrent of cheap sex she usually emitted had taken on depth and mystery. That was the power of beauty.

It was impossible to carry on a long conversation but Andrea kept trying anyway, leaning forward at so sharp an angle that the collar of her sweater fell open and the soft swell of her cleavage, with its smattering of chestnut freckles, gleamed like ripe pears, as she shouted: "Sorry, what? *What?*" Ivy watched Gideon. But it was hard to tell what he really thought of Andrea. In a way, he reminded Ivy of her aunt Sunrin. Such impeccable manners. But where Sunrin's polish emitted superiority—her difference set her apart—Gideon's included you in its intimacy, like a gentle guide whispering the answers in your ear so that you felt very clever when you said the right words. Ivy could see the magic of it on Andrea's glowing face—how special and beautiful I am, Andrea was thinking. Ivy wondered if that was how she looked talking to Gideon. Every twitch of his brow, cock of his head, curve of his lips signaled, to her, lust, incredulity, contempt. She imagined

Gideon harboring these emotions because these were the emotions she harbored herself.

"Do you have any single friends?" Andrea asked Gideon after her second glass of sparkling lemonade. She wasn't drinking, but Ivy could hardly ever tell the difference between drunk and sober Andrea. Probably alcohol wasn't allowed on her diet.

"There's my cofounder, Roland," said Gideon.

"How old is he?"

"Twenty-seven. No wait. Twenty-six."

Andrea shook her head. "I'm thirty-three."

"What?"

"She's thirty-three," said Ivy.

"Twenty-six is still a baby," said Andrea. "I need a man"—she tapped her finger—"to put a ring on it."

Gideon nodded sympathetically.

"Andrea's becoming very practical these days," said Ivy.

"All men want these days is sex. You know what Chris said to me the other day? He said, 'Why should I want to get married now? The longer I wait, the more my stock goes up.' And he's right!" Andrea shook her head helplessly. "Time's running out for me but he hasn't even reached his prime yet! Why should he want a thirty-three-year-old with decaying eggs when he can have a twenty-two-year-old fresh from college?" She wagged a finger at Gideon. "You'd better not be wasting Ivy's time. Two years with Daniel! She just wanted to meet his mom. What a chickenshit."

Ivy dragged Andrea to the restroom. She listened to Andrea struggling with the zipper of her pants before going into the stall to help her.

"You're the best," said Andrea, leaning a hot forehead against Ivy's shoulder. "Gideon should know he can't mess with my best friend."

With a best friend like you, Ivy thought, who needs enemies? She brushed Andrea's bangs back from her temples.

"You have to make him work for it," Andrea went on. "Ask him if he's seeing other women . . . demand that he give you an answer! Men need ultimatums. Gideon seems like a good one but you can't always tell by their clothes . . . remember that South African guy I was with last year? He had that pet python? He asked if he could strap on a . . . well, anyway, I was like 'No, honey, you can't insert that rocket into my a-hole,' and then he dumps me the next day. This was the same man who told me he wanted two of our own kids, then we'd adopt our third because there's so many babies who need a good family. I cried when he said that." Andrea gazed up at Ivy in pity, as if Ivy had been the one who'd cried when a man said he wanted to have three children with her, one adopted. "You're the innocent type. Men love to take advantage. If Gideon asks you to do anything you don't want to, tell *me* and I'll give him a piece of my mind. If he respects you, he would respect your boundaries."

Ivy considered the woman before her. The indignant expression meant to express feminine loyalty, the simmering anger that seemed to be universal to all single women over thirty. Neither the loyalty nor the anger had anything to do with Ivy; she was simply the persona upon which Andrea's ideas of life refracted themselves.

She washed her hands and went back outside.

The band was playing a sultry rendition of a Billie Holiday song. Gideon was watching the saxophonist. The man swayed with each velvety vibrato, his chapped lips exhaling into the mouthpiece through brute force as beads of sweat formed, quivered, then dripped down his temples. Gideon closed his eyes. He picked up his drink and downed it in one mouthful. His Adam's apple was very prominent when he swallowed.

Ivy reached the table. She leaned down and kissed the side of Gideon's neck where his pulse throbbed. The tumbler slipped from his fingers.

"Are you having fun?" she asked.

"Yes!" He glanced behind her shoulder. "Is Andrea all right?"

"She's just freshening up." Ivy brought her stool closer so their knees knocked together when she sat down. "I'm sorry about her grilling you earlier."

"Not at all. She seems like a great friend. Very protective of you."

"Her therapist told her she tends to project her emotions onto others."

"I can see that." He added something she didn't catch.

"What's that?"

"I said—it's not every person who can be that honest with what they want."

The quartet began an upbeat rock number. Andrea came back. She seemed excited, almost hectic.

"Whee! I peed for almost two minutes. And guess what? I got my period! I was almost a week late . . . it must have been my diet throwing me off. Can you imagine if I was *actually* pregnant? . . . It's not like Chris and I are ready *at all* to be parents . . . God, it's hot in here . . . I need a drink!" She ordered an extra-dry martini and took out from her purse a large Japanese fan, flapping it vigorously toward her crumpled, ecstatic face. Ivy and Gideon averted their eyes. Even honest Andrea couldn't be honest about everything.

IVY LAY ON her bed waiting for the Lins to arrive. It was almost dusk. Shadow puppets flitted side to side with the incoming draft, and the sweet smell of dying irises and white jasmine tea candles, flickering in every nook of her room, transported her back to Sylvia's bohemian apartment—had it only been three months ago?—where her memories of the party had taken on a dazzling glow, all the faces sneering and beautiful, the clamor of disparate voices blending into a single sonorous voice. She hadn't enjoyed herself at the party. But it'd also been one of the best nights of her life. The two were not always in opposition.

It was her birthday today. She'd been alive for twenty-seven years. What had she done with her time? I'm a first-grade teacher, she thought. It seemed incredible. Meifeng always said that everyone had a great future in their past. How had she let hers slip away?

It'd seemed natural postcollege, after a year of waffling over law school, to concede that she would never make it as a lawyer and slide onto the easier path of getting her teaching certification. A lot of girls from her sorority became teachers. Ivy didn't like children but that didn't matter. Being a teacher wasn't actually about teaching. Most jobs have nothing to do with the day-to-day work and everything to do with what they represent. Teachers made good trophy wives to wealthy men. Why struggle to climb the corporate ladder yourself when you can retire after marriage to volunteer at puppy shelters and color-code your sweater drawers? One of her colleagues, Christine Masterman, started a cooking blog the day she got engaged. Now Christine walked around school in her fifties-era starched skirts and little ballet slippers, pushing gluten-free brownies on all the other teachers—they tasted like dried avocado, which they were—and bursting with so much Mary Poppins smugness Ivy wanted to smack her across the back of the head the way Shen used to smack her and Austin when they got carried away. Only patience had tempered her resentment: one day, she'd thought, her time would come. But what she hadn't realized was that unlike herself, the other teachers at Kennedy already had a pool of future husbands to choose from. Family friends, childhood playmates, church members, best friends of older brothers, their dads' golf partners' nephews. For the Christines and Sylvias and Arabellas of the world, an acceptable job was just another task to tick off on the life list, no different from choosing the right hat to wear to a polo match in Newport. Ivy had been their friend, she'd hooked up with their exes, but she had always been different. She had no family to back her.

Gideon said last week at Dresdan's that not everyone could be honest about what they wanted. Was he hinting that *she* wasn't honest? That she was "guarded," that he couldn't see himself marrying her?

With one arm, Ivy pulled out a cigarette from the pack in her nightstand and lit it on the flame of a candle. She blew tepid smoke rings onto the ceiling and watched them dissipate, thinking dully that her dreams were just like these smoke rings: they rose one by one, died without ever taking form.

The doorbell rang. She got up very slowly and looked out the window. A bright nickel-colored van was parked on the curb. It was Nan's new car. Ivy suspected her mother felt guilty about such a large purchase because Nan had talked about nothing else during their last few phone calls. A van was safe, spacious, and because it was paid for up front in cash, Nan said they'd gotten a good deal. "Always bring your cash when you buy a car," Nan had advised her. As if Ivy had thousands of dollars lying around to spend on new cars, when she could barely afford repairs on her shitty Camry. I should stop sending them money each month, she thought resentfully.

"A-ya, you look so skinny!" Nan greeted Ivy, bursting through the doorway carrying several bags of heavy groceries. "I need to refrigerate these right away—" She swept past Ivy toward the kitchen.

"Where's the bathroom?" Austin asked. His face was dripping with sweat; when Ivy hugged him, she smelled a musky, sour odor, like clothes left in a suitcase for too long.

"There are gangsters over there," said Shen, pointing across the street to where the usual pair of tattooed men stood in front of parked SUVs, chewing tobacco and spitting loogies onto the pavement. "Why do you live here? Why? If you need money—"

Meifeng tapped Ivy's leg with her cane. "You should put more effort into your looks. Even your father wears better-quality pants than these. The crotch hangs down to your knees!"

Ivy ignored the rabble and glanced at the fifth guest, a stocky Chinese man in a bomber-style coat, standing on her doormat, untying the shoelaces of his duck boots.

"Who's that?" she hissed at her grandmother.

"Come in, Kevin!" Meifeng called. "Sit. Sit. Don't mind the mess." From one corner of her mouth, she muttered to Ivy that Kevin Zhao was Ping's friend's son. He went to medical school in New Jersey. His parents lived in China and had asked the Lins to look after him on the weekends. "We told him we were coming to see you in Boston. He's never been to Boston. He's only been in the US five years."

"You guys invited a stranger here?" said Ivy.

"Don't be a child." Meifeng sniffed the air. "I thought Shen hadn't smoked in the car."

Kevin took off his coat. Underneath he was wearing a black sweatshirt that said COUTURE in blocky white letters. He introduced himself to Ivy as "KZ" in a strong Chinese accent. "I've heard a lot about you," he said.

"Like what?"

"Your mother says you're a great writer. She showed me your room. So many books! You must have been a child prodigy. Are those notebooks all full? May I read one of your stories?"

Ivy said she didn't write stories.

"Articles?"

"No."

"My friend is applying to business school," said Kevin. "If you have time, can you look over his essay?"

FOR DINNER, IVY took Kevin Zhao and the Lins to Shangri-La, a Chinese restaurant in Belmont. During her family's prior visit, she'd made the mistake of taking them to a fancy Italian restaurant in the North End. Carbonara is a pasta made with raw eggs, she'd explained to a horrified Nan. Meifeng ate too much beef braciole and moaned over an upset stomach. Austin, the one person she'd thought would appreciate the food, had sat slumped in his chair, refusing to even order an entrée because he didn't have an appetite. This had launched Shen into a diatribe about Austin's petulant stubbornness that'd lasted the rest of the trip.

From that visit, Ivy had seen firsthand just how wrong things had gotten with Austin. He'd been an energetic and eager—sometimes too eager—boy, and the sullenness that had seized him in high school had been attributed to teenage hormones and a bad attitude. But instead of improving in college, he'd become positively unresponsive. He gained an enormous amount of weight, stayed up all night playing computer games, switched from one major to the next, often having to retake classes because of poor attendance, until he finally dropped out last summer ("he's resting for a year," Nan excused). Nan took him to their family doctor, a Chinese woman from Suzhou, who diagnosed him with vitamin deficiency and wrote a flurry of prescriptions for nutritional supplements. "I had the same health issues at his age," Nan told the family. "Anemia. I slept all the time. I couldn't even finish my *gaokao* exams because I fainted. Not enough to eat. My son's inherited my weak constitution." No one pointed out to her that Austin was not anemic and had plenty to eat. It was easier to believe that good grades, enthusiasm, intelligence, and motivation could all be solved with vitamin D pills.

"At least I don't have to worry about you anymore," Nan would sigh to Ivy after these long rants. Irked by this hypocrisy, Ivy said, "Weren't you the one who threatened to commit suicide if I came to Boston?" To Ivy's surprise, Nan said Ivy had been right, her daughter was strong and wise, wiser than Nan herself, who was only a stupid, uneducated country woman. This flagrant display of humility had only made Ivy more cautious. Her mother's approval might be even harder to bear than her disappointment.

IVY KNEW NOW why her parents were so chummy toward Kevin Zhao: they were trying to set her up.

This should have been obvious to her from the get-go but it hadn't been. She'd let her guard down, thinking that Austin's problems were enough fodder for her parents' meddling, and that her own life would be spared.

She sat, humiliated, through the free peanuts and spicy pickles, through the twelve dishes Shen had ordered, which the waitress had to push another table to hold, through the dessert course of boiling-hot pumpkin pastries, which, in her rush to end the meal, she'd eaten too quickly and burned the roof of her mouth. The conversation was all but a farce. Nan would ask Kevin a question like: "How often do you call your mother?" To which Kevin would glance at Ivy, then downplay his filiality: "Once a week." Nan would correct him: "Ping says you call home every day. She says you save up all your money to visit them in China. Ivy only lives a few hours away and never visits us." Occasionally, Meifeng would chime in comments like: "Ivy's not a *ting hua* child like you are."

The cycle would start again: "Ping says you exercise every day?" "I play basketball sometimes." "And you swim, too, I heard! Healthy habits . . . Ivy likes to swim, too, don't you? . . . You don't? Well, you like the outdoors! You go on those camping trips. I think it's so dirty sleeping outside, but our Ivy's tough . . ."

And again: "Kevin, what do you do when you're not studying?" "I like to travel. I was in Berlin visiting a friend over spring break." "Berlin! Where's that? . . . Germany! Ivy's never even been to Europe . . . Ivy, I hope you learn from Kevin. You can't get through life just from reading books . . . Kevin, did I tell you Ivy's a great writer? Her mind is so busy with new ideas . . . she is very independent, our Ivy . . ."

It was a bizarre form of matchmaking. Nan couldn't seem to decide whether she was trying to talk Ivy up to Kevin, or shame Ivy into being a better person. Perhaps love and shame always went hand in hand, even in romance.

Shen finally asked for the check. Kevin went to use the restroom. All five Lins watched him go.

Nan said, "What do you think of Kevin?"

"Mama—*no*."

"He's in medical school—you can be good friends—"

"*No.*" Ivy looked at Meifeng accusingly. Meifeng picked her teeth with a toothpick.

"How are you going to meet a man surrounded by women teachers all day long?" Nan flared, abandoning her innocent act. "Listen to me. Kevin's father is a wealthy businessman back in Hangzhou. They're *da fang* people. Not stuck-up or stingy like the Shanghainese. I already asked him if he thought you were pretty—"

"*When?*"

"Your aunt Ping says he doesn't have a girlfriend. This is your chance."

"I have a boyfriend," said Ivy.

"You said his parents were divorced."

"This is a different boyfriend."

Nan looked at her suspiciously. "Chinese?"

"American."

"Then it won't last. Haven't you learned by now?"

Ivy slammed her teacup on the table.

Kevin returned to the table. He said he had a few friends in Boston who were going to meet him in front of the restaurant. Nan insisted that they wait with him at the curb until his friends came. Ivy knew her mother wanted to see if these "friends" were female. Ten minutes later, a matte black Acura greeted them at the curb. When Kevin opened the door, a blast of hip-hop music—*shake, shake, shake your money maker*—reverberated into the quiet night. "Bye, KZ." Ivy waved. "Happy birthday, Ivy," Kevin said cheerfully before sliding into the front seat. The Lins blinked in surprise. They'd all but forgotten it was her birthday.

Her family left the next morning. Nan had a dentist appointment—she'd just bought dental insurance—and Shen said he was meeting with someone who would be helping out part-time with the packaging and inventory. Ivy cut him off before he could go into details. She despised hearing anything about the family business. She associated all that with those dark years when they'd first moved to New Jersey. Andrea's therapist would probably tell her it was PTSD.

During their goodbyes, Ivy gave Austin a stiff hug. "Be cool," she said. He looked down at his shoes.

"Your brother really wanted to be here for your birthday," Nan said, something strangled about her tone that made Ivy turn away.

Shen was overly hearty as he patted Austin on the back. "Soon, you'll be living on your own in some city and we'll drive up to see you like we do with your sister."

"I doubt it," said Austin. They were the first words he'd spoken since the restaurant.

On each of these trips, Ivy told herself she would sit Austin down for a long, private siblings-only chat, but there never seemed to be the right circumstances or opportunity, and after they parted, he never responded to her texts or calls. She was seized with an impulse to give him something, to convey both her affection and inadequateness, so she took off her scarf and wrapped it around his neck. "It's really expensive," she said. "Cashmere and silk blend."

She held the door open for Meifeng as her grandmother hoisted one leg into the car, then another. "My knees haven't stopped hurting since we got here," she said.

With a pang of conscience, Ivy thought that she should visit Clarksville more, at least to see Meifeng, who had raised her, and Austin, who was shutting down like an overloaded computer—

Meifeng beckoned her close. "Do you really have boyfriend or was that lie for your mother?"

"I do."

"Listen. Kevin isn't so bad. I know you think he's ugly but looks aren't everything. Look at your father. Beauty is the wisdom of women; wisdom is the beauty of men. Jojo's son is already three—"

Ivy slammed the passenger door shut. I'll never leave Boston, she vowed.

NAN'S PHONE CALLS the next few weeks were peppered with references to Kevin. He'd brought over expensive ginseng for Meifeng.

He'd called to ask after Shen's cold. He took Austin to play basketball at the YMCA.

Ivy thought of the black Acura, the pulsing sounds of bass and rap as the tires screeched haughtily into the dark night, and bitterness filled her at the idea that even filial posterboy Kevin led a wilder life than she. Ten times a day, she would glance at the little plastic clock hanging above the classroom calendar and agonize over each passing minute . . . and yet when she looked back on the month, she thought it'd gone by quickly. But to where?

Only on the weekends with Gideon would she feel truly alive. Everything was vibrant, the sensory pleasures—licking melted butter off her fork, crushing grapes beneath her toes, the red globes bursting like fish roe—raw and exciting. The grape crushing had taken place during a wine-making tour outside the city. There were many excursions to wineries that April and May, for wine tasting and wine bottling and wine buying. Sometimes, she and Gideon went alone, sometimes with Tom and Marybeth. Those weekends were a blur of dark cellars, laughter echoing through pungent air, Gideon's constant hand on her arm—steady now, he'd say, smiling, his crooked teeth beautiful, and she would bite his cheek, emboldened by fumes, he tasted like salt and soap.

Then there were the clubs: the Yacht Club, the Racquet Club, the Algonquin Club, the UClub. Tom had memberships to all of them and often dragged the group along for a morning of squash or tennis. Drinking commenced at noon. Later, Ivy would recount to Andrea the pompousness of these places—gold-framed paintings of cocker spaniels, ancient documents displayed in glass safes, various suits of armor standing guard at the bottoms of spiral staircases carved with Latin crests—but it was easy to fall back on middle-class sensibilities and ridicule the wastefulness of the rich while standing with Andrea at a buffet line in Quincy. Ivy found it impossible to feel anything but fumbling ineptness when socializing among these old-moneyed *Mayflower* families, who held tradition as life's highest tenet. Tom Cross could laugh at his own pretensions but Ivy couldn't laugh. She didn't know the difference between tradition and pretension. Laughing here would only reveal her own obtuseness.

But as long as she was amenable and admiring, there were many new experiences available to her. On the last Saturday in May, she and Gideon went with Tom and Marybeth to a horse ranch Marybeth's aunt owned in New Hampshire. Ivy was flying—she literally flew into the air, holding on for dear life, but she managed to clear her first fence on the back of her glossy chestnut-colored mare. Time slowed down: the glossy strands of Marybeth's ponytail streaming in front of Ivy like a torch, Tom and Gideon cheering from the sidelines, their faces blurry and handsome, the smell of grass and sounds of birds chirping, and the image of her own figure, smartly dressed in jodhpurs and riding boots, reflecting back at her in the split second the mare leapt. "Today was my perfect day," she told Gideon later when they were back at his place getting ready for bed.

"You were so brave jumping that fence," he said. "The look of pure determination. I've never seen anything like it."

Ivy couldn't hold it in anymore. "We *are* serious about each other, aren't we?" she said.

He seemed surprised. "Of course. Sorry, were we supposed to have *the talk*?"

"Talk is for losers." She swung her leg to straddle his lap. He'd exchanged his contacts for black-framed reading glasses and when she slid them off his face, she saw the indents on his skin from where the nose pads had pressed, in the shape of little footprints, and her heart nearly broke with love to glimpse him unexpectedly in such nakedness.

He lifted a strand of hair from her neck and let it slip through his fingers. "I'm going to take a shower."

Ivy listened to the sound of running water. Her entire body ached from riding all day but still she felt restless. Since Valentine's Day, she and Gideon had slept together eleven times, all sober, earnest, do-you-like-this-or-that sex, and if she thought really hard, she could even list every single kiss. After all, she'd initiated most of them. Gideon was rarely physically demonstrative with her in public, but in her experience, men like that tended to be wild creatures in bed. But for whatever reason, he was holding back. Sometimes, like tonight, when he looked at her with eyes hooded, arms crossed, mouth tight with self-control, she was sure he was suppressing his desire for her, but she did not know why. In her crazier moments, she wondered if Gideon had such bizarre tastes that he was afraid to lose himself in front of her. His deference, his courtesy, his decorum—traits she'd once loved about him—now stood in the way of her getting closer to him.

She walked over to the window and rolled it open. The cool air felt good on her skin. The moon was fat and pale orange, like a Ping-Pong ball hanging low in the sky between two steepled rooftops. Gideon's street was much quieter than her own; other than the occasional rush of tires and rustling of leaves, there were no sounds. She could have been anywhere, in any city or suburb or countryside. She wished for a cigarette, for a drink, for something to break or someone to scream.

Gideon came back, rubbing his hair with a towel and wearing his favorite pair of pajamas, the pale blue ones with his initials embroidered in white thread on the breast pocket. She'd teased him mercilessly about them at first. But they're so comfortable, he'd explained sheepishly. And it was a Christmas gift from Grandma Cuffy, on the Whitaker side; Sylvia had a matching set.

"Everything good?" he asked.

She smiled.

"I'm exhausted. Should we call it a night?"

She climbed back into bed. He was asleep within minutes but she could not sleep for a long time.

"IT'S NOT GOING THROUGH," SAID THE CASHIER AT THE CO-OP.

"I'll get this one," said Andrea, fumbling for her purse. Ivy shook her head and pulled out her second credit card—the one she'd opened for the "onetime expense" of the ski trip back in January—and handed it to the cashier. He looked embarrassed. Resentment warmed Ivy's face. What was the big deal? The whole country was in debt.

But when she got home, she regretted buying the grapes—who knew a small bag could be so expensive, and also the organic milk. She could have bought regular. She steeled herself to check her credit card balance, then lost her nerve. Instead, she spent the night giving herself a manicure with an old bottle of nail polish. The effect was so gruesome she went to the corner nail salon the next morning. The Korean girl did a beautiful job trimming her cuticles so Ivy felt compelled to leave a large tip. Anxiety twisted her insides. She did not see how she could cut back further—she had already stopped going to movies and paying for books, coffee, restaurant delivery. Her cigarettes were her main indulgence, but each time she tried to quit, her expenses only increased because she would throw out a perfectly good pack, then immediately rush out to buy another one after her self-control ran out. All those good cigarettes, rotting in a dumpster! She'd only bought the grapes for the vitamins. She would stop buying fruit.

Ever since summer break began, she'd felt torpid and lazy, without appetite. When she stood up too quickly, she grew light-headed and had to lie back down. Her meals consisted of Andrea's chocolate stash, eaten in a supine position, the box balanced on her chest, and cold Italian subs from the diner down the street, where, to extend the meal, she'd tear off little pieces of the stale bread and dunk them in instant coffee, letting the dough bloom in her mouth until it disintegrated. Every week, she received another email from an overachieving colleague organizing do-gooder events like repainting the gymnasium or volunteering at TeachU. She never responded.

Andrea said she was getting too thin and made Ivy weigh herself. She'd lost six pounds. "Eat this right now," said Andrea, pushing the last bites of cheesecake across the table. Crumbs dotted Andrea's lips; a moist tongue covered in congealed graham cracker darted out to lick them. Ivy shook her head. "How do you have so much self-control?" Andrea lamented. Ivy went outside for a smoke.

The gangsters were still there, guarding whatever precious cargo was inside their indestructible SUVs. Ivy thought of her mother's shiny new van. Everyone needed something to live for.

She spent the day shopping at her favorite boutiques and, on a whim, bought a digital camera for Austin. Nan said he was doing better and Ivy wanted to reward him. He'd been taking his vitamins, said Nan, and Shen had put him in charge of the yardwork so he could get some sunshine every day. He was going to resume classes at a local college, where they could keep an eye on him and wake him up for his classes. Austin didn't want to go back to school but eventually they'd persuaded him. Shen had sat down with him and they'd drawn up a schedule together: what time Austin would rise, what time he'd exercise, what time he'd eat and sleep and shit. "He just needs some discipline," said Nan. "Even I'd get strange thoughts if I stayed locked up in my room all day long. It's unnatural." Ivy hadn't left her house for four days at that point. She felt this would be futile to point out to her mother.

The digital camera had been a splurge but she justified it by asking herself when was the last time Austin received a nice gift. That month, however, she didn't send the usual three-hundred-dollar check to Nan. She pushed her calls from home to voicemail.

ON A SCORCHING afternoon in July, she stopped by Gideon's office for the first time. His company rented a corner unit on the tenth floor of a coworking space, furnished with Ping-Pong tables, secretaries in horn-rimmed glasses, colorful egg-shaped chairs. She met Gideon's cofounder, Roland Wellington, a pale man with a thin nose and nasal voice, along with their ten employees: fresh-faced boys right out of Ivy League schools, and the only female employee, a pretty Indian girl in a mustard-colored turtleneck who'd just graduated from Oxford. The topic of discussion was a barbecue one of their investors, Dave Finley, was hosting the next day at his house in Wellesley. There were rumors that Mark Zuckerberg might make an appearance.

Gideon invited Ivy to come, but warned her that she might find it boring as it would be an older crowd.

"I'm happy to come," she said.

"You'll love Dave and Liana," Roland added.

"Everyone loves Dave and Liana," said Gideon. Something about his tone made Ivy's ears perk up. These people whom he'd never mentioned until now were special to Gideon in some way. Each new member of his social circle was a potential key that might allow her further access into his interior life, a place she saw as a series of rooms through a long corridor, of which she had only frequented the outermost rooms. She thought she would feel more secure since they'd made their relationship official six weeks ago, but actually, it was the opposite. Their intimacy hadn't caught up with the proclamation, and in fact they became more unnatural around each other because both felt the pressure to appear closer—in one horrible instance last week, she'd tried out *Giddy-Bear* as a nickname and could see, even in her tipsy state, that he was taken back. "Y-y-yyes?" he'd stammered in response. She was embarrassed, he was embarrassed, and she'd reverted back to calling him by his proper name. It was easier to display affection in front of Tom and Marybeth and Andrea. When they faltered, they could simply fall back on familiar group dynamics. Alone, however, there was nothing to defuse the underlying awkwardness, as if they were two actors in a play, trying to cue the other into remembering the right lines, only their scripts were slightly different.

Dave Finley's barbecue turned out to be the kind of gathering that made Ivy glad she had splurged, after an agonizing hour debating with herself, on an expensive blowout at a downtown salon and a new pleated midi dress with a high ruffle neck. A prim-and-proper trophy wife. She'd taken her cue from Gideon—he showed up at her house in a linen seersucker suit, that particular shade of Easter blue lightening his hair to a creamy almond blond so that she wanted to lick him.

On the way over, Gideon told her the basic facts: Dave was his longtime mentor and one of the partners at the largest VC firm in Boston; his wife, Liana, was a human rights lawyer turned philanthropist; they had a five-year-old daughter named Coco. Because of Coco's age, Ivy imagined Dave Finley in his late thirties or early forties, powerfully built, with cunning eyes and dark stubble over a cleft chin. But when a lithe, white-haired gentleman cut across the lawn to welcome them, Ivy realized she'd pictured the Dave Finley from twenty years ago. This Dave wore jeans, striped espadrilles, and a sports shirt of some terry cloth material. No one else at the party was dressed so casually. It was one way of displaying power: to show you didn't have to dress up for anyone. A maze of laugh lines covered his deeply tanned face, the kind of face you immediately pictured on boating catalogs or ads for senior homes in Florida.

"You look marvelous, my dear," he said, his blue eyes bright and admiring as he enveloped Ivy's hand with his own. When he leaned forward, she could smell the alcohol on his breath, along with something medicinal. Within minutes, using the same twinkling charm, he managed to extract from her her age, education, job, pay grade, all without coming across as presumptuous or nosy.

"Teaching is a noble calling," Dave said, flashing very white, very straight teeth. "If only they weren't so underpaid and overworked. I was just in Korea last month. Teachers over there are *deities*. The parents bombard them with gifts—electronics, vacations, sometimes good old cash—and they're asked to become godparents and host baptisms. Forget tenure, there's a *shortage* of qualified teachers there. The good ones can work wherever they want. Over here, teachers live like church mice, off the scraps of public funding and are forced to plagiarize shoddy research papers to make a name for themselves."

"I suppose that's true," said Ivy. He seemed to be under the impression she was a professor of some kind. "My first graders sometimes bribe me with Girl Scout cookies," she joked.

He appeared not to hear her.

"And most of our teachers are quite stupid. The folks in Utah are telling their students that the theory of evolution is created by the devil to discredit Jesus. And just look at the state of our STEM education compared to other countries. Disgraceful, is what it is."

"Well, not *everyone*—"

"Of course not. Like I said—a noble calling. You've a golden heart, my dear, I can see it beating as we speak." Dave's gaze roamed around the lawn. "Where is Liana?"

It seemed impossible to Ivy that Dave would be able to spot his wife through the throng of guests in elaborate blazers and summer dresses, fluttering from group to group like butterflies methodically pollinating every flower in the garden, while the catering staff, severe in their black vests and white gloves, hovered around them like giant moths carrying trays of canapés and cold drinks in various sherbet colors.

"There she is." Dave called out to a tall Asian woman standing on the upper deck holding a child in her arms.

Holy hell, thought Ivy.

Liana Finley had one of the ugliest faces she'd ever seen. Wider than it was long, and asymmetrical, with one cheekbone higher than the other, the jawline neither round nor square. A shimmering pink-

and-white silk *qipao* hugged every long line of her erect stature, the slit up to the hipbone revealing a muscled bronze leg. Spray tan? No, that was just Liana Finley's skin tone. No wonder Dave had been able to spot her. She would be eye-catching in any crowd, the fierce Chinese-Amazonian.

Liana walked toward them, still carrying the girl. She greeted Gideon with a warm kiss, then shook Ivy's hand. Ivy found it impossible to determine Liana's age or accent, which was clipped and sounded vaguely German.

Gideon said, "How old are you now, Coco?" The little girl held up five fingers. She was dressed in a lime-green tutu and white tights, and much fuss was made about the green glitter on her chubby cheeks in the shape of a dragonfly. "What's a dragonfly called in Chinese, Coco?" said Dave. No response. "You learned it this morning." Everyone waited. Coco whispered something Ivy was pretty sure did not mean dragonfly. "You are so smart, my love," said Liana. Dave gave his daughter three exuberant smacks, pulling away with glittering lips. I was five, Ivy thought, when the flight attendant left me at Logan Airport.

"I read the other day that toddlers can learn up to four languages with relative ease," Liana said to Ivy, handing the girl to the nanny. "So Coco is a little behind."

"She seems smarter than many of my six-year-olds," said Ivy.

"She *is* precocious," Liana conceded, "but maybe everyone feels that way about their own child."

A waiter came around with a tray of mojitos. Both Ivy and Liana took one. Liana stirred the mint leaves in her glass until the rum turned muddy. "Before Coco," she said, "I thought having children would be tiresome. I would be tied down. Lose everything I've worked for. But actually it's the opposite—she's given meaning to everything I do. You'll understand when you have your own."

Ivy nodded earnestly. So this was Liana's main theme. Powerful human rights lawyer, gave it all up for the charms of motherhood.

Not a new story. Yet, for the rest of her life, Liana would still feel compelled to demonstrate that she regretted nothing, she was in no way diminished or lesser than her ancient, white-haired husband, whom everyone secretly believed she'd married for his money (*had* he supported her through law school?). All women, Ivy was beginning to understand, had a theme. The story they constantly told themselves. The innermost wound.

When Liana stopped talking, Ivy complimented the other woman on her satin slippers—"They're so intricate, and they go so well with your dress"—but actually, she thought they looked like those dollar shoes they sold to tourists in Chinatown, red and shiny, with a black plastic sole, the cloth embroidered with cherry blossoms.

Liana smiled kindly but the kindness felt condescending. So we're back to this, the smile seemed to say.

"They're by this amazing designer, Ralph Li-Ping. I try to support Asian designers and artists."

Ivy smiled. Both women took a long sip of their drinks.

"Dave, what are you looking at?" Liana asked, clearly finished with playing the role of mentor. Ivy felt like a new toy passed around from Dave to Liana, neither of them particularly interested in playing with it, but obligated to feign minimal enthusiasm for Gideon's sake.

Dave was showing Gideon something on his phone. "We're not supposed to tell anyone yet, but Liana will be the face of Christopher Zhu's fall campaign. This is a video he sent me of Liana at Tokyo's fashion week. He said he hoped I didn't mind sharing her—he called her his muse."

Gideon and Ivy bent their heads over the screen. There was Liana, her face announcing itself like a blazing sun amongst moons, sitting in the first row with two willowy models on either side. Her deep voice carried over the chatter of the room to the person recording the video. She was speaking Chinese to the black-haired companion on her left, but badly. Her pronunciation was even worse than Austin's.

Dave beamed expectantly. Ivy murmured her praise.

"You know," said Dave, cocking his head from Ivy to Liana. "I didn't notice it until just now, but you two could be sisters."

"We look nothing alike, sweetie," said Liana. "I have at least ten years on Ivy."

Gideon replayed the video, listening with surprise. "I didn't know you could speak Chinese, Liana."

"Kindergarten level," said Liana. She explained how she'd been taking classes twice a week to learn Mandarin. She was expected to make a five-minute speech for her charity foundation that would be broadcast on CCTV.

"When is this?" asked Gideon.

"September."

"You still have time. Will it be recorded? I'd love to see it."

Liana said she would try to get someone to film her. She and Gideon smiled at each other.

Liana turned to Ivy. "Do you speak Mandarin?"

"Not well."

"Say something," said Dave.

"Like what?" said Ivy, feeling a new degree of sympathy for Coco Finley.

"Say, 'The weather today is seventy degrees.' "

Ivy said the phrase in Chinese.

"Your accent is good!" Liana said in surprise—too much surprise, Ivy thought resentfully. "Maybe you could go over my speech with me. My Chinese tutor has been insufferable lately, I'd be thrilled to make some real progress for once."

"If it would help," said Ivy. She stared and stared. She could not fathom the idea that any man, let alone Gideon, would find such a face attractive—and yet Liana had inspired a designer to artistic glory! He'd called her his muse!

"Have *you* ever been to China, Ivy?" Dave asked.

"I was born there," said Ivy. "I came to the States when I was five. But I went back once when I was fourteen." She briefly described her one vacation in Chongqing, but when she realized she was holding court for the first time—Dave and Liana's interest seemed genuine—she began to embellish this one summer to many summers, speaking of a childhood spent in both rural villages and glittering metropolises, of the discrepancy between the rich and the poor, the abject poverty, the ostentatious excess, families of four squeezed onto a single motorbike, fields and fields of rice paddies. She described Jojo, Aunt Hong, Sunrin and Sunrin's *ayi*: where they lived, where they worked, how they viewed people from America, reducing her relatives to avatars for the poor, the rich, the Chinese. As she spoke, Gideon took her glass from her hand and signaled a waiter for another.

"What you said about the class and gender discrepancies really struck home with me," said Liana. "My great-grandmother was sold by her parents to a peddler so they could feed her brothers. She still came from the foot-binding generation but she taught herself how to read. She raised my grandmother to be the first woman to attend a previously all-male engineering school in Beijing. If you're interested, I have this book on how Chinese women overcame the class barriers in the pre-Mao era. I can lend it to you."

Ivy said she would love to read it. Liana suggested that Ivy come to her next book club.

"Am I invited?" Gideon teased.

"Women only."

"Even I can't get in," said Dave, his white curls bouncing around his temples as he shook his head. "They lock the doors for hours and all I hear is nonstop giggling. You must be our mole, Ivy. Give us the inside scoop."

Liana placed her arm around Ivy's waist. "She'd never betray her fellow women."

Ivy felt something loyal and protective emit from the heat of Liana's hand, something that inducted her into Liana's inner circle, even if she barely understood how to navigate such a circle in which her Chinese-ness wasn't something to hide under the tablecloth like an unseemly dog, but flaunted in a *qipao* with a slit up the thigh. Suddenly, she felt ashamed of her earlier simplification of Liana's life, of her relatives' lives. Maybe there were no new stories, only your story. But what did the real story even matter, when most people judged you based on the shallowest surfaces?

After they'd eaten their scallop ceviche and pistachio tapenade, Dave suggested that Liana show Ivy the roses. "Everything's blooming wonderfully this year"—he tapped Liana's hip—"all thanks to you, my dear."

"It's all thanks to Francisco," said Liana, taking Ivy's arm. "I just write the checks."

They walked toward the well-manicured garden near the gazebo, not speaking much. Liana occasionally waved to a friend or pointed out vegetables to Ivy she was particularly proud of: the bright red tomatoes, splitting with juices, and the fat zucchinis as long as an arm. "We used to have so many problems with parasites and rabbits. But after we hired Francisco, almost everything we eat is homegrown."

"What a time commitment," said Ivy. "And you're so busy already, with Coco and your charities."

"Just throw money at the problem," said Liana. She frowned and bent down to pluck a weed that had been wrapped around the stem of a red rose. When she straightened up, a black-vested staff member appeared from thin air to take the weed from Liana's manicured fingers, handing her a wet napkin with his other hand.

"I like you, Ivy," Liana said frankly. "I can see why you're special to Gideon. You two make a beautiful couple. Let me know if I can be of help to you in any way . . ."

It was almost midnight when Ivy and Gideon left. All the lights in the mansion were still ablaze. Dave and his friends were playing bridge in the foyer; Liana sat on the terrace surrounded by wives from her book club, debating fervently about the oil crisis, as if the president himself were waiting breathlessly for their phone call, to tell him exactly what needed to be done.

Just what was this cloak called privilege and how did it protect you? Was it visible to the wearer or just to onlookers on the outside?

"We'll get dinner with them sometime," said Gideon in the car. His smile, thrown into relief by the headlights of a passing truck, looked particularly sweet. "Liana's great, isn't she? You two have a lot in common."

"Really?" Ivy murmured.

"I saw her in court once," said Gideon, "back when I was an undergrad . . . The way she took control of the jury—'If we don't dare, then who will dare?'—I'll never forget that line. It made me want to change the world." He shook his head. "She was something else."

Ivy said, "Yeah. I love Liana and Dave. Who wouldn't want to be like them?"

They fell quiet. The radio crooned its top ten love songs; an announcer awarded concert tickets to the fiftieth caller of the night. A slow acoustic song began playing . . . *and you know . . . for you I'd bleed myself dry* . . . and in the man's soft timbre voice, Ivy heard her own longing.

By the time Gideon pulled up into her driveway, she'd made up her mind to quit teaching and become a lawyer.

11

In the weeks following the Finley's barbecue, like the tide pulling back and forth from shore, Ivy's confidence waxed and waned. She purchased a test prep book and spent her days struggling to solve convoluted logic problems—*There are exactly three recycling centers, exactly five kinds of material are recycled at these recycling centers, each recycling center recycles at least two but no more than three of these kinds of material. The following conditions must hold . . .* —which made her feel frustrated and inept, as if she were back in high school, afraid of Nan's scoldings for bringing home abysmal test scores. At night, while Gideon slept beside her, Ivy replayed the day's events like a film reel: golden-eyed, broad-shouldered Gideon in soft crew sweaters and double-breasted blazers, with his irresistible grin that felt like a present; Gideon with the clean, square hands, the birthmark on his shoulder in the shape of an apple, and the blue-green veins running up his arm when he held her, raised and pulsing with blood, was enough to make her knees weak. But also: Gideon of the smiling mask, Gideon going days without calling, working himself to death at the office, without complaint or explanation, working with the still determination he'd had since childhood. The Celtics had lost in the playoffs, he'd taken her to Game 7 against the Magic back in June and they'd screamed themselves hoarse, wishing, cheering, stamping, clapping, and still it was not enough; the entire arena went home despondent, many weeping, and it seemed to Ivy now like a bad omen. Each morning when she looked in the mirror, the shadows underneath her eyes were darker. She lamented the fading of her hard-earned beauty; her heart grew uneasy.

One afternoon in August, Sylvia texted out of the blue. *Let's catch up! Can we get together for dinner tonight?* Ivy immediately agreed. She'd been waiting for something like this for a while, and had been getting antsy, wondering if Gideon's sister's silence was a form of rebuff. It'd been raining since daybreak. What would have been a fifteen-minute drive to the restaurant Sylvia had suggested took an hour through the crawling traffic. Ivy's Camry was in the shop again, for brake replacements this time, so she hailed a cab but they got stuck behind a fender bender four blocks from the restaurant; she got out of the cab and ran. Sylvia wasn't there. Ivy waited another fifteen minutes before Gideon's sister arrived, wearing a navy trench coat over a low-cut black dress, the glass beads around her neck rubbing together in a pleasant clinking sound as she walked across the room. Men's eyes followed Sylvia but in a different way from how eyes followed Andrea. It was the difference between wanting something obvious and wanting something impossible, which was only a more distilled kind of wanting.

"The Haymakers Theater is in the middle of nowhere," Sylvia apologized, her white-gold head still glistening with a halo of raindrops. "I had to wait forever for the driver to find me, he'd driven all the way to *Amherst . . .*" She kicked off her heels underneath the table and waved the waiter over with requests for "the Chiang Mai, please. And for God's sake, make it strong. Did you order yet, Ivy?"

"Not yet."

"The curries here are excellent. I'll have the Massaman."

After they placed their orders, Sylvia explained the reason for her tardiness—she was at a rehearsal concert for her close friend Victor Sokolov, a cellist. He was a modern Stravinsky, more lively than Elgar but with the same beautiful themes. She said she'd met Victor while he was at Juilliard. He trained afterward at the Vienna Music School, he was brilliant, he was the real thing.

"My friend Andrea is a violinist," said Ivy. "She plays for the Boston Symphony Orchestra." Sylvia's expression revealed neither admiration nor curiosity. "I'll let her know about the album," Ivy added. "I think she would love it."

"Victor's very experimental," said Sylvia, "so I don't know if a pure classicalist would enjoy it. Now with that said, I think Victor's arrangements . . ." Like Gideon, she was so good at small talk that Ivy almost believed Sylvia had invited her to dinner solely to discuss classical music. The waiter brought over their curries. Sylvia waited until Ivy had placed her napkin on her lap before exclaiming, in somewhat breathless amazement, "So! . . . You and Gideon!"

Ivy smiled. "You hold your chopsticks really well." Even this tiny amount of power—withholding a second longer information Sylvia wanted—felt like a win. This comment detoured them on a tangent about how Sylvia learned to use chopsticks—she loved sushi—and their favorite Japanese spots around Boston.

"Anyway," said Sylvia, "back to Gideon. He won't tell me anything about you! I only found out you two were still seeing each other when I saw the cupcakes you left in his fridge. 'Ivy brought them over.' That's it. They were delicious by the way, you *must* give me the recipe. You know, it's so typical of Giddy . . . all this hush-hush. I bet you're the reason he's skipped the last few dinners with the parents. Didn't want to lie when they ask about his love life. They'd know by his stutter."

"We're keeping things on the down-low," said Ivy. "Both of us are private people . . . everything feels more special this way." She almost meant it. Since they'd had the talk-that-was-not-a-talk back in May, she'd cautiously waited for Gideon to invite her to one of his parents' Sunday dinners in Beacon Hill, or even a casual weekday dinner. But every Sunday afternoon, as she got dressed to return home, he never suggested that she might stay, nor had he asked her to be his plus-one for a cousin's wedding back in June. This had upset her at first, but she knew better than to pressure him. Pressure only worked on easily manipulated men, and she had never been able to respect any man she could easily manipulate.

"There you go," said Sylvia, leaning back in her chair with her arms on the table, like a cat stretching its limbs in a satisfied yawn. "You two are perfect for each other."

Ivy looked up.

"You don't think so?"

Her flustered pause brought a roguish glimmer to Sylvia's eyes.

"You're sweet and beaaauutiful *and* smart. I could tell immediately back at my house Gideon was interested in you. The way he avoided you that night! . . . Let me tell you a secret—Giddy's overly cautious around people he likes. Do you sometimes get the feeling he's keeping you at a distance?" Ivy gave a little gasp. "It's a fear mechanism," Sylvia said with a small smirk. "It's also why he's keeping you all to himself for now. It's like you said—he doesn't want Mom and Dad to butt in."

"Did he s—"

"And Arabella! She just gushed about you during Ellen's Easter lunch. Aunt Ellen's the youngest of seven so everyone spoils her. She's claimed the big holidays. Mom gets the leftovers: Memorial Day weekend, Labor Day. They're the only girls of the Whitaker bunch—you wouldn't *believe* how many uncles and second cousins I have—but their relationship is more like a divorced couple fighting for custody over the rest of us. We're such a large family, and Dad's side is big, too . . . don't look so scared! Gideon's very good at organizing all of us into a neat little diagram for when you meet everyone. I think you'll get on with Uncle Jack. He's very fond of interesting people, so he'll love *you*."

Ivy continued to smile and nod. Agree with everything. But the girlfriend was usually supposed to butter up the sister. The role reversal unsettled her.

Sylvia's phone made a quiet buzz. "Excuse me—I forgot I was supposed to meet my mom today . . ."

Ivy looked away politely as Sylvia made her call. She took a bite of her kabocha pumpkin, which had gone cold. She could hear Mrs. Speyer's lilting voice through the speaker; it was like listening to two wrens chitter to each other.

"So—where were we?" said Sylvia after she hung up.

"Easter brunch."

"Right!"

They took turns sharing stories about Gideon. Every word, every laugh, every conspiratorial joke was filtered through the knowledge that everything either woman said would be conveyed by the other to Gideon . . . *Sylvia told me . . . Ivy said this about you . . .*

Halfway through dinner, Sylvia said, "Here she is," and waved at someone at the door. Ivy turned around, paling.

Mrs. Speyer was standing in front of the hostess booth, brushing the rainwater off the lapels of her coat. As with her children, there was a distinct elegance about the way she held herself, her frame as narrow as a girl's, the long neck supporting a head full of ash-blond hair blown out at the crown and smoothed back into a low chignon. "Why on earth are we meeting here?" she asked Sylvia when she reached their table. "The show starts in fifteen minutes."

"Mom," said Sylvia, "this is Ivy Lin."

Ivy half-stood up in her seat, still holding her chopsticks dripping with curry sauce.

Two spots of pink dappled Mrs. Speyer's almost translucent cheeks, like rose petals floating under a frozen pond. "Yes, of course! Gideon's friend from Grove. Of course I remember you, dear. How *are* you?" Instead of a handshake, she leaned in and gathered Ivy to her chest, her grip surprisingly strong.

Ivy said she was well, thank you. "And how have you been—Mrs. Speyer?" Of all the possible scenarios she'd imagined her first meeting with Gideon's mother, this chance encounter, without Gideon present, wasn't one of them.

"Oh, please. That makes me feel so old. Call me Poppy."

"What show are you two watching?"

"*One Thousand and One Nights*—it's a *beautiful* production—I've already been twice . . . do *you* like ballet, Ivy?"

"I've never been," said Ivy.

"Oh, you really should go."

They beamed in the ensuing pause, having run out of safe ground.

"We should get going," Sylvia said finally as she extracted her wallet from her bag.

Poppy suddenly lit up. "Would you like to join us? I'm sure we can get an extra ticket."

Ivy hesitated.

"I'm sure Ivy has better things to do," said Sylvia, glancing at her for confirmation.

"I'm just *suggesting*," said Poppy, "and, oh, isn't it summer break now . . ."

"Well, let's make up our minds soon," Sylvia said, almost rudely, and Ivy felt this rudeness was directed at her.

She murmured she really would have loved to join but she had other plans, unfortunately. Had she been asked in advance, she surely would have accepted, but Poppy's and Sylvia's demeanors seemed strained, simultaneously eager and reticent, as if they were coming from an exuberant evening in which further plans felt both necessary and exhausting. The Speyers nodded in unison, their smiles the same exact shade of sympathetic regret. Just who knew what and how much?

THAT WEEKEND, OVER dinner, Ivy brought up the run-in with Poppy to test Gideon.

"Right! Yeah, she told me," said Gideon.

"Sylvia told you?"

"Well, both of them did."

"Your mom hasn't aged a day since I saw her back in middle school," said Ivy.

Gideon laughed. "She'll be happy to hear that."

"*I* probably looked like a drowned dog . . . we should get together properly next time so she doesn't think you're dating a crazy person . . ."

"That'd be nice," he agreed, but didn't suggest a time or place in his usual take-charge way. Ivy immediately changed the topic to demonstrate how trivial her suggestion had been.

"By the way, I've been mulling it over for a while now, and I think I'm going to apply to law school." That got his attention. She'd never seen his brown eyes so large and keen across the rim of his wineglass.

"Really? What spurred this on?"

Self-conscious pride made her adopt a droll tone as she explained how she'd always wondered about the path not taken—"I worked at a law firm, as you know, and loved it there"—and that she'd recently decided that it wasn't too late to change careers, especially after speaking with Liana. Gideon questioned her about the specifics: when, why, how sure was she? "On a scale of one to ten," she said, slicing into her steak and watching the pink juices flow out onto the bone china plate, "I guess it's a ten." How warm his fingers felt over hers! And how wide his smile, glowing in the lamplight with encouragement and admiration. "I haven't gotten in yet," she said, and he said, "You will," as if he owned law school as well.

"Other than Liana," he said, "my uncle Bobby would be a great person for you to speak with. He's a partner at Fenton and Heath. I believe they do a lot of work in international law. Would you like me to connect you guys?"

"That'd be *wonderful*, thank you."

"And I suppose you'll have to let the Kennedy School know."

"What do you mean?"

"I just assumed you'd want to spend this year exploring different options and studying for the LSATs . . . but of course one can't simply just quit one's job," he added quickly, seeing her blank expression. "And you can always study nights and weekends. It's still early days yet."

Ivy wouldn't have refuted him if not for the faint blush forming on his face, a blush that revealed his embarrassment at having embarrassed *her*, in presuming that she had the means to do whatever she wanted, now that she had a goal, as if all this time she had been teaching not out of necessity but out of an idle indulgence whose only purpose was to allow her time to come to terms with her natural, inevitable path in life.

"No, you're absolutely right," she said, not quite fully grasping what she was committing to, only knowing that she was about to say something very, very foolish. But there was no helping it. She must always "save face," no matter the cost. "The timing works out if I leave now," she said, ticking off the months on her fingers, "I'll have five months to prepare to take the test in February."

"Ah, is that so?"

"And there's a prep class I want to sign up for in September. I can even schedule coffee meetings without worrying about school hours!"

Gideon tactfully refrained from commenting. He refilled her wineglass, fixing his gaze on the little vase of flowers at the center of their table.

"If you need—time off—to figure things out," he said, "I'm sure my parents would be perfectly happy to help out . . . the interest rates banks charge these days are practically criminal." Their eyes met.

Ivy would never be able to forgive herself for the garish smirk that automatically formed on her face, somewhere between a sneer and a frown, out of sheer shock once she realized what he was offering.

"Wow . . . that's . . ."

He waited, his head slightly cocked. So this was what Gideon looked like when he lied, she thought. No, not a lie. He meant it. He would ask his parents to lend her money. Money he himself did not have or was unwilling to give. Perhaps he was offering only because he knew she would refuse.

". . . Crazy," she finished, half-laughing, dismissive, the whole thing a great amusing joke. "Your parents are saints if they really would just—give away—their money to someone they barely know. It's a kind thought, but completely unnecessary."

Both now certain of her refusal, he continued to warmly suggest ways he could be helpful, the perfect picture of poise and attentiveness.

After the waiter came and took their dessert orders, Gideon leaned back in his chair and seemed to take a proverbial stretch, like a driver taking a break from the wheel. Ivy imitated his pose, looking around the room, pretending to admire the restaurant's grand atmosphere, oxblood walls and fresco ceilings and waiters in tailcoats; she and Gideon were probably the youngest guests by two decades.

"Ivy?"

She turned, beaming. "Yes?"

Humbly, he asked if she was willing to join him and his family at their beach house in Cattahasset in two weeks.

"*Wei*?"

"Hi, Grandma."

"Why haven't you been answering our calls?"

"I wanted to explain about the checks. I haven't been mailing them home because I've decided to apply to law school next year. I'll need to save money."

There came a disbelieving snort. "You want to be a lawyer now?"

"Yes."

"Haven't you already tried that?"

"That was different. I was just a secretary."

"When are you going to stop jumping around like a harebrained rabbit? Have some focus in life. You'll be thirty soon! When I was your age, I already had Hong and Nan. I was carrying forty kilos of rice home every day, strong as a horse. Look at you now . . . both you and Austin have your mother's genes—soft."

"You say the same things over and over again," said Ivy.

"Do you think I like saying them?"

"I don't have time for this. I called because"—she braced herself—"I was wondering if Baba could give me a loan. I'll be leaving my job," she rushed to explain, "because I need time to study for the LSATs and find an internship to gain more experience. The loan would just be for a year. If Baba can't, that's fine. I just thought I'd ask first because the interest rates banks charge these days are practically criminal."

It wasn't as bad as Ivy had feared. Meifeng only clucked her tongue, iterated a few of her old proverbs about appreciating one's parents in times of need, and asked how much she needed. Ivy impulsively added five thousand dollars to the number she had prepared. Guilt made her stern. "I'll be super busy from now on," she said, "so tell Mama to stop calling me about that Kevin guy." Meifeng tried to protest but Ivy cut her off. "If either of you mention him again, I swear I'm going to elope with the first man I see on the street." She hung up to the sound of her grandmother's angry squawk.

SEASIDE NEW ENGLAND always invoked a sense of nostalgia, like life viewed from a Polaroid. The slim beech trees, clapboard houses with steeply pitched roofs, the sun fading everything to a washboard white. A year ago, she'd been with Daniel in a similarly sleepy town in Rhode Island. She'd booked them the king suite at a famous bed-and-breakfast reviewed by Condé Nast as one of the most romantic destinations in America. During the day, Daniel had trailed after her as she went into one vintage shop after another, cooing over wind chimes shaped like doves and necklaces made of prayer beads, while Daniel held her little straw basket sagging with apricots and nectarines they'd bought from the farmer's market. By the third day, they were so bored after brunch they resorted to eating another late lunch, at three o'clock, of fried oysters, followed by gelato, eaten sitting on a bench at the small park that made up the town center, watching two boys rollerblade around an oak tree. Ivy had tried to maintain her gaiety—*Look at these clouds! How was your gelato?*—but Daniel tapped his foot in the grass and said, "Now what?" and she'd had no answer because they'd already done everything on her list. Magic, she'd realized then, was not inherent to a place, it emanated from the person viewing it. This trip would be different, it would feel special and beautiful, because Gideon thought it was special and beautiful and he was the altered lens through which she would view the world. On the drive down, he'd steered with one hand and pointed at landmarks with the other, talking about the nice weather and the places he wanted to take her. "Look at that," he said as they pulled into the driveway, "the Walds are here, too. I should hop on over and say hello!" Ivy had never seen him so peppy. It almost troubled her. Had he been unhappy, all this time, in Boston?

The Speyers' cottage, Finn Oaks, was a typical beach house of the area, with green shutters and trimmings and a narrow pebbled walkway that led up to the front door with round latticed windows like those on a boat. It was empty when they arrived. A note from Poppy was pinned on the fridge underneath a seashell magnet: *We have gone into town. There are leftover meatballs in the fridge if you darlings are hungry from the drive. See you soon. xx Mom*. They ate the meatballs with the crusty baguette someone had left out on the counter, washed down with two beers.

When Ivy inquired after the origin of the cottage's name, Gideon said that his great-granddad's dog was named Finn and when Finn died, they'd buried him under the oak tree in the front yard. "Is this him?" Ivy asked, peering at a black-and-white photo on the fireplace mantel of a handsome man in a wide-brimmed hat. Gideon nodded, then pointed out other photos of grandparents, great-grandparents, aunts, uncles, great-uncles, dogs, cats, babies. Since then, said Gideon, the house had been repurposed as a summer home. Growing up, he and Sylvia had spent most of their summers here, fishing on the sailboat or swinging on the rubber tire tied to the oak tree by the beach. Despite the pride in Gideon's voice, Ivy privately thought the house showed its age—the wooden planks along the ceiling were bent and cracked; the wall of windows in the family room were stately but the velvet curtains looked as if they hadn't been aired in decades. The decor was also oddly shabby and provincial: straw and felt hats hung on pegs, woven baskets and clay pots strewn in various corners among rattan chairs, a Native American tapestry served as the centerpiece, and everywhere Ivy looked were wooden mobiles dangling with shells and pebbles, like those a child made at summer camp. Down the hall, they came to a yellow alcove lined with rickety bookshelves, the spines of old leather-bound books etched with cursive titles packed tightly between two gargoyle bookends. Gideon walked to the corner and yanked back an enormous yellow knit cover. Dust billowed around in the air before settling on the gleaming black lid of a piano. Gideon sat on the bench and played the beginning of "Chopsticks." The piano was badly out of tune.

"They bought this for Sylvia so she could pick up an instrument," said Gideon, "but then they found out she was tone-deaf. So they had me take lessons instead. No one really comes in here except Dad when he has to take calls." He switched to playing a sonata in the minor key. There was no sheet music but his fingers moved swiftly across the keys without hesitation. He'd never mentioned he played the piano. Each day they were together, Ivy learned something new about him. It was marvelous, really. Perhaps this was the secret to a lasting marriage: to always uphold a veil of mystery between each other, like a silk screen dividing a bedroom chamber. If Shen had an ounce of mystery about him, maybe Nan wouldn't look down on him so much.

"This is the best room in the house," said Gideon, bringing her to the first bedroom upstairs. There was a four-poster bed with a crinkly linen duvet, a drop-leaf writing desk, two slender maple nightstands, and a heavy wooden chest at the foot of the bed, the lid open, displaying matching towels. Fresh flowers were abundantly displayed, green-tinged carnations in jugs, various bouquets, lavender pots, and on the nightstand, a water bowl floating with a cluster of peonies. Ivy walked over to the bowl and dipped her hand into the water. One petal broke free at her touch and floated away from the others. She had the urge to bring her fingers to her mouth and lick the peony-flavored droplets.

"Mom loves coordinating flowers with the furniture," said Gideon. He noticed her funny expression. "What's wrong?"

"The peonies. I thought they were fake. They looked *so perfect*." In the vanity mirror, she caught their reflection: light head, dark head. We would have beautiful babies, she thought. She went over and kissed the tip of his nose.

"Sometimes I wish I could bottle up the way you look at me," he said. "When I'm old and amnesic, I can take it back out and relive the look on your face."

She reached down and found the cold metal buckle of his belt, and in one motion, pulled the end tip through the loop. His fingers moved to rest on top of hers. "They'll be back soon."

She withdrew her hand and went to stand by the window. Outside was a terrace overlooking a sloping lawn; beyond that was the surf lapping the sand.

"Do you like your room?" Gideon asked.

She turned around. "*My* room?"

"It's tradition. I'm down the hall."

She waited to see if he was teasing. He wasn't. She toyed with a tassel on the curtain. "Are you going to sneak in at night?"

"Unfortunately, Mom has ears like a bat's." He gazed at her very seriously. "Are you upset?"

"I'll miss you," she said, shaking her head but smiling nevertheless. "Your mom is very sweet and old-fashioned. We'll have a great week." Her eyes drifted back to the peonies. "I can feel it."

IVY STEPPED OUT of the shower to hear a woman's clear soprano calling out Gideon's name. Gideon shouted that they'd be right down. He turned to Ivy and asked if she was ready. She was changing into yet another outfit, a calf-length dress of a clingy jersey material. When she'd tried it on at the department store, surrounded by their three-paneled mirrors with soft overhead lighting, it'd seemed perfect for an evening dinner. But here in Poppy's guest bedroom, the somber textiles sucking the light from other fabrics, the dress looked cheap. She could see the outline of her underwear through the thin material. The zipper snagged on her hair as she pulled it off. "Goddamn it."

Gideon waited. Under his polite silence, she sensed a growing irritation. He'd already been sitting on the edge of her bed for fifteen minutes, but for once she couldn't appease him. Vanity took priority. Sometimes she had nightmares, true, sweat-inducing nightmares, of being late to some important event, a first day of work or a job interview, while trapped in the vicious cycle of *choosing the right thing to wear*, but unable to make up her mind, panic pressing her every which way.

"The dress isn't very comfortable," she explained breathlessly to Gideon, shimmying into a pair of cropped khaki trousers and a sky-blue top with a more modest neckline. It wasn't perfect but it would have to do. She plastered a smile on her face and wiped an eyelash from the corner of her mouth. Her fingers were cold and clammy.

Gideon's parents were unloading groceries in the kitchen when they came down. Like the rest of the house, the kitchen seemed to belong to a different era. The cabinets, the refrigerator, even the microwave were painted the same muted teal, giving it the kitschy feel of an old movie set. Poppy said, "Hellll-oo, Ivy, it's *wonderful* to have you here." She kissed Ivy twice, smelling of rosewater and talcum powder. Ted Speyer shook Ivy's hand over the countertop. His skin was pink and pale, like ham, his hair had gone mostly gray, and the outline of a small belly protruded through his striped polo. A faint aura of charisma clung to the crevices where vitality had once resided. "I remember you, kiddo," he said. "I never forget a friend of Gideon's. You came over to our house once. How're your parents doing?"

Ivy lowered her gaze and murmured that her parents were fine. She resisted the urge to add "sir" or "Mr. Speyer." It was agonizing that Ted still remembered the sleepover incident; even Gideon had never brought it up with her.

"Is that a new shirt, darling?" Poppy asked Gideon.

"Sib got it for me in Majorca." Gideon leaned over the island and kissed his mother on the cheek.

"Do you need help with dinner?" Ivy asked.

Poppy shook her head. *"Not at all."* Everything she said was a grand proclamation, yet her voice was so girlish and warm it was hard to think her affected. "I'm going to roast some veggies and Ted will grill the steaks. We'll eat around eight. Sylvia called to say she'll be late and to start without her."

Dismissed from the kitchen, Ivy and the men migrated to the family room. Ted picked up the newspaper and settled onto a woven rattan armchair. Gideon opened his laptop. He and Ted placed their beers on wooden coasters carved with the subway map of Boston. How unified and comfortable they looked, thought Ivy, in their clean-pressed clothes and large, American bodies—unlike whenever she saw her own father and brother together, like two bristling pit bulls forced into the cockpit. She tried to read the book Liana had lent her but she couldn't concentrate. Perhaps it was a side effect of the nicotine patch she'd plastered onto her inner thigh after her shower. She'd never used one before but she'd never risk bringing cigarettes to the Speyers' beach house. The patch left a metallic coating in her mouth, like the residue of cough medicine, and her right pinky finger spasmed every so often on the armrest of the sofa. Thoughts of the past also kept cropping up. Perhaps it was because Finn Oaks itself felt frozen in time, no sign whatsoever of technology, not even a television, and the faces of long-dead Speyers staring at her from every crooked picture frame. She half-believed she was fourteen years old again, fearful because she was somewhere she wasn't supposed to be, watching over her shoulder for Nan to show up and drag her back to Fox Hill. She checked her phone. A handful of texts from Andrea, four missed calls from home. Nan still treated cell phones like landlines—she simply kept calling until the person picked up. She probably wanted to verify that Ivy had received the money, that the check hadn't gotten lost or stolen in the mail. Ivy turned off her cell and went back to her book, counting down the minutes until Poppy would call them over to dinner.

THE PLACE MATS were laid, the wine poured, and everyone minus Sylvia, who was further delayed due to car troubles, sat around the table. They closed their eyes and held hands while Ted said grace: "For what we are about to receive may the Lord make us truly thankful."

"Amen."

Ivy added her own prayer: *And please God let this week go well and I'll be a better person and daughter in the future. Thank you, Amen.*

JUST BEFORE THE clock chimed ten, the front door swung open and Sylvia's voice called out, "I'm here," accompanied by a light, silvery laugh.

"Sylvia's here," said Gideon. The voices downstairs grew louder. "Should we go down and say hi?"

"You go first, I'll be right there," said Ivy, having just changed into a rather revealing teddy pajama set. She was disappointed—she'd anticipated some precious alone time with Gideon to go over the day's events: How'd you think it went? Did your parents like me? That sort of thing.

Ivy heard Poppy's loving scolding, Sylvia's apologetic tones. There was the sound of a man's voice greeting Poppy and Ted. Gideon's voice joined in the fray. The man's voice came again—"Good meeting you finally"—and Gideon's response: "It's about time." Ivy listened with renewed interest. It comforted her to know that there was another non–family member in the house. Sylvia must have brought her boyfriend.

"Did you call the dealership?" Poppy was saying indignantly. "Really, to have a new car stall on your first day!"

"It's a refurbished car," said the boyfriend, "from 1930. I think I can cut it some slack."

Sylvia explained it was the faulty gauge system, but because the car was so old, the dealership couldn't find the parts. "Roux loves cars almost as much Giddy loves boats. But Roux gets seasick. You and Gideon might just hate each other."

Polite laughter.

"You'll have to teach me to sail," said the boyfriend. He went on, but Ivy's heart had risen to her throat. She threw on her robe and floated to the top of the staircase, barefoot, one hand on the banister.

Everyone looked up. Amongst a sea of gold heads nestled a dark one, all too familiar under the chandelier's glaring light. Roux Roman.

12

THAT NIGHT IVY DREAMED OF A LACQUERED RED DOOR WITH A gold handle, the ray of light from under the door a brilliant orange, as if a fire blazed on the other side. The handle was cool to the touch; it drifted open without sound. The room was dark, she could see nothing, yet she was sure something extraordinary was waiting for her inside, calling out her name. She woke hearing the echo of a man's voice. The clock on the nightstand read five minutes to ten.

Her room was streaming with unfiltered sunshine. A gust must have blown in through the night and pushed open one of the terrace doors; there came the cheerful chirping of birds and the faint sound of waves, which had bled into her dreams and become part of the white noise, constant but no longer distinguishable. She lay there for a while until a clamor of shouts and laughter drew her outside onto the balcony. The Speyers were throwing around a Frisbee on the back lawn. Poppy was quite good, Ted atrocious. Sylvia caught the disc, then dropped it with a pained cry. Gideon went over to inspect her hand. Their foreheads touched, two fused flaxen heads, the flaxen of romantic oil paintings: *Picnic on Summer Day*. A flutter of black caught Ivy's eye. It was Roux's hair blowing in the breeze. He was directly beneath her balcony, staring up at her, unsmiling. Their eyes locked. How long had he been there?

Last night, her knee-jerk reaction after seeing him had been to gape stupidly in shock, wondering if she was seeing his doppelgänger; he shattered this illusion by saying her name: "Ivy?" Then there had been the back-and-forth with the Speyers of *You two know each other?* and *What a small world!* followed by the inevitable questions of just *how* they knew each other (same hometown), and to what extent (neighbors). Then Poppy had ushered Roux and Sylvia away for a late dinner, and Ivy had retreated back to her bedroom.

She'd slept fitfully, half-hoping Gideon really would sneak into her room, but also relieved he hadn't so she would have more time to get her story straight. She thought back to that summer day thirteen years ago, the blinking computer monitor, the dusty windowsill, the sound of the leaf blower, and felt once more the dampness of Roux's skin, the flutter of black lashes, the look on his face, scrunched, as if in pain. No doubt Roux would recap it all for Sylvia as a bedtime story. Men loved to talk about how they lost their virginity. It was different for women. Ivy had lost her virginity at fourteen. Fourteen was two years below respectable. Fourteen was trashy territory, for girls who got themselves impregnated and had to drop out of school. Gideon thought she'd had a strict and sheltered childhood, that her parents were well-to-do entrepreneurs who'd insisted on an all-women's college, that she'd been a virgin until eighteen: she knew he imagined the incident had come about through a chaste kiss on a fifth date, that perhaps she'd cried a little into her pillow afterward. We were only children, she'd say to Gideon. So many of life's mistakes could be swept under this magnanimous explanation.

She took extra care in dressing that morning: white cotton shorts, a lacy scalloped blouse, navy ballerina flats. She pulled her hair back into a ponytail at the base of her neck and pinned her bangs to the side with bobby pins. A touch of concealer, bronzer, blush, lip gloss. She looked as firm and new as a poached egg.

When she came down, the Speyers were nowhere to be found. Roux was sitting in Ted's armchair with a mug of coffee and a box of donuts. He wore a white tee and blue jeans ripped around the pockets and knees, as if he spent his time working on his hands and knees.

A mechanic. A construction worker, perhaps. Definitely blue-collar, judging from the clothes and donuts.

She said his name, startled at how natural it still felt: "Hello, Roux." At her voice, he stood up to his full height. Nothing gangly about him anymore. The traits she'd disliked about him as a boy—his unkempt-ness, his contempt, his familiar way of looking at her—were now the very signs of his manhood; any woman would remain aware of him long after he entered a room. Ivy felt something warm and joyful leap from his smile and latch on to her skin; she recoiled slightly, mostly out of embarrassment.

"When I saw you last night," he said, "I couldn't believe my eyes. Are you real? Or a ghost from my past come to haunt me?"

"I'm real."

They stood around awkwardly until she sat down, rather primly, and he followed her lead.

"How are you? What are you doing here?" Then, without waiting for a response: "You look exactly the same."

"So do you," she said, though this wasn't remotely true. She nodded at the donuts. "You still love your Dunkin'."

Roux said he had to drive around for half an hour to find it. "It's in this old brick building that's supposed to look like some fancy establishment. I mean—it's goddamn donuts. Who're you trying to fool? Tastes the same. Want one?"

She shook her head. She noticed that Roux's left sock had a large hole at the heel. This detail comforted her. It bridged the gap between this Roux and the seventeen-year-old one of her memories.

He asked about her life. She explained how she'd moved to New Jersey for high school and the trajectory that brought her back to Boston.

"You ended up a *teacher*?" He seemed to find this funny. "Damn, I feel sorry for your students!"

She laughed. "I just quit, actually. I'm going to apply to law school." I'm having fun, she thought in amazement.

They were just getting into a comfortable rhythm when Sylvia came into the room, her hair still damp from the shower and smelling strongly of coconut oil.

"Baby, are you ready? We have to go pick up some swim trunks for you—oh, hello, Ivy." She perched herself on the side of Roux's armchair and wrapped an arm around his shoulder. "How are you liking Finn Oaks?"

Ivy parroted the usual adjectives—beautiful, sweet, cozy—but her mind was reeling at the sight before her: Roux Roman and Sylvia Speyer, arms and legs entwined, flashing their pearly teeth at each other like a stock couple from a Hallmark card. Was there a more incongruous pairing in the entire world? Or was the clichéd allure of dating a man from the wrong side of the socioeconomic line at play here on Sylvia's hormones? Sylvia asked Roux if he took out the car that morning and they began carrying on a side conversation about car mechanics in their bedroom voices. Sylvia nuzzled her head into Roux's neck, calling him her "little kangaroo." He pinched her ribs. Sylvia emitted a loud squawk. Roux cooed *You like that, don't you . . . don't you . . .* as if he were talking to a dog. Some forms of seduction were more thrilling in front of an audience, perhaps Roux and Sylvia were into that sort of thing. But as they carried on . . . and on . . . and on . . . Ivy thought that no self-respecting adult would behave so embarrassingly on purpose. Other people had a sense of themselves in the larger context of some objective world. For Roux and Sylvia, there was no larger context, no objective world. And thus they lacked all self-consciousness.

"So you never finished your story yesterday," said Sylvia, finally turning to Ivy. "About how you two know each other. Neighbors, was it?"

Ivy hesitated. Was Sylvia being facetious?

Roux said, "Good old Fox Hill. You ever go back and visit?"

"Never."

"In New York?" said Sylvia.

"Right here in Massachusetts. In shitty West Maplebury." He smirked at his girlfriend. "You've probably never heard of it."

Sylvia made a face. "Childhood friendships are the sweetest," she said, and began telling a story about her best friend from first grade. She really doesn't know, Ivy thought, mostly in relief, but there was also a tiny prick of petty irritation that Roux hadn't thought it, thought *her*, worth mentioning.

"I haven't seen Natalie in more than twenty years," Sylvia was saying, "but each time I see a pink bicycle, especially with those handlebar streamers, I think of her."

"Every time I see a Kmart," said Roux, "I think of Ivy. She used to be quite the—"

"How did *you* two meet?" Ivy interrupted, her breath catching.

Sylvia said something about an art institute and Italian painters but Ivy was barely listening. The word *Kmart* rang in her mind like a death toll, the shy optimism she'd felt for Roux only moments earlier skewered through the heart by his casual betrayal.

"Roux is the main patron of that exhibit," said Sylvia. "He's got brilliant tastes, and a killer instinct for undervalued art."

"All I did was donate a carload of money," Roux clarified. "They give you a certificate and a title, like 'Friend of the Museum.' But I get terrific tax deductions—"

"Roux curated the collection himself." Sylvia spoke over him. "He even helped us borrow a piece from a notoriously stingy museum in Florence. *I've* been writing to them for months—"

"I know the director there. He comes by my pizza shop when he's in New York. I renovated it to look like the one we used to eat at, remember?" He grinned at Ivy. "They'd give us free slices if we went after ten. You'd bring a Tupperware to bring some home for your brother. Boy, could that kid eat."

Ivy said she didn't remember the pizza shop. She could barely look at him.

Roux's smile turned quizzical. "Really? What about Giovanni? His retarded son, Vincent? We'd go around selling pepperoni slices to the drunk people in the park. We wanted to save up for those inflatable boards to use in the pool."

"Did we? Kids want the strangest things. I really can't remember."

His expression changed, a slight tightening. "I bet you can't," he said slowly.

"So you're an *art collector* now," said Ivy. "*And* you run a pizza shop? That's an unusual combination."

"Not only that," said Roux, leaning forward. "I also own laundro-mats, dollar stores, ATMs, and vending machines. Big moneymakers, those ATMs. Especially in motel chains. The art thing is just a hobby. I enjoy procuring what everyone else wants."

There was something about the way he said this that made Ivy cross her legs in self-defense. She'd been mistaken. He wasn't poor at all. Somehow this didn't surprise her. He'd always had a hard streak when it came to money. One of those ambitious hustlers destined to either succeed wildly or end up in jail. He might even have more money than Sylvia. Gideon's sister would probably only date a man with a bigger bank account. And also she'd been wrong about the jeans: they were probably so expensive even the rips and tears were handcrafted to resemble the real working-class man, which Roux clearly wasn't anymore.

Roux said he was also looking to get into the car industry. He asked Ivy if she liked cars.

"Not really."

"That's because you've never been in a good one. We'll go for a drive in the Bugatti. Sylvia chose this one. She thought it was the color of my eyes. What do you think?"

Ivy had no answer.

He waved at the driveway. "Just look."

"I really don't care."

"Don't be rude."

Ivy wanted to hit him.

"Roux, cut it out." Sylvia frowned. She was speaking to him in a normal voice again.

Ivy stood up from the sofa and said she was going to find some breakfast. Sylvia invited her to join them for crab cakes at the Red Barn. "Can you believe Roux's never had crab cakes before?"

"*You're kidding,*" said Ivy.

Sylvia looked at her coldly.

"Next time," said Ivy.

"See you later," Roux called on his way out. "It was good running into an old . . . neighbor."

IVY BROUGHT HER coffee and croissant to the beach. She couldn't stand to be in the living room a second longer, trapped by the wooden walls expanding in the heat with occasional creaks and groans, and the outdated furniture, striped futons and round-legged consoles, giving the impression of a life lived in miniature. A dollhouse life. Or maybe it had only been Roux's presence, unexpected and overwhelming, that had made her feel so constricted.

Poppy and Ted were sunbathing beside a large striped parasol. Gideon was a beige seal dipping in and out of the waves. A chirping chorus welcomed Ivy: *Come, come! Sit. Join us! Did you sleep well?* "They're not as fresh as I'd like," Poppy said about the croissant in Ivy's napkin. "I got to the bakery a bit late this morning and those were the only ones left." Ivy reassured her the croissants were delicious, she'd never slept better. She placed her towel next to Poppy and pulled off her dress, acutely conscious of her childish proportions, all rib bones and spine and a large bruise on one kneecap from banging it on the edge of the wooden chest in her room. Ted was wearing a Harvard T-shirt and gray swim trunks, the mellow backdrop to Poppy's vibrant one-piece, her figure as firm and perky as a young banana. People said that Asian women aged well, but Ivy thought that past fifty, American women who went to the gym and cared for themselves looked much more youthful.

When Ivy complimented the beautiful scenery, Ted pointed out the palm-sized flowers with the crinkly fuchsia petals and serrated leaves growing in the underbrush. He said they were rugosas; they'd been brought over from eastern Asia in the mid-1800s, the first report of them occurring on Nantucket. Ivy expressed her admiration at his intimate knowledge of the land. That's what she called it, the land, because it seemed the only word to match the solemnity with which Ted had spoken about beach roses.

"Some of our friends are horrified by the idea of vacationing in the same spot every year," said Ted, "but we're creatures of habit. We wouldn't trade this for any spot in the world."

Ivy said Nan was the same way, she preferred domestic comforts to exotic destinations. And by domestic comforts, she meant Nan's house, which she never left except for her annual trip to visit Ping's family in Doylestown, Pennsylvania.

"And where do your folks live now?" asked Ted, propping himself onto his elbows.

So it began. Context, subtext. Clarksville was *near Princeton*, *self-employment* implied tax write-offs, a *small shop* meant commercial real estate. This last part wasn't even a lie—Shen had recently purchased a large warehouse so they could fit all the used junk they could no longer store in their house. Nan complained all the time about their tightening cash flow. Ivy imagined her parents sitting at the kitchen table, punching numbers into Nan's little plastic calculator—which deserved a spot in the *Guinness World Records* for its durability—jotting down the little red and black figures into the checkbook, year after year, day after day, until death.

"You and Gideon are the same age?" asked Poppy.

"I'm three months older," said Ivy. She could see the calculations in Poppy's head. Twenty-nine for the first kid. That left ten years to pop out three more before she turned forty.

"Gideon says you're thinking of law school," said Ted.

"Yes."

"That's quite a time, not to mention financial, investment."

It was hard to gauge from his tone whether he approved of this plan. Ivy nodded in a vague sort of manner that she hoped conveyed both agreement and optimism.

In her tactful, chattering way, Poppy kept them entertained with stories about her eldest brother, Bobby, the uncle Gideon had mentioned who was an attorney in California, until Gideon came back from his swim.

"How's the water?" Ted asked.

"Frigid," said Gideon, shivering as a breeze flapped the edges of the parasol.

"Ivy here was telling us about law school," said Ted.

"Ah," said Gideon.

What did that *Ah* mean, Ivy wondered.

"Do you think you'll apply to nearby schools?" Poppy asked innocently.

"Absolutely," said Ivy. "I love Boston. I can't imagine living anywhere else."

Poppy placed a hand on her arm. "It's *so* nice that Gideon brought you here. We haven't met any of his girlfriends in, why—it's been years! Since—well. He's always been so *coy* when it comes to his private life."

"Now, now, Poppy," said Ted quietly. "Gideon can make his own decisions."

Gideon jumped to his feet and declared he was hungry, he was going to go back inside.

"Let's all go," said Poppy, blushing.

They collected their things in silence. Gideon walked ahead, followed by Ivy, finally the two older folks loitered a few steps behind, speaking with each other in hushed tones.

After lunch, Gideon napped in his room with a headache, and Poppy and Ted went to visit their neighbors down the street. Ivy found a shaded spot on the porch swing to study. She turned the earmarked page of her test prep book and began to read: *Evidence + Assumption = Conclusion is the bread and butter of LR. Remember to use keywords as well as critical thinking to locate the conclusion FIRST. Then ask "Why is the conclusion true?" and identify the evidence, ignoring any filler or background. The assumption is what's missing, what the author takes for granted . . .* She woke up with her cheeks burning. The sun had moved across the sky, low and blinding, facing her head-on. Roux's precious Bugatti was parked behind Gideon's car, the convertible roof curved snugly over a little blue body, with headlights so circular and protruding they looked like two eyeballs atop antennae. It was a toy car and Ivy understood that Roux had bought it for that very reason, to show he had no need for practicality, it was simply for amusement.

From the open window of the laundry room out back, she could just make out Sylvia's voice saying something about air-conditioning. Ivy gathered her book that'd fallen onto the ground and went back inside.

Everyone except for Roux was gathered around a black-and-white cat pawing a sock across the tiled floors. It was obviously a stray. One of its ears was shriveled like a mushroom; its tail was dirty and matted with missing sections of hair. Sylvia was telling Poppy how they'd found it outside the bushes at Tom's Market, trying to eat a jalapeño pepper. "He obviously used to belong to someone because he's so sweet around people—he's not feral at all. He kept rubbing up against my leg and purring for food. I'm going to bring him to the vet tomorrow to get him checked." She thrust the cat at Ivy, who gingerly pet the top of its normal ear. It seemed neither to like nor dislike humans. When her hand neared its belly, it let out a long hiss and Ivy quickly retracted, brushing away the cat hairs floating in her face.

"Don't get too close," Poppy said, hovering by the door. "Not until we get him checked for diseases."

"I've already decided to keep him," said Sylvia. "I'm going to call him Pepper."

Poppy pressed a hand to her cheek. "Are you sure you have time for a pet, Sylvia? Getting your doctorate is challenging enough without the added responsibility of a cat."

"It's maybe too much for *you*," said Sylvia, "but thankfully I take after Daddy."

Ted said, "You'd better think this through, Sib. Mom's right, you *do* travel constantly. Who's going to look after it when you're gone?"

"But—"

"She'll handle it," said Gideon, exchanging a look with his sister. Countless times, they must have tag-teamed Ted and Poppy in this fashion, thought Ivy, maneuvering through their parents like two acrobats whose mutual trust was implicit and uncompromising.

Sylvia brought the cat to the living room, where Roux was nursing a scotch and flipping through one of Poppy's coffee-table books about historic landmark homes, and began to tease it with one of the wooden mobiles. Gideon jingled the shells together and the cat swiveled toward him, both the normal ear and the shriveled one flattened on its football-shaped head, its tail switching low on the ground like a ratty mop. "I've always liked cats," said Gideon. "I was quite fond of Tom's old cat, Beaver. He used to drink water straight out of the faucet Miriam even taught him how to pee in the toilet. Quite smart, cats."

"Do *you* want to take Pepper?" Sylvia asked.

"Should I?"

"Your place is quite small—" Ivy began just as Sylvia said, "Oh, *you should!*"

"Are you sure you have time for a pet?" Ivy asked, realizing, too late, that she'd used the exact line as Poppy only minutes ago. Gideon and Sylvia exchanged another look.

"I hate cats," said Roux, snapping his book shut with a bang. "And this one's ugly as hell. I don't know that it's actually tame. It looks like it could take a swipe at an eyeball when you're asleep."

Ivy couldn't help it—she laughed.

"You're heartless," said Sylvia. "How on earth your parents raised you."

Roux said, "Like a stray dog."

When it didn't look like Sylvia or Gideon were going to do anything else other than lie on the ikat rug and pet the cat, Ivy suggested that they head back down to the beach.

"I actually need to finish up an email," said Gideon. "I'm going to go grab my laptop." He got up and left.

Shortly after, Roux finished his drink and got up as well. He looked at Sylvia as if expecting her to follow him, but she stayed put on the rug. Their earlier lascivious affection seemed all but a figment of Ivy's imagination. She wondered if something had happened over crab cakes. But then again, maybe this was just the norm for Sylvia and Roux, who both seemed like the sort of people who'd be attracted to volatility.

"Can you please hang up your clothes?" Sylvia called out to Roux's retreating back. She frowned at Ivy. "You're lucky Gideon's relatively tidy. Roux's barely unpacked anything yet somehow our bed is covered with his shit."

"You guys are sharing a bedroom?" said Ivy.

"Why wouldn't we be?"

"It's just—I thought your mom didn't like it . . ."

Sylvia actually laughed out loud, dimples flashing. "Ivy! You're such a duck. Mom's looked the other way since I snuck Tucker McDermott through my window in tenth grade. What a proper upbringing you must have had. No wonder Giddy loves you."

STARING AT GIDEON across the table, Ivy thought: Either Sylvia's lying or Poppy does mind, but Sylvia doesn't care about her mother's feelings while Gideon is more considerate. He would never sneak some slut through his window. This explanation was plausible, yet it did nothing to mollify the sting of rejection. Ivy could not bear to contemplate the third idea, which was that Gideon simply had grown tired of her but was too much of a gentleman to say so outright. Since arriving at the cottage, they'd barely had any alone time and even amongst others, he didn't stay by her side like a protective boyfriend nor did he seem overly concerned about making her feel comfortable. She'd thought this was a sign of their bond, from the man who'd said *Sorry, were we supposed to have the talk?*, and that he trusted her to hold her own among his family, the same way she had with the Crosses and Finleys. But perhaps the distance she felt between them was just that—distance.

Lost in her own thoughts, she was quiet throughout dinner and ate very little. She felt she might be coming down with a cold. The spasms in her little finger had spread to her face, which felt stiff and tingled as if she were on the verge of sneezing. Halfway through the entrée, interrupting Poppy's summary of her volunteer work at the local museum, Roux glanced over at her and exclaimed: "Ivy—your eyes."

"What about them?"

"Oh my," said Poppy, covering her mouth. Everyone turned, forks pausing in midair.

"They look really red and—puffy," said Gideon.

Ivy got up and fast-walked to the restroom; Gideon and Poppy were on her heels. When she looked in the mirror, she let out a squeak. Her eyelids were so thick they looked like two angry blisters on top of her black pupils. "What's happening?" she lamented, closing her lids and rubbing them to clear the watering. This made it worse and the skin around her eyes began to tingle, then to itch.

"Should we go to the hospital?" Poppy asked, clutching her throat. She called over her shoulder, "Ted, can you come here? We need you."

Ivy said she thought she might be having an allergic reaction. She'd had one when she was very young, to a bee sting, only less severe. That time, her throat had been itchy as well. She swallowed to check her reflexes, which seemed intact.

"The cat!" said Gideon. "Ivy, are you allergic to cats?"

"I don't know," she said through rubbery lips, beneath which, even as she looked into the mirror, she could feel the blood beginning to pulse.

"Is everything all right?" Ted asked, switching places with Gideon, who'd gone to fetch the Benadryl.

Poppy explained the situation to her husband. "Should we take her to the ER? Is this like a peanut allergy? Do we have an EpiPen on hand? How's your breathing, Ivy?"

"What's going on?" asked Sylvia, joining the fray.

"Ivy's allergic to your cat," said Poppy. "She's been playing with him all evening. Look at her eyes."

Sylvia frowned. "You're allergic to Pepper?"

"I don't know," Ivy said again. She felt it was her fault she didn't know anything about her own allergies.

Ted asked if she'd been around cats before.

"Not really."

Gideon returned with a Benadryl and a glass of water. After she swallowed the pill, she said, "I'd better stay in my room in case it gets worse."

"Oh yes," said Poppy, "stay upstairs until the cat leaves tomorrow."

"Pepper's not leaving," said Sylvia.

"We can't keep him here if he makes Ivy sick."

"We don't even know she's allergic to cats."

"It's not a food allergy," said Gideon. "We've only had salad and steak. Have you been touching your eyes after petting him?"

Ivy tried to remember if she had done so; she wasn't sure.

Sylvia said, "See—it might not be Pepper."

Poppy, a tad shrill, said, "Really, Sylvia, now is not the time to argue about this."

Sylvia's cheeks flushed; she whipped her head around and disappeared down the hallway.

Gideon asked again about going to the hospital.

"I'm fine—really," said Ivy, embarrassed at everyone's attention. "This happened before when I was young. My throat feels fine. I'm just going to go shower and wait for the Benadryl to kick in. You guys go and finish your dinners." She tried to smile but the effect was gruesome. With great effort, she convinced the Speyers to return to the table. Roux hadn't moved a centimeter from his chair. He glimpsed her face on her flight up the stairs; she thought she saw his lips twitch. But of course he would laugh at her misfortunes. What had she expected? Concern?

Upstairs, she took her second shower of the day, careful to avoid scrubbing the sunburned spots on her nose and cheeks. The steam soothed the itchiness; when she stepped out, some of the swelling in her lips had gone down. Looking in the vanity mirror, she said, "I'm a troll," and turned away.

A few minutes later, Gideon came up holding a breakfast tray. One plate held the remains of her steak and potatoes; the other plate had a slice of apple pie, the filling congealed on the bottom like amber-colored slime. Ivy thought woefully of the hours she and Poppy had spent that afternoon slicing the apples, simmering the bourbon, rolling the dough, brushing egg wash onto the beautiful lattice pattern of the crust as the house filled with the wonderful aroma of cinnamon and butter. How she'd looked forward to that pie.

"So much for making a good impression," she intoned.

"What are you talking about?" said Gideon.

"This evening was a nightmare. What your family must think of me."

"They love you."

"Do they?" It wasn't rhetorical, she really wanted to know. But Gideon only patted her leg as a gesture, meant to convey his support, but already she could sense his thoughts leaving her, waiting for the proper moment to retire to his room, where he could shed his boyfriend duties and resume his primary relationship with his laptop.

"Tomorrow will be better," he said. "We'll go to the hospital first thing if your rash doesn't improve."

But what about tonight? she thought at him. But with a face like boiled crabmeat, she was in no position to demand anything just now. There were women who went their entire lives without letting their husbands see them without lipstick and perfectly drawn-in eyebrows. Perhaps she'd gotten complacent. Once you saw something, you could never unsee it. People were shallow that way, no matter how they tried to convince themselves otherwise.

13

IT RAINED ON AND OFF ALL WEEK: BLEAK SKIES AND A MONOTONOUS downpour kept them indoors all day reading, drinking, listening to Gideon play the piano, helping Poppy bake endless trays of oatmeal raisin cookies that they gave away to the neighbors. Ivy's allergies grew so bad that she began medicating with two kinds of antihista- mines, which made her feel as if a weight hung on each individual eyelash. Gideon offered to leave the cat with the Walds but Ivy didn't want to cause any more of an inconvenience. Instead, Sylvia kept the cat in her and Roux's room. Every chance she had, Sylvia expressed her doubts that Pepper was the cause of Ivy's allergies, but not to Ivy herself, though she always said it within Ivy's hearing. Emotions ran high all around. Every gesture, tick, personality quirk, all normally be- nign, quickly became small but continuous irritations under the con- fines of a single roof.

Roux and Sylvia seemed embroiled in a low-key fight. It started when Sylvia took a dig at him about his morning donut runs. "Other guys would be thrilled to get three home-cooked meals a day," she said, "but you don't eat a thing because you fill up on that junk." Roux finished chewing, then wiped the sugar powder from his mouth with the back of his hand. "One person's trash, another's treasure," he said. "Maybe you can stop bitching all the time." Everyone except for Gideon, who was outside taking his usual morning swim in the ocean, rain or no rain, was still at the breakfast table drinking the last sips of cold coffee. Ted's face went through a comical range of expressions from shock to anger to resignation as decades of training to pretend pleasant deafness kicked in. Ivy expected Sylvia to implode at Roux, but Gideon's sister only said in a strained voice, "I wasn't implying anything." Poppy pressed her lips together in a quaking frown, her only outlet for what must have been internal fury, as she scurried over to Sylvia to smother her in frivolous sentiments. Roux asked Ted if he had any cigars. Ted said, "No, Roux. I don't have cigars lying around."

Roux's rough demeanor almost reminded Ivy of Tom Cross, only Tom's rudeness was condescending, meant to prove a point, whereas Roux's rudeness held no contempt. That was why Roux could speak that way to Sylvia, even to Ted and Poppy (Roux and Gideon did not speak unless it was in a group setting, and even then, the neutral politeness was obviously a mask for mutual disinterest), and they tolerated him—because he didn't look down on anyone. He didn't know any better.

Sylvia pushed her mother away with a petulant scowl. It was impossible to reconcile this sulky girl with the sophisticated, unflappable Sylvia at her dinner party all those months ago. Maybe everyone reverted back to infantile habits around their family members.

It seemed like things were on the verge of an implosion. However, that very evening, Roux and Sylvia were drunk and intertwined on the armchair, cooing at each other in their baby voices. The next day, when looking for a quiet place to study, Ivy came upon them in the piano room, sitting cross-legged on the floor. An Italian film was playing in the background on Sylvia's computer. Ivy apologized for interrupting, but Sylvia waved her in. "I'm glad you found us. This movie's a snooze. I don't understand a word so Roux has to translate everything, but I think he's making it all up."

"*Perché sei ignorante,*" said Roux in a passable accent.

"What are you guys working on?" Ivy asked, noting the paper and pencils scattered over the coffee table.

"My coloring book," said Sylvia, showing Ivy her pages filled with geometric flowers and castles, the same sort of coloring book Ivy kept in her classroom for her first graders. "Roux's working on a new sketch," she added in afterthought.

Ivy glanced at the drawing on the table. A gas station, Ferris wheel, what looked like a woman in a baseball cap pumping the gas.

"It's Vegas," said Roux.

"I get that," said Ivy, though she hadn't.

"Never mind. It's garbage."

"It's amazing," said Sylvia coldly. "Tell him, Ivy."

"It is," said Ivy. With minimal black-and-white strokes, he'd managed to capture a specific mood and emotion on the page: the moment before violence descends. And here she'd assumed his interest in art, much like his interest in vintage cars, was a nouveau riche status thing, without any appreciation other than for the price tag. He'd said it himself that first day: I enjoy procuring what everyone else wants. "I really like it," she said again.

Roux shrugged. "You want it?" He tore the page from the spine and handed it to her.

"How generous of you, kangaroo," said Sylvia. At first Ivy thought she was being flippant—how presumptuous of Roux to assume anyone would want his silly old sketches—but when she glanced over, Sylvia was practically frozen with anger.

They heard Gideon coming down the hall. Ivy folded the drawing and quickly slid it into her book; she excused herself from the room.

That'd taken place Monday night. It was Thursday now, and Ivy noticed that Sylvia had pretty much stopped speaking to her after that. Overnight there seemed to have sprung an invisible force field that prevented Gideon's sister's head from physically turning in her direction. She wasn't even rude; Ivy had simply ceased to exist for her. Was this punishment, Ivy wondered, for the cat? Could a person be that petty? Or was this just another amplified symptom as a result of being cooped up together?

Gideon was, of course, oblivious to the undertones between his girlfriend and sister. Sometimes, Ivy would hear Sylvia's low voice coming from the alcove speaking in low, unbroken murmurs to Gideon about some important private topic—or to give the impression of speaking about an important private topic, to prove a point, Ivy thought. Her Giddy, his Sibbie. And as Ted's only hobbies were reading the newspaper, his golf magazines, and his five o'clock beers, that left only Poppy as Ivy's sole remaining ally. They'd spent a happy hour that morning looking through Gideon's baby photos, a rite of passage for any girlfriend and one that Ivy hadn't expected to come so soon. She especially loved the photo of a toddler Gideon wearing a pink tutu, one ballet slipper, and a gold tiara on his head, pushed on a swing by an identically dressed Sylvia, "when you have a sister"—Poppy laughed in little hiccupping sounds—but a few photographs struck Ivy as being distinctly strange, mostly because of Poppy's explanations.

"Sylvia was always a bad sleeper," said Poppy, referencing a photo of Gideon and Sylvia sleeping underneath a striped blanket, crown touching crown, one of Sylvia's arms thrown over Gideon's chest. "They shared a bed until high school. When Sylvia finally asked for her own room, it almost broke my heart." She pointed out another photo of Gideon and Sylvia soaking naked in a freestanding white tub. "And they *loved* their bath time. After every softball game or beach day, they'd beg for their rubber duckies and vanilla-scented bubbles."

Ivy saw no bubbles or rubber duckies in the photo. The smooth brown of Sylvia's back, the sinewy back of a teenager, was sliced in half by the surface of the water. Gideon's brown legs were tucked between his sister's in the small tub, which was a normal-sized tub but felt small in proportion to the long-limbed siblings inhabiting it. Ivy and Austin had never been allowed to sleep side by side, only head to feet, like sardines, and Nan always took great care to inform them that the genders were never to mix, Ivy should never let a boy see her nude, even her own brother or father. Was this perversity, then, this freedom between Gideon and Sylvia? Or innocence? But the innocent were often perverse, the perverse innocent.

Later that afternoon, the roof began to leak, staining the old floor-boards in dark gray rivulets. Ivy and Gideon had been eating a cold pasta salad in the alcove when Poppy cried out, "Oh! Oh! Someone get me a bucket!" They hurried to the living room. Sylvia was covering her head with the coffee-table book Roux had been reading the other day. Roux, for some reason, was naked from the waist up and wringing his shirt into a potted plant. Ted came running down from upstairs, his hair flattened on one side, clearly having just awoken from a nap. "A bucket, Ted, hand me a bucket," Poppy cried. Ted picked up one of the woven baskets by the fireplace. "A *bucket*, not a *basket*." Ted's face turned as bright as the tomatoes in the fruit bowl. Roux began to laugh. He draped his wet T-shirt like a towel around his neck. "You look like the plumber," Ivy informed him. Soon they were all laughing, Poppy the hardest, shrieks of uncouth laughter emitting from her dainty bird mouth.

The small leak had the effect of a thunderstorm in clearing the stifling air. They placed basins to catch the drops falling from the ceiling and mopped up the remaining puddles. "Our old cottage has been showing its age," said Poppy, "but we haven't gotten around to repairs." She gave a regretful sigh. When Roux said he knew a contractor in Boston who could do the job, Poppy said, "What a *wonderful* idea, I *must* think it over," which was her way of deflecting unwanted suggestions. Afterward, they ate ice cream sitting on the porch, listening to the pitter-patter of the rain while Poppy and Ted regaled them with anecdotes about the storms their "dear Finn Oaks" had weathered throughout the years. The way the Speyers spoke about old objects, chipped teacups, rusted silver spoons, the old gramophone they found in the attic, as if they were living creatures, was absurdly charming to Ivy. Sylvia sat beside her on the love seat. "The ice cream made me so cold all of a sudden," she said, shivering and dropping her head onto Ivy's shoulder. Ivy felt an unexpected thrill, not unlike the feeling when the boy who'd bullied you in school suddenly confessed he'd done so because he liked you. She closed her eyes and breathed in the scent of rain and salt and soft female warmth, all the while keeping pace with Sylvia's breaths rising and falling against her arm.

I must have been overreacting, she told herself. Sylvia has no reason to begrudge me.

The good mood carried over to the next day when they finally woke to a broiling sun and cloudless blue skies. The younger crowd decided to take the boat to Coven Island and go clamming for that night's dinner. Poppy packed them turkey sandwiches and a huge Tupperware of new strawberries. Gideon filled the icebox with beers.

It was not yet ten o'clock on Friday morning and already the marina was teeming with families, dogs running off-leash, fishermen perched on the yellow and orange rocks jutting into the harbor. At the edge of the water a gray shingled shack had a placard that read CATTAHASSET YACHT CLUB. Farther up the road was Cattahasset Point Club, a multilevel estate with two enormous white wraparound decks in which couples and groups of middle-aged women brunched underneath striped umbrellas.

"It gets more crowded every year." Sylvia frowned, narrowly avoiding being barreled down by two boys in matching sailor shirts. "When we came here as kids, there was hardly anyone around. Now look."

She was right about the summer tourists, but Ivy was delighted rather than put off by the crowds. Vacation, in her view, *should* be a little excessive sometimes—it couldn't always be solitary beach walks and books and restrained dinner conversations about politics and art—and the loud, happy voices of people in flip-flops and open-collared shirts drinking iced lattes seemed the perfect antidote to the hushed atmosphere of Finn Oaks. She slipped her arm through Gideon's. He said, "Hey there," and she said, "Hey there," and they smiled at each other. He led them to the pier where the boats were bobbing up and down on the water, indistinguishable to Ivy's eyes.

The Speyers' boat was small and white except for two green stripes running along the side. The four of them fit quite comfortably with Gideon taking the driver's seat, Ivy perched on a bench in the cockpit, and Roux and Sylvia up front on the deck. A small set of stairs led down to a tiny cabin. Soon they were swerving past the other sailboats, the little yacht club where Gideon had parked shrinking into a flat square in the distance. Their boat was fast and light in the water. Gideon pointed out various landmarks on the coast; on the bow, Roux's arm was draped around Sylvia's waist. She'd already taken off her cover-up and was sunbathing in a black lace bikini.

Twenty minutes into the ride, Roux clambered to the back of the boat, clutching the handrail. He took a seat on the bench across from Ivy and lay down on his back. Sylvia arrived shortly afterward. She murmured something in his ear, he shook his head, she smoothed out his hair. After a while, she crossed over to Ivy's side of the boat. Ivy asked if everything was all right. "He's just feeling a bit nauseous," said Sylvia. "He took some motion sickness medicine this morning but it's not working."

They looked over. Two buttons of Roux's shirt had come undone, revealing a tuft of black chest hair, stark against his pale skin. His one leg was bent upright on the bench and his right arm was thrown over his eyes. "I hope he'll be okay until we get to the island," said Ivy. She felt little sympathy for Roux; her only concern was that he shouldn't ruin their day. His sour moods could be toxic, even more than Sylvia's, whose sulkiness could usually be ignored, while no one could ignore Roux when he made up his mind to be unpleasant.

"It's probably all the sugar he eats every morning," said Sylvia with an arrogant toss of her hair. "Sometimes I envy how easy things are between you and Gideon. You guys are basically the same person. You like the same food, read the same books, you even talk in the same bookish vocabulary. Pretty soon, you'll be going around in matching outfits."

But you two already do that, thought Ivy, thinking of the monogrammed pajamas.

"You and Roux seem close, though," she said, sensing danger. "Sometimes it's better to be complementary than similar."

"I guess that's true," said Sylvia, mollified. "I tried to figure out our anniversary the other day. It's confusing because we've taken so many breaks. I think it's around eight months next week . . . Christ, only eight months! With all the fights we've had, I feel like I've married and divorced him twice over."

Ivy asked what they fought about.

"I never remember afterward. He's got a temper. But I hate fighting so I walk away until he cools down. He calls me the ice princess. I suppose both of us are stubborn. Our fights can go on for days."

"That seems normal."

"Actually, it's not," Sylvia said with a tolerant smile, as if Ivy had been trying to be unnecessarily uplifting. "My parents *never* fought. And there were some serious issues, believe me. Dad was gone most of our lives, commuting back and forth from Boston. He rented this house over in Back Bay. White walls, everything straight-edged, like a ruler, and boxed in. Every time Mom would bring us, we'd go to our bedrooms and everything—the bed, the desk, the windowsill—would be covered with fruit flies and gnats. And still Dad refused to get a housekeeper. He said it made him look *elitist*." She paused to let the word, *elitist*, settle in the air. It was a common habit of the rich to talk about elitism and privilege, as if by pointing out the fact, they were disarming future accusations of being so.

"Mom didn't like that," Sylvia continued. "When they got married, she gave him all her inheritance so he could get into office, but he was always ashamed of her family background . . . there were some scandals, sure—our great-grandfather was rumored to have eaten human meat on his tour around Kenya . . . but in the end, Ted's the real hypocrite. . . . our mom's his second wife, did Gideon tell you about that?" Ivy shook her head. Sylvia said, "Yeah. Well. He was married once, for two years, after the navy. But we don't talk about that . . . Anyway . . ." She laughed, a little pained ironic laugh. "I suppose you agree with Roux. I'm just a spoiled girl complaining about her frivolous problems." Ivy was a beat late in her protests and Sylvia said disappointedly, "It doesn't matter. I've long stopped giving a shit what people think about me."

"No family's perfect," said Ivy, unsure what tone to adopt to contain the damage and settling for briskness. "Plus, you and Gideon turned out so well."

"You've no idea how narrow-minded Ted and Poppy can get. She's been a monster toward Roux all week. Yes, she has," Sylvia insisted, seeing Ivy's incredulity. "They hate that no one they know has ever heard of Roux. Did you know they tried to get my cousin Francis to look him up? Francis works for Governor Patrick. And she won't shut up about how he never went to college. All week, it's been 'but he doesn't value education' and 'he doesn't treat you right because he has no role models.' What does she expect him to do—walk around holding his Boy Scouts badge?"

Ivy had no idea all this had been going on while she'd been engulfed in her own stupor of allergy meds and insecurity.

"Were you there for that?" Sylvia asked.

"For what?"

"Roux said he dropped out of high school his senior year to support his mother. She'd gotten cancer."

Ivy said she'd moved to New Jersey way before that. But Sylvia already knew this so why was she pretending otherwise?

Sylvia nodded.

"But he's so successful now," said Ivy. "Surely Poppy must see how far he's come?"

"You think Roux's successful?"

"Isn't he?"

The two women looked at each other in surprise. When Sylvia didn't say more, Ivy returned to the subject of family.

"I've always wished my parents had higher standards for me and my brother. We don't agree at all on what makes a good life . . . and I don't think Poppy and Ted are narrow-minded. They have—tradition—" Sylvia rolled her eyes. Ivy said, "I'm serious! Meaning comes from the importance we attach to the small things. If there are no standards, then there's no culture or—even society!"

"That's one way to look at it," said Sylvia with a curious smile. "It's so nice sometimes to talk everything over with an outsider. Oh, I don't mean it *that* way," she added. "I just mean you're such a good listener. You give us all—perspective." She brushed her fingers over Ivy's wrist to undercut the implied insult of her words. Physicality, Ivy was beginning to understand, was Sylvia's power and one that seemed to work on men and women alike.

"Actually, I've been meaning to ask you a favor," Sylvia went on, lowering her voice. "My parents will want to usher us all along to St. Stephen's on Sunday, and I know Roux won't come. He says he'll never step foot inside a church. Can you talk some sense into him?"

Ivy's eyes darted over to Roux. He hadn't budged from his limp-doll position and was sleeping with his mouth slightly open. "Why would he listen to me?"

"You're the other significant other here and I presume you're not religious. He'll see you're willing to play along. If we all just corral him . . . make it seem like a group activity . . ."

For all of Sylvia's talk, she was surprisingly compliant with her parents' wishes. "Does your family usually attend church?" asked Ivy. Ted said grace before dinner but that was the extent of any religious displays Ivy had seen so far.

"*Oh, yes*," said Sylvia. "Our faith is very important to us."

"I'll try and talk to him." To say no was a power, too, one Ivy had learned long ago but seemed incapable of using on any Speyer.

Sylvia clapped her hands with childish delight. "Have I told you already how happy I am you're here? You made Mom so happy. You two looked as thick as thieves the other day, laughing over Giddy's baby photos. She absolutely *adores* you."

Ivy laughed with the bashful gratitude expected of her. When she flattered Sylvia, she felt like an ingratiating panderer, yet when Sylvia flattered her, she felt beholden and vaguely patronized. She couldn't win.

A gull was circling overhead and they watched it for a while as it dove into the water, dipped back up, dove back in, trying to catch the fish that kept flopping and squirming out of its large yellow beak. I'm the fish, Ivy thought, and Sylvia's trying to peck me to death. Death by a thousand pecks.

"You know," said Sylvia, still observing the bird. "Roux didn't want to come on this trip at first. But when he heard you were coming, he changed his mind."

"I didn't know that." *Why?*

The boat cut a wake too quickly and water lapped the sides of the boat.

"Giddy's such a speed demon," said Sylvia, standing up. "I'll tell him to slow down."

THEY ANCHORED IN a tiny pebbled beach, surrounded on three sides by rocky cliffs and wild grasses. Gideon and Sylvia immediately undressed and dove in, swimming in a diagonal to the shoreline, arms dipping in and out in synchronized lines. Ivy buried her toes into the sand and waded in slowly; the waves crashing up to her chest were so cold her ribs shuddered in protest and her breath came out in shallow gasps. Gideon's and Sylvia's dark blond heads bobbed up and down in the waves. Ivy watched the siblings talk and splash each other, their carefree laughter carrying in the wind but the words themselves unintelligible. Gideon gestured at her to swim closer. He and Sylvia were both treading water, the ocean around them black and endless. Ivy shook her head with a laugh, hoping he'd swim over to her. When he didn't, she thought she must look stupid just standing there, neither swimming nor playing, and so she made her way back up the beach where Roux was sitting on their picnic blanket, still fully dressed with a cigarette hanging from his mouth. He offered her one, but she declined. She could hardly sit still. Sylvia said Roux had known she would be on the trip. But he had seemed equally surprised to see her that first night. He'd kept secrets from both her and his girlfriend. That made him risky, if not just a bit compelling. Ivy felt painfully anxious, like a girl about to go on a first date, but also primed for disgust, as if she expected nothing good to come from an honest conversation. She decided silence was the best option, as it was for most delicate situations.

They gazed out at Gideon and Sylvia in the water.

"Creepy, isn't it?" said Roux. "How lovey-dovey they are?"

"You have a filthy mind."

"There's an aphorism somewhere here: something about a kettle . . ."

She left him. She hadn't thought to reach for a cigarette since she'd arrived in Cattahasset—she even managed to convince herself she'd really quit this time—but breathing in the secondhand smoke made her realize her indifference had been a pretense to fool the ragged beast in her that craved a smoke so violently her hands shook. She even fantasized, walking away on the beach, about stealing a few cigs when Roux wasn't looking; she would keep them dry in her sunglasses case, smoke them all at once later in the night.

She spent the next half hour exploring a small cove by the cliffs, to give the appearance of amusing herself. When she got back, the siblings had returned.

"How was your walk?" said Gideon.

"Marvelous. Look what I found." Ivy showed him the little seashells and dead mollusks she'd collected. She was relieved to see that Sylvia and Roux had moved on to their own towels a little ways away. Sylvia was lying on her belly, tickling Roux's nose with a feather. Ivy looked away but she sensed every one of their movements and she felt she was suffering.

She snuggled her head into the crook of Gideon's shoulder. His hair, normally neatly combed, was curly and coarse with sand and the tip of his nose was pink from where he had missed a spot applying sunscreen. She flipped over onto her stomach and leaned in for a kiss. Gideon gave her a quick peck but she prolonged the contact, leaning her weight into him and running her tongue over the ridges of his teeth. She could feel his surprise in the stiffness of his chest. For once, she didn't stop herself. Why should she? She was his girlfriend. She had rights. Needs.

Gideon wrangled free from her grasp with a bemused smile.

"I love you," said Ivy.

He opened his mouth. A second passed. There came the sound of waves lapping at the rocky cliffs. She flipped over onto her back and let her eyes drift. This isn't real, she thought. None of this is real.

"I care about you a lot," came Gideon's tender voice. The tenderness was meant for himself, she knew, and not for her, tenderness meant to reaffirm the position he was determined to take. She felt his hands over hers, his soft lips lingering on the center of her palm. She didn't move. Then his face filled her vision, he was on top of her, kissing her mouth with a fervor she had never known. Instinct made her draw her arms around his neck and arch her back off the sand. His hand was on her lower back, something wild and frantic released in her—she slipped one hand down the cold, wet waistband of his swim trunks, cupping between his legs. He was completely flaccid. He continued to kiss her, his tongue wet and hungry, running his hand down her back. Above them, the sky darkened. It was Sylvia's shadow blocking the sun.

"Sorry to break up the show but we should get going soon if we want to catch any clams—we're going to miss low tide."

CLAMMING—OF ALL THE ridiculous activities WASPs loved, this one took the cake. Ivy had imagined that clamming would involve a boat and nets, similar to catching lobsters or crabs, but really, it was just pulling a rake through the sand until you hauled in something, and more often than not, it was a pebble or a shell, and not anything edible. They arrived at the Great Pond to kids splashing around little tide pools while their parents, in large sun hats and rolled-up chinos, dug for their dinner with a Puritan work ethic that would have made Ivy's yam-digging farmer ancestors proud.

It was the golden hour, the sky a haloed blue with wistful streaks of pink and orange, a sliver of a moon high in the sky. After they collected enough clams, they headed to a nearby park for the bake. Gideon got out Poppy's aluminum stockpot and set it on the outdoor grill; Roux and Sylvia dumped the clams inside with an entire stick of butter, half a bottle of Albariño wine, and a bunch of bayberries. They all gathered on the grass, getting rapidly drunk, brushing sand from their legs and the hollows underneath their ankles. When the shells popped open, they feasted, all of them starving, and no one talked much as they chewed on Portuguese bread, driftwood-smoked clam meat, another bottle of wine. The sky slowly darkened. Moths flittered toward the streetlights. Everyone was beautiful but their beauty had a sinister quality, like the beauty of Venetian masks that might hide the glorious or grotesque. The sight of Roux and Sylvia sharing a kiss was enough to bring sudden tears to Ivy's eyes. *I care about you a lot.* But caring a lot was not love. Caring without loving was only pity. Roux looked at her. It was too late to rearrange her expression. His eyes were dark and stormy and honest—the only honest thing around her!

At ten o'clock, Gideon said they had to get going if they wanted to make it home before the tide turned. He held her hand very tightly on the walk back to the boat. She felt like telling him to cut it out, he didn't have to mollify her in these cheap ways, as if she were such a simpleton, like Andrea, the kind of naive girl who'd believe in such apologies. It occurred to Ivy that she and Gideon had never before quarreled. He'd never had a reason to apologize. Now he did and she was the one who was sorry.

Immediately after they boarded the boat, she went down into the cabin area and lay on the trundle bed. It was hard, cramped, and smelled of seaweed. From the little window she saw the hazy brushstrokes of the Milky Way: burning stars millions of miles away, where she wished she could be, if only she could be reborn as something other. She counted two hundred stars before she fell into a deep and dreamless sleep. The next thing she knew, she opened her eyes and Gideon was murmuring, *We're back*.

14

THE NEXT MORNING, IVY WAS IN THE KITCHEN MAKING BREAKFAST before anyone else was awake. Roux was the first one down. He took one look at her appearance—fully made-up, her hair clasped back in a mother-of-pearl clip, a new apron tied around her skirt— and asked whose body she'd buried. "Gideon find out and put you in the doghouse?" he added, pouring himself a cup of coffee. Instead of leaving for his usual morning donut run, he sat on one of the barstools and watched as she arranged the raspberries in concentric circles atop a bowl of yogurt. "You missed a spot here," he said, plucking up a raspberry and popping it into his mouth. "Better start again."

She picked up the paring knife and began slicing a kiwi into quarters. "On the boat yesterday," she said calmly, "Sylvia wanted me to ask you to go to St. Stephen's with us tomorrow."

"Why?"

"It's important to her parents."

"No. Why'd she tell *you* to ask me?"

Ivy gave him a sharp look, but he seemed genuinely ignorant of why his girlfriend would assume Ivy had any influence over him. Maybe she'd been the only one tiptoeing around him, imagining a shared history that he found so inconsequential, it hadn't even been worth mentioning to Sylvia.

"Anyway, I'm not going," he said, eating another raspberry.

"Doing the opposite of what everyone wants—it's childish. And not amusing whatsoever."

He eyed her coldly. "Who says I want to be amusing?"

She felt his desire to pick a fight and resisted by adopting her "teacher" tone, which she sensed would most irritate him.

"Suit yourself. But if your girlfriend asks, can you please tell her I tried to convince you?"

"You're so . . ."

"Yes?"

"Never mind. It's too fucking early for this."

"You clearly want to say something to me. It's not healthy to hold things in."

"You know those monkeys who clap and screech when their owner cracks the whip?" He made a snapping motion with his wrist. "That's you with the Speyers. Cooking them breakfast. Running their errands. When'd you become such a goddamn ass-kisser? It pisses me off just looking at you."

She asked if he was done. He wasn't.

"You're being played a fool and you don't even know it. You really think these people *care* about you? They care more about the stray cat. They just want you to clap, monkey, clap."

Ivy brought the knife to her mouth and licked the flat surface of its juices. "You know what your problem is?" she said quietly. "You just wish you were the one holding the whip."

She turned her back to him toward the stove, turning the sausages one by one, her hands trembling with rage, until she heard him turn and walk away. When she came to her senses, the sausages were burned, streaked with char and unsalvageable.

The Speyers came down around ten. Ted and Poppy praised the food as if no guest had ever toasted bread and scrambled eggs for them. Ted kept asking what Ivy had put in the eggs, they were just so delicious. "A lot of butter," she said ebulliently. She gave Gideon a light kiss on the lips. He spoke to her in a normal, cheerful tone. No degree of discomfiture could survive the unassailable force of inane morning chatter. It was why she'd gotten up early to cook breakfast. She spooned out a portion of yogurt into a bowl, drizzled with honey, and handed it to Gideon with a wide smile. To show you were wounded from battle was to lose the war.

Roux returned to the table. He pulled Sylvia aside to the porch, speaking to her in a harsh voice, which they all pretended not to hear through the thin sliding doors. Sylvia remained still; Roux was a pacer. They went back and forth for a while. Roux, his voice louder, said, "You know what I'm talking about, you do this—"

Sylvia returned inside, heading straight upstairs; Roux remained outside, lighting up a cigarette.

"These eggs really are just delicious," said Ted.

"Enough about the eggs," said Poppy.

After helping Poppy load the dishes into the dishwasher, Ivy went to her bedroom to grab her prep book. To her surprise, she found Sylvia standing by the window. When Sylvia saw her, she quickly removed her hand off Ivy's table.

"Pepper got out of my room. I was looking for him."

Ivy gazed around the empty room. "Is he here?"

"Not that I've seen. I checked the bathroom and he's not in there either."

Ivy asked if she'd checked underneath the bed. She dropped to her knees but only saw dust balls rolling underneath the wooden slats of the bed frame.

"I'm going to check the attic," said Sylvia. "Let me know if you see him."

Something didn't sit right. Ivy went to her desk. Her test prep book was wide open on its spine in a section she didn't recognize. She thumbed through the pages, then shook it down by the spine. Roux's sketch, the one she'd stuck inside for safekeeping, was gone.

★ ★ ★

IVY FOUND GIDEON working in the foyer after his swim. She asked him if he'd seen Sylvia's cat, it'd gotten out of its room. He said he hadn't seen it.

"Are you really going to bring it back with us to Boston?" she asked.

"I think so."

"I guess we'll be spending our time at my place from now on . . ."

He glanced up briefly from his laptop to reassure her he'd keep his apartment clean of cat hair, she would hardly notice Pepper's presence, and besides, she seemed to be doing much better on her allergy medications and he'd heard from Tom's mother that tolerance could be built over time. As he spoke, his fingers kept on typing as if they were separate entities from his brain.

"It's just that Sylvia found him," said Ivy. "And she seems so attached already. Why doesn't she keep him?"

"Her apartment doesn't allow pets. And she has her heart set on rescuing Pepper. It's the right thing to do." His decisive tone allowed for no further discussion.

Ivy felt a scrunching sensation between her eyes, as if she were trying to squint at something far away.

"Should you really always be humoring Sylvia like that?"

"Like what?"

"It feels like she takes your attention for granted. She expects you to talk to her even when you're busy with work or when we're together. She says she wants to spend more time with you but you guys go off alone all the time. You're basically at her beck and call."

"I wouldn't say that," said Gideon, his hands finally stilling. "Sylvia and I have been through a lot together. It's made us close."

"So I've heard. It's difficult being a senator's kid." This wasn't fair, Ivy knew. Gideon had never complained.

"If Sylvia's behavior has been bothering you," Gideon said in measured tones, "I can talk to her—"

"*I'm* not the one who's bothered, *she* . . ." For a split second, Ivy thought to tell him about catching Sylvia snooping around her room and stealing Roux's drawing. But she caught herself. Was she stupid? Gideon had chosen a cat over her. He'd never believe her over his sister.

"Either way. It upsets me to see you two at odds," said Gideon, sounding exactly like his father the time Ted had chastised Poppy on the beach: *Now, now, Poppy.*

Ivy stood up. "We're not at odds. I'm sorry." Roux's voice echoed in her ears: clap, monkey, clap.

"I'll be upstairs napping until dinner," she said. Would he stop her? No. The clacking of the keyboard resumed before she even reached the stairs.

SHE VEERED TO the left into the laundry room. She didn't want to run into Sylvia upstairs or, even worse, see Roux's face leering at her in triumph, proven right in his assessment of her meek servitude, which hadn't even made a difference at all, in the end. It was obvious to her now that Gideon was going to dump her. He didn't love her, he didn't desire her, he was only biding his time until the end of the trip. Soon she would become just another story the Speyers would tell around the dinner table next summer: *Remember that Ivy Lin? Very nice girl.* Then they would coolly tuck her away like a postcard of a forgettable town they'd once vacationed in. Ivy burned to remember how she'd felt she'd almost won Poppy to her side, especially in light of Sylvia's obnoxious behavior. Poppy, prefer Ivy to her own daughter? Ridiculous. The Speyers' graciousness had lured her into thinking she was making progress, when in reality she had made no more impact on these people than a ball bouncing off a foam pad. Ivy remembered a phrase Meifeng used to say: *A gentleman's friendship is insipid as water.* Yes, that was the right word to describe the Speyers. Insipid. Wishy-washy. Without form. Things without form were, by definition, impossible to hurt or penetrate.

She slammed her fist onto the washer lid. The metallic sound rang through the room. She heard a furious snarl echo from the depths of the room and jumped back in fright.

Sitting in a pile of dirty clothes inside the laundry basket was Sylvia's cat, his legs tucked underneath him. He raised his squashed head and blinked lazily at her.

"You scared me," she said.

The cat widened his jaw into a large yawn, revealing teeth like blades, and jumped out of the hamper. He walked straight to the back door that led to the yard, turned his head, and fixed unblinking yellow eyes at Ivy.

"You want to leave?"

He rubbed his head on the door, then began walking toward her, ears flattened, tail low and swishing against the floor like a duster.

"Oh, shoo, shoo!" She kicked at him. He jumped aside, hissing.

She reached over and pushed the outer door open. He didn't move. She picked up a broom from the corner of the closet and jabbed it toward him. The cat sprang out the door and onto the grass. He looked back at her once; when she made a threatening gesture with the broom again, he turned and streaked away down the sidewalk.

DINNER THAT EVENING was on the lawn. The table was set with Poppy's decorator's eye: freshly cut roses in Mason jars, starched white napkins, champagne flutes next to flowered placeholders. The smell of butter and herbs, sage, rosemary, thyme, wafted over from the charcoal grill. Poppy had spent the afternoon sticking mushrooms and peppers onto wooden skewers while Ted tended to the fire. Ivy wore the navy calf-length dress, the one she had deemed too revealing on her first day at Finn Oaks. A middle finger to giving a shit. Sylvia said she no longer cared what people thought of her. It struck Ivy now this wasn't true. Sylvia cared that people thought she didn't care.

Poppy, resplendent in a floor-length floral skirt with her gray-blond hair pulled back in a low ponytail, corralled everyone for a photo in front of the porch. Roux was the photographer, on Poppy's request. He shrugged, the offense sliding off his shoulder. *One—two—three—* The flash went off, blinding.

They took their seats. Ivy was sandwiched between Roux and Gideon.

"You look nice," said Gideon.

"Thank you."

"Do you want a glass of wine?"

"God, yes. White, please."

When he left, Roux turned to her. "Look. Sorry about this morning. I was out of line."

His words caught her off guard. She'd thought he was going to say something clever and biting again. She opened her mouth to make a condescending retort; she couldn't speak. Unexpected kindness often made her cry, whereas cruelty never did. "How are you going to make it up to me?" she asked after she'd regained her composure.

He scanned her face to gauge her seriousness. "How about I go to this—church thing—with you guys tomorrow. It seems important to you."

Through the screen door, Ivy saw Sylvia standing beside Gideon in the kitchen. They were deep in conversation. Gideon shook his head. Sylvia placed a hand on his shoulder as if consoling him: *I know it's hard but you have to tell her it's over.*

"Forget it," said Ivy, her eyes sliding back to Roux. "I could care less."

Gideon returned, empty-handed.

"Where's my drink?"

His mouth opened in surprise. "I'm so sorry. I'll be right back."

She turned away. "Never mind. Ted's about to say grace."

When Ted finished, Poppy picked up her glass. "I am so happy to be here with everyone in this special place. Ivy"—Ivy looked up—"we wish you the best of luck on your upcoming exam. Thank you for making the time to join us. What a special week this has been."

Everyone clinked glasses.

Poppy had not mentioned Roux at all in her toast. Ivy could see where Sylvia's spitefulness had originated from. She glanced over to see if Roux had noticed. He looked the same as always: wooden. She felt a new benevolence for Roux, her fellow outsider, whose crassness she could now appreciate as a kind of confidence and maybe even superiority. She felt his reticence as her own revenge.

She poured herself a glass of wine and finished it in one go. Ted offered her another pour. She reached for a slice of focaccia. Roux handed her the basket; their knuckles bumped and a few bread rolls tipped out. He picked up one of the fallen rolls from the table and put it on his own plate. Then he put one of the clean ones on her plate. Over his shoulder, Ivy glimpsed Sylvia's face, the veneer of indifference gone, replaced by a slab of frigid anger like the time Roux had given Ivy the drawing. A sensation of wondrous astonishment, like oxygen, ballooned in Ivy's chest. Sylvia Speyer was jealous of *her*.

"That's *so* lovely to hear, darling," said Poppy after Sylvia finished telling them about her upcoming project with her advisor, restoring a sixteenth-century sculpture. "Teamwork is very important, as I've learned throughout my years of charity work. To go fast, they say, you must go alone, but to go far, you must go with others."

"Did you read that from a Hallmark magnet?" said Sylvia.

"From a bookmark Cynthia gave me. It's a very truthful saying—one I agree with a hundred percent."

Sylvia said, "Giddy, remember that one time Mom went to Cynthia's house and came back with a swallow tattoo and told us it was real?"

"Your mom was a real rebel back in the day," said Ted. "When I met her, she was an activist protesting the Vietnam War. She was in a rock band for a while. She had the leather jacket and pink hair. I had to talk her out of a tattoo of Led Zeppelin."

Poppy said, "Oh, hush, Ted." *Huh, huh, huh*, went her laugh.

"We've heard all this before, Daddy," said Sylvia. She smiled sweetly. "There aren't any journalists around."

Ted's smile quivered on his pale pink face like a man who's just been told he'd missed the last call for drinks.

Jealousy didn't suit Sylvia, thought Ivy. She was loveliest when she was high and mighty.

"Have I mentioned how good you look?" Ivy said to Roux, purposely keeping her voice down. "Like a sleek black panther."

"Is that a compliment?"

"How do I look?"

He eyed her. "Drunk."

"I'm not drunk at all. And you shouldn't call a girl out for being drunk even if I was."

"Why not?"

"It's not very gentlemanly."

"Do you want me to be more gentlemanly?"

"Of course."

"You sure about that?"

They were flirting. It was a nervy, bewildering sensation, this new way of being with Roux, a previously reprehensible character. Yet the sensation of being struck by those attentive gray eyes felt vaguely familiar, like a song she'd once heard but had forgotten.

"I've wanted to ask you something all week," she said.

"Yes?" He refilled her water glass. They were almost whispering now, their heads bent close.

"Was I better in bed or was Sylvia?"

Roux regarded her coldly. "What's the matter with you?"

Ivy snapped back. To cover her embarrassment, she reached for her wineglass and gulped it down too quickly, spilling some from the corners of her mouth. Roux handed her a napkin.

"Never mind," he said gruffly.

After dinner, Ted brought out lawn chairs from the garage and arranged them around the crackling fire on the beach. Gideon collected pieces of driftwood and added them to the pit. Everyone consoled Sylvia about losing her cat—was it Ivy's imagination or had Gideon flashed a few inquisitive looks her way? She stared at the thin white foam near the shore, all that was visible of the Atlantic. Such an expansive ocean but most of it invisible, swallowed by a fluid and heavy darkness, like a wet towel pressing down from the sky.

Shortly, Roux disappeared into the house to take a phone call. Ivy announced she was getting chilly, she was also heading in for the night. "Want me to come up with you?" Gideon asked. She told him to stay.

The lights were off in the house. From the porch, the roaring bonfire on the beach looked no larger than a basketball. She made her way up the stairs in the dark. The only light in the hallway came from the crack under Roux and Sylvia's room. She rapped the door with her fingertips.

Roux did not seem surprised to see her, or if he was, he didn't show it.

"Packing for tomorrow?" she asked, closing the door softly behind her. On the bed was an open duffel bag half-filled with Roux's scant belongings.

"I'm leaving now."

All the thoughts Ivy had been so carefully corralling scattered like ash. "Why?"

"An electrical outage at one of my factories in Brooklyn. I have to assess the damage."

"You're going to *New York*?"

"That's where Brooklyn is, yes."

"Right now?"

"Yes."

"What about Sylvia?"

Roux shrugged. "I told her to get a ride back with you and Gideon." He spoke in a flat, distracted sort of way, giving the impression of hurrying though he hardly moved. He zipped up his bag and scanned the room before his gaze finally settled on her. "Best of luck with everything," he said, obviously waiting for her to move out of his way. But she didn't want to move. She wanted to place herself in his way.

"Don't you want to know why I came to see you?"

"No, not really."

"Why didn't you tell Sylvia what happened between us?"

"What *did* happen between us?" His apathy was impenetrable.

"Sylvia told me that you knew I'd be here," said Ivy. "But you pretended to be surprised when you saw me."

He didn't answer.

"Did you come here because of me?"

"Everything always revolves around you," he said coolly. "You and Sylvia have that in common."

"I was glad to see you again," she said.

"I must have missed the signs."

"We used to be good friends."

"*Friends?*" He glared at her like one of the Speyers' gargoyle bookends and dropped his duffel on the floor, both of which seemed like promising signs to Ivy. "Do you even know what happened after you left that summer? I went to your house. Got cursed by your grandmother. Your mom told me to never come near you again. Your dad was there—he had to translate but I got the gist. I was a bad person—*I* had corrupted *you*. Isn't that funny? Parents really don't know their children at all." Ivy tried to defend herself—she was out of the country, her parents moved without her knowledge—but Roux snapped, "You could have sent a damn postcard when you returned—*Hello, it's me, Ivy; I'm alive.*"

"I didn't think you cared!" she exclaimed. This was a lie. She knew he'd cared. But it hadn't mattered to her then.

"Were you actually glad to see me here?"

"Of course I was." She hesitated. "After all—you were my first. I haven't even told Gideon that."

His mouth contracted. "You said I wasn't."

"I lied."

"I lied, too. I want to know."

"Know what?"

"Why you came here tonight."

There it was. The voice from her dream. Exhilaration made her legs tremble. She saw clearly now that people could be divided into two categories: those who acted, and those who were acted upon.

She went to him. Roux's eyes, descending toward her, looked like the scales of a beautiful fish; her heart trembled with pain. He brought his lips to her eyelids, one, then the other, leaving a trail of kisses down her temple to her mouth, softly at first, then, when she bit his bottom lip, he gripped the sides of her neck with both hands and kissed her so hard their teeth mashed together, neither breathing, until they were tearing at each other to get closer—closer! Her hands scrabbled to pull up his shirt. She pressed her palm flat against the center of his belly, feeling his breath rise and fall beneath her hand. He seized her wrists and pushed her hand down on his skin harder, until she could feel the bottom of his rib cage. He made a sound, as if he were in pain, and the noise seemed to signify his total surrender. She knew then that she had pulled him over with the force of her will. The sound set something off inside her: a sticky, inflamed need as her spine dissolved beneath her, a sudden wetness between her legs that made her legs go weak, her eyes falling into the back of her head. He picked her up by the butt cheeks and took two steps backward. They fell back on the bed; she landed on top of him.

With one motion, he pulled off her dress and tossed it to the floor. She straddled him and unclipped her bra herself, flinging it next to the dress. That it wasn't their first time seeing the other's body made it more exciting—they didn't have to go through the introductory motions. He sat up, took her nipple into his mouth. She released a small breath, her fingers pulling his hair away from his scalp until his head drew back and she kissed him again on the lips, then lower, where her teeth sank into his neck. Somewhere along the way, his shorts and boxers disappeared. Their eyes met. She shifted her weight onto her knees; he adjusted her torso over his lap, the mattress creaking underneath them, and then she lowered herself on top of him.

Their heads drew back simultaneously. Ivy let out a hissing noise as she swiveled her hips over his, the tiniest of movements that sent tremors throughout her entire body. She leaned forward and placed her hands over his, then drew them over his head. She squeezed her legs tighter around his hips—any moment now, she would burst—and began rocking front to back. Roux's mouth was twisted in an oval. She was covered in sweat, her hips slid over his, their skin smacking together and apart, together, then apart. Each time she undulated, she drew a sound from him that filled her belly with a fever to push further, faster, to bring him to the edge of desire and push him off again. She opened her eyes; Roux's head was lying back on the pillow. His eyes were closed.

Slowly, she let out her breath, the room coming back into focus. Her first thought was to check the window—thank God it was closed and their sounds, quiet as they were, hadn't reached the beach. Her second thought was that it wouldn't be long now before the Speyers came back inside to get ready for bed. Still, she allowed herself to lower down to rest her cheek on Roux's chest.

"Do you have any cigarettes left?"

Roux motioned at his crumpled jeans. Ivy fished out a battered pack of Camels from his back pocket. He lit hers, then his own. He smoked with his left hand, his right hand draped in the valley between her chafed thighs. She picked up a coffee mug from the bedside table and placed it on the bed between them as an ashtray. "I'm going to break up with Gideon tomorrow," she said as the flood of pleasure released from the nicotine reached her brain. "Stay tonight. I have nothing on my schedule next week. I can go with you to New York tomorrow."

It was startling to see Roux's smile without any of its usual derision or irony or scorn. His smile was just that. A man smiling because he was happy. "You're beautiful," he said, running his hand down her leg. Her heart fluttered with delight and sorrow. *Beautiful* . . . Roux was the first person ever to have called her that.

"What are you going to tell Sylvia?" she asked. For a second, as his hand paused in its caresses, she was afraid. But then he frowned and said he would tell her the truth, that it was never that serious to begin with. His dismissal of his girlfriend, contrary to Ivy's expectations, felt like a letdown. She would rather it had been a struggle for Roux to choose between them. "Why were you even with her then?" she asked.

"Why else? Her face."

Ivy looked out the window, where the shadow of the oak tree brushed up against the glass like gigantic palm fronds. "I should go. They'll be coming up soon. Will you wait for me until tomorrow?"

She heard the thrum of his voice reverberating against her eardrums as he brushed his lips on her temple: "Of course." Ivy suddenly saw that life could always be easy like this. A postcoital cigarette. Pillow plans. Honest duplicity, instead of the infinitely more exhausting duplicitous honesty.

I CONSIDER THAT *our present sufferings are not worth comparing with the glory that will be revealed in us.* Romans 8:18. The priest closed his Bible. *Let us pray.*

Ivy closed her eyes. Uncertainty gripped her. Had she done another stupid thing last night? She pictured Gideon's downturned face working on his laptop, distant and unbothered, oblivious—or indifferent—to her sufferings. Her heart hardened. Then she tried to imagine the glory awaiting her with Roux. They'd leave New England, forsake its frigid winters and maddening rotaries and crumbling brick buildings, for . . . for what? She pictured the hole in Roux's sock. The faded workman jeans. At least he had some money and a nice car. Maybe they could go on a road trip across the country, eat burgers and chug beer while drifting through gambling towns like the lovestruck couple in a country song music video. They'd make their way to California, buy a ranch house, plant a lemon grove. It was a version of someone's success, somewhere in the world.

Around her, the congregation stood as one, hymn books open. Their voices rose through the dome: *Shall we gather at the river . . . Where bright angel feet have trod . . .* Ivy glanced down the pew where the four Speyers' heads were bent, sunshine halos around their crowns, their sweet voices singing together in harmony. If you love me, she thought at Gideon, you'll look at me. If one couldn't ask for a sign in a church, then where could one ask? But he didn't look at her. He didn't look.

GIDEON ASKED IF she wanted to take one last walk down to the beach, he said there was something he wanted to say to her. She almost wished to save him the effort; he looked so pale and serious, still dressed in his black Sunday suit, as if returning from a funeral, with two frown lines between his brows. But then her eyes met Roux's across the kitchen countertop. He gave her an imperceptible nod and she smiled bravely to show she understood.

She followed Gideon across the lawn, which over the past week had become as familiar to her as her own house. Down the narrow trail with its vivid fuchsia rugosas, the bushes lush and overgrown from days of rain, and the sand, damp and soft, between her toes all the way until the water's edge. Gideon walked barefoot, his pants rolled up to midcalf. She stepped inside the lines of his footprints. Even with sandals on, her feet could not fill the indent.

They didn't talk much. Gideon occasionally pointed out a neighbor's house: *See that flat-looking one facing us? The Scollocks live there year-round . . . They don't have kids and mostly keep to themselves . . . Mr. Scollock takes a swim every morning for his arthritis . . . the Clarks are in that one . . .* Always small talk first. Then business. There was an order to everything for people like the Speyers.

"It's nice that you're close with your neighbors," said Ivy.

"This"—Gideon waved his arm at the ocean—"is in my blood. I get homesick all the time for this place. When I was little, I'd make my parents drive here from Andover in the dead of winter just so I could climb these rocks. My best summers were here. My first kiss, my first, well, you know." They'd stopped by a part of the beach hidden from view of both the Clarks and the Scollocks. Tangled strips of seaweed draped over a piece of driftwood like a rotting carcass. Ivy tried to imagine a young, naked Gideon rolling around in this smelly, dead stretch of beach. Such self-abandonment was beyond her comprehension of him. But he had been that way once. Just never with her.

"That was a long time ago," said Gideon, picking up a pebble and tossing it into the water. "But honestly—I wouldn't mind raising my kids here. Did you have a good time here?"

People had been asking Ivy that all week: are you happy, did you sleep well, are you having fun? And no matter her state of mind, she would always respond with honest conviction: Yes, I love it here. Because access was always preferable to no access.

"It feels like I've been waiting to come here my entire life," she said, her throat swelling. What was the point of pretending otherwise when it was so close to the end anyway?

They made their way farther down the shore to a rock formation jutting several hundred feet into the water, wide enough for someone to walk straight out into the sea. The sun had disappeared behind gray clouds. A violent wave crashed into the stones and sprayed them with salty droplets, and this reminder from the sea, so stark and indifferent to her pain, flung Ivy's resolve to the surface like the piece of seaweed splayed on the driftwood. Better to be the one doing the leaving. "There's something I wanted to say to you." She turned around. Gideon was on one knee.

The hand that gripped hers was cold and hard. Gideon's voice, while right below her, sounded as if it were being broadcast from a faraway place, one with a muffled signal, so that she only understood humming disjointed phrases: "—unexpected—you told me the other day that you loved me—unprepared—I did some—rather—don't want to lose you—" His voice came back in full near the end: "I want you to be my w-wi-wwiife. W-will you m-m-marry me, Ivy?"

Was he joking? she wondered. No, no, not Gideon. He would never play a joke of this magnitude. And his face was so white, his lips so drained they appeared almost purple.

Then a hot licking happiness drenched her like a bucket of steaming water on a chilly night. Her shoulders convulsed, one hand rose to cover her gaping mouth. But how to thank him? How to express her leaping gratitude?

"Ivy?"

"Yes! Oh, yes!"

Then they were in each other's arms, laughing. He took out a black velvet box from his pocket and opened the lid. The stone was a brilliant blue sapphire, rimmed with little diamonds. He took her left hand and slid the ring past her knuckle. It was too big. She closed her fist to keep it from sliding off.

"We'll get it resized," said Gideon.

"Did you have this with you the entire trip?" Had she been wrong about everything?

"It's Grandma Cuffy's," said Gideon. "Mom's been keeping it for me . . . I asked her for it this morning." Ivy made a small gasping noise, drinking in every word. "As for Sylvia," Gideon went on, "I know she really does like you. She's been telling me all week how wonderful you are, how much you fit into our family. I hope you'll give her a chance."

"That doesn't matter," said Ivy. It really didn't. "I was just in a bad mood earlier. Imagining things on my own."

"Her heart's in the right place."

She placed a finger on his lower lip. "Do you know . . . I actually thought you were bringing me here to break it off with me." She felt his surprise in the twitch of his neck.

"Why?"

"When I told you I loved you, you said you *cared about me a lot*." He began to clarify but Ivy added, "And then we had that fight yesterday about the cat."

"*Was* that a fight, really?" His tone made it clear he did not think so.

Ivy tried to justify her earlier certainty—why had she been so angry, so sure that Gideon was pulling away from her?—but like a person at the end of a twelve-course meal who could no longer evoke the sensation of hunger, she could not bring to mind a single piece of solid evidence of how Gideon or his family had wronged her. A flicker of stubborn pettiness held out, insisting it'd not all been in her head, but the voice was instantly quashed under the undeniable reality of Gideon's warm, reassuring embrace.

"And you didn't let me finish the other day," he said into her hair. "I love you."

"You what?" she whispered.

"I love you." He placed a hand on her arm. "Don't move. I think a seagull just crapped on your shoulder."

"My grandmother says getting shit on by a bird is one of the luckiest omens . . . We've been blessed by the Chinese gods, Gideon!"

They laughed until their sides hurt.

POPPY'S MASCARA-LESS EYES were wide with anticipation. "Are you. . . !" Ivy held up her hand. Poppy made a humming sound in the back of her throat. Gideon said, "We're getting married!"

Gasps echoed through the room. Poppy stammered, "Oh, my little boy!" Ted rubbed his wife's back. "Did you know about this, Poppy?" he asked. Sylvia came over and kissed Ivy's cheek; *I'm so glad*, she whispered. Then Ivy was swept up by Poppy's embrace; there was nothing delicate about it, Ivy felt all her ribs pressed against Gideon's mother's, the bony points of Poppy's shoulders digging into her chest bones. Gideon and his father were embracing. "I'm proud of you, Giddy," Ted said, and Gideon, for a split second, looked like the mischievous boy Ivy remembered from middle school. She knew then that

Sylvia had been wrong about their childhood, at least her brother's version. Gideon had probably been proud of his father, proud of being a senator's son, and wanted to walk the same, unassailable path as his ancestors before him, those people in the black-and-white photos whom he'd so proudly spoken of that first day at Finn Oaks.

After Poppy turned away, Ivy found herself standing on the outskirts of the circle. The Speyers congregated around Gideon, laughing and crying and finishing each other's sentences. Through the commotion, Ivy became aware of Roux, standing a few paces apart from the others, taking in the sight with the air of one observing a great farce. She walked over decisively.

"I'm guessing you won't be going to New York with me," he said.

"Listen," she said softly, glancing around to make sure no one was listening. "We did something stupid last night. We were both wasted. Can we just agree that it never happened and never mention it again? . . . It's not worth hurting others and ruining this moment." Like all people blinded by their own happiness, she looked at him with the frank certainty of impending forgiveness and goodwill, for how could anyone object to anything during the sacred matrimonial celebrations?

Roux leaned down. Ivy thought he was going to kiss her. She took a step back. His smile was drawn and white around the edges of the lips; somehow, this was more shocking to witness than his anger would have been. "You haven't changed at all," he said in a loud, clear voice.

"Think about Sylvia," she hissed.

"What about me?" Sylvia called out.

Roux glanced at his girlfriend. "Let's break up." Sylvia's expression faltered, then straightened into a kind of mechanical sneer. It was the most human face Ivy had ever seen.

"It was never going to work," said Roux. "Come get your things from my place when you get back." His scornful gaze swept over all of them before lingering on Gideon, who had taken a step forward in front of his sister.

"Is this really the time and place, Roux?" said Gideon.

Roux shook his head. "You poor sucker." Then he swung his duffel bag over one shoulder and left, the front door slamming shut behind him.

None of them moved. Then: "Good riddance." It was Poppy, brushing invisible lint off her skirt. "I told you this would happen, Sylvia," she said crisply. "Why do you never listen to me? Why does no one listen?"

PART FOUR

15

ASTOR TOWERS CONDOMINIUMS WAS ONE OF THOSE NEW HIGH-RISE
developments along the river, towering and vaguely threatening, with
the amenities of a five-star hotel—Jacuzzi, conference rooms, dry
cleaning, heated floors—all advertised on their enormous billboards
Ivy passed every day on her way to her prep course. And yet whenever
she came, the elevator was always empty, the carpet on the twenty-
eighth floor hallways vacuumed to a stiff bristle with no footprints
besides her own. It was Thanksgiving afternoon, already a quarter
past three, and she still hadn't eaten anything all day. Afternoon light
streamed through the floor-to-ceiling windows, hitting the wooden
bowl of fruit—peaches, apples, pears, on the slate countertop—about
as appealing as wax fruits from a still-life painting. She was thirsty. The
touch-responsive refrigerator came with three settings for water: boiling, room temperature, ice. She spooned three tablespoons of matcha powder into a large mug and pushed the button for boiling water.
There was milk in the fridge but she couldn't find sugar in any of the
cabinets. She brought her tea over to the breakfast table and watched
the pedestrians below, bundled in their dark winter coats, looking like
bloated ants, scurrying, hurrying, eternally busy. Autumn had come
and gone like a vivid wet dream, three short glorious weeks of orange
and red foliage giving way to November's dreary cold rains, the sharp
pinpoint sky so magnified it felt you were viewing it through the lens
of a telescope.

As she sipped her tea and smoked a cigarette, she ran through her mental list of never-ending wedding to-dos for the next week. Decor. Cake. Flowers. Music. All this should have made her happy, but it didn't. She was tired. Trying to study for law school while planning a wedding for two hundred guests made her feel as if she were supporting a bag of bricks while balancing on a tightrope. It'd been three months since her engagement and with each day that passed, her fear grew that something would snatch away her happiness. Gideon would change his mind about marrying her. Sylvia would convince Gideon that she was unacceptable. Her family would humiliate themselves in front of the Speyers. She would get into a car accident and become a cripple. Gideon would die. Every night before bed, hives spread from her back and belly all the way to her eyelids; she developed heartburn and the doctor told her to refrain from lying down after eating. But because she was so tired all the time, she chose to refrain from eating in order to lie down.

The impending wedding seemed to affect Gideon not at all. In the weeks following their Cattahasset trip, she'd scrutinized him for any signs of change, thinking that now he could finally relax around her. She didn't know when it was that she started to think of Gideon as tense or anxious or whatever was the opposite of relaxed. When she'd first seen him at Sylvia's party, she'd thought of him as soft. Easygoing. And yet this soft easygoing conduct, meant to convey an uncomplicated interiority, felt to Ivy like prison bars that guarded Gideon against her, against everyone, in a way that was hard and impenetrable. Since the engagement, he'd become even more gentle and considerate toward her. He never so much as snapped at her. "What *don't* you like about me?" she'd asked him once. "I like everything about you," he'd said.

This gentleness had lured Ivy into a false sense of security. On their last date at a popular burger chain, she had asked the cashier for a cup to fill with water at the vending machines. But when she got to the vending machine, she'd changed her mind and filled her white plastic cup with raspberry club soda. Back at the table, Gideon had taken a sip and said, "Isn't this cup for water only?" At first, she hadn't known what he was talking about. Then she realized she hadn't paid for the soda. The white cup for the water was free. The blue cup for the soda was two dollars. Gideon reassured her that it was an honest mistake, no harm done. He got out of the booth and went to go pay the two dollars. That incident had deeply shaken her. It'd been an impulsive act born of opportunity, like keeping your neighbor's misdelivered packages or not telling the cashier that they undercharged you—no one would see you do it let alone point out it was wrong; people like Meifeng would even applaud you for your quick thinking. How many of these corner-cutting things had she always done that she would now have to eradicate? Gideon had assumed this time was an honest mistake, but what about next time? How many times would it take before he started to realize that his fiancée did not have the sort of upstanding moral characteristics he so esteemed?

Ivy sometimes felt she was two different people—the kind, generous, moral citizen she tried to be with Gideon, and her unsatisfied, practical, opportunistic self. She would have given anything to be like Gideon naturally—to be *good*—but she was not good. She was jealous, petty, vengeful; experience had taught her to hide these characteristics behind a veneer of sweetness and humility. The more diligent she was in the Speyers' presence, the more difficult it was to rein in her lesser impulses when she was alone.

Depressed by this unflattering portrait of herself, Ivy finished her cigarette, rinsed her mug, and went back to the bedroom. The entire apartment was set up like an art gallery, the rooms separated not by actual walls but by a bewildering display of glass, steel, onyx marble, free-floating furniture, and a handful of art pieces—a racetrack, sketches of human anatomy, a series of black-and-white photographs, blown up, of various hands veiny with age. All meant to appeal to a specific type of self-congratulatory bachelor. The bed sat on an elevated glass platform, not unlike the lazy Susans installed in every Chinese restaurant, and beside it was a nightstand containing the only personal items in the apartment: a large stack of papers, legal documents, yellow notepads, unopened envelopes. Underneath all that was a small silver case that Ivy had once opened to find a handgun, snugly packed between the black velvet like an expensive piece of jewelry. She picked up a particularly fat yellow manila folder and withdrew a stack of cash. She counted ten hundred-dollar bills, then placed the rest back in the folder.

"Roux. Are you awake? I have to get going."

Roux squinted up at her before he turned over and fell back asleep. She watched him for a few more seconds. Gideon was a light sleeper, prone to insomnia, which he regulated with a half milligram of melatonin every night. Roux's sleeping habits rendered the handgun in his nightstand useless because the intruder would have shot him before he realized anything was amiss. "Happy Thanksgiving," she murmured. The heels of her boots thumped softly along the floor all the way to the elevator. When she exited the lobby, she looked up once more at the towering facade. All the windows were dark.

SHE HAD INITIATED the affair.

Back in September, she and Gideon had dinner with Tom and Marybeth at a Spanish tapas restaurant to announce their engagement. She'd expected the drunken revelry that had accompanied the Crosses' engagement announcement, had looked forward to it even, imagining Tom's waxing nostalgia and Marybeth's gloating triumph. But upon taking her seat at the table, Ivy knew immediately something was wrong. Tom could barely manage a grimace; Marybeth was aloof and distracted. They did not seem surprised when Gideon announced their engagement.

"Well, that was fast," said Tom.

Marybeth said, "I suppose you'll be moving in together?"

"Not until after the wedding," said Gideon. "Ivy's lease is up around then anyway and we don't know which school she'll end up at."

There was a lull as everyone studied the menu. Ivy tried to fill the silence by telling funny stories about their vacation—The roof leaked! I was comatose because of a stray cat!—but she was met with tepid smiles, and she soon fell quiet, aware that her enthusiasm was as far from the current mood as a raucous football crowd from the hushed solemnity of a tragic opera.

For the rest of the night, Tom and Gideon spoke mostly about work, Tom's arm draped on the back of Gideon's chair like a balding freckled uncle giving advice to his earnest nephew. Ivy tried to insert a question here and there but whatever opinion she expressed, Tom would undercut her by stating the opposite opinion in a supercilious tone that began with "Where did you hear that . . ." or "But isn't it true that . . ." or "Do you *really* think . . ." Trying to establish a rapport with Marybeth instead, Ivy asked for advice about finding a local wedding venue.

"Oh, I don't think I'll be much help," said Marybeth. "We've decided on a destination wedding in Kauai. We wanted to keep our anniversary date in March, so that limited the venue to somewhere tropical. My parents wanted to do it at Palm Beach, where my grandparents live, but Tom and I already went to *three* weddings in Florida last year. Miriam—Tom's mom—doesn't like traveling out of the country so Hawaii it was. Though why a twelve-hour flight to Hawaii is better than an eight-hour one to Italy, I have no idea."

Ivy saw Tom's eyes flicker their way when Marybeth mentioned his mother, but his voice didn't break from his conversation with Gideon. Men with men. Women with women. The same thing had happened at Dave and Liana's house the previous week. Ivy had gone to the library with the other housewives for their book-club meeting, served with Darjeeling tea, crustless sandwiches, little wispy greens picked from Liana's garden, and Dave had whisked Gideon out for tennis with other partners at his firm. Even with the Speyers, more and more, it was Poppy and Ivy, Gideon and Ted. Perhaps there was some unspoken code about matrimony, that it meant the separation of the sexes, like joining a social club whose sole existence was to take your spouse off your hands.

"As long as we have the full Catholic ceremony at Saint Mary's Cathedral," said Marybeth, "and William can golf the Princeville Course, everyone's happy." She picked up a slice of the grilled tomato bread, sniffed it, then dropped it onto her plate indifferently. "Not to be a nag, Gideon," she said, wiping her fingers on her napkin, "but have you sent in your RSVP yet?"

"Not yet. Uh—"

"I'm really sorry about the small guest list," Marybeth said to Ivy.

"Why?" said Ivy.

Marybeth blinked at Gideon, but before he could respond, she said, "Since we decided on the new venue, we had to limit our guest list to married couples."

"Oh!" said Ivy, a beat too late as the implication hit her. "I totally understand." And to overcompensate for the warmth flaming her cheeks, she began to justify Marybeth's actions, on Marybeth's behalf, to the entire group. "You both have such large families," she said, nodding at Tom to include him in her overreaching benevolence, "and so many old friends. And small weddings are so much better than inviting randos." A ripple of invisible winces went across Marybeth's and Gideon's faces.

"I was going to tell you, but it totally slipped my mind," Gideon said quietly.

"It's not a big deal." Ivy laughed again, picking up her sangria.

Tom smiled. "Don't be mean, sweetheart," he addressed Marybeth. "Now that they're engaged, it's not too late to add Ivy to the guest list, is it?"

Marybeth hesitated. Ivy could tell she was embarrassed to be outed as the decision maker. Ivy felt a pain deep in her heart. She'd thought that she and Marybeth were friends. That Tom was the bad guy.

"It's not necessary," she said, truly sweating now through her thin cotton dress. "*Really.*"

"This is dragging on," said Gideon in a clipped way. "Why don't you two go home and think—"

"No, Tom's right," said Marybeth. "We'd be thrilled to have you there, Ivy. I'll get your address from Gideon later."

Ivy considered protesting but felt drained by the effort.

"The banana flowers in Kauai are beautiful in March," Tom said to Ivy. "Or so Marybeth keeps insisting. They sound like something you smoke. And they're not even yellow, they're a neon pink. Me, I say— who gives a shit about banana flowers?"

"I do," said Marybeth, clearly still resentful that Tom had thrown her under the bus.

"My mom has her heart set on Cattahasset," said Gideon as the waiter set their tapas around the table. "Or Martha's Vineyard. Remember the summer before college, Tom?"

"Do I! Your Finn Oaks is a dinosaur compared to the setup we had going on." Again, he addressed Ivy alone. "We had a heated pool, the living room converted with futons, Ted's oldest bottle of whiskey— to this day, he thinks a raccoon came in the middle of the night and knocked it over. We had Blake Whitney pee around the glass. For some reason, only *his* piss resembled that exact shade of expensive-ass scotch."

Ivy laughed gratefully, letting herself sink into the oblivion of being carried along with the conversation. So Tom could be considerate, she thought.

She was mistaken.

Tom picked up his glass. "I gotta admit—I underestimated you."

"What do you mean," she said, smiling gamely in preparation for one of his jokes.

"You sure work fast. Got Gideon locked down. *Good for you.*"

"What?"

"You're one to talk," said Gideon, pointing his fork in Tom's direction. "Marybeth has you tied by the—" but Tom was still talking to Ivy, his tone growing increasingly merry.

"I remember you now. From the eighth-grade yearbook. Ivy Lin. It jogged my memory. You used to follow Gideon around back in the day. Real quiet and mousy. Now look at you. Grabbing the bull by the horns, eh? Hustled your way up like—who's that Asian lady married to old Murdoch? Anyway, I bet you couldn't wait to get knocked up—"

Gideon stood up. "Watch your mouth," he said, enunciating every syllable with no trace of a stutter, though he was pale with emotion. The waiter hurried over to ask if they needed something.

Ivy tugged Gideon's arm. Gideon remained standing.

Tom wiped his face with his soiled linen napkin, smeared yellow with a bit of horseradish from the smoked anchovies.

"Come on. You know I'm joking. I'm *happy* for you two. No hard feelings, right, Ivy?" He held up his hand in midair.

Ivy realized he was waiting for her to high-five him. She did it, despising herself, but despising Tom more.

"See, Gideon? Ivy and I are best friends. Sit down, sit down . . . I'm just *thrilled* . . . Isn't it wonderful to be alive?" He brought his fist to his eyes and, to Ivy's shock and disgust, began to cry.

"I'm sorry about Tom," Gideon said on the drive home. "He wasn't always this way."

Yes he was, thought Ivy. "It's fine," she said, immediately changing the subject. If Gideon spoke about the matter even a second longer, she would start crying.

"Do you remember Henry Fitzgerald, from Grove?" said Gideon. "He was on the lacrosse team with me and Tom?"

"No."

"Henry's dad was the CEO for Biogene Pharmaceuticals."

". . . Okay."

"Some years back, when Dad was still senator, he uncovered some suspicious practices at Biogene, so he called in the FTC to investigate them for antitrust violations. Long story short, Mr. Fitzgerald was not

only fired but sentenced to serve a few years for restricting drug dis-
tribution to jack up the prices. Henry's family lost everything. Henry
began acting out. He quit the team, skipped school. He was caught
smoking marijuana in the bathroom at senior prom. Most teachers
look the other way, but Henry was already in deep shit so they ex-
pelled him. Columbia rescinded its admission offer. A week before
graduation, Henry and some other guys tried to jump me outside the
parking lot. Tom had heard them talking about it in the locker room,
and he showed up with his family's lawyer. He drew up a restraining
order for Henry and the others. If they came within ten feet of me,
I'd press charges. It would have been a felony because Henry and the
others were holding their lacrosse sticks and Tom's lawyer said that
would constitute a deadly weapon."

"How clever of Tom's lawyer."

"Tom's always protected me. I think it's made him paranoid all
these years. He thinks everyone who didn't grow up with us is an
enemy. It's hard for him to trust new people and their intentions." The
car stopped at a red light. Ivy felt Gideon's gaze on her profile but she
kept her gaze straight ahead.

"Anyway, it's no excuse for what he said. I wish . . . well, we don't
choose our friends based on worthiness."

"I understand," said Ivy. That was Gideon, loyal to the last. She'd
always thought loyalty necessitated a certain blindness, like religious
faith, yet Gideon saw Tom for who he was, and still he chose to defend him. Was that love? She wondered how Gideon would defend *her*,
if the time came. Then, recalling Tom's and Marybeth's cold, unsur-
prised expressions when Gideon announced their engagement, she realized that time had already come and gone. Gideon had just shielded
her from it until tonight.

Moments later, she felt warm fingers brushing her cheek. The
touch nearly broke her. She quickly turned to face the window and
pinched her wrist to keep the tears from falling. By the time they arrived at her house, she'd composed herself. Her street was empty; the

gangsters had retired to wherever gangsters retired to on a quiet Tuesday night. Or maybe they were making their rounds around Boston, robbing people and inflicting violence. Silence did not mean peace.

Inside, she checked the mail, drank a glass of water, refilled the vase of Casa Blanca lilies that Andrea's admirer had delivered to their house, the large star-shaped petals curled outward like a woman's exposed throat. Finally, she allowed herself to go to her room. She proceeded to slam her pillow onto the mattress in strangled yelps until Andrea came running in alarm, her face dripping sludge from a mud mask. "Go away!" Ivy shrieked at her roommate. "Go away! Go away!" Andrea went.

It was so unfair, Ivy seethed, her anger past the point of tears. *Watch your mouth.* Of all the things Gideon could have said, he'd chosen that. Probably he'd picked it up from Poppy. Surely Sylvia would have had better retorts in her arsenal. Sylvia, who had stolen Roux's drawing. Sylvia, who always took what she wanted, who never would have high-fived Tom. Meifeng used to say that men would respect you to the extent that they feared you. But Ivy had basically called herself a random person to Gideon's best friends. A passerby in his life. Not worth respecting. She'd done it to herself.

It was the first time she seriously entertained the fantasy of breaking off her engagement. The only thing greater than her desire for Gideon was her vanity. Instead, she dug up Roux's phone number from where she had written it in her planner back at Finn Oaks. A month had passed since they'd slept together. She called and asked him to meet her for drinks. "I want to explain what happened at the cottage," she said. After a long pause on the line, he agreed.

He chose a bar in a seedy part of town. It was midnight by the time she got there. She remembered the time because she'd checked her phone, pathetically, to see if Gideon had called. She played her old game: if he calls, I'll go home. He didn't call. Posters of old bands hung on every inch of the bar's walls, the wooden surfaces sticky from spilled beer and oil residue in a way that could never be cleaned.

Burly men with long beards and steel-toed boots sat alone over their frothing pints of draft beer. The kind of man Roux was when he wasn't driving his million-dollar Bugatti with its bug antennae lights and dolphin-shaped tail.

Four vodkas later, Ivy couldn't remember how they'd gotten back to Roux's condo. She only remembered the feeling of seeing Astor Towers for the first time: a contemptuous admiration. *Well done*, she wanted to say, but instead, she took off her dress.

That night, on the cusp of a terrible hangover, she was filled with self-loathing. "This is a onetime thing," she said coldly.

"Sure is," said Roux.

Six days later, she was back, this time because Gideon had canceled their dinner date after she'd spent the entire afternoon stewing Italian cioppino, all those tight-lipped mussels she'd shucked gone to waste in the garbage, as she hated mussels and Andrea was on another one of her fruit-only diets.

By their third meeting, she didn't even bother with the pretense that this was a fleeting affair. When she arrived, Roux picked her up by the waist and tossed her down on the bed. When she tried to scamper away, he got hold of one ankle and bit down on her calf, leaving neat lines of teeth marks on her flesh. She couldn't remember the last time she and Gideon had had sex. She, who had once been so skilled in drawing a man in with a twitch of her brow, now found herself lying helplessly beside her fiancé in the dark, a chilly breeze blowing through the open window, and the sound of his light breathing in her ear, waiting for sleep to come, was enough to slice her heart into ribbons. Back she went into Roux's bed . . . Roux, who spread her limbs out on the bed, admired her naked body and told her: "There's nothing here to be ashamed of. You're lovely . . . here . . . and here . . . and here . . ." Yes, she enjoyed it. She enjoyed every second of it. It was a lowly pleasure, one that left her gasping and exhausted and empty. But what of the soul—that fickle creature that was not so easily satisfied?

During her fifth meeting with Roux, they sat outside on his balcony overlooking the river, smoking and nursing warm whiskeys. That was when he told her about his mother. "Lung cancer," he said when Ivy asked how Irena Roman had died. When it'd happened, he'd just been released from prison and was working in New Mexico. Ivy spat, "Wait—you were in *jail*?"

"Only for eight months. I was barely eighteen so they shortened the sentence."

She was astounded. "Did you assault someone?" For some reason this was the first thing that came to mind.

"Theft. Guess I wasn't as good as you."

"What were you stealing?"

"Cars. Mostly in the newer developments they were building around West Maplebury. Their old shitty vans, people would park in the garage. The Ferraris and Porsches, they'd leave out in the driveway so the neighbors could see." He jiggled his tumbler at her. "Actually, I got the idea from you. Remember how you used to tell me about stealing from yard sales with your grandmother? That rich people didn't value anything?"

She snorted, then shook her head. "We stole old belts and bent spoons. How could you be so dumb?"

"I learned my lesson, believe me. There are far more efficient ways to earn a living."

"Like pizza shops?"

"Like leverage."

She thought about that. What was leverage, anyway, but unused power? It was the potential of power that was powerful. Potential, which she'd always known to be more exhilarating than even the most triumphant outcomes.

"What's the gun for?" she asked. "It freaks me out. You could just shoot me in my sleep."

He rolled his eyes and told her to quit being dramatic. "I keep it out of habit."

"What kind of fucked-up habit is that?"

"Leverage, then." He smirked in what he thought was a cocky way but she saw right through it. He was only trying to impress her, to say, see, I have leverage over you.

Something occurred to Ivy. "Did Sylvia know about you going to jail?"

"I don't hide that stuff."

But Sylvia had told Ivy that Roux dropped out of high school to support his dying mother, not because he'd gotten arrested. So even brazen Sylvia Speyer was capable of shame.

"You're not involved in anything—illegal—now, are you?" she asked.

"Ah . . . work talk is boring."

"You can tell me, kangaroo," she said in a baby voice. "I can keep a secret."

Roux stubbed out his cigarette and turned to her with burning eyes. She thought he would take her, right there on the balcony.

"You don't have to be Sylvia," he said, and stood up to go back inside.

THE NEXT TIME she went over, Roux continued his story. In New Mexico, after his release, he'd found a job at a ranch shoveling horse manure. The secret money he'd stashed away from the car sales he now invested in a fertilizer company that used horse manure as part of a formula that multiplied grain production, the same horse manure that Roux's farm was producing, and whose owner had given Roux 2 percent share of the farm's initially nonexistent profit as opposed to paying him an actual salary. Eventually, every shovel of horseshit earned Roux around five hundred dollars on the stock market. When Irena finally got hold of him with the news of her illness, she was already on her last weeks of life, sustained by an oxygen machine. All this time, she'd never stopped being Baldassare Moretti's mistress, the main cause of contention between mother and son. Baldassare had set up an apartment for her next to his house with a private nurse in the second bedroom; the apartment was always filled with flowers and casseroles from all of Baldassare's relatives, including his wife and his son, Ernesto. They were apparently one big fucking family at that point. "I'll always remember the smell," said Roux, "right before she passed. Flowers." Roux said he'd been moved by the way Baldassare's entire family had come together for Irena—they paid for the funeral, the cremation, the urn, even offered to let Roux continue living in his mother's apartment. One thing led to another, and soon Roux was managing payroll at Moretti's restaurants, then promoted to GM, then given the green light to launch his own businesses; the division of Roux's money and the Morettis' money became as murky as their living situation.

"He sounds like the Godfather," said Ivy. She laughed nervously but Roux did not. She could have pressed him for more details but she didn't really want to know. So much of Roux's life felt ominous and repulsive to her. The gun, for one thing. Only extremists kept handguns in the house. Rifles would have been preferable, especially displayed in a glass cabinet. Rifles were classier, for sport, while hand-guns hidden in a drawer were sordid things. Then there were the envelopes of cash stuffed in his drawers and wrapped in wax paper underneath the sink. The old-fashioned cell phones as blocky as cement. No friends or family besides the Morettis, and Ernesto Moretti could hardly be called a friend. He'd been an angry, churlish kid back in West Maplebury, with the kind of fragile ego and prideful blub-ber that made him an easy target of bullies but also a bully himself, the weak preying on the weaker, and Ivy heard the same ridicule in Roux's voice when he spoke of Ernesto now. Under the sheen of his luxury goods, Roux's life, current and past, was an ugly black hole, one she drew away from, the same way she still avoided looking at the vagrants on her street too closely.

But if she forgot these unsavory details, she could enjoy their ar-rangement. Roux liked everything modern, convenient, and preferably unattainable. He wanted the best service, the best food, he wanted to *feel* rich. Ivy obviously preferred her fiancé's brand of cultured breeding, but that didn't stop her from making ample use of Roux's hedonistic profligacy. After sex, Roux would put on a foreign movie on his state-of-the-art television and order a feast of Maine lobster, Wagyu steak, fatty bluefin tuna shipped out that morning from Tokyo. When the weather turned cold, they soaked together in his Japanese-style tub with the heated salt rocks, their hips and legs stacked together like Tetris pieces, and afterward he would rinse out her hair with a little wooden spout he'd coaxed from a Tibetan monk who'd used it as a rice-measuring cup. Ivy fancied her and Roux as two separate but amicable pirates taking a break from plundering the world. He had his toys, his money, his art, his businesses, and she had Gideon. Rules, God, society—nothing applied to them in the impersonal sanctity of his apartment.

A month into their affair, she began to pilfer money from Roux's manila envelopes—twenty dollars at first, then hundreds, then thousands. If he ever asked her about it, she planned to say she only wanted to buy nice clothes for herself. He, himself, took great pleasure in dressing the part of the millionaire bum: low-collared sweaters, ripped jeans, white T-shirts, tan leather boots. But he liked to indulge her with presents. It made him happy when she squealed over a beautiful pair of earrings or a necklace, although she never wore any of it outside of Astor Towers. She didn't want Gideon noticing her sudden extravagance.

It was impossible that Roux did not know she was stealing from him—once a person knows hunger, he'll count every grain of rice, as Meifeng would say—but he never said a word. This was because Ivy was the one with leverage now. She could stop coming to him any time she wished, but he could not stop himself from desiring her. And desire, Ivy knew, was the strongest form of leverage. Roux would always be willing to do what she said. She enjoyed his admiration for her, which she knew to be genuine, and she liked the way he looked at her, his eyes soft pools of gray, like the sea before a storm, and his mouth curved into a smile that seemed to sing *Beautiful, beautiful!* At times like those, she felt benevolence well up within her, and she was extra gentle with him those nights, extra affectionate, to give back a little of what she'd taken from him.

16

Two hours after she left Roux, Ivy arrived at Ted and Poppy's town house in Beacon Hill. The entire street was a row of navy oak panel doors with gold knockers, like a line of schoolgirls in uniform. Poppy greeted them from the kitchen, dressed in a blue cashmere sweater and fitted khakis that grazed her bony ankles. Ivy wore an almost identical outfit except that her sweater was polka-dotted and her khakis were black. Both women wore pearls around their necks and enormous jewels on their ring fingers.

"You're shrinking a little more each time I see you!" Poppy said, rubbing Ivy's spine and eyeing her son. "Has Gideon not been feeding you?"

"Excuse me, I am a *wonderful* cook," said Gideon, placing his hands on his hips. "I take out the pizza from the box, put it on a plate, and spin it in the microwave for three minutes. Very arduous. Ivy loves my cooking."

"I caught a cold last week," said Ivy after the chuckles died down. "Plus, I had to make room for tonight, knowing how good *your* cooking is, Poppy."

"I wish I'd had your foresight," said Ted, patting his slightly protruding belly. He walked around the kitchen island to hug Ivy. "How are you, kiddo?" he said warmly.

"I'm great," Ivy responded, just as warmly. "*Thank you* for having us tonight."

They were all standing around the kitchen island, rosy-cheeked and jocular; this prolonged ritual of greetings that Ivy had once found affected in its unnecessary exuberance—they'd only just seen one another at lunch a few days ago—now felt as natural and automatic to her as a handshake. Though she and Ted never had much more to say to each other than these stock phrases, her affection for him increased each time he called her *kiddo* and asked how she was doing. That sheer repetition of superficial interactions could breed intimacy, in a different but no less meaningful way than did deep vulnerability, was a lesson the genteel had learned early.

The men shortly went to the living room to watch the football game. Ivy rolled up her sleeves to help Poppy assemble the cranberry goat cheese salad. It felt like stepping back into Finn Oaks. The kitchen was thick with the smells of butter and roasting meats; a sports announcer, the same announcer, it seemed, for every sports game ever broadcasted, was shouting from the TV.

"I'm *so* happy we decided to do this," Poppy said as she piled the butter lettuce into the salad spinner. "With Sylvia in Belize with Jeremy, Ted and I felt so abandoned. We thought we were going to have to accept my sister Ellen's invitation last-minute . . . We'd love to see darling Arabella, of course, but Ellen gets so *out of hand* during the holidays. Her husband, John, you know, is . . ." She kept up a steady stream of talk about her various family members—Ivy was not sure if she was expected to follow along—interspersed with questions concerning the Lins' food preferences, like if Nan liked butter on her corn.

Ivy had never known Nan to like anything other than Chinese food. "Whichever way you like is fine," she said. She checked her watch. Ten minutes to seven. She prayed the Lins hadn't run into traffic. She had warned Shen, no less than three times, to leave before noon.

"With an extra pat of butter then," said Poppy. After finishing with the corn, she opened the ovens, releasing a blast of fragrant heat, and

Ivy saw the twenty-pound turkey basting in its juices, the green bean casserole warming in the lower shelf.

"This looks amazing, Poppy," Ivy remarked as she shredded mint leaves into tiny sections. She checked her watch again. "My brother will worship you. He's a huge foodie."

"Thank you, darling. Ted and I used to dine out all the time but I've come to love cooking so much since he retired. There's something about your husband eating your food that feels very special." She winked at Ivy. "You'll know soon enough." She began to help Ivy with the mint. "How many years apart are you and your brother?"

"Four."

"He's just out of college then."

"Actually, he's taking this year off." Ivy had told Poppy this before, and Gideon's mother had an impeccable memory.

Poppy nodded vaguely. "Sylvia took a semester off from Yale for a screen-printing apprenticeship in Florence. That's how she knew she wanted to get her PhD in art history. Does Austin know what he wants to do after graduation?"

"He likes computers. He's always tinkering with gadgets in his room. He prefers to build stuff and learn through hands-on experience instead of sitting in a classroom."

"Your entire family must be *very* gifted," Poppy marveled. "Austin will make an incredible engineer"—Ivy blinked in embarrassment—"and *you're* so brave, chasing after your dreams of becoming a lawyer"—Ivy was blushing in earnest now—"and *your parents* must be very smart to have started their own business from scratch."

"I think it's more hard work than talent," Ivy demurred. She could never tell if Gideon's mother was only being excessively kind or if she actually held these glowing opinions of her friends and acquaintances; if it was the latter, then the world was a very rosy place indeed for Poppy Speyer.

"If Austin's interested in computers," Poppy said thoughtfully, "maybe he can do an internship at Spencer's—my cousin's—company. They hire every tech-savvy person they can get their hands on. But perhaps Austin will think the work is too boring. He sounds very advanced."

Ivy said she would talk to her brother about it. She doubted Austin was capable of much more than sleeping these days. The Lins' optimistic plan for Austin—the local college, thirty minutes of reading a day, early-morning jogs around the neighborhood—had lasted all of two weeks before everyone conceded that perhaps Austin was still too anemic for such a vigorous schedule. The vitamins, Nan admitted, hadn't worked at all.

Thankfully, before Poppy could insist on asking her cousin right then and there—it was hard to extricate an idea from Poppy's mind if she thought about it for too long—the doorbell rang.

"Oh, that must be them," said Poppy, smoothing out her hair with an endearing pat. She called out to Ted and Gideon.

Nerves seized Ivy all at once. She trailed after Poppy with her best game face: chin up, eyes crinkled into a welcoming smile. The smell of butter was overwhelming—she'd only had that matcha tea at Roux's house—and she had to swallow the acid rising up her esophagus.

"*Hello there!*" said Poppy. "Thank you for making the drive all the way up! Come in, come in!" She ushered the four Lins inside with bear hugs, which the Lins returned with an air of fumbled slowness consistent with people unused to physical contact.

When Ivy saw her parents walking toward her, her jaw dropped: they were decked out head to toe in designer clothes. Almost every article of clothing had a brand in an obvious placement: the breast area of Shen's patterned sweater vest, the cuffs of his crisply ironed button-down, the large silver clasps on his loafers. Nan wore a heavy beaded jacket over a red silk blouse; the purse she carried had a giant designer logo sewn in onyx and gilt. Thankfully, Meifeng looked no different from her usual getup: a stiff jacket buttoned up to her neck, gray trousers, black walking shoes. "I called to warn you but you didn't pick up," Meifeng muttered, waving aside Ivy's gesture to help her with her cane. "Leave it. I need it these days, my knees are killing me." She smiled at the Speyers and said in broken English, "Hello! Welcome!"

"Welcome," said Poppy, and Ted said, "Welcome indeed."

"Do you like my jacket?" Nan whispered to Ivy in Chinese. Ivy grimaced. When they stepped aside, she saw Austin lurking in the back, wearing an ill-fitting tweed blazer over a black crew sweater. He had lost a lot of weight and was, for some reason, sweating profusely even though he'd just stepped inside. Ivy stood up on tiptoes to kiss one ashen cheek, feeling sad in a way only Austin evoked in her, a sadness that included both anger and guilt. They'd grown up with the same parents. Why couldn't he adjust, as she had?

"Do you like the camera I got you?"

"I haven't used it yet," he said.

Gideon was smiling and uttering all manner of compliments to Shen and Nan. Ivy could tell he was nervous because he stammered more than once, though his face betrayed no embarrassment. Shen seemed equally nervous, ducking his head into his shoulders and nodding vigorously at everything Gideon said. Nan alone remained unmoved, staring Gideon up and down, not even bothering to hide the judgments forming in her gleaming black eyes.

After many starts and stops and interruptions and polite laughter, Poppy led them to the living room and served aperitifs and little bite-sized cheeses and fruits she called "nibblers."

"Your house is beautiful," Nan commented in a thick-accented English, looking up at the chandelier dripping crystals like a waterfall, the ornate fleur-de-lis frieze molding, the white marble head brought back from Greece atop a small bronze drawer. To her husband, she said in Chinese, "Look at their ceilings. We should do something about our ceilings."

"How long have you lived here?" Shen asked.

"Let's see . . ." said Poppy. "We moved here almost four years ago, is that right, Ted?"

"That's right."

"How much it cost to buy?" said Nan.

Poppy blinked. "Oh, um, the house? Rent for our place is around four thousand." She tittered at Ted. "It's very affordable for what we're getting."

"We sold our place back in Andover," Ted explained to Shen. Ted seemed incapable of keeping his gaze on Nan, smiling at her with a kind of diffident trepidation, mingled with little nods, before looking back at Shen. "It was too big once the kids moved out. We wanted to be in the city and we liked the freedom of renting. We can pick up and go whenever we want."

"Like homeless people," sniffed Meifeng in Chinese, her understanding of English having vastly improved since she'd started watching reality television. Her head swiveled around the Speyers' living room until Poppy said, "Ivy, would your family like a tour?"

"Yes," said Meifeng loudly, pushing herself up on her cane. Ivy, despairing, stood up as well.

Poppy led the four Lins plus Gideon from room to room. Ted had elected to remain on the couch with Austin. Nan's sharp eyes took in every detail—the two modest but tasteful bedrooms, the corner library, the solemn parlor with russet curtains—and made humming sounds of approval in her throat, but Meifeng would point to a table or lamp and ask abstract, one-worded adjectives, like "Old?" or "Real?" Poppy would rush to answer with a detailed explanation about the origins of each piece and Ivy or Shen would translate. "Everything is falling apart," Meifeng said to Ivy in Chinese. "Their wealth is made of dung. Not useful even when spread." She flicked a knob of plaster off the wall, then sniffed it. "It's an old house," Ivy hissed back, wishing Meifeng had stayed back in Clarksville. She noticed Poppy glancing over at them in nervous anticipation, listening so hard her neck was strained forward. Ivy smiled weakly. "My grandmother said she loves your—paint color."

"It's called *Sherwood Green*." Poppy lit up. "I can write down the color number for you. When we first moved in, we went to Benjamin Moore . . ."

Ivy felt as if her heart were anchored by an arrow to Poppy's every movement. If Poppy's brows rose in incredulity, Ivy felt her heart jerk up, and if Poppy's eyes widened with interest, so, too, did Ivy's. She quivered whenever Poppy looked confused or agitated and then rushed to make Gideon's mother feel at ease. When Nan or Meifeng spoke too long in Chinese, she would tell them in sweetly venomous tones to speak English. By the time they returned to the living room, Ivy felt as if she'd just come from teaching an enormous group of illiterate, rambunctious first-graders. She longed to hide in the bathroom but was too afraid of what might happen in her absence.

Things calmed down slightly once the Lins began munching on Poppy's nibblers. Austin ate one cheese cube, then another. He ate them so fast that soon there was only one cube left, and as he reached out for the last one, Meifeng hit his hand smartly with the back of her cane.

Poppy said in a high voice, "There's more in the fridge. Please, eat up!" and practically flew to the kitchen. Ivy shot her grandmother a black look of death, to which Meifeng, interpreting her look correctly, simply said, "The doctor told us your brother has high cholesterol. No fatty foods."

"We were friends in middle school," Gideon was saying to Shen, who was sitting on the sofa with his hands clenched into fists, resting atop his knees. "Ivy used to be my little cousin's teacher. My sister, Sylvia, recognized her and got us back in touch."

"Men who grow up with sisters," said Shen, "know how to treat women. Like my son here. He has the softest heart." He patted Austin's knee and began telling a story about how Austin used to follow Ivy around everywhere—he even used to cry in stores because he wanted to go to the ladies' room with Ivy instead of with Shen to the men's room.

Poppy came back with three times the amount of cheese on her platter, setting the plate directly in front of Austin. "Here you go, sweetheart," she said brightly. Austin blushed to the roots of his hair.

"Ivy and Gideon's love story is very romantic," Poppy told Nan after she'd settled back down. "Of course, I was surprised by how much of a—whirlwind—it's been. But considering they were child-hood friends, I feel there's a *trust* there you don't have with someone you just met."

"In Chinese—we call it—*mìngyùn* . . ." Nan looked at her husband.

"Fate," Shen supplied. "My wife says Gideon and Ivy have a shared fate. They are destined. When we were still living in Massachusetts, I remember coming to get Ivy from your house once."

"That's right," said Ted, as if he'd also just remembered. His eyes darted to and away from Nan. He cleared his throat.

"She didn't tell us about Gideon back then," said Shen. "My wife was very strict—more studying, less boyfriends. But Ivy snuck out and went to your house. She was so angry when we showed up!" He glanced fondly at Ivy, who was burning in humiliation at her father's revisionist history.

"Gideon and I were only friends back then," she said pleasantly.

"Well," said Poppy, her eyes misty with emotion. "I don't know about destiny, but I would call it God's will that you two found each other again."

"God's will," Shen echoed.

"Are you folks Christian?" asked Ted.

"We are," said Ivy before her father could respond. "My parents used to take us to church every week when we were kids." She did not say it was to pick up her mother from her English lessons with the local Chinese pastor.

Poppy picked up her glass. "To Ivy and Gideon! Ivy, we are *so* happy to have you as part of the family. Here's to our two families coming together and learning more about each other's cultures."

Ted said, "Shen, Nan, Grandma Lin, Austin—thank you for joining us this Thanksgiving. We have so much to be grateful for." Everyone clinked glasses. Meifeng let out a small burp, which they all pretended not to hear.

"My wife and I were childhood friends," Shen said after downing his glass. "We met in high school. She came to my village. She was the most beautiful woman I ever saw. I always knew I would marry her."

Nan colored with pride.

"Ted and I met in college." Poppy giggled. "He chased me for two years before I agreed to go on a date with him. I thought he was too popular with the ladies."

"Now, now," said Ted. "I was no such Casanova."

"When you know *you* love Ivy?" Nan asked Gideon.

"I've always admired Ivy," said Gideon, clearing his throat. "Even back in school, she was the nicest, smartest girl in our grade. And she's grown into an even more amazing woman."

Ivy smiled gratefully and reached for his hand.

"Ivy is *very* smart." Nan nodded. Shen translated the rest: "My wife says when Ivy was little, all the other kids would ask their parents to buy them toys, but Ivy would go around shoveling snow and mowing lawns for money. All to buy this toy airplane she wanted. She never asked us for anything. She was always independent."

"*That was me*," Austin snarled. Everyone turned to him in surprise. He looked down, seemingly shocked at his own outburst.

"I guess we all remember things differently," Ted offered kindly. "You don't want anyone taking your credit, right, kiddo?"

Austin sank further back into the sofa.

"Were you that hardworking?" Shen joked, slapping Austin on the back of his head. But Austin knocked his father's hand away with such force that the Speyers averted their eyes. Nan admonished her son in Chinese. Austin said nothing.

"Let's move to the dining room, shall we?" said Poppy.

★ ★ ★

THERE WAS A great deal of fuss made over the seating. After much shuffling, Ivy was next to Gideon and Austin, across from her parents and Meifeng; Ted and Poppy were on opposite ends of the table. Laid atop Poppy's finest tablecloth was a magazine-worthy feast: the pear-thyme brined turkey roasted to a perfect crispy brown, rosemary and bourbon gravy, Brussels sprout gratin, two different kinds of salad, apple-walnut stuffing, brown butter mashed potatoes, French green beans with garlic and almond bread crumbs. Nan and Austin refused Ted's vintage Cabernet but everyone else took a glass.

Shen praised every bite of food he ate, taking a second helping of everything. Ivy and Gideon took turns telling the story of their engagement, mostly for the Lins' benefit, as Poppy and Ted had already heard the story many times. The topic then came to the wedding. The ceremony would be held at St. Stephen's, the reception on the top floor of the Millennium Hotel. Ivy had hired a wedding planner back in September, but that had proven to be unnecessary as Poppy had taken everything under her gracious but unassailable command. She'd been the one to suggest the venue, the date, the guest list, emailing Ivy the names of every Whitaker and Speyer in a massive, four-columned spreadsheet that'd included their age, address, and exact relation to Gideon. "Wouldn't it be marvelous," she'd said to Ivy at their last coffee date, "if we incorporated some aspects of your cultural traditions in the reception—perhaps a small show or ceremony?" Ivy had promised to get back to her with some ideas. With no one to guide her on the traditions involved in a grand American wedding, Ivy had readily acquiesced to letting Gideon's mother decide everything, which now apparently had to include a tribute to Ivy's Chinese heritage.

Nan gave Shen a significant look. Shen's face turned grave.

"My wife and I—we want to pay for the wedding." In the startled silence, Shen said, "In Chinese culture, it's our duty to provide this for our daughter. She's our responsibility. We would be honored to do this as her parents."

Gideon looked at Ivy. Poppy looked at Ted. Ted looked at Gideon.

Ted cleared his throat. "That's very generous of you, Shen. It's just, uh, in our culture, we assumed Gideon and Ivy would be financially responsible for themselves . . . it's their decision, of course . . . it's very generous of you folks . . ."

"*Very* generous," Poppy chimed in.

Ivy felt about as gut-punched as Ted and Poppy sounded. She said, "Let's discuss it later," but Nan began to insist over Gideon's grateful response that they would think on it.

Gideon turned to Ivy. "What do you think?"

She smiled and nodded, trying to hide her bewilderment. "In that case. Thank you. Mama. Baba." Gideon reiterated his gratitude, getting up to shake Shen's hand.

In the background, Ted began explaining how *his* child-rearing philosophy had always leaned toward financial independence, but that he understood all too well—he gave Poppy a wry glance—how a little generosity from the older generations could go a long way.

Ivy didn't know what flustered her more—that her parents, thrifty as they were, had offered to foot the bill for two hundred guests, or that Poppy, for all her firm suggestions on how the wedding should be arranged, had not planned on chipping in at all. It'd been a delicate procedure planning the wedding thus far, since Ivy could never bring herself to speak frankly about dollar figures with any Speyer. It'd been especially awkward when dealing with tactless people like Meifeng, who nagged her at least once a week about how much money Gideon made, to which Ivy would respond with evasive, nonnumerical answers delivered in irritated tones. In reality, she had no idea how much Gideon made or the size of his trust fund (if any)—he spent money easily and decisively, saying no to small expenses as often as he agreed to larger ones, thus revealing nothing about his inherent wealth—and

Ivy felt annoyed that this should be such an obsession on Meifeng's part when even Nan hadn't thought to ask Ivy about such private matters.

Poppy said, "I hope the reception will be up to *your* high standards, Nan. You have impeccable taste, that wonderful Chanel jacket . . ."

"All those checks you've been sending us these years," Meifeng whispered to Ivy under her breath. "Your mother's been saving them for you. And more."

Ivy could only nod stiffly at her grandmother. Was this where she was supposed to prostrate herself in gratitude? First the loan to cover her year's rent. Now this. I'll pay every cent back after I become a lawyer, she vowed, feeling very flat all of a sudden. The conversations continued on around her in pairs, everyone looking old and tired and gray, their skin drooping like papier-mâché under the dim light of the crystal chandelier. Gideon was speaking: "The slopes are very icy on the East Coast compared to Colorado—do you enjoy skiing, Nan?"

Nan's head snapped back in surprise. "Call me *Mom*," she said firmly. "You're my son now."

There was a sharp sound of a chair scraping. Everyone's heads followed Austin's figure striding out of the dining room. "Are you looking for the bathroom?" Ivy called out at his retreating back. But he was already gone.

Nan didn't take her eyes off Gideon.

"Ah—right," said Gideon. ". . . Mom." He took a large mouthful of goat cheese and winced, reaching for his water.

"See how he squirms," Meifeng muttered.

Nan beamed and turned to Poppy, making a wide circle with her hands. "Now we are all family."

"Yes . . ." said Poppy, her almost invisible lashes fluttering in double time.

Ted cleared his throat. "You can call me Dad," he said to Ivy with a twinkle in his eye.

"That won't be necessary," said Poppy. She looked around with an air of resolute gaiety. "Should we bring out the pies?"

FIFTEEN MINUTES LATER and Austin still had not returned to the table. Ivy excused herself. She found him sitting on the staircase, scrolling listlessly through his phone.

"What are you doing? Come back to dinner." No movement. "Come on," she said more insistently. Silence. She grabbed the phone from Austin's hands but it slipped and landed on the floor with a loud clatter. He didn't bother to pick it up.

"It's better that I'm not there." He was sweating again, his pallor white and ashen, like the underbelly of a fish. A bead of sweat trailed down his neck and disappeared into the tight collar of his dress shirt.

"Let's go," she said, tugging at his elbow. He was too large now for this to have any effect. There came a burst of laughter from the dining room; Ivy could hear Poppy's distinct *huh huh huh* carrying on the longest. "*Austin*," she snapped. "You need to come back to the table."

"Why?"

"You're part of the family."

"I wish I wasn't."

Familiar words rose to Ivy's throat. She hated him for making her sound like a broken record all her life. "Just be . . ." She couldn't finish. Austin's face was twisting, his chin quivering, one hand over his eyes. *Just be cool*, was what she was going to say, this childish phrase seemingly the perfect advice that encompassed all she wanted for Austin: ease, assurance, knowledge of what mattered and what didn't.

Before Austin could compose himself, Poppy was walking toward them, smiling her eager hostess smile. "Is everything all right here? I wasn't sure if you two got lost."

Ivy said "Everything's fine" just as Austin said "I'm sorry."

Poppy sat down beside Austin on the stairs. "I was talking to your sister about this earlier. I hear you're interested in working with computers?"

Austin glanced at Ivy. She nodded.

"Uh, I guess," he said.

"My cousin Spencer is looking for an intern for his software company in New York. Would you be interested in something like that?"

"What kind of intern?"

"You know, I never asked about the specifics. But I'm sure he'd very much like to talk to you about it."

Austin mumbled something about not being qualified. Poppy said, "Oh, I'm sure you can learn on the job. They don't expect you to come in with prior experience . . . I think you'd be *fantastic* at it . . ." When Austin didn't respond, she said, "That's settled then. I'll get your email from Ivy and have Spencer send some information over to you." She picked his phone up off the floor and handed it back to him. Austin stared at the cracked screen without moving. Poppy slid one arm around his hulking shoulders, tentative at first, then more firmly when he didn't stiffen but instead lowered his head. "There, there," Poppy soothed. Ivy was confused by this remark until she saw the steady drops of tears sliding off the end of Austin's nose into his lap.

"Get some tissues for us, will you, Ivy?" Poppy whispered.

By the time Ivy returned, Austin was wiping his face on his sweater, his blazer draped over his legs. Poppy was speaking to him in quiet tones; he nodded, twisted his hands in his lap. Ivy only heard the last few sentences: ". . . between us . . . nothing to worry about. Why don't you get freshened up in the bathroom and we'll go have some dessert. Do you like apple pie?" Austin mumbled that he did. When Ivy caught her brother's face on his way to the bathroom, she saw that he looked as if some knot had finally unwound inside him. He even managed a small grimace that was supposed to be an apologetic smile.

Ivy's astonishment was so great it erased all other emotions. All those flunked classes, meticulous plans, doctor visits, vitamin injections, and all Austin needed was a motherly shoulder to cry on?

Poppy's butter-soft hands to pat his back and say, *There, there*? She couldn't believe that the respect and understanding her brother had sought all his life had come from, of all people, Poppy Speyer, the woman who worried about things like where to find a rare 1830s Georgian sterling silver spoon to complete her collection.

For the first time in her life, Ivy saw how her marriage to Gideon, which she'd guarded from the Lins like a dragon over its most precious treasure, could lead to a new identity not just for herself but for her family. It was something that Meifeng used to tell her: one successful marriage feeds three generations. Only now did she believe this.

17

AUSTIN STARTED HIS NEW INTERNSHIP IMMEDIATELY AFTER THE New Year. Every morning, he caught the seven forty train into Manhattan, and he returned in the evening with the commuter crowd. Shen took him to the outlet malls to buy four suits in muted shades of blue and gray, striped silk ties, thin cotton socks that Austin colorcoordinated with his ties. He needed a new cell phone, because of the cracked screen, as well as a new laptop because the fan had stopped working on his old one. The internship was unpaid, so Nan gave him a credit card for his daily expenses. He liked to pick up a bagel and a yogurt smoothie at Penn Station for breakfast, then lunch at a popular sushi place in midtown. And because he felt guilty about living at home while his new friends at the company had to pay their own rent, he would often treat them to sashimi platters as well.

"You should see your brother now," Nan bragged to Ivy on the phone. "He was born to work. He goes to bed right after he gets home and sets his own alarm. He bought an ironing board to iron his suits every night. And he's finally making friends. They want to take a trip together to Mexico. He's never been invited on a trip before. Baba's worried that Mexico's too dangerous. What do you think?"

Ivy wondered how her parents could afford all these additional expenses. Over Christmas, Nan had mailed her the money for the wedding, made out in four separate checks, with specific instructions for Ivy to cash them a month apart so "the banks won't be suspicious."

Suspicious of what, Ivy did not care to ask. Long gone were the days when she had access to her mother's checkbook—the Lins were probably cutting back in other ways—and so she repressed her conscience and said, "Austin will be fine in Mexico . . . I'm glad he's adjusting." Indeed, her brother returned her calls now and seemed to be in a state of giddiness every time they talked about his new job. He said he fetched coffee, conducted market research, wrote up long, twenty-page reports; everyone praised him for his great attitude. "My manager, Allen, says if I keep doing well, maybe after I graduate, they'll offer me a full-time position." Ivy told him not to expect anything. She was afraid for him, afraid of his fragile hope.

Perhaps she was unfit in giving this advice as she'd just taken the LSAT and bombed it so badly she'd deleted the email announcing her score from her inbox, then deleted it again from her trash folder. When Gideon asked about her results, she told him she wasn't happy with her score—he had the delicacy not to ask the precise number—and that she was going to retake it in September. He pulled her into his arms. "I'm proud of you for not giving up," he said.

That evening, they went for drinks at Dresdan's. Ivy didn't want the evening to become a pity party, so she wore her favorite dark brown taffeta dress with ball-gown sleeves and a black velvet choker that had a little bell attached to it, like a cat's collar, and whenever she turned her head, the bell went *da-ding da-ding* and it was the sound of merry church bells. Ivy downed one cocktail after another while Gideon nursed a beer, laughing, telling her to slow down. His voice seemed deeper than usual, this abstract beautiful man in a white button-down, rolled up at the cuffs, the gleaming face of his watch emitting a rainbow onto the wall of liquor bottles behind the bar. All evening, he kept saying, "Are you happy? Are you happy?" and she'd say, "Of course. I have *you*."

She told Roux about bombing the LSAT as well. His reaction was, expectedly, entirely different from Gideon's.

"Of course you flunked. You'd make a terrible lawyer."

"Why?"

"You have no deductive reasoning skills. You act on your whims and passions. You're easily intimidated by others, and you're swayed completely by outward appearances. I never understood why you even *wanted* to go to law school. I mean, you were probably a mediocre teacher but you'd be an even worse lawyer. Trust me, I've met a whole bunch of them in my life and they all see the world as one big booby trap. You couldn't see a freight train coming until it ran into your face."

Normally, Ivy would have been seething at Roux's poor assessment of her character, but it was such a relief to finally talk to someone about Dave and Liana Finley and Gideon's other ambitious friends who looked down on her lack of achievements, and how was she ever going to score high enough to get into a good school?

"Dave Finley?" said Roux, pulling her legs onto his lap and massaging her calves. "The VC guy?"

"You know him?"

"I've seen him at some art auctions."

Ivy rolled her eyes and smeared some caviar onto a bagel chip. Roux loved to hint once in a while of his comings and goings amongst the one percent, to remind her of his new social status. Gideon never name-dropped. Gideon was allergic to all forms of self-promotion. The private clubs, the yacht, the shabby-chic beach house, the Celtics season tickets—all this was a result of Gideon's natural tastes, tastes that had been refined and handed down through generations of education, unlike Roux, who liked to know how much everything cost, how many copies had been printed, how many people were on the waitlist before he made a purchase.

"Look," said Roux, handing her a napkin. "What did you want to be when you were little?"

What had she wanted to be? "I don't know." The only thing she could remember wanting to be was popular. And to get away from her parents.

"How'd you get into teaching?"

"Oh, same as anything else. It came my way and I thought it would be an easy job until I figured things out."

Roux looked at her shrewdly. "Why don't you just do what all women used to do for a living—cook, clean, look after the kids. No woman I've ever met has complained about having a husband as breadwinner."

"The women *you* know," said Ivy coldly, "are probably too dumb to do anything else. Thankfully, I have more enlightened friends."

"And here I thought you were a resourceful woman. If it's money you need . . ."

"Are you offering to be my *patron*?"

"It's one solution."

"Not the kind I want." She reached for an olive, popped it in her mouth, then spit it into her napkin. Too briny.

Roux pushed her legs off his lap. "You know what your problem is? You've never really worked hard at anything. You've gotten by on lies and cleverness. You think you've had a hard childhood, but you've always been privileged . . ."

Ivy turned on the television.

For weeks now, he'd been like this, hot, cold, tender one moment, angry the next. He'd always been moody, but the swings felt even more extreme than usual. It tried Ivy's patience. More and more, he expressed his unhappiness when she refused to spend the night; he insisted on taking her for drives in one of his fancy cars, which he kept covered in Astor Towers's private garage, and though Ivy always turned him down, afraid she might run into someone she knew, now Roux's face would sour after her refusals and he'd remain cranky until she soothed him in other ways, most of the time through sex. He also had a new habit of proposing exotic getaways. He complained about being overworked—running errands for Baldy (the nickname Ivy had given Baldassare Moretti) had him frequently flying out of town—and he wanted to take Ivy to Cuba, to Tuscany, to Marrakesh, where his friend Andre Pascal lived and had invited him to spend a week at his family's villa. Roux pulled up photos of Marrakesh right then and there on his laptop. Ivy obligingly cooed over the photos of blue umbrellas under a hazy sand-blown sky, crumbling orange-red villas the color of a ripe mango, mosques with stained-glass windows inside which olive-skinned men knelt, praying over braided rugs. She was practically there, she said, she could smell the fig and date trees bending over the garden walls.

"I'll book tickets right now," said Roux.

"No."

"Why not?"

"I have to study, Roux. I just bombed my LSAT, remember?"

"It's just a week."

"I said no."

His grasp tightened on her wrist. "How long are you going to make me wait?"

She slapped his hand. "I'll make you wait as long as I want."

All of this theatrical martyrdom, Ivy only took for the flashing of feathers of a man exuding his dominance on any woman, something she could safely laugh off, instead of seeing it for what it was: a desperate man running out of patience, waiting for a prize he believed he'd duly paid for and belonged to him.

IN THE BEGINNING of March, one of the start-ups in Dave Finley's portfolio announced their impending IPO at a market value of a billion dollars. To celebrate, Dave rented the penthouse suite at the Gonford and invited everyone in Boston, it seemed, to the extravaganza. The email he'd sent Gideon was literally to "bring your Ivy-girl and all your friends. Send names to Nancy to add to guest list." Everyone at Gideon's company was going and he'd also invited Tom and Marybeth as well as Sylvia and her new boyfriend, Jeremy Lier, who also happened to work "in tech," though his work, when he'd described it to Ivy, seemed to consist of filming himself playing video games and launching things off the roof of his apartment building. He said he was a documentary maker.

Ivy had not planned on inviting Andrea. It was Gideon who'd suggested it. "I think she'd have fun. At the very least there'll be a ton of single guys. Not to mention they'll all be newly minted millionaires by next week." His tone was humorous but not cynical. He didn't care about newly minted millionaires but understood how a single woman of a marriageable age might value such things. Ivy suppressed her instinctive reluctance and said she would ask her roommate.

Andrea had cut her hair, an elongated bob that fell in feathery waves around her jawbone, and she'd swapped out her shrunken skin-tight wardrobe for high-waisted trousers, men's cuffed shirts, black patent leather loafers with tassels. She'd gone to see a color consultant who told her she was a "cool autumn" and should therefore stop wearing light colors and bright patterns. Ivy, according to Andrea, was a "clear spring," which meant she should avoid black clothing, which happened to make up half of Ivy's closet. The evening of the party, standing side by side in front of the trifold mirror in Andrea's room, Ivy told herself that Andrea deserved this night. Andrea's father had recently had a heart attack and she'd flown back to Toronto to care for him for two weeks; on top of all that, she'd been occasionally sticking her finger down her throat after one of her binges, coming out of the bathroom with a swollen face and bloodshot eyes. Ivy told herself that if she paled tonight beside Andrea, who was ravishing in her high-collared navy jumpsuit, her hair a rippling sheet of taffeta, it didn't matter because none of it was real; sooner or later, the real Andrea would ooze out of her pristine shell to ruin the beautiful illusion.

When they arrived, the penthouse was already packed with people, squeezed shoulder to shoulder like on the dance floor of a nightclub, with groups of scantily clad women pressing behind Ivy, braying, "Excuse me, *excuse me*," and men in sweatshirts and sneakers balancing four drinks in their hands. Holding hands, she and Andrea pushed their way across the room to the huge flag etched with the startup's logo (a prismatic cube) fluttering over their heads like a war banner. The breeze came from massive wind generators stationed in the corners of the suite, blowing white smoke that smelled like watermelon Jolly Ranchers. Gideon had texted that he and the others were under the flag. Ivy found Gideon, Sylvia, and Tom standing around a frosty white cocktail table shaped like a tulip. The surface was hardly big enough to hold even a handful of wineglasses.

"Cute jumpsuit." Sylvia nodded at Andrea after Gideon introduced everyone. "Very aggressive."

Andrea decided to take this as a compliment and beamed with friendly eagerness. "*You* look amazing! That salmon color suits your skin tone perfectly." She began to regale Sylvia with details about her life-changing appointment with the color consultant. From Sylvia's impassive eyes, not quite focused on Andrea's face but somewhere beyond it, Ivy could tell Sylvia wasn't taking in a single word.

"Andrea's my violinist friend I told you about," Ivy injected.

Sylvia smiled blankly.

"She plays for the Boston Symphony Orchestra?"

"Right, I remember you saying something . . ."

"Sylvia's friend composed the album I gave you, *The Watchmaker*," Ivy said to Andrea.

"Oooh!" said Andrea. "I just *loved* . . ."

Ivy turned to Gideon and Tom. "Where's Marybeth?"

"She couldn't make it," said Gideon regretfully.

"She hates these things," Tom sneered to demonstrate his own concurrent disdain. "I just spent twenty minutes listening to a group of jackasses shit on each other for not 'thinking big enough' and wanting to 'disrupt this' and 'do good' and 'better humanity.' All the while, they're telling these girls how much equity they have in this little venture. In banking, at least people say what they mean: *I want to make money*. A pile of dogshit money." He glanced at Gideon's disapproving frown and his expression softened. "I know, I know—you guys are different. Nonprofit health care . . . I suppose you've resigned yourself to living like a barefoot monk for the rest of your life . . ."

Beside Tom, Sylvia and Andrea had stopped talking, or, more precisely, Sylvia remained silent and Andrea wasn't so slow on the uptake that she couldn't sense another woman's blatant disinterest. She smiled at Ivy across the cocktail table in a kind of vague, bright way that Ivy knew was nervous dread.

"How's Jeremy's documentary coming along?" Ivy asked Sylvia.

"His vision's expanded," said Sylvia, drumming her red-manicured fingers on one of the tulip petals. "He's going to branch out past the start-up view and also film larger organizations to see how teams function. He wants to film the Boeing machinists' strike in Oregon. If he pulls it together in time, the film will debut at the Berlin Film Festival next year."

"That sounds amazing," said Andrea.

"He's brilliant," Sylvia dismissed. "A true visionary. He does everything deliberately. He doesn't suffer from the inertia that afflicts the rest of the world. Most people are just sheep masquerading as intelligent beings, waiting to be slaughtered."

Andrea laughed uncertainly. "You're so right."

Tom said, "That sounds just like the pile of dogshit I was talking about."

Sylvia grinned. It could have gone either way. She might have thrown her water in Tom's face. Sylvia's eyes slid past Tom and she waved to the man walking toward them holding frothy cocktails adorned with various slices of fruit. Ivy thought that Jeremy Lier, besides his green eyes, looked remarkably like Roux—tall, slim, the smooth line of his broad shoulders tapering to a thin waist. Also like Roux, he dressed with a kind of slouchy indifference, sneakers and gray beanies and corduroy messenger bags, but Ivy knew better now than to think Jeremy a struggling artist. With that crowd, the presumption of expendable wealth was a given, the exact means never addressed.

"Oops, didn't realize there were two more," Jeremy said as he handed out the cocktails. Andrea offered to go get her and Ivy drinks to save Jeremy another trip. Ivy said, "I can come," but Andrea said there was no need. She seemed relieved to have a purpose. Before she even made it ten feet away, a scrawny-looking young man in black-framed glasses had approached her with a simpering smile. He was wearing one of the free yellow T-shirts they'd been handing out in the lobby, with the tagline SWINGBOX TO YOUR NEW REALITY.

"Aaaand we'll never see her again for the rest of the evening," Ivy murmured to Gideon.

"Will she be okay?"

"She's a big girl." Ivy smiled keenly. "Let's not hinder her fun."

A famous DJ ascended the stage and everyone began swarming toward the dance floor. Sylvia and Jeremy left to find the heated pool. Tom was arguing with a silver-haired man about the ethics of selling social media data. Gideon was on his phone, probably checking email. He seemed tired tonight; the light reflecting off their frosty tulip table cast his prominent cheekbones in a cold marble glaze. Ivy nuzzled up beside him and wrapped her arm around his waist. It was always during moments like this, in a crowd of noisy strangers, that she felt most compelled to seek his touch, as a kind of self-assurance.

On a trapezoidal platform across the room, she saw the towering figure of Liana Finley swinging her hips in an elaborate silk kimono. A feather boa was wrapped around her neck, like some nesting black-blue ermine creature. Gideon said he needed to use the restroom. "Will you be all right?" he shouted into her ear.

Ivy gestured at the platform. "I'm going to go dance with Liana."

"I'll come find you there." Gideon released her elbow.

Ivy fetched her own drink from the bar, then squeezed her way across the throng of sweaty bodies. Liana pulled her up onto the platform. Without speaking, she wrapped the end of her boa around Ivy's neck and began dancing up to her, arms raised, head tossed back. Catcalls came from a distant corner. Someone shouted, "Yeah Liana!" The music swelled even louder. Ivy was laughing, champagne fumes pleasantly tickling her throat. She felt the admiring gaze of hundreds of people on her gyrating figure, pressed against Liana's. If only she could always feel this way, as if she were flying in a dream, her eyes roaming the room in a detached, wondrous way, evaluating those evaluating her, in mutual satisfactory evaluation. Glaring neon lights began flashing from the ceiling, girls erupted in screams, and in one of those flashes of perfect illumination, Ivy saw Roux in the corner, watching her dance.

It was definitely him. Wasn't it? Perhaps she was mistaken. The lights flashed again, and again she saw Roux's face, the mop of black hair, the pale, tall figure in a white T-shirt and black jeans.

She stopped dancing. Liana's hip bumped into hers with a painful jolt. The other woman guided Ivy's chin to face her. Strange how inhuman people looked when viewed from close up. All judgments of attractiveness became irrelevant, reduced to shapes and curves and lines; it was like looking at the face of a farm animal, utterly deprived of meaning. Ivy tried to move her body in sync with Liana's but she'd lost her focus and could no longer hear the music or people screaming. Roux's gaze had trapped her in an invisible box, isolating her from the outside world. She unwound herself from Liana's scarf and jumped off the platform. A man's arm darted out with the pretense of trying to steady her landing but really to slide his hand down her backside. She tried to spot Roux again but was too short, even in her four-inch heels, to see much more than the giant flag blowing in the fake wind. She'd lost him.

She made her way one by one through all the rooms of the penthouse before catching sight of Jeremy and Sylvia soaking in the Jacuzzi next to a raucous pool party.

"Where'd you guys get the swimsuits?" she asked, stooping down stiffly in her short dress.

"They're giving them out over there," Sylvia said, waving to a table along the wall where two Eastern European girls in maid's uniforms were handing out fluorescent one-pieces and swim trunks. A few men near the end of the line decided they could wait no longer, stripped, and cannonballed into the pool stark naked.

"Disgusting," said Sylvia. "This is why we didn't go into the pool." Her eyes flicked at Ivy, who was still kneeling awkwardly over them. "Jump in," she suggested.

Ivy hesitated. She didn't want to stay still but she didn't want to be flung back into the crowd either. The warm, musky smell of chlorine reminded her of being back in a school gym. It felt safe. She took off her shoes, sat on the edge of the Jacuzzi, and dipped her legs into the bubbling water. Jeremy and Sylvia spoke to each other in casual, drifting sentences, making minimal effort to include Ivy in their conversation. She didn't mind. Her mind wandered here and there, watching girls pose for photographs with pasty young men in yellow T-shirts; men who would, according to Gideon, become millionaires by next week. Already the arrogance was forming, preceding the money itself, and could be seen in the reckless way they were grabbing and pushing each other into the pool, conscious of being watched, straddling floaties shaped like flamingos. Ivy was only half-listening when Sylvia said to Jeremy: "—at least he was a great supporter of the arts. You two would have gotten along."

"Is this the Italian guy from the mob?"

"He was Romanian."

Ivy's neck snapped toward Sylvia. "Who is this?"

Sylvia said, "This guy I used to date, Roux Roman. Oh, right, you've met him . . . Ivy came to Cattahasset last summer," she explained to Jeremy. She seemed to have completely forgotten that Ivy and Roux had known each other long before Sylvia had met him. "Anyway, my cousin Francis works at the DEA and looked into him. He works for a bunch of loan sharks. They own some restaurants—a cheese shop in the North End, some sandwich shops—as a front. They have those casinos in Vegas, too. I was surprised at first they'd let in an outsider like him, but I suppose the family line is thinning . . . then there was the thing he did with those old warehouses, buying them out and converting them to bodegas—oh shit, here he comes again . . . Do you think he's stalking me?"

Indeed, Sylvia's sharp amber eyes had spotted Roux standing near the clusters of yellow and white balloons on the periphery of a small crowd.

"You think he's here for *you*?" Ivy asked, unable to hide her disbelief.

"Why else is he here?" said Sylvia, her eyes narrowing. "I've had to file restraining orders before."

"Has he approached you?"

"Not yet," Sylvia conceded. "I saw him come in a while ago. But I know he never goes to these things . . . and he *knew* I'd be here tonight to support Gideon."

"You're making me jealous," said Jeremy, kissing Sylvia's hair. Sylvia scratched under his chin.

Jeremy's green eyes widened with glee. "Do you think the guy's ever *killed* anyone?"

"I'm sure he did," said Sylvia. "The one time I visited his house in Evansville, there were these workers, two of them, only they were dressed in suits and ties, pouring concrete onto the basement floor. Underneath the cement was dirt, nothing else. At least nothing that hadn't already been buried . . ." Her eyes bored into Roux's back, as if challenging him to come over and contradict her, but he didn't turn their way, though Ivy was certain he'd seen them the moment he entered the room.

"The Boston mafia world would be interesting to film," said Jeremy. "If I could get access somehow—to the head boss. You think this guy would want to talk to me? For an interview?"

"I doubt it, puppy," said Sylvia. She fanned her face with her hands. "I'm boiling alive. Let's get out."

★ ★ ★

IVY FELT SHE had to keep moving, like a shark that would die the moment it rested. She remembered that Gideon would be looking for her on the platform where she'd been dancing with Liana. How long had it been since they'd separated? She went back to the dance floor, but Liana was gone and in her place a gaggle of women wearing the free swimsuits was dancing wildly, barefoot, droplets of pool water spraying from their long hair onto the chanting crowd.

Gideon was not part of the crowd. She made a beeline for one corner of the room, then another, to maintain her air of purpose. She glimpsed Andrea on one of the inflated sofa beds beside the scrawny young man from before. Sitting down cross-legged, he looked like Andrea's little brother or teenage son. A fleshy woman with lavender hair barreled into Ivy. They struck up a conversation about the dangers of indoor pools. The woman held out her weed pen. Ivy took two long puffs before handing it back. "Love the hair. My roommate would dub you a 'dashing winter.'" The woman grinned. "Come on." Ivy followed her into the stairwell. They climbed and climbed, holding on to the wrought-iron railings that seemed to spiral forever beneath the domed glass ceiling. "Ivy-girl!" a man's voice boomed from overhead. Dave Finley stood on the top step in a tangerine-colored suit, the collar open to reveal his speckled, old-man skin.

"So happy to see you, my dear! I haven't congratulated you yet on your engagement."

He had, multiple times, but she thanked him anyway. She looked over her shoulder. The lavender-haired woman had abandoned her.

"Have you seen Gideon?" she asked.

"I told Gideon last summer, I said, 'You've caught yourself a unicorn, Gideon. A woman with beauty, brains, *and* common sense. An absolute rarity.'" He raised a yellow toy gun—it shot out streams of soap bubbles—and aimed it at Ivy's hair.

"Stop it," she said, inhaling a bubble.

He pressed the trigger again and again and again.

"*Stop.*"

He grabbed her and mashed their mouths together. "How beautiful you are," he breathed. "I have a suite here on the eighth floor if you'd like a tour."

"You're so drunk." Ivy laughed, attempting to treat the entire thing like a joke. "Have you seen your wife's feather boa? It's fabulous."

"What?"

"Is it made of fur or bird feathers? People don't like to wear fur these days, they say it's inhumane. Anyway, Liana looks like a beautiful ostrich. That long neck and small, sleek head—"

As expected, Dave could not stand a talkative woman when he was this drunk into the evening, and he interrupted Ivy by shooting his gun into the ceiling and calling his wife's name.

Ivy fled. She finally reached the rooftop. There, sitting on cushioned lawn chairs underneath a heating lamp, were Gideon and Tom. "I've been looking for you everywhere," she said breathlessly, feeling as if she might, at any second, burst into violent laughter.

"You should thank me, Ivy," said Tom. "I've just saved your fiancé from being mauled by a group of hungry cougars. We've barely managed to get away."

"*Thank you,* Tom. Thank you for always saving Gideon. You're such a *hero.*"

Gideon moved his lips but she couldn't focus on what he was saying. A rushing sound filled her ears, like wind blowing over a field of grass.

"I can't hear you up here," she said, motioning with her hands. "Can we go talk somewhere else?"

Gideon stood up and took her arm. "Let's go in here." He led her to the waiting area for the restrooms. "Are you feeling all right?"

She said she had had one too many and was feeling queasy. She saw a dark-haired figure behind Gideon—her heart jerked. But it was only one of the maids holding an armful of towels stained with what looked like Kool-Aid.

"Let's splash some water onto your face," said Gideon. When she didn't move, he led her into the women's room himself.

"I ran into Dave in the staircase," she said.

"Yeah, I was with him earlier. He's quite drunk."

"Did you know he has a suite here on the eighth floor?"

"Really? That must be nice."

He knows, thought Ivy, staring at Gideon's carefully blank expression. He knows and he doesn't want me to tell him. "Come here." She pushed Gideon into one of the stalls and closed the door behind her. He was more confused than stunned; then, grasping what she wanted from him, his face went slack. He took her hands and pressed them to his lips. But she didn't want tenderness. She broke away and slithered down to hip level, pulled down his pants, and took him into her mouth. She was extra rough, both aroused and sickened by the cool, spongy tissue of him hardening, pressing against her tongue. The hands encircling her head were warm and snug, it felt like a crown. A minute later, she came back up and guided him into her, one leg over his hip, her back pressed against the stall. They moved as one, in gentle motions, then, her violence building, she stepped her other foot onto the edge of the toilet seat. He slipped out. She tried again but as they struggled, Gideon banged his elbow on the wall and made a soft cry. "Get a room, *gross*," a woman said from the next stall. Gideon froze. His face paled, his mouth closed in shame. Ivy looked upon her fiancé as if from very far away. His humiliation seemed sad to her. She was sad that he was humiliated and sad that she'd been the one to bring it upon him.

Without speaking, he pulled up his pants. She unbunched her dress. Like thieves making their separate getaways, they snuck back out to the party to blend into the anonymous crowd.

18

"Why'd you go last night?"

"I was invited."

"By whom?"

"The mayor himself. A gold-plated invitation delivered on a dinner tray. Want to see it?"

"That's not why you went."

Roux splayed his hands out in front as if to say, *You got me.* "You're right. I wanted to see you in your natural habitat. The slutty dress. Dancing on the table. Salivating over the *abundance* of rich men. Throw a lasso and you'll catch one. Did they stuff tips into your underwear? . . . Oh, wait. You weren't wearing any." He was smirking but his eyes were cruel and not one bit amused.

"It's called a platform," said Ivy.

"What?"

"I wasn't dancing on a table."

Roux laughed in disbelief. "Was Gideon even there?"

"Yes."

"What a pathetic man."

"You're green with jealousy," Ivy said pleasantly, "and it makes you look like a filthy, green kangaroo."

"Don't call me that."

She deliberately took her time lighting a cigarette, blowing the smoke right into his eyes. "Why not?" she said. "That's all you are with your dirty money and gold-plated invitations from the *mayor* of crime town. A filthy green kangaroo."

He slapped her. A great big *thwack* on her left cheek. Ivy's head snapped to the side. She was conscious of the cigarette falling out of her hand and rolling onto the pillow. Her hand drifted to her cheek. The skin was warm and sticky, the pain nonexistent at first, then ferocious.

She launched herself at him, arms raised, going for the hair. She fought like an animal, eyes pinched shut, swinging blindly, silent except for the staggered breathing emitting from her nostrils. Roux wrenched her hands away, pinned them to her sides. She tried to bite his arm. He pushed her facedown onto the bed. Her legs thrashed around but only kicked air. "Enough!" he shouted.

When he realized she wasn't struggling anymore, he slowly released her. Oxygen returned to her lungs in embarrassing wheezes. She told herself to move, to react, but she couldn't move a muscle. Over the thump of her galloping heart, she heard the ticking of the clock in the living room.

Roux shoved his face into her line of sight. "Are you okay?"

"Get away from me."

"Look," he said aggressively, showing her his profile. "I'm bleeding." He was. She saw the gashes down his cheek in two parallel curves, like red ski tracks, which he was cupping with one hand to keep the blood from dripping onto the sheets.

He reached for her hand but stopped when she flinched. "I'll get you some ice," he said flatly, disappearing to the kitchen.

She heard him rummaging around the refrigerator, opening and closing cabinets. What just happened, she wondered. Was there a manual for how to react when your lover slaps you? What would Sylvia do?

She lay there for a minute before morbid curiosity made her walk out to inspect herself in the entryway mirror. The left side of her face was blotchy pink with mascara and lipstick smeared all over. She tried to comb her hair with her fingers but found that her fingers were too stiff. She looked like a ravished woman. Or a ravaged woman. It was basically the same thing.

Roux came back with an ice pack. He had wiped off his blood but the scratches and dime-sized chunk of scalp, where the hair was missing, looked white and lumpy, like tofu, and spotted with smeared blood. Their eyes met in the mirror; both paused for a second, taking in this wanton portrait. The unsentimental gray eyes, in tune with her every movement, seemed to say she'd deserved it, that he wasn't sorry, that he could do it again, and maybe worse.

Sylvia would be cold and indifferent, Ivy decided, recalling the mechanical way Gideon's sister's expression had straightened after Roux had dumped her in front of her entire family. Maybe Roux, not Sylvia, as she'd assumed, had been the source of their volatility. Roux, who had had no father growing up and could only resort to sordid violence.

Ivy walked into the living room. Roux followed.

"Want to watch a movie?" he asked, seeing her look toward the television screen. She'd only been trying to see her own reflection.

"All right."

Roux dimmed the lights. It was a French movie they'd already seen, about a high school girl who falls into prostitution out of boredom and ends up accidentally killing her seventy-year-old client during sex. Halfway through the film, Roux reached his hand underneath her shirt and cupped her breast. They had sex on the sofa, swift, urgent, without preamble. The flames from the gas fireplace flickered over his naked body, illuminating the marble-white skin, the powerful chest, the body that was so much larger than her own. Bone for bone, flesh for flesh, he could crush her if he wanted. He could beat her senseless, suffocate her with his pillow, bash her skull against the wall, he had the power to do all this and she wouldn't have the strength to stop him. He grabbed her leg and hitched it over his waist. They tumbled onto the floor. *I love you*, he whispered, piercing her neck with his teeth. She dug her nails into his fleshy thighs, slick with sweat, until he groaned with pain and pleasure. When they finished, he rolled away and they lay side by side on the ground, several feet apart, panting up at the ceiling. The movie's theme song began playing in the background. Ivy caught the last scene—the lithe French virginal heroine who was a prostitute lying in bed with her dead lover beside her, smoking a cigarette, as the police cars pulled up in front of her house—before the screen faded to black. She and Roux often watched foreign films like these. The unfamiliar language, the characters' detachment, the portrayal of sex as a clinical act—all of it depressed her, yet she also found the films comforting in some ways. They portrayed, more or less, her own reality.

AFTER ONE OF her mother's beatings, Ivy could, at least, count on being left alone for a few days. If the beating was particularly vicious, Nan might even cook Ivy's favorite dishes and allow her to watch television before starting her homework. Nan neither justified nor apologized. Roux's guilt, on the other hand, made him truculent. He wanted Ivy to know exactly why he'd behaved thus, why he'd hit her, why he was driven crazy by her—it was all because he loved her. He'd told her so in the heat of their lovemaking, which, like anything said during sex, didn't count. But admitting it seemed to have unlocked some previously untapped source of male possessiveness. He had never before wooed her, never tried to be her boyfriend, but now his romantic gestures were unrelenting.

The morning after their fight, Ivy received a same-day FedEx package with no return address. Inside was a black velvet box holding a pair of earrings. They were shaped like origami cranes, each the size of a thimble. The lines of the crane's beak, the right angles of its wings, the jutting plane of its tail, were all molded in forward movement, as if the bird was about to take flight. She knew immediately who'd sent them. What frightened her was how Roux had gotten her address. She glanced across the street to where the men with the SUVs stood smoking in their usual spot. She'd seen them come in and out of the house and thought they must be running some kind of business from there. Now she wondered if Shen had been right when he'd called them gangsters. And if they were gangsters, might they be associated with Roux? She hurried inside and drew the curtains.

Roux called every day the following week, asking to see her. She picked up at first, making excuses about having her period, prior engagements, car troubles. He accused her of lying—*You're fucking pathological, you know that?* She accused him of being a savage woman-hater. She finally demanded that he stop calling; when he refused, she threatened to block his number. "Do that and see what happens," was his chilling reply.

She sold the crane earrings he gave her to a pawnshop. With the money, she went to an upscale boutique in Back Bay and bought a cocktail dress of pink organza, patent leather Ralph Li-Ping stilettos, and a crocodile-skin clutch. It would be her outfit to the Cross wedding, an event she had dreaded for months but which she now looked forward to as a means of escape from Roux. Now that he knew her address, she lived in perpetual terror of his showing up on her doorstep when Andrea was home, or, more disastrously, when Gideon was over. The city itself seemed to press against her, hostile in its harsh noises, the drills of construction sites, police sirens. Every night, she crossed off another day on her calendar. May 22, her wedding day, was circled with a red heart. Only seventy-two days away, she told herself. She said it like a prayer: Seventy-two days. Seventy-two days. Seventy-two days.

IT'D RAINED THAT morning in Kauai when they landed but by early afternoon, the sun was streaming through the stained-glass windows of St. Mary's Cathedral. Sitting beside Ivy in the dark cherrywood pew was Marybeth's aunt, the one whose ranch they'd visited in New Hampshire last year. She kept bumping into Ivy's elbow as she raised her compact mirror to powder her face with an almond-scented bronzer. "Are you a friend of the bride or groom?" she whispered, and Ivy almost said, *Neither*. She said she was the fiancée of the best man. "The splendid blond one?" the aunt asked. Ivy nodded with pride. Standing at the altar with the other groomsmen was Gideon, looking splendid indeed in his tailored gray suit, his hands clasped somberly in front of him. Certainly he looked better than the groom, who wore his tux like a straitjacket, his arms rigidly pressed against his sides.

As Ivy waited for Marybeth to walk through the doors, she felt her phone vibrating inside her clutch. Marybeth's aunt adjusted her hearing aid, looking around for the source of the noise. The organist began playing Mendelssohn's "Wedding March" and the crowd stood. Ivy followed suit, a second late as she silenced her phone. A gasp of delight rippled through the room. Dripping from head to toe in lace and pearls, Marybeth looked like a Pre-Raphaelite painting with her burnt-orange hair rippling under a sixty-two-inch ivory silk tulle veil, the culmination of a thousand hours of Chinese labor hand-embroidering all those cascades of delicate flowers. Her gloved arm was threaded through her father's, a jolly-looking man with round blue eyes spaced very close together. Tears were already streaming down his face into the bow tie around his fat neck. People said that daughters wanted to marry men like their fathers and Ivy could picture how in twenty years or so, Tom could develop the same thick neck, the red freckled cheeks. But age would never soften Tom to jolliness. He was one of the most unhappy people Ivy had ever met. Yet she couldn't pity him. His unhappiness, unlike Andrea's and Austin's and even Roux's, contained malice. It had the need to hurt others. In that way, Tom Cross and Nan Lin were alike.

Ivy had once asked Marybeth what it was about Tom that had first attracted her to him. Marybeth said, "He hates dumb women, loud women, flirtatious women, fat women, Catholic women, Jewish women, women who snore, women who can't drink . . . you get the idea. I thought, 'At least I'll never have to worry about him running off with some bimbo.' The opposite, actually. You should see the stack of HR complaints against him from his secretaries. Anyway, when he kept on asking me out, I thought there must have been something special about me. So I decided to give him a chance. I've always wondered, though, why me? I guess I'm marrying him to find out." Ivy thought of this now, watching Marybeth float down the aisle in a daze of serene happiness. What a reason for marrying someone. But then again, plenty of people got married for less.

The ceremony was tedious—there had already been the processional when they'd arrived at St. Mary's, and they still had to sit through the biblical readings, exchange of vows, exchange of rings, another prayer, the nuptial blessing, more prayers, singing. When Ivy wasn't looking at Gideon, her eyes kept returning to Tom's father, whose deep baritone voice was the loudest in the room as they sang "Ave Maria." During mass, he closed his eyes but his lips fluttered continuously without sound; every so often, he'd gesture at the ceiling as if conducting an invisible orchestra. When giving his speech at the reception, the elder Cross spoke about his son's devotion to God, his faith in the sacred matrimony in upholding God's will, his expectations for Tom in remaining a leader for the parish. Not once did the elder Cross mention Marybeth, who had long drained her champagne and was chewing ice cubes from her empty water glass.

"That was beautiful," Ivy whispered to Gideon as everyone clapped.

"It was lovely," Gideon said unsmilingly.

Then Gideon made his best man's speech—a short, lighthearted roast followed by funny stories showcasing Tom's finer traits. Near the end, Tom's face scrunched up like a dried apricot. Ivy thought he would start weeping again but he didn't. The guests laughed. Clapped. Toasted As soon as Gideon took his seat, white-gloved waiters served their appetizers out of heated gold platters. Contemporary American food with a Hawaiian twist. The portions were tiny, meant to take a backseat to the exotic garnishes: sprigs of emerald green, bright fuchsia spirals, a cluster of unnatural aqua-colored beads—"liquid nitrogen," someone explained to his neighbor. After they finished eating, the younger guests milled onto the makeshift dance floor on the sand,

surrounded by real torches, as a seven-piece band powered through rock renditions of traditional ballads. The star of the show was the Hawaiian pahu drum, played by a thickset Hawaiian woman in a grass skirt with two coconut shells for a bra and a pink-and-white lei swaying over her voluptuous breasts. It was as if she had looked up on the Internet what she was supposed to wear to look the part of who she was.

Ivy went to use the bathroom. A headache was forming as a result of mixing her liquors, and the pain throbbed harder with each beat of the drums. When she came back outside, Gideon handed her back her clutch. "Your phone's been buzzing this entire time," he said. "I was worried it was an emergency so I checked who was calling. Someone named Kang Ru?" Ivy nearly fainted from her idiocy. "It's one of my college friends," she said quickly. She took the phone from Gideon—twelve missed calls. She said a short prayer of gratitude that Roux wasn't the texting type. "I'll call him back later," she said, and turned off her phone. "Let's dance."

They joined the others on the dance floor. Gideon took off his jacket. Underneath he wore a light gray vest with satiny black buttons. She placed her hands lightly around his neck. They swayed slowly, foreheads pressed together. The last time they'd been this intimate was in the rooftop bathroom at the Gonford. It was another one of those things, like her LSAT score or Ted Speyer's first wife or Dave Finley's philandering ways, that they would never speak of. People like Roux and Nan thought love was speaking your mind—in the most forceful, unrestrained manner, the more unrestrained, the more loving—but Ivy had been with Gideon long enough to understand how delicate silence and restraint, that careful distillation of one's most unseemly thoughts, was the most loving and respectful gesture one could make toward one's spouse. Once upon a time, she'd found his careful control unsettling; now she found it not only admirable but also heroic. Anyone can lash out from anger. But it takes a special kind of man to gently declare to his fiancée: "I like everything about you," and devote his life to upholding the principle.

A group of Tom's cousins came and pulled Gideon away for a photo. Ivy saw Marybeth's aunt on the dance floor, twirling in circles. Ivy walked over, took the withered hands in her own, and began a jig. Through the terrace doors, she heard the chants of *shot, shot, shot, shot* and glimpsed Gideon's blond head tipping back. She glanced around the tables. There was no one else she knew at the wedding besides the bride and groom. This old white-haired woman who smelled of almonds was her only friend here.

Gideon came back four songs later, decidedly less steady on his feet. He was holding two glasses of champagne and spilled a little when he gave her one.

"Gideon, you're drunk!" She never thought she'd see the day.

Gideon rubbed his face. "I've had some shots. Tom made me. I can't remember how many."

A couple in matching purple and white leis danced over and tapped Gideon on the shoulder. Their names were Nettie and Hilton. They were from Ann Arbor. When Gideon introduced Ivy, they both shook her hand with two firm pumps and the same aw-shucks grins. It was something Ivy had noticed throughout the evening: how the couples at the Crosses' wedding resembled each other, in their speech patterns, coloring, temperament, if not directly in looks.

Nan used to talk about qìzhì, as in: "That woman has the best qìzhì among her siblings," or "You can't buy good qìzhì no matter how rich you are." Nan meant that this elusive quality was not something one could learn or imitate, but an aura you unconsciously emitted. Ivy didn't know if couples could grow to have the same qìzhì—like developing a similar taste for exotic foods—or if they purposely found partners with similar qìzhì, like how the most attractive man and woman in a room will instinctively gravitate toward each other. Then Ivy wondered whether her and Gideon's qìzhì matched—or did people see a couple who didn't quite fit together?

An old Grove alumnus came and said goodbye to Gideon. Ivy was reminded of the girls of her youth. Like faces from a storybook, she saw once more the svelte daisy-haired Satterfield twins, creamy-skinned Liza Johnson with the wide lips and catlike eyes, only they didn't seem like fourteen-year-old girls but fully formed women entirely capable of inflicting upon the present Ivy the loneliness and embarrassment she'd felt throughout her preteen years.

"Are you guys still friends with Nikki and Violet?" she asked Gideon. "And Liza Johnson. Didn't she date Tom for a while?"

Gideon's eyes went perfectly round. "That's right—you don't know."

"Know what?"

"They're dead."

Ivy said stupidly, "Who's dead?"

"Nikki and Liza."

"*What? How?*"

Gideon stopped jiggling his legs. "It was right before high school graduation. A freight truck came out of nowhere and T-boned their car. Jordan—Jordy, he's here somewhere—was driving. Chris was in the car, too. They were going to Panera. The guys were okay, but both the girls . . ." He gripped her shoulder. "Sorry, I thought everyone knew by now . . . The whole town came to the funeral. Nikki had an open casket but Liza's face was too badly mangled . . . Nikki, you re-member, had that long, blond hair? It was woven in braids around her head. Before they lowered her, Violet placed a flower crown on top of her hair. She looked like an angel . . . I'm sorry, that was morbid. Were you close friends with the girls?"

"No," said Ivy, "I barely knew them . . . It's so sad." A sensation like little icy feet pattered across her heart. Just seconds ago, she'd been jealous of them, these imaginary rivals. But these girls were dead now. Had been dead for years, for no reason at all.

"What about Una Kim?" she said. "What happened to Una?"

"Who's Una?"

Ivy shook her head. "Never mind."

Gideon was watching her with his head cocked. "You're a nice per-son. One of the nicest I've ever met."

"I'm not nice at all," she said, turning away.

"Well, I think you are." He mussed the top of her hair. This gesture felt so tenderly protective, so *brotherly*, that she was struck with the impulse to tell him everything. Her strong, dignified Gideon who would never hurt or disappoint her, who would know exactly what to say, and whose benevolent dignity would perhaps atone for her own mistakes and depravity. She would tell him she loved him, had always loved him, he'd been her idol and our childhood idols are evergreen. She was lonely, and sorry, and she wanted—wanted—

"I don't feel well," said Gideon. He placed one hand on his stomach, took a step back, and puked his dinner all over her patent leather Ralph Li-Ping stilettos.

THE NEXT MORNING, Gideon was in poor shape. He apologized profusely for his poor behavior, insisting that he would buy her the same pair of shoes when they got back to Boston, as she had thrown out the ones he'd puked over—the smell had been too offensive to pack into her carry-on. Then he choked down two Advils with a bottle of Perrier and slept the entire flight home.

After landing at Logan, he kissed her goodbye and took a cab straight to the office, as if in penance. Ivy waited until his cab rounded the corner before hopping in her own cab. "Astor Towers, please. On the corner of Summer and Hawley." She turned on her phone and called Roux.

She thought he would pick up on the first ring, having waited breathlessly all week for her call, but in fact, her call went twice to voicemail and she almost told the cabdriver to change destination before he finally picked up on her third try.

"Where were you?" he snapped.

"Hawaii."

"You don't have time to go on a trip with me but you have time to fly to fucking Hawaii?"

"I'm coming over," she said.

Tendrils of clouds drooped from the sky like shaggy gray sheep. From her cab window, she saw a woman in an arctic winter coat walking beside a teenager in a cropped jean jacket. March and April in Boston was a strange in-between time when people fell sick, dogs barked furiously at the sky, one day it was sunny and hot and the next, a blizzard was coming. She checked her phone's calendar. Sixty-nine days.

"Here's fine." She got out at the florist shop two blocks from Astor Towers. With great care, she selected one stem after another, the owner stating the names of each flower as if they were the names of her children: freesia, lisianthus, white spray chrysanthemums, penny-cress, eucalyptus, pittosporum.

"Sixty-nine eighty-six, please."

Ivy pulled out a hundred from her wallet. It was Roux's money, the money she'd stolen from him, which would now be used to buy his own consolation flowers.

He opened the door before she even rang the doorbell. "I saw you coming into the building," he said wanly, a cigarette stub hanging from his cracked lips. Brushing past him, she smelled the familiar rank odor of a hangover, and something foreign and fragrant. Roux was shirtless and wearing, of all things, blue hospital scrubs for pants, the ends of the cotton drawstrings hanging down to his thighs.

"Where'd you get those?"

He glanced down. "The hospital."

"You were in the hospital?"

"No."

"Then whose are they?"

He shrugged.

Then Ivy understood the reason for his odd, disheveled manner. She'd thought the strange fragrance came from the flowers but now she realized the scent wasn't one bit floral but entirely synthetic and distinctly *female*, like the smell of a department store makeup counter.

"Wild night?" she said.

"Why haven't you been answering my calls?"

"What's her name?"

He refused to answer.

"I guess you didn't ask. And here I was going to console you." She thrust the bouquet at him. He didn't take it. "Let's stop this, Roux," she said. "It's not fun anymore. I'm getting married in sixty-nine days. You've obviously moved on as well. Let's call a spade a spade."

He eyed her with bleary exhaustion. "Calm down."

"I am calm." She placed the flowers on his coffee table and went to the kitchen to fill a vase with water. He followed her.

"I was drunk last night."

"You're always drunk."

"I don't want to fight this early in the morning."

"It's not a fight. It's goodbye."

He opened the fridge and poured himself a glass of orange juice, drinking it in large gulps with a little bit trickling down the corners of his mouth.

She couldn't believe she had ever found this man attractive.

"I mean it," she said. "I never want to see or hear from you again. It's over. I came here to tell you that in person. For the sake of our friendship."

He wiped his lips on the back of his hand. "*Our friendship?* We're back to that? When are you going to stop *lying*—"

"You *knew* I was marrying Gideon—"

"I thought you would leave him!"

Ivy opened her mouth, closed it. "When have I ever said that?" she said finally.

"Last summer. At the Speyers' house."

"That was before I was engaged."

"You came to me a month later. You couldn't stay away. You hate your life. You bitch about the Speyers, about their goody-goody friends. You wanted me to *save you*."

"That's ridiculous," Ivy snapped. "I've never asked you for anything besides sex. I thought we were in agreement about that part."

He eyed her compassionately. "You're punishing me. For the other day."

She denied this with an impatient toss of her head. "Don't be ridiculous. I was always going to end things with you before my wedding." She could tell by Roux's glazed obstinance that she wasn't getting through to him. Never does a woman lie in a more cunning way than when she tells the truth to a man who doesn't believe her. Frustrated, she turned on the tap and began filling the vase with water.

"You tell Gideon you're leaving him or I'll tell him myself."

She turned off the tap. "What did you say?"

"You heard me."

For a moment, she didn't take him seriously. And then, she did. An incredulous fury rose in her, the fury of a master in the face of mutiny. She could tolerate violence but she couldn't tolerate violation.

"If you do that," she said, "it's over between us. I'll hate you. I'll *hate you.*"

"*Ah,*" said Roux, "but I thought it was already over between us." Her anger had reanimated him. Given him the impression he had the upper hand.

"Let me tell you how this is going to go," he said. "You'll get married. I'll go away like a dog with my tail between my legs. Once you get bored playing house, you'll call me. It's the same shit over and over. Stop deluding yourself about your fake marriage."

Ivy took two steps forward, raised her arm, and let the vase fall from her hand.

"What the—"

Glass shards splattered across the kitchen floor. Roux, barefoot, leapt back, his ears glowing red like two coals on either side of his pale head. "Are you crazy?"

She didn't respond. There came the sound of ice cubes tumbling in the freezer. "Going to slap me again?" she asked.

Roux shook his head over and over, cursing under his breath. The thought floated through Ivy's head that she might stop by Gideon's office later to bring him takeout from his favorite Greek place. He'd probably be working all night again. They had a big meeting coming up in Costa Rica with some important minister. Roux was on one knee, picking up broken glass with fistfuls of napkins. Broken glass on a kitchen floor—that was Roux's world. Meaningful work, efficient tasks, decisions based on logic and clear-cut goals—that was Gideon's world, the place he carried with him wherever he went, a place immune to the sordid, the trivial, the violent, the shameful, the poor. And Roux was trying to take it away from her.

He was still ranting, all threats no doubt, as if she needed some tough love to come to her senses. Like most men, he'd liked her passion when he was the cause of it, but her own passion, passion that had nothing to do with him, was dismissed as foolishness. Nothing she would say now could convince him to take her seriously. He couldn't afford to.

Ivy remembered something. "If you ruin my marriage," she interrupted, "I'm going to ruin your life. I know the Morettis are part of the mob. I'll go to the police, the Feds."

He actually started to smile. "*The mob?* Ivy, you don't know shit about what I do."

"All money is traceable, virtual or real." It was something Sylvia had said during the launch party, when she and Jeremy were still discussing how the mob operated.

Roux's smile froze.

Ivy's instincts zeroed in on the bullseye. "I'll go on record against you. I know about the house in Evansville. The cement you poured over your basement. The casinos, those converted warehouses." She tossed out all the jargon she'd ever heard: *testify, witness, mob, racketeering, embezzlement, gambling* . . . She watched his body straighten, the arms uncross, the fingers curl in the air as if grasping at an invisible handle. The mouth could lie but the body never lied.

Roux leaned in. "Have you ever seen what a gun looks like up close?" He saw her slap coming and grabbed her wrist. Their eyes locked.

"You disgust me," she said. "You're an animal. You're worse than an animal. You're a—a criminal."

"I'm a gambler," he said curtly, turning his back to her and walking to the sofa. She unwillingly followed him. He stared out the balcony for a long time. She was afraid to break the silence lest he was in the midst of some epiphany concerning the truth of her words.

"I'll make you a wager," he said finally. "Tell Gideon about our affair. If he still marries you—I'll give you half my net worth."

Ivy couldn't contain her guffaw. She should have seen this coming. With Roux, it always came down to the price tag.

He gestured toward the bedroom. "You think I haven't noticed you've been stealing from me? Who else would accept you, Ivy, if they knew the real you? You fumble around your life like a deaf-mute person. You can't pick a career, you can't pick a man. You have no idea what you want."

"Do you hear yourself?" she exploded. "The *real me*? You—don't—know—me. We've *literally* just met again after a decade."

"People never change."

"Oh, for fuck's sake."

Roux strode to the door and pulled it open. "This is becoming tedious."

Her face contorted. Control was a zero-sum game between them: one had to suck it from the other.

"Two weeks," he said, propping the door open with his foot. "If I find out you still haven't told precious Gideon, I'll have a talk with him. My offer still stands. If you tell him—"

"Roux—"

"*If you tell him* and he forgives you, then I was wrong about everything. I'll gladly pay up. And if he *doesn't* take you back, well, I guess my money won't seem so filthy after all."

"You're so—"

"Go."

"Fuck you."

"*Go.*"

She reached down, pulled off one shoe, and flung it with all her might at his head. The heel struck the wall near his left shoulder, leaving a black smudge the size of a quarter.

"That's more like it," he said. "You're more honest when you're angry."

She flew at him but he was ready. He practically tossed her into the hallway, barring her way back inside with his steely arms. Dignity abandoned, Ivy called him all manner of names, insulted his mother, his lowly birth, called him corrupt, berated his corrupt mind, his disgusting habits, his cowardly nature, his lack of integrity. At her last insult, Roux pulled out his wallet and showered her with a fistful of crumpled bills. "There's your integrity," he said, and slammed the door.

SEX WAS A kind of sickness, Ivy realized, and that sickness began and ended with Roux. Maybe there was a kind of logic to Tom's father's fanaticism with God, worshipping an honest and righteous deity who would never betray you. She wondered if such devotion stemmed from willpower or from something else, a deeper secret to life she had never known. All her life she had had secrets. They had held her up like stilts on quicksand, without which she would have sunk long ago, just another one of Sylvia's sheep waiting to be led to slaughter. She felt she had to take control of her life. But how? *I am the one controlling my life, am I not?* she asked herself.

These thoughts ran through her head, without beginning or end. She told Gideon to stay away so he wouldn't catch her cold before his big meeting. Then she threw all pride out the window and called Roux. Begging was also a form of taking control. She pleaded with him to see the futility of his demand. This will change nothing, she said, you're only hurting innocent people. "Are you referring to Gideon or your-self," said Roux, "because neither of you are what I'd call innocent." Just *listen* to me, Ivy had shouted, *just listen!* He stopped answering her calls after that. In the stifling afternoon silence of her bedroom, her eyes strayed to a different day now on the calendar—the deadline Roux had given her to expose their affair to Gideon, unmarked on the page but permanently emblazoned in her mind with a large black X. Twelve days . . . eleven . . . ten . . .

She received an email from a law school consultant, one of Liana's friends. For an affordable rate of eight thousand dollars, she could provide services such as essay and interview preparation and weekly online study sessions for the LSAT. Ivy half-heartedly agreed to think about it but then she lost the consultant's phone number. Studying, in the midst of such a crisis, felt as absurd as trying to toast bread as the house was burning down. She took to stalking Astor Towers, pounding on Roux's door—"Goddamn it, I know you're in there!"—but he never answered. No matter how long she waited or how hard she pressed her ear to the door, she heard nothing from the other side. Reckless plans flew through her mind in lieu of sleep. She and Gideon could go off the grid and live with-out computers or phones so Roux would never be able to find them. She could fake their deaths. She could go to the FBI and enroll in the Witness Protection Program in exchange for giving them informa-tion on Roux and the Morettis. But Roux could still make calls and send letters from prison, couldn't he? When she realized that there was no way to prevent two people from making contact in this day and age, her hope of changing Roux's mind turned into fantasies of how to punish him afterward. Tarring and feathering. Chinese water torture. Taking a machete to his precious cars—but no, he could just buy more. *Afterward.* What a terrible word. She couldn't stop herself from looking down the fissure that would soon divide the before and *afterward*, the Confession itself. In how many ways could Gideon leave her? In one version, he was angry, he called her a slut, a whore, an immoral woman, he shouted that he hated her, that he never wanted to see her again. In another version, he was heartbroken—he hadn't thought she was capable of causing him such pain, he would never forgive her, he wished they'd never met. The last scenario—the one that kept her tossing into the night—was the one where he was indifferent. *I never really loved you. You're not the girl I thought you were.*

One evening, the thought came to her that if she quit smoking, she would be able to regain control of her life. Since she'd lit her first cigarette in Roux's bedroom at fourteen, she'd never gone longer than a week without smoking. She decided to quit cold turkey. Impose her will upon her weak body. She took to walking the streets. Every corner she turned, every back alley, in front of every bar and club and café, she saw people smoking in their warm circle of companionship and commiseration, a commiseration she was now excluded from. Without even thinking, she drifted up to an old man with a tattoo sleeve and a chef's apron and asked if she could bum one off him. He stuck his cigarette in his mouth and pulled out a pack of Lucky Strikes from his back pocket. The decisive way he clicked his lighter and shielded her flame from the wind felt like the greatest kindness she'd ever been shown. The minute she threw the stub into the sewer, she hurried into a pharmacy and bought her own pack of Lucky Strikes, practically salivating, her hands shaking, pupils dilating. She smoked half the pack walking back home, one cigarette after the other, overcome with a wonderful oblivion. When she finished, she called Roux. He didn't answer. This was expected. She had, after all, failed to quit smoking. Tomorrow, she thought. Tomorrow I can quit.

Andrea came home from her date at two in the morning and found Ivy playing solitaire in the living room. An empty bottle of red wine was lying on its side on the carpet. Andrea sniffed the bottle, then made a face. "Is this what I used to make beef bourguignon last week?" Ivy shrugged. Maybe it was the alcohol blurring her vision, but Andrea appeared to be radiating lustful vigor, her shiny hair tumbling in loose waves, carrying her flesh not with her usual self-consciousness but with a sensual ease that spoke of a delightful evening around a fire, with copious bottles of wine, having sex until dawn, sex Ivy was no longer having with anyone.

"He asked me today how a person knows if they've found the right one," said Andrea.

"Who is this?" Ivy was in the middle of contemplating if she could pay one of the gangsters to stand in front of Astor Towers and send her updates on Roux's whereabouts so she might ambush him.

"The guy I've been seeing, Norman."

"I can't keep track of your man parade," said Ivy.

Andrea, too giddy to be offended, was only too willing to relay to Ivy everything about Norman Moorefield she'd probably already said countless times before. They'd met at Dave Finley's party two weeks ago. He was involved with the start-up in some important capacity, blah, blah, he was so romantic, she had never felt this way about anyone, and did Ivy think they were moving too fast, or if you know, then you know? A warm cheek pressed against Ivy's shoulder. "I want to have children so bad," came a tortured whisper . . . Ivy struggled to open her eyes; she felt something wet on her skin . . .

She woke up the next day gasping from another sweaty nightmare. She'd fallen asleep on the sofa. Andrea must have covered her with the throw. The deck of poker cards was splayed out on the coffee table in a perfect fan except for the queen of hearts, which had been torn into little pieces and piled on the side. Had she done that? She vaguely recalled being unable to stop moving her hands, shuffling cards, painting her nails, picking at her cuticles until they bled. She went to the bathroom and observed the ghastly sight, thrown into relief by the harsh midday light: a white and bloated face, red-rimmed lids, swollen lips, a monstrous pimple growing on her chin. Checking her phone, she saw it was already three in the afternoon.

She couldn't remember the last time she'd eaten. The gnawing pain in her stomach suddenly pierced her from belly to head, leaving her doubled over the sink. She went to the kitchen and dug out a can of Progresso soup and an old packet of oyster crackers from the takeout drawer with all the delivery menus. Food tasted strange these days—tinny, everything flavored with anchovy. Her teeth felt tender, she chewed the crackers very slowly; when she brushed her teeth afterward, her gums bled and wouldn't stop until she stuffed cotton balls in her mouth.

Gideon came over Saturday evening . . . or was it Sunday? Ivy peeked at her phone underneath her pillow. It was Sunday. One week left. Seven days. One hundred and sixty-eight hours. Maybe she could beg Roux for more time, say she was ill. Surely he would grant her that at least.

Outside, it was hailing. The weatherman that morning had announced that another cold spell was coming from the north. Heavy snowstorms all week. The weatherman was her only companion these days; he talked to her for hours in his repetitive but soothing voice, always delivering warnings: cloudy skies . . . visibility poor . . . lows around twelve degrees with windchill . . .

There was a deep V between Gideon's brows.

"Sorry?" said Ivy.

"I said are you feeling better?"

"Yeah."

"Those look quite itchy."

Ivy covered the hives around her wrists with the sleeves of her bathrobe.

"What happened?"

"Allergic reaction to a bracelet," she said.

"I noticed you had something similar on your neck last week."

Ivy's heart lurched. She'd thought she'd covered all the bruises and marks from her fight with Roux with concealer, but had Gideon seen through it? Had she not been careful enough? But his attentive, serene face revealed nothing.

"Have you been eating? You look thin." He sniffed the air. "Is your neighbor having a cookout? It smells like something's burning."

"I think Andrea was cooking earlier."

"Have you seen a doctor yet? You feel a bit feverish."

"No."

"You might need antibiotics to kick this cold."

"I said I'm fine!" Instantly engulfed with remorse at the way he recoiled from her, she softened her tone. "I don't have a fever. I promise I'll go see the doctor if I get one . . . Anyway, tell me about your day."

But her attention immediately wandered away from Gideon's voice. She studied his face. Such a wonderfully symmetrical and *right* face. She traced in her mind the aristocratic brow, down the slope of his nose, brushed invisible fingers over his long, brown lashes, the sharp point of his chin, the plump dent of his Cupid's bow . . . Shuddering, she realized she was memorizing his features for future recollection.

It was silent. Gideon was looking at her. Ivy realized he was waiting for a response.

"Should I let you sleep?" he said quietly.

She squeezed her eyes shut. Did she want sleep? Yes, she wanted to sleep and wake up and have Roux Roman be dead.

"I feel bad I won't be here for the next two weeks."

Her eyes flew open. "Wait, where're you going?"

He smiled ruefully. "I suppose it's dreadfully dull to listen to me talk about work all the time."

Ivy dropped her gaze guiltily.

"But yes. Two weeks in Costa Rica with the team."

"Oh, right . . . Is there cell service down there?" She was thinking that if Roux tried to contact him, he wouldn't be able to answer his phone.

Gideon assured her that he had international coverage; plus the resort had fiber optic Wi-Fi, so all her calls would come through. Ivy's teeth began chattering. The torpor of procrastination had given way to adrenaline-pumping panic. Gideon would be gone for two weeks. Past Roux's deadline. She would have to confess now if she wanted to tell him about Roux in person. She felt like that cartoon roadrunner who'd suddenly come to the edge of the cliff.

"Hey—what's wrong?" said Gideon, noticing her agitation. "This isn't just because you're sick. What is it?" Her chin quivered. "Tell me, sweetheart." It was the first time he'd used this endearment. There was a pain in Ivy's heart, she recognized it as despair. She was out of time, she would have to tell him. She tried to speak, but she only took shallow inhales.

"Is it the wedding? Has Mom been inserting her oar too much?"

"No," said Ivy, "it's not that." Inserting her oar. How she would miss his old-fashioned phrases. "It's me," she said. "I've . . ." Her tongue stuck to the roof of her mouth. She reached for her water and chugged the entire glass down, praying for courage. "Do you remember last summer? Since we got back from Cattahasset, I've been feeling kind of confused and lonely. So I . . ."

"I'm listening."

"I . . ."

"Did you cheat on me or something?"

Ivy jerked away with the same instinct as a child too near a fire. "*What?* Why would you say that?"

"Never mind," he said hastily, patting her knee. "Poor joke. What were you saying about Cattahasset?"

But the unexpected directness of Gideon's question had completely rattled her.

"I was saying how—" Her mind seized onto the first thing to confess, a truth of a different kind. "I'm not going to retake the LSAT. I don't want to be lawyer."

There was an almost comical pause as both of them took in her words in equal surprise. Could he hear her heart pounding its traitorous beat from her rib cage?

Gideon crossed his arms in the way he did whenever he was about to have a serious discussion. "Really? What made you change your mind?"

Now that that particular Band-Aid had been pulled off, Ivy found sweet relief in pouring out her honest feelings. She said she'd been lying to herself, she didn't think she was cut out for law, she didn't like the long hours, the tedious reading, the cutthroat environment.

"So you want to go back to teaching?"

She hesitated, trying to read in his attentive expression whether this would be acceptable. ". . . No."

"Then what do you want to do?"

"I want to . . ." But she was *tired*, goddamn it, she didn't want to *do* anything. She rubbed her aching eyes. "Honestly, no one's really asked me that before. I took on teaching to avoid having to go to medical school. My parents always wanted me to be a doctor. They were worried I wouldn't be able to find a job. That I wouldn't marry well."

"What does marriage have to do with it?"

Oh, Gideon! How could she expect him to understand? And how fiercely she loved him for not understanding. "You're not mad at me?" she said.

"About not wanting to go be a lawyer?" He frowned. "Why on earth would I be mad at you? You can do whatever makes you happy . . . *This* is what's been bothering you this entire time? What do you think I am, an ogre? Listen, you don't want to be a lawyer or teacher—fine with me. You're smart and resourceful"—Ivy flinched—"so why don't you take as long as you need to figure out what you really want to do?"

"But timing-wise . . ." She trailed off in embarrassment, because she couldn't say that the money her parents had given her for rent, for the wedding, was running out and she couldn't possibly ask them for more. Unless she accepted Roux's offer, in which case she would lose Gideon and what would be the point of having money *then*? . . . Money, money, accursed money, that rabid, tenacious hound that'd been nipping at her heels all her life, so that she could never, never get ahead.

"After we're married, we'll move in together so you won't have to worry about rent, at least," Gideon said, neatly reading her mind in his tactful way.

After we're married . . . ! If there had been a knife on her table, she would have picked it up right then and plunged it into her heart. The pain would have to be in proportion to her remorse.

Gideon was rubbing her back in smooth circular motions, as if he was soothing a skittish horse. "In the future," he said, "just talk to me. There's nothing we can't get through together." She nodded feebly. "That's settled then." He picked up her empty glass. "Orange juice, tea, or more water?"

"Tea, please."

After he left, Ivy decided she had no choice left but to kill herself. When a young person dies, their love remains pure and everlasting. People go to their funerals and say poignant things about them. Call them angels. She could be Gideon's angel. Perhaps Roux might even kill himself in repentance. The only thing Ivy knew with absolute certainty was that she would rather face death than betray Gideon's trust, and what the hell was that sound—

Her phone was buzzing. Both hoping and fearing it was Roux, she lunged to see the caller ID. It was only Nan. Ivy ignored it. Nan called three more times in succession. Ivy was about to silence the call for the fourth time when the idea popped into her mind that somehow Roux had gotten in contact with Nan. Perhaps they were in on it together. She picked up.

"Now's not a good time, Mama. I'm in bed with a cold . . . Hello?"

There was a clamor of voices followed by beeping sounds. "Hello? Hello? It's Mama. Can you hear me? Grandma's in the hospital. You should come home."

19

MEIFENG HAD SLIPPED IN THE SHOWER AND FRACTURED HER HIP. She's fine, said Nan, but she needs hip replacement surgery. Gideon insisted that he drive Ivy to Clarksville. "You've been sick all week," he said firmly, "and besides, your car's always acting up. We're supposed to be getting a lot of snow."

"But your trip . . ."

"There's time."

The supposed storm brewing from the Atlantic hadn't yet hit Boston, but Ivy could smell the sharp cold of something big coming when she rolled down the passenger window, somewhere in upstate New York. "I'm getting nauseous," she said to Gideon, who sensed the emergency right away and pulled over. She opened the car door and threw up the soup, the oyster crackers. She rinsed her mouth with a bottle of spring water and Gideon kept driving.

They arrived at Presbyterian Hospital just past midnight. Nothing about the Jersey landscape had changed: the same potholes on Route 1, the smell of cow manure, the flat strip malls, the smog blowing over from the factories in Elizabeth. Nan met them at the elevator on the fourth floor. Her face seemed to have aged a decade, two ashy streaks of hair pulled back on either side of her head like bleached straw, the broken green veins pulsing under her pallid skin. She seemed flustered by Gideon's presence, touching her neck often as she spoke in Chinese, glancing over her shoulder as if expecting Shen to translate her awk-

ward explanations to fluent English. "Grandma just came out of surgery," she informed Ivy. "She's still under sedation, but you can go in.
They said only one person can be in the room at a time." Gideon tactfully left to fetch them some coffee. Ivy went in. Meifeng was asleep
with an oxygen tube in her nose. Her lips were slightly opened and
cracked. Occasionally the devices attached to her arms made strange
beeping sounds, but no nurses came hurrying in. The heart, that wondrous heart, continued to beat on.

She held her grandmother's dry palm until Nan stuck her head in
the room in a state of overblown panic—"The doctor's here, come,
come! Oh, your baba had to go use the bathroom *now*. His weak
stomach . . ." Ivy went back outside to translate for her mother. The
attending said everything went smoothly, it'd been a fairly standard
procedure. He launched into a detailed, convoluted medical explanation neither women could follow. Nan kept tugging Ivy's hand—
"What's he saying, what's he saying?"—and Ivy would hush her
mother. "He said she'll be fine . . . let me listen . . ." Indeed, Ivy gave
every appearance of listening intently, but blossoming under her relief for Meifeng's well-being was the furtive, murmuring observation
that this doctor was young and handsome, with curly, light brown hair
and a cleft on his chin, like Superman. Standing in a deferential line,
two feet behind him, was an entourage of nurses, residents, students.
Every place where humans gathered, there would be a food chain.
Someone had to be on top.

The blue scrubs the doctor wore were the same ones Ivy had seen
on Roux a week ago. She tried to picture Roux here at Presbyterian,
a surgeon, giving them reassuring updates on Meifeng. If she married Roux, Nan would be pleased. "My son-in-law is a surgeon," Nan
would brag to her sisters. Ivy would massage his shoulders after his
operations. She would organize hospital fundraisers, like Liana Finley, and open gift baskets Roux's grateful patients would send to their
house. This pretty scene made Ivy's heart lighten for a second. Then
she remembered. Roux wasn't a doctor. On him, the scrubs had been

a costume. Roux hadn't even finished high school. Roux's mother had died in the apartment her married lover paid for. Roux was the opposite of a healer, he inflicted violence.

She felt like being sick again, but there was nothing left to puke up.

"Considering her age," the doctor concluded, "we'll have to monitor her here for a few days. Not to worry—we'll do our best to get her home as quickly as possible. The longer her stay, the higher the risk of infection . . . I'll just take a quick look . . ." He stepped into Meifeng's room and performed his perfunctory checkup while the rest of his entourage crowded at the threshold of the door, scribbling down every word he said. Soon after, the horde of white coats departed like the tide pulling back to the sea, leaving behind an emptiness that was not yet relief, only the deflation of action. Nan asked Ivy if she and Gideon had eaten yet.

"No . . . we drove straight down after you called."

Nan clucked with worry. "You two should go to our house and heat up the leftovers."

Ivy said Gideon had to drive back right away for an early flight the next morning.

"Here and back in one night. Won't he be tired? What if he falls asleep and gets into an accident?"

Ivy didn't argue. She was exhausted, even though she'd done nothing. She'd done nothing all week. How draining futility was.

Nan spotted Shen hurrying down the hall. Her expression morphed from concern to irritation so fast it gave Ivy whiplash. "*Where* have you *been* . . ."

Gideon was walking a few strides behind Shen. "I'm sorry to be rushing off like this," he said, handing Ivy a Styrofoam cup of coffee.

With that same superhuman liquidity, Nan's face smoothed into a motherly smile. In broken English, she thanked him for coming all this way and apologized for being such a bother. She told him to drive slowly on the way back and to let them know when he arrived in Boston.

"I'll call you tomorrow to see how things are," Gideon said quietly in Ivy's ear.

"I love you," she whispered painfully. He kissed her, shook Shen's hand, then kissed Nan's cheek. Nan colored; her hand rose again to her neck.

They all remained standing until the elevator door closed on Gideon's smiling face.

"He's a good man," said Shen.

"Very reliable," Nan agreed.

Ivy touched her eyes. They were wet. Nan eyed her daughter suspiciously. "Go get us some water," she told Shen.

"She has coffee."

"*I* want some water. We'll be in the waiting room." She marched Ivy down the hall. The minute the door closed behind them, Nan said, "What's wrong with you?"

Ivy sank into a plastic armchair and reached for the box of tissues on the rickety side table. She felt as if she were trapped in one of her garish nightmares. Six hours ago, she'd been lying in her own bed in Boston. Now her grandmother was breathing through an oxygen tube and she was stuck with her mother in the waiting room of a hospital, watching a late-night talk show with the volume muted on the little television set mounted in the corner.

"You look even worse than Austin," Nan said severely. "No color in your face at all. Have you been trying to lose weight?"

"I'll stay the night here with Grandma," said Ivy. "Why don't you and Baba go home."

Nan's face softened. "Grandma will be fine. American nurses are very capable. We can come back first thing tomorrow morning. Is that why you're crying?"

"I don't know."

"Did you fight with Gideon? Is he mistreating you?"

"What? No. We don't fight."

Though they were alone in the room, Nan lowered her voice. "Is it another woman? You can tell Mama."

Ivy blanched. Not for the first time, she wondered from what twisted depths her mother's thoughts bubbled from.

"*A-ya*, are you still so thin-skinned? . . . Sit up straight!" Nan pounded Ivy's spine reproachfully. "You look like a hunchback. Don't think you can just become ugly after you get married."

"I'm not getting married."

"What are you saying? Not getting married!"

"Gideon's going to call off the wedding."

Nan's brows rose to her hairline. After a brief silence, she said, "What have you done?"

"You probably can't even get your money back for the wedding."

"Bah—money. Who cares about that?"

Ivy laughed hollowly and pointed out that Nan had *just* been complaining about Meifeng's hospital bills.

"They're two separate things," Nan dismissed. She snatched away the pen Ivy had been fiddling with. "Money isn't the only indicator of success. It's a man's breeding that counts. The goodness that runs in his veins. Money can't buy that."

"Oh for God's sake," said Ivy, "not this *qizhi* crap again." She retrieved her pen and clicked it furiously into her palms.

"It takes more than love to make a good marriage," Nan went on, not listening to her. "Only a fool would think otherwise. Rich people are no fools. Don't underestimate your man. He's ambitious, I can tell. No one is that careful if they don't have grand plans. He walks with such importance, always watching all of us to see how we fit into his life. I see him look at you sometimes. Trying to see if you can help him on his way."

"On his way to *what*?"

Nan waved this aside. "Men rarely talk. They only act. Do you remember Aunt Ping's friend's son, Kevin Zhao?"

"No."

"Do you remember anything in that thick head of yours? He's that boy who came up to Boston to meet you last year."

"So?"

Nan's voice held a trace of pride as she announced that Kevin was married now to a girl from Yunnan. "A ballet dancer. He just finished medical school and got offered a job at the hospital. They just bought a house, right in Clarksville. Only twenty-nine years old." She shook her head nostalgically. "It took me and Baba until we were in our forties to buy our first home. And we still had to borrow money. But Kevin's bought his wife a house. He sends money to his wife's parents . . . What has Gideon done for you? You come to Baba for money because you don't trust your future husband. He should have at least offered to help you pay for law school."

"He did offer." This was technically true.

"Really?"

"But I've changed my mind. I'm not going to law school anymore."

Nan didn't seem one bit surprised. "There's a saying in Chinese: 'Husband and wife are like birds in the woods, when trouble comes, they flee separately.'"

"That's optimistic," said Ivy. "Did you get that one from Grandma?"

"You know what the secret is to a lasting marriage?"

"Separate bedrooms?"

Nan weighed this seriously for a moment. "No. I'll tell you everything . . . Before Baba, I was involved with a young man from my village. You've heard the story from Grandma?" When Ivy dropped her gaze—she was recalling the time back in high school when she'd screamed, *You died with that boyfriend of yours back in China, we're just your replacement family!*—Nan said shrewdly, "What did Grandma tell you exactly?"

Ivy was too embarrassed to go into the intimate details—she still felt mortified at the idea of speaking to her mother about any topics related to sex or romance—and so she summarized Meifeng's story as, "She said she forced you two apart by sending you to live with your aunt. You never forgave her. Your boyfriend ended up dying in the work camps . . . someone killed him for stealing a sweet potato." This last detail had been the source of many nightmares growing up.

Nan frowned. "*That's* what she's been going around saying this en-

tire time? Even after all this time, my own mother still can't understand me." Ivy snorted but the irony went right over Nan's head. "The
truth is," Nan went on, "I did love him for a while—Anming Wu. But
it wasn't what my mother imagined."

"I'VE NEVER CARED that much about looks, but I was told my whole
life that I was pretty. I had ideas, too, about what I wanted for my
life. You have to understand what those times were like. Everyone we
knew was being carted off. Relative against relative. Neighbors turning
into spies. The Wus—they were a corrupt family. They bribed officials in Beijing to keep their *qipao* business afloat. Anming thought that
made him immune to the dangers of his background. He went around
talking about his money as if it were a bulletproof suit. I was young. I
was taken in by his promises of a future where I would be the *taitai* of
his family, living an easy life. Oh, I fell in love with him all right, at least
the version he presented of himself.

"One night after the school festival, we were alone in the changing
room, he threw himself on top of me. I tried to fight him off, but he
was strong and convincing. I told myself it was all right, he loved me,
he would do right by me. I was so dumb it seemed inconceivable that
this was anything other than the first step to a marriage proposal.

"After that incident, I waited for his words of love and promise. I
waited for months. Then one day, I was walking back from the factory
and I saw him behind a tree with another girl from school. His hand
was up her shirt. I saw him clearly for the first time. I realized I had
been used. He never had any inclination to marry me—why would
he? My parents were poor farmers, without money or connections,
supporting four daughters. I had nothing to offer his family.

"I was scared out of my mind. Another woman in the village had
been driven away for getting caught with a boy in the rice paddies. Her
shame was known in three counties. Her father—the village butcher—
lost all his customers; her mother committed suicide. I was terrified

this would happen to me, and then not only would my prospects be ruined but my sisters' as well. Also, Anming had a big mouth—look how much he bragged about his family's secrets, their money, their government connections. I had to get him far away from me. I thought about how to do this for days, and finally came up with the solution.

"There was a staunch Communist who lived in the outskirts named Mu Xiao. She was a fanatic Mao follower desperate to prove herself to rise in rank. In an anonymous letter, I wrote down everything Anming had told me about his family's corrupt ways—which officials they had bribed, how much money they had hiding underneath their floorboards, his family's right-wing political sympathies, all of it. She used the letter to orchestrate his family's arrest to get herself promoted to section leader. The Wus were sent to prison—the government officials they had dealings with were executed—and all the children, including Anming, were sent to the countryside. You could say that I singlehandedly ruined the Wus. Who knows? If not for my letter, maybe their protection would have lasted past the revolution. I was sorry when I heard he died. I cried bitterly and prayed for my soul for months afterward. But I would do it again if I had to.

"Around this time, I became aware of a boy in my aunt's town who I knew had been pining for me. He wasn't the best-looking man but he was smart, from a long line of scholars. His mother was a nurse; his father was the chairman of a hospital. I liked Shen Lin immediately. He didn't speak much but he was reliable. He came to the factory every day and gave me a hard-boiled egg. I cursed him for it at first. I told him if I ate too much, I got hungrier, and he said that was all right because he would give me all the eggs I could eat, as much as I wanted. I told him I wanted twenty eggs. The next day, he came with a bag of twenty eggs. I told my mother I found the bag on the side of the road.

"Many girls liked Shen, or they liked his family's circumstances, but he didn't look twice at them. He had heard the rumors that I was in love with a dead man, but curiously, it made him want me more.

"After asking around, I found out that the Lins were known for two things: their hard work ethic, and their weakness for gambling. They would work themselves to death to attain something, only to bet it all away on a whim. Shen was on track to become a doctor in the local hospital, and I was sick of Xing Chang, sick of taking care of an ailing father, sick of my sisters, and most of all, sick of my mother, who had worshipped the Wus all her life, licking their boots and fawning over their children. I wanted to get away from her most of all.

"One day, when Shen passed me on the street, I made sure he heard me telling my friend how badly I wanted to leave China to go to America. That I wished there was a man who had ambitions of living abroad. I heard rumors shortly afterward that Shen told his father he wasn't going to become a doctor, he was going to take the TOEFL exam. After he passed, he came around my house and proposed. I made a bit of a fuss about it, then accepted.

"You used to ask how your father and I got married. That's how. It was because I willed it. If I had been a stupider girl, your father never would have looked at me. But I saw my chance and made a story for myself—even if it was a false story. You have to give a man something to fight for. That's the secret to a lasting marriage."

WHEN NAN STOPPED speaking, Ivy could only stare. She dug the pen deep into her palm.

Meifeng once told her a bedtime story about the frog who lived in an old well. The frog was born in the cold and dark well; all it knew of the outside world was the faint light far above it, which it took to be the sun. One day, a bird flew down into the well and said to the frog, "Come up to the outside world where it is bright and warm." The frog laughed at the bird, thinking that the well was, in fact, the entire world. Ivy could see that she'd been the frog, thinking her suffering unique, specific to her Chinese family, her particular circumstances. But she was just another desperate girl who'd dreamed of beautiful things, dreams Nan must've also had at her age. Nan, who, like Ivy, had fought to escape. Not only to escape but to thrive, she'd fought with everything she had to *get what she wanted*.

"I admit—I was disapproving at first when I heard you weren't marrying a Chinese man," said Nan. "But you've always known your own mind. So don't worry—your family won't disappoint you. We won't get in your way." Nan's voice cracked. Ivy realized that her mother assumed the Lins were the reason Gideon was calling off the wedding.

"Stop that!" Nan snatched the pen from where Ivy had been digging it into her palm. She took Ivy's hand and ran the tips of her fingers down the web of grooves.

"Don't ruin your hands. You've always had beautiful hands. Look at this. A long life line." She traced the bottommost line. "A fractured love line. A precarious wealth line. That's the luck you were born with." She closed Ivy's fingers into a fist. "You know how we picked out your name? In Chinese, Jiyuan means 'to chance one's luck.' Now is no time to turn lazy. Pull yourself together. Now—what are you going to do about your wedding?"

IT WAS HALF past two in the morning when Ivy stepped foot in her old bedroom in Clarksville. Everything was the same as she'd left it when she'd gone off to college, vowing never to return. Her old clothes were folded neatly in the drawers, the boxy T-shirts with yellowing collars, shiny theater costumes from Drama Club, rubber flip-flops and canvas shoes flattened in a cardboard box. In the bottommost drawer of her desk was her old Baby-Sitters scrapbook where she'd glued cutouts of skinny white girls with braces, pretending they were her friends.

She ran a finger over the photo frame on the nightstand—she and Austin standing at the bus stop in their oversized winter parkas—and her finger brought up no dust. There was no dust, either, on the plastic clock or the little glass dog figurine on her desk. Meifeng had given her the figurine when she went to college. Nineteen eighty-two was the year of the water dog, Ivy's Chinese zodiac sign combined with her elemental astrology. Water dogs were supposed to be brave, self-centered, selfish. "You're brave, self-centered, and selfish," Meifeng always told her.

Ever since Meifeng's knee troubles caused by her days as an *ayi*, Nan had taken over the Lins' housekeeping. Ivy pictured her mother wiping down the furniture, the clock, the glass dog, with the striped dish towel she always used, rinsing out the towel in the plastic basin Ivy had once used to destroy her diary. She felt anger. She blamed Nan. Only stupid people would work so diligently to clean a room no one occupied. Just what was it that her mother had tried so hard to slap into her growing up? Ivy suspected even Nan didn't remember.

The next morning, out of habit, she checked her phone for any calls from Roux; the little jerk in her heart beat to the rhythm of *six days, six days.* But there was only a text from Gideon asking after Meifeng.

As Nan cooked breakfast, Shen showed Ivy all the upgrades they'd made to the house: the tiered chandelier shaped like an upside-down wedding cake, the elaborate ceiling moldings that looked suspiciously like the ones at Ted and Poppy's townhome, the patio they'd built in the yard, having finally uprooted the chicken shed, with smooth stone tiles and a row of young trees trimmed into lollipops. Ivy had to admit that this house, which in her memories retained the decrepit dankness of a cellar, was much improved, and—dare she say it?—quite tasteful. The kind of house she might have been proud of growing up in. The kind of house that might have saved Austin.

Ivy still had not yet seen her brother. There'd been a light under his door when she got back from the hospital last night, but when she knocked, there was no answer. She'd knocked again that morning and again he ignored her. When Ivy asked about him at breakfast, Nan's face suddenly collapsed, as if some linchpin that'd kept her composure in place had come undone at the mention of Austin's name.

"Your brother stopped going to work."

"Why?" Ivy asked, her heart sinking. Last she'd heard, he was living his best life.

"Two weeks ago, he slept through his alarm and was late to work. His manager scolded him. The next morning, the same thing happened. He didn't want to get out of bed. Baba said he had to go in and face the consequences but Austin refused. He said he didn't feel well. He hasn't left his room ever since. Baba had to send an email on his behalf saying he was resigning to focus on school." Nan sighed and handed Ivy a pork bun hot from the steamer. "What can we do? He'll never grow up. Why are both my children so frail?"

Ivy remembered now why she'd stayed away all these years. Home was a load you could never put down, once you were back in its orbit. "Is he coming with us to see Grandma?" she asked.

"We asked him to come yesterday," said Shen, shaking his head as he gulped down his rice porridge. "He said he couldn't. I don't understand. This is his flesh-and-blood grandmother who raised him. What's wrong with that boy? We should have sent him to the army. He's never been disciplined. That's the problem."

"That's hardly the problem," said Ivy, slamming her chopsticks into the table. Neither parent contradicted her.

They drove to the hospital in near silence. Meifeng was awake when they arrived, and cranky. She was hungry, the hospital food tasted like spoiled milk, she wanted to eat noodles, drink real tea, not this tepid Lipton stuff, she wanted her own bed, the woman beside her wouldn't stop mumbling, she had a mahjong game she was supposed to attend at Xiaoxing's house. When she said to Ivy grumpily, "So it takes near-death for you to come visit me," Ivy decided to take her father up on his offer to give her a tour of his new warehouse. On the drive over to the hospital, Shen had brought it up twice already, which was how she knew he was eager.

"Tell Mimi she has to email back that woman who bought the watch," Nan called at their retreating backs. "Tell her *no refunds*."

"Who's Mimi?" Ivy asked in the car.

"Our employee," said Shen.

"You guys have employees?"

Shen didn't respond. After a while he said, "Since when did you start smoking?"

Ivy denied it.

"I saw you on the patio last night."

"It's only once in a while. It's all this wedding planning stress."

Shen handed her the pack of Marlboros he always carried in his jacket pocket. Ivy took it, seized with a curious shyness at this stranger sitting beside her, an old man, offering her a cigarette. Probably no more than a few hundred words had been exchanged between them in all their lives. What did she really know about Shen Lin other than what Nan and Meifeng had told her? What private identity did he have outside the ones shaped by the family? She noticed the gray stubble underneath his curved chin; the lips holding the cigarette were thin and purple. She could not imagine a world where marrying him was the shining achievement of Nan's life. But if her mother hadn't done that, Ivy would probably be in Chongqing, living in the squat unit next to Jojo, clerking in Yingying's store. Girls still married young in China, around twenty-two or so, and she would have been no different. She might have had a kid already. Austin wouldn't have been born, due to China's one-child policy.

"Do you remember what you told me when I went off to college?" she asked. "You said I'll always find people who'll be better than me."

"Did I?"

She found herself shaking. "How could you say something like that to your own daughter? Weren't you afraid I'd develop self-esteem issues? Why do you think everyone is better than us? *Why?*"

Shen flicked his ash out the window. "I don't see anything wrong with my advice. You've grown into an independent woman. Learned to be humble. Life has rewarded you with a good husband, distinguished in-laws. What more do you want?"

Ivy's anger turned to forlorn disgust. She would never be able to make this plain, undeviating man understand that the most fragile inner parts of a woman were compiled from a million subtle looks and careless statements from others; this was identity. The desire for a different identity had made Nan ruin a man, marry another.

"Never mind," she said cynically. "You'll never believe it even if I told you."

"We're here," said Shen.

He pulled up to a whitewashed corner building on a tree-lined street. There were corporate buildings on either side, identical placards with names of dentists and private law firms. "That's our accountant's office," he pointed out. "Very convenient."

The warehouse extended much deeper than it appeared from the outside. It was a soaring space, high ceilings, newly painted windows stacked on top of one another; steel shelves, fifteen rows tall, were lined with cardboard boxes labeled in six-digit codes and equipped with sliding ladders to reach the higher shelves. There was a section of old furniture in the back, all shrink-wrapped, which Shen said he and Nan bought in bulk at estate sales. He showed Ivy the glass cases of jewelry, the gilded oil paintings, the spacious office in the back, furnished in all mahogany furniture, with two enormous computer monitors, a laser printer, and stacks and stacks of flattened cardboard boxes. An Asian girl in skinny jeans and a white turtleneck sat typing in the leather chair. When she saw Shen, she jumped up and said in Chinese, "Three emails already about the Sony—" Then she saw Ivy. "I've heard so much about you," she said, blushing.

"Only good things, I hope," said Ivy.

The girl lit up. "You should hear the way *Taitai* brags! I'm so sorry to hear about Grandma. *Taitai* said she'd be okay. I'm so relieved. Congratulations, by the way."

"For what?"

"Your engagement."

"Oh! . . . Thank you."

"I just bought my dress the other day . . . I can't wait for your wedding. *Taitai* says there'll be two hundred guests, and that your fiancé's dad was a senator . . . I've seen photos of you two. Your fiancé is so handsome, he looks like Brad Pitt . . . I heard you two went to Hawaii on vacation. How romantic!"

Ivy had not known this girl, Mimi, had existed until that morning, and yet this girl knew everything about her and Gideon, she was a guest of Ivy's wedding, she called Meifeng "Grandma."

Shen asked Mimi to show Ivy the workstation where items were photographed and cataloged. They headed to a small room where a fancy tripod camera was set up in front of a green screen on one side of the wall. "*Taitai* would stay here working all night if she could," Mimi confided. "Your dad installed a camera system so she can feel safe working here alone. See?" She pointed at the little screen showing the various exit doors and sidewalks. "*Taitai* has an eye for angles. She knows how to place and style each item so it looks brand-new in the photos. Her personal taste is so elegant as well. Your house is decorated exquisitely."

Ivy could tell Mimi wanted to impress her with her intimacy with the Lins; this only brought out in Ivy the instinct to withhold. She smiled tepidly, a little twitch of her cheekbones that could hardly be called a smile, and looked somewhere to the left of Mimi's earlobe. I guess I've learned a little from Sylvia, she thought.

"I'm getting hungry," she said to Shen when they returned.

"Should we get some hamburgers on the way back to the hospital?"

"I brought some dishes over to your house yesterday," Mimi jumped in. "Not that fancy though," she added, blushing again.

"Mimi is a great cook," said Shen. "She often brings dinner to our house. Your mom and I get home so late, sometimes around midnight, and you know your mother—she never liked cooking. She doesn't even have time for housework anymore."

"So who does it then," Ivy said bluntly.

"One of the women in your grandmother's mahjong group comes once a week to clean. We pay her twenty dollars an hour, and she always stays for tea."

So along with an employee and accountant, the Lins could also afford a housekeeper. A stranger, not Nan, had been dusting Ivy's glass dog. Ivy thought of the designer clothes her family had worn to Thanksgiving at the Speyers' house, a display that had horrified her at the time as a gaudy attempt to impress. But the new clothes, the upgraded, barely recognizable house, the credit card that Austin used indiscriminately, the checks Nan had sent Ivy to pay her rent and the wedding—it was clear now that none of these things had been face-saving gestures, as Ivy had assumed, but simply her parents' real lives.

Mimi embraced Ivy when saying goodbye. "You're even prettier than your photos," she said.

Ivy recognized in the girl's wistful voice a bad case of family crush. She was the object of a family crush.

Somewhere along the way, Shen and Nan had become business-people with a bit of wealth and power. The lie Ivy had been telling all along had come true.

STILL NO RESPONSE from Roux. Strange how one could get used to anything. The blind panic of before had receded, leaving behind a muted detachment. It was not resignation but a kind of gearing up. A feeling she was familiar with. She'd first felt it, at fourteen, rapping on Roux's window with an orange-sized bruise on her head.

Meifeng was discharged on Tuesday morning. To celebrate, Nan ordered from the local Sichuan restaurant a feast of the Lins' favor-ites: braised pork ribs with sweet potato, cold eggplant soaked in gar-lic and fresh chili peppers, marinated beef tongue, little oval slices of glutinous rice cakes glistening with oil atop a bed of leeks. Austin was coaxed down to dinner by the combined pressure of the entire family. He made an effort to shower and shave, arriving at the table wearing a pin-striped suit, silk tie and all, as if the clothes would trigger him into a different mode of living. Ivy had never seen anything so feeble in all her life. Nan smiled hopefully and Shen spoke in hearty tones about how much weight Austin had lost. None of them commented on the impracticality of eating oily food dressed in one's best suit.

Shen drank too much. Nan heaped meat into her children's rice bowls. In other words, nothing had changed. At least on the surface. And yet Ivy saw that her father was drinking expensive liquor, not generic beer, and Nan wore a thin gold necklace over her turtleneck. Nan never used to wear jewelry. This new jewelry-wearing Nan ordered eighty-dollar takeout meals instead of scolding Meifeng for buying Austin a McDonald's Happy Meal. There were a host of other flyers and coupons for Chinese restaurants clipped on the fridge, suggesting this was a usual occurrence. What luxury. Maybe she and Austin would have been different people if they'd grown up eating eighty-dollar Chinese takeout meals. Maybe this. Maybe that. Who knew what made you *you*. Ivy wished she knew.

She could hardly eat. She watched as Shen chuckled to himself over something Nan said. When Nan complained of a headache, he got up and went to fetch her a glass of water. They snapped at each other over various past grievances, not in a serious way, it was just how they talked, without awareness of the other person as *other* but only as an extension of speaking to themselves. Ivy wondered if she and Gideon would ever learn that intimate language of marriage. Would they have fights about laundry and cooking, pee in front of each other, argue about where to go on vacation? She could not imagine such a life with Gideon. Happiness with him had always been like an impressionist painting—one had to take a step back to appreciate the scene. Their marriage, if they married, would be like the peonies floating in the water bowl back in Ivy's room at Finn Oaks: tranquil, elegant, unmarred by strife. What did it matter if she never experienced the mundane familiarity of the sort between her parents? She had never wanted that kind of love anyway. She had only ever wanted the picturesque, the heroic.

GIDEON SAID THE meeting with Costa Rica's health minister had gone well. They would receive their funding check at a formal dinner on Friday. He asked after Meifeng's recovery.

"Nothing can slow *her* down," said Ivy. "She ate more than all of us combined, and was complaining that she wasn't allowed to drink liquor."

"I hope I'm that spirited when I'm eighty."

"Eighty-seven."

"Wow."

Ivy heard a man's voice in the background and Gideon turned away from the phone briefly to respond to him. It always made Ivy lonely to hear noisy gatherings in Gideon's background. His life always seemed so busy without her; her phone line was always clear.

"How's Costa Rica?" she asked.

"Humid. These mosquitoes are eating us alive down here. One of our engineers was sick all night from dinner."

"You want to practice your speech with me?"

"You don't mind?"

"Of course not."

She waited as he went to fetch his computer. When he returned, she lay down diagonally on the bed, closed her eyes, and let the soothing cadence of his voice wash over her like a warm bath. Nan said that the secret to marriage was that you had to give a man something to fight for. But Gideon was not Shen Lin. He was not a fighter or a gambler, and he would not believe that a woman who'd been with another man could truly love him, could love him *more* purely because she had been with another man, to spare him her own depravity. Five days. Ivy tried to imagine the future waiting for her in five days. A Gideon-less future. It was as unimaginable to her as a formless desert upon which she would wander aimlessly, running through the shimmering heat toward golden palaces and lush palm trees that were not there.

SHE CRAWLED INTO bed that night with Meifeng. She wanted to lie still and lick her wounds, like a sick cat. Meifeng was surprised but pleased. "Just don't kick me," she warned. "I might break my other hip."

Ivy asked if it'd hurt when she fell.

"A pinch. I called out for help but Shen wasn't home, just your mother. She carried me on her back to the car and drove me to the hospital." Meifeng sighed. "Nan's not a young woman anymore. I didn't think she'd have the strength. It's good to have children, Baobao. They're insurance for old age."

"I don't want kids," said Ivy.

"To understand a parent's love, you have to have kids yourselves."

"It's too risky. You have no idea what kind of monster will pop out of you." Ivy knew now what kind of blood ran in her veins. It was no kind to pass on.

"Monster! What kind of stupid idea is that? If you don't have kids, who will take care of you then if you fall in the shower?"

"A live-in nurse. Nurses don't expect anything from you. You pay them to do a job. It's clean and fair."

Meifeng snorted. "There's no outtalking you when you get like this." She reached for her mug of tea, wincing a little with discomfort. "You've always had strange ideas about children. Remember the time you wet the bed because you saw that little ghost girl? You begged me to leave the light on."

"I'd just watched *The Exorcist*." Ivy laughed, then shivered. "I thought the devil that had possessed the girl would come through the TV and get me." Her eight-year-old self had been frozen at the image of the black spirit entering her, turning her into a thrashing child-monster.

"But I didn't keep it on," said Meifeng. "Too wasteful, I thought. I've always regretted not providing you comfort that night. I keep imagining how scared you must have been to wet the bed. It's strange to be old. All the little regrets keep you up at night."

Ivy huddled her head reassuringly into Meifeng's shoulder. After a silence, she murmured, "Do you believe that the bad things we've done come back to haunt us?"

"I can't say I do. I've done plenty of bad things. I've been punished for some of them but overall, I've had a good life." Ivy felt Meifeng's body rise in a shrug. "Ask me after I've died. Maybe the punishment comes in the next life."

"What bad things have you done?"

"Ha What haven't I done?" She began to list her sins in a grim voice that betrayed a hint of pride—Meifeng, at least, hadn't changed much from the grandmother of Ivy's youth. She still believed her wrongdoings were another form of survival, a method of getting the upper hand on a world that had always tried to get an upper hand on her.

All day long, Ivy's mind had been a buzzard circling around something she couldn't yet pin down. She thought of Roux, of the gun. She thought of Nan's past, of Shen's stoicism and ignorance, of Mimi the employee who was probably a better daughter than Ivy was to Nan and Shen, and of Austin's fancy suit, and of family and money and past mistakes, and of Gideon, most of all, of Gideon.

"Have you ever killed anyone?" she interrupted Meifeng's nostalgic monologue.

"Once," said Meifeng, adjusting the blanket around her hips.

Ivy stilled. "You never told me that."

"It was when your grandfather and I were just starting out on our farm. Your mother hadn't been born, just Hong. A thief came into our house, probably looking for food or money. It was so dark I couldn't even see where I was going. I heard him rustling in the kitchen. I could smell him, too. He was making this gurgling sound and when I screamed at him to leave, he came toward me. I stabbed him with our carving knife."

"He died?"

"Your grandfather carted him in the wagon to the little hill by our house and we buried him."

"Did anyone come looking for him?"

"He was a homeless man. No one knew he existed."

Ivy's sudden pulse of exhilaration frightened her, it made her speak with a severity she didn't feel, to mask her agitation. "Didn't you feel bad? You *killed* a person."

Meifeng chuckled darkly. "In China, a single life can feel insignificant. I've seen hundreds of people die—kids, old people, women. They simply dropped over from hunger or disease. And then we'd walk past their bodies until someone thought to move them out of the way to keep them from being trampled. My sister died while shitting on the toilet. My best friend died when a vegetable seller blunted her on the head for short-changing her a yuan. Lives are like rivers. Eventually they go where they must, not where we want them to go." She groaned suddenly. "My leg is hurting now. Let's sleep."

20

NAN DROPPED IVY OFF AT THE TRAIN STATION THE NEXT MORNING. They didn't speak at all on the drive over, but as Ivy got out of the car, Nan asked suddenly if Ivy could speak to Gideon's mother about Austin. "Tell her he's just been very sick with the flu . . . can you see if she can ask her relative to give him another chance at the company?" Under a dark, overcast sky, Ivy thought that Nan looked more than ever like Meifeng. Yet whereas she had always seen toughness in her grandmother's face and weakness in her mother's, she now realized it was the opposite. Meifeng was weak. She had always been driven by fear. Nan was strong and hard. She had been driven by greed.

"Austin's depressed," said Ivy.

"What?"

"Depression. It's a disease. He doesn't need another job or school or one of your schedules. He needs to see a psychiatrist. Stop pretending he's anemic or weak or whatever else you and Baba tell yourselves."

A myriad of expressions flickered over Nan's face before settling on stoic cynicism, the preferred armor of millions of Chinese immigrants.

"What does he have to be depressed about? We're all depressed. *I'm* depressed."

"No you're not."

Nan licked her lips. "What have we done wrong? We always tried our best."

"Sometimes you can't help it." And because the rims of Nan's eyes were turning pink, Ivy said, "It's not your fault." A faint screeching in the distance announced the arrival of the train. "I have to go." She walked up the platform and slid into the first available seat. From the window, she saw Nan's silver van, as shiny as the day she'd bought it, sitting in the parking lot until the train pulled away and Ivy could only see her own wan reflection in the windowpane.

They stalled for an hour in Connecticut, rain slamming sideways onto the windows, followed by the pattering thuds of hail. She put her book away and sent Roux a single text: *My grandmother's in the hospital—call me.* She prayed the past week had softened his resolve—there were only four days left until his arbitrary deadline.

When she arrived home, it was already twilight. In the kitchen, Andrea was drinking tea with an effeminate young man. There was something familiar about the man, who could have been one of Gideon's employees in his faded gray sweatshirt, tan corduroys, black-frame glasses sliding off a rather snub nose. He introduced himself as Norman.

"I saw you at the party," he said.

"What party?"

"The one for Swingbox."

"What's that?"

"Oh. Uh. We're a file hosting service—"

"At the Gonford, Ivy," Andrea tittered. "Norman and I were together all night."

"Right, yes," said Ivy. "Your new friend." The man in the yellow T-shirt who'd floated after Andrea all evening like a spindly balloon attached to her tailbone.

Norman finished his tea and went upstairs to use Andrea's computer to take a video call—"just a short interview with TechCrunch," he said self-consciously.

"We're going to Machu Picchu next month," Andrea whispered, squeezing Ivy's forearm with both hands as if it were a massage ball.

"You *have* to come shopping with me. I'm so happy you guys finally met . . . I think he's going to propose on the trip! Oh my God, I can't believe I just said that out loud—*sshhhhhh*." Andrea made a low, frightened giggle. ". . . Sorry, I thought I heard him coming down. Can you believe how fast things have been happening? When he came up to me at the party, I thought, 'He's not my type at all,' but then we kept talking—he's *so* smart—and then I realized how much we had in common—"

"I'm going to make a sandwich," said Ivy, standing up. "Want one?"

Andrea looked glum. "Shit, I'm going to regret this in a few hours when my face bloats up before rehearsal." She shrugged. "Oh well, make me one, too."

Ivy spread the marshmallow fluff and peanut butter onto four slices of white bread. It wasn't the low-calorie kind Andrea bought, but she didn't tell her.

Ivy turned around to hand Andrea her sandwich. There were two Andreas.

"Yooo-hoo? Ivy?"

Ivy blinked and the vision went away. "I think I'm coming down with something. I'm going to stay in bed this week. Can you make sure no one bothers me? I want to sleep it off."

Andrea swore she'd keep a lookout, promising to bring takeout pho on her way back from work. In a moment of fondness, Ivy leaned over and brushed her fingers over Andrea's cheek. "I'd marry *you* if I could," she said.

Andrea laughed, then launched into another story about her and Norman's last date at a rave club where they'd dropped acid together—drugs really lowered your guard—and Ivy was so right, you had to teach a man how to treat you . . .

It was exhausting to watch someone try so hard to get such ordinary things. Andrea wanted to be wanted, to be validated, for someone to say, *I'll take care of you.* "I'll be the one taking care of you," said Andrea, and Ivy realized she had spoken out loud. Andrea licked the corners of her lips of marshmallow fluff and lowered her voice in what Ivy knew was sure to be some confession that Andrea thought of with utmost secrecy but was, in reality, utterly insignificant.

"You know, and I didn't even know he was—you know, when I met him . . ."

"He was what?"

"The founder of Swingbox."

Something clicked in Ivy's mind. "Wait—the company that IPOed. The billionaire founder?"

"He hated that *Times* article," Andrea said proudly, reaching for a spoon and eating the peanut butter straight out of the jar.

Norman returned from his call. He pulled his chair closer to Andrea's before sitting down, draping one arm around her shoulder. Both of them assumed a posture of grinning anticipation, as if waiting for Ivy to say *Cheeeeese* and take their photograph. She excused herself. Moments later, she heard their footsteps tread quietly up the stairs. She lay on her bed, waiting. It soon came. The rhythmic squeaks of a mattress, thumps of a headboard hitting the wall, a woman's muffled moans—sounds of passion that Ivy might once have mistaken for sounds of love. Or maybe it was both. Love. Passion. Money. That they could all coexist in the ordinary, unspectacular bodies of Andrea and Norman seemed to Ivy the most miraculous of things.

PERHAPS BECAUSE OF the hair and corduroys, Andrea's new boyfriend reminded Ivy of Daniel Sullivan, the man she, too, had thought would propose on their big trip to Vermont, but who instead told her she wasn't wife material, that she was guarded, he didn't know who she really was. Daniel was the only man she'd ever begged for love, perhaps the only true heartbreak of her life thus far. And still he hadn't trusted her. She'd thought he was going to propose and he'd dumped her. She thought Gideon would dump her and he'd proposed. So why couldn't Andrea have Machu Picchu with her new billionaire?

Early on in their relationship, Daniel had taken her on a weekend hiking trip to the White Mountains in New Hampshire. They'd hiked for six hours until her heels were bloody and her toes blistered under her wool socks. She hadn't complained because she'd still been trying to impress him by embracing his hobbies as her own. Andrea would soon see for herself—all that sweat and blood women spilled, it was usually for nothing.

The trail they followed that day was one Daniel had created on one of his solo mountaineering trips. Ivy could still see it because he had made her memorize it in case they got separated. There was no cell service, no forest ranger for miles. The mountain had many sharp turns and mossy holds, he said, but it would be worth it because the view was spectacular. And it was. At the top of that cliff, the sky was the most beautiful thing she had ever seen.

On the way down, Daniel had boasted that only adventurous hikers could brave such terrain. "Do you know how many people have died in these mountains?" He listed the dangers around them: snakes and bears, drowning on the river crossing, a simple misstep that would lead to a hundred-foot drop over the cliffs. She'd had the thought that he didn't value her life much, to bring her here so early on in their relationship, without having taken any precautionary measures for her safety. Looking back, however, she only felt thankful for the experience. Danger often created unique opportunities. Daniel had understood that.

That night, the thumping noises of hail hitting the window became, in Ivy's dreams, the sound of Daniel's hiking boots striding in front of her over the narrow, rain-soaked path. The backs of his heels were coated with mud and dry grass, a little mud even smeared on his herringbone gray wool socks. Once more she saw the yellow dust around the muddy, curved bend; the tiny wildflowers that poked through the underpass; the hidden platform off the top of the ledge; the V-shaped ditch, a hundred feet below, lined with ragged boulders and spires, impossible to climb back up once a person fell *down down down*.

* * *

SHE WOKE WITH the taste of mud in her mouth. Her room was so dark she thought it was still night, but when she flicked on the lamp, her clock read half past noon. She checked the weekly forecast on her phone. Little frost symbols lined the calendar. *Three days*, pattered her heart. She called Roux. She didn't expect him to answer; in fact, she was already rallying herself to get up, dress, and drive over to Astor Towers to pound on his door. She was unprepared for his short but resigned "Hello?" Her mouth hung open in silence until he said, "Look, don't get any ideas. I just wanted to ask about your grandmother."

"My grandmother?"

"You texted me that she's in the hospital. What happened?"

"Oh!" Choked up with gratitude at his concern, Ivy told him about Meifeng's surgery.

"I'm glad it wasn't more serious," he said.

"Did I tell you about my parents' new warehouse?" Without waiting for his reply, she began rambling about the Lins' business in a bright, showy tone, like a person suddenly thrown onstage with the threat of being stoned to death if she didn't keep the audience's attention.

"So they've pulled themselves into middle-class respectability," said Roux. "Just like you've always wanted."

"I guess."

"Good. I'm happy for you."

"Roux?"

"What?"

The aggression in his "What?" made her withdraw what she'd been going to ask, which was if he'd reconsidered his ridiculous blackmail, and instead the words "We never did take that trip we talked about" slid glibly off her tongue, as if they'd always been there, simply waiting until her denial and futile prayers fell away like the last dead leaves on a brittle tree branch.

There was a long pause. Then—"You mean *I* wanted to take. You never did anything but make excuses."

"What about Sunday?" she said. "Are you free on Sunday?" That Sunday was the deadline he'd given her for telling Gideon was not lost on either of them.

"Depends on where we're going," he said grimly.

"It's a surprise. There's something I want to tell you."

Even his breathing sounded cantankerous. "If you think—"

"Just come. Please."

"Don't expect it to change anything."

"I know."

"Fine."

Ivy's entire body began to tremble. The momentum of it all left her light-headed; she felt both out of control and certain of absolute power.

"Believe me," she said, "it'll change everything. This place is a bit of a drive, but worth it. I promise."

He asked if she would be driving.

"My car doesn't have four-wheel drive. Can you pick me up? Dress warmly. And bring a bottle of your best whiskey."

"What for?"

"We'll be celebrating." She squeezed her eyes shut.

SNOW FELL ON Friday. Softly, blanketing Newbury Street with a new-born fuzz. In the distance were the sounds of sirens, of people dying and others rushing to save them. Ivy walked on, numb with cold, the sky bleak and empty and vast.

At the pharmacy, she purchased her usual Lucky Strikes, cold medicine, a six-pack energy drink, sourdough pretzels that were on sale, and a little bottle of red nail polish called Alight in Flames. Next to the pharmacy was a sleek little hair salon with cushy red velvet chairs and floors polished to a gleaming marble white. Suddenly, nothing seemed as important as getting a haircut. She went inside. Underlying the overly perfumed air was the smell of synthetic chemicals. The stylists, in black leather jeans and black Doc Martens, were more beautiful than the clients sitting in the chairs.

"What are we doing today?" asked the stylist as she ran her fingers through Ivy's limp black locks, four days unwashed, hanging to her breasts.

They stared at the same reflection, the stylist with professional astuteness, Ivy with bone-deep loathing. She was so sick of the face staring back at her: the hard practicality of the brown-black eyes, the once round cheeks now sunken into two crescents, a puckered bloodless mouth, a smoker's mouth, aging her a decade.

"I want a change," she said. She evaluated the stylist's sleek, platinum-blond hair. The stylist was an Asian woman, yet she had platinum-blond hair because no one had told her she couldn't, and it was arrogantly resplendent. "I want *your* color," said Ivy. "That exact shade."

The stylist rubbed Ivy's hair between her thumb and index finger. "Is this virgin hair?"

"Yes."

"Might be tough." She walked Ivy through the difficulties of lightening black hair—there would be bleach, many processes of bleach, it would take multiple sessions—

"No, it's got to be in one go."

"I wouldn't suggest it. It'll fry your hair."

"Can you do it?"

"It's possible, but—"

"Do it."

Nine hours later, Ivy walked out of the salon, unrecognizable to herself. Her hair was the color of wheat, an ashy flax that somehow made her face appear sharper, her skin fine and thin over the small bones, her eyes blank and cavernous. The stylist had even colored the eyebrows a nutty brown. Ivy liked it. She looked like an alien—not quite Asian, not quite white, somewhere in the middle, a girl of mixed blood, or perhaps some true freak of nature. She imagined what Mei-feng and Nan might say if they saw her now. Probably that she had made herself ugly, disfigured herself in some irreparable way. Austin was depressed and Ivy was irreparable. It's not your fault, she'd told Nan in the car. She'd only said it to make her mother feel better. Now Ivy knew it to be true. Hair was reparable, but her need to destroy, escape, remake was a darkness the combined forces of Meifeng and Nan hadn't been able to fumigate.

GIDEON EMAILED HER a clip his employee had recorded of him and Roland accepting the check. The stage behind them was lit fluorescent green. An old woman in a sequined, floor-length gown took the podium to talk about the impact Gideon's company had had on her country. When she walked over to shake Roland's hand, she tripped over a wire and stumbled a few steps. Gideon steadied her, making a joke to lighten the mood. Ivy could tell he was enjoying himself, utterly in his element, championing a cause that had nothing to do with him, a purely altruistic cause. There were people in the world who were born that way: altruistic. Not everyone would have stabbed a homeless man rummaging in their house for food. As Gideon leaned in to the microphone to speak, Ivy heard a ripple of anticipation, that sound of people collectively leaning forward and drawing breath. Gideon spoke of making an impact on the lives of others, in bringing about the change you wanted to see in the world, of kindness, of humility, of hope. His voice became impassioned when he spoke about the work his company was doing to improve the lives of the most impoverished. Everyone was mesmerized. Ivy was mesmerized. In the middle of the speech, while he was taking a sip of water, the person recording the video panned to the audience. Dark-skinned men in tuxedos and busty women with perfect blond highlights sat around circular tables laden with silverware and champagne flutes. There were the occasional glints of sparkling jewelry, a bright red lipstick; one woman was dabbing her eyes with her cloth napkin. The camera panned back to Gideon. As she watched him through the screen of her laptop, Gideon had never felt farther away from her—and yet she had also never felt such ownership of him, fingering the sapphire on her ring finger while recalling the way he looked fresh out of the shower, his shoulder muscles rippling as he slid one arm into his monogramed pajama shirt. All of Ivy's pleasure lay in this gap, that elusive divide between familiarity and admiration, intimacy and enigma.

ON SATURDAY MORNING, she saw that someone had parked their car in her spot in front of the house. It was a black Audi, covered with a fine dusting of snow. She wondered which of her neighbors had come into sudden wealth—perhaps the gangsters across the street had been rewarded by their boss—but mostly she was irritated that they had taken up her spot.

When she walked out to get the mail, she discovered a bubble envelope with her name written on the front in black permanent marker. No return address. She ripped the package open. Out fell a set of two identical keys. There was nothing else. Her eyes wandered to the Audi. She raced inside, dug out her phone from underneath her pillow. There was one unopened text, from Roux: *You drive.*

SUNDAY. SHE WOKE and immediately checked the forecast. Chance of snow: 100 percent starting at three o'clock.

It was still night, the moon a faint watermark on an ashen sky misty with the pale clouds that would bring the promised snow. She heard the groan of pipes upstairs as Andrea turned on the shower; twenty minutes later, her roommate's footsteps thudded down the stairs, the front door opened, closed, leaving behind the sudden hushed impotence of an old house.

Ivy sprung into action. She dressed in the clothes she'd laid out the night before: black joggers, old hiking boots, multiple layers of thermal wear, a Red Sox cap she'd dug out of the umbrella closet. She left the light and heater running in her room and closed the door. The air chewed at her exposed skin as she hurried to unlock the car and slide into the Audi's leather seats, made brittle by the cold. She knew nothing about cars but she knew this one was a beautiful piece of machinery. The seat curved perfectly against the contour of her back; a slight tap on the gas and it sped to sixty without any effort or noise. The sensation of driving an expensive car through a deserted city, with beautifully clothed mannequins staring at her through dark shop windows, tall skyscrapers looming on either side of the broad avenue, and the immovable sense of an earth built for her and her alone, made Ivy feel reckless and free. Roux said cars were a man's domain, that women, especially Asian women, shouldn't be allowed near fine cars. As a passenger, yes. As a driver, no. But he'd let her drive this Audi. It was his olive branch.

By the time she got to Astor Towers, the diner across the street was just opening its doors. She put on her emergency lights and texted Roux she was outside. Minutes later, he ambled out from the lobby dressed in loose slacks and a brown fleece jacket. From afar, his face was a closed door, she could read nothing in his gray eyes, narrowed against the sun, or his perfectly set mouth, taking a long drag of his cigarette before tossing it into the gutter.

She'd planned an entire greeting composed of light banter, but he saved her the effort by immediately bursting into laughter after sliding into the passenger's seat. "What have you done?" he said, touching the ends of her hair.

"Do you like it?"

"What was wrong with it before?"

"You know I've always hated my hair."

"You look like an albino. Or a radioactive mutant."

"Whatever." She smiled charmingly and brought her fingers to his jaw. "You shaved."

"Yes."

They kissed quite naturally.

"Thanks for rolling out of bed before three," she murmured.

He pressed his fingers on the back of her skull and gently brought his forehead to hers. They stayed like that a second longer than their breezy conduct allowed for.

What was this feeling? Ivy wondered. Fear, confusion, tender hate, all mixed together and tinged with the sense of impending danger. Like a hostage trying to please her captor. But who was the captor and who was the hostage?

"Well?" said Roux, releasing her. "How do you like the car?" He inspected the gears, opened the glove compartment, patted the dashboard with a paternal air.

"It's beautiful," said Ivy. "Thanks for letting me drive it."

"You can have it."

"*Seriously?*"

"You're always complaining about your car breaking down."

"I'll ruin this one before long, with my history." Then a terrible thought struck her. "Is it registered under *my* name?"

Roux's eyes flicked over her sardonically, mistaking her agonizing fear for childish petulance. "Obviously not—*I* bought it—but if it means that much to you, I can transfer the title over—"

"No!" She grinned bashfully, relief making her brisk and overly eager. "Let's get going." She flicked on the turn signal. Roux strapped on his seat belt.

"Where exactly *are* we going?" he asked as she merged onto the freeway.

"Hiking."

He frowned. "Isn't it the wrong season for that?"

"I told you to dress warmly. I'll have to speed a bit. It's supposed to snow later."

He took her lead and didn't speak much, fiddling with the radio, rolling down the windows to smoke. The wind blew his disheveled black hair over his eyes; he didn't look so much like a handsome man riding in a sports car as an actor playing a handsome man riding in a sports car. She, too, felt as if she were acting out a scene from an old movie, perhaps a scene near the credits, where the couple drives away from the city and bursts through a tunnel in their getaway car. That's what this is, Ivy thought. A getaway car.

The sides of Route 93 were brown with slush and ice. Occasionally they saw a carcass of a dead deer or rodent, dragged to the side of the road and half-buried in a mound of fresh snow. Each mile away from Boston, the temperature outside dropped a fraction of a degree. The radio turned staticky, and then she drove with only the hum of the engine as backdrop. The Audi seemed to drive itself, responsive to her lightest touch, without any jerky movements or bumps when they went over potholes. Roux reached over and took her right hand, holding it limply in his lap while she drove with her other hand.

The roads turned narrow and winding; she made ascending circles around the mountain. Their breaths thinned; the view gave way to purple mountains and the brown lines of treetops. They hadn't passed another car in the last thirty minutes.

"Cold today," said Roux, rolling the window back up. "You sure about this hike? We could just go there"—he pointed at a billboard whizzing by, for Red Wingz Sports Bar and Grill, two for one, at the following exit toward Stocksfield—"and call it a day." Despite his cultivated appetite for the luxurious, Roux truly liked places like that, roadside diners, Vegas casinos, hot dog stands, he was very American in that way. Places like that suited him, the way boats suited Gideon and rose gardens suited Liana Finley. "I want you to see this special spot," Ivy said firmly. "It's got to be today."

Ten minutes later, she pulled off to the side of the road. It was a small lookout passengers used to photograph the view. In the summer, tourists could follow a set of rickety stairs to a tiny waterfall that trickled down the mountain. Of course, now everything was frozen. "This is it," she said, cutting the engine.

Roux took in the absolute isolation around them. The few sur-rounding trees were bare and laden with icicles, thick with the smells of pine, frost, wet asphalt. "I never thought you were the outdoorsy type," he said, rubbing his arms vigorously.

"I'm just superstitious. I wanted it to be—here."

He didn't ask the obvious: want what to be here? Since the time he'd slapped her across the face, he'd begun to mistake her deception for discretion.

"Where's the start of the trail?" he asked.

"There is no trail."

"You know your way up?"

"I've been here before."

"With Gideon?"

She winced at the first break of code. "No."

They walked half a mile from the parking lot and stopped by a nondescript junction with a small STAY IN YOUR LANE signpost. Ivy consulted her hand-drawn map. "This is it."

"Lead the way," said Roux, his mouth twitching in resigned good humor.

They began their ascent.

Underneath her coat she wore three layers, but he only had on a cotton zip-up under his fleece. "Give me your phone and wallet," she said, "I'll put them in my backpack so you can put your hands in your pockets."

They walked on, slowly, because they were both smokers and out of shape, and because Ivy sometimes grew dizzy, her vision blurry with white spots, when she stopped to get a drink of water. The clouds momentarily parted and the sun peeked out, strong and distant, burn-ing the backs of their necks. Sometimes she flapped her collar to let some of the heat escape from underneath her thermal shirt, and other times she walked with her hands tucked underneath her armpits.

"Are we almost there?" Roux asked at the two-mile mark. He took off his fleece and tied it around his waist. The first leg of the hike had been

steep and unforgiving. During certain parts of it, they'd had to scrab-
ble around snow-covered boulders, tripping over branches. Her hiking
boots were sturdy but Roux wore thin suede shoes. He stamped his feet
on a boulder to shake off the snow that'd collected around his ankles.

"You want my gloves?" she asked.

"I'm fine."

She clasped his hands between hers and warmed his fingers with
her breath. She wished she had told him to bring gloves.

"Do you hate me, Ivy?" he said keenly.

"Why would I hate you?"

"For what I made you do."

"Let's talk about it later," she said quickly, pulling her hands away.
"We're almost at the halfway point."

Their breaths came out in shallow pants, sometimes with wheezing
sounds during a particularly steep climb. The path that Daniel charted
had little red triangular markers he'd tacked on the trees. Ivy lost sight
of them for a moment and panicked that she wouldn't be able to find
the ledge. As Roux rested on a fallen log, she looked for telltale marks.
A strong breeze parted the branches, revealing the faint glint of red on
a branch not fifty feet away.

"I thought we were lost," she breathed, placing a gloved hand on
her chest.

"I trust you," said Roux.

FINALLY, A CLEARING opened up to their left, a flat expanse of rock
overlooking a view of mountains that seemed to go on forever. There
was no sign of technology or roads or civilization; the vast silence felt
prehistoric, as if they were the first people to have ever looked upon
this section of earth and graced it with human voices.

"Is this it?" asked Roux.

"Almost. We have another half mile or so. I thought this would be
a good spot to stop for lunch."

They admired the view for a moment. Then Roux laid the fleece blanket over the rocks and Ivy pulled out their lunch from her backpack: peanut butter and marshmallow sandwiches, a thermos of coffee, trail mix. Roux took out the whiskey—a deep, amber-colored bottle of 1942 Dalmore, which he twisted open and poured into a leather flask, giving her the first taste. "Jesus," Ivy gasped, pounding her chest. A few more sips and she might start to believe that this poignant magic cast by the mountains was real.

As they ate, Roux told her the history of the Dalmore. He'd won it in an auction from a Scottish lord who'd also been auctioning off his castle where the Dalmore had been stored for decades in its cavernous wine cellars. "But what the hell am I going to do with a crumbling wall of bricks?" said Roux. "Better to have ten more of these bottles. Exquisite, isn't it?" His cheeks were pink, his eyes lively and relaxed. Ivy told him to drink up—"It'll keep the cold at bay," she said. She picked the crust off her sandwich, made a little hole in the ground, and buried the crumbs.

"What are you doing?"

"Nothing. Just restless." Roux always gave her the best of the best: whiskey, jewelry, a car. He would probably buy her that damn castle if she asked for it. "How are your businesses doing?" she asked.

"I opened a laundromat in Roxbury last week."

"Exciting."

He noticed her tone and said dryly, "Do you know how much revenue a laundromat brings in?"

"A hundred K?"

"A single one can bring in a million a year."

"I should tell my father to open one," Ivy said, only half-joking. Then, when he actually began listing out figures pertaining to the initial investment, she said in exasperation, "Why are you so obsessed with making more money? Aren't you already a millionaire?"

"So?"

"When's enough enough?" It was not a rhetorical question—she really wanted to know. But Roux only shrugged.

"I wonder," he said, gazing into the distance with the brooding expression he always wore when thinking of his dead mother.

"So what's the plan, then?" she said. "Are you going to work for the Morettis for the rest of your life?"

He searched her face. "Does it bother you?"

"Not at all." She looked him straight in the eye. "You know me—when have I ever cared about things like following the law?" She pretended to take another swig from the flask.

"Come here," Roux said tenderly.

Ivy went. She sat between his knees; his arms encircled her waist and she leaned back into his chest, feeling his heartbeat through the layers of their clothes. His hair tickled her cheeks as his soft voice, gruff with alcohol, whispered elaborate promises in her ear: they'd marry, he'd take his money and they'd start fresh, somewhere far away from the Morettis, maybe in Asia, and he'd take care of her, her family, their children's future, and he'd never hurt her again—all promises of a man who is very nearly drunk, spilling the rawest dreams of his heart. "You know me," he vowed, as if he could hear her unspoken doubts. *"you know* I always keep my promises."

"You once told me you weren't the marrying type," she said.

He laughed, then sighed, then laughed again. "Trust you to remember every shitty thing I've ever said."

Ivy let herself relax into the hard body supporting her, the strong arms wrapped around her like chains, and she looked up at the white-ribboned sky, the weak sun. She would never again mistake physical strength for strength.

"Roux," she said. "What would you do if I said that I'd told Gideon about us and that he's forgiven me? That we're still going to get married?"

"That's impossible."

"How can you be so sure?"

His grip tightened around her waist. "Look at the way he treats you. He still thinks you're that little girl who liked him back in middle school. You probably trailed after him trying to tie his shoelaces. That's what he wants from you—a wife to tie his shoelaces for the rest of his life." He turned her head with one hand until she was looking at him. "Maybe I was harsh when I said all those things last summer at the beach house. But you needed to hear it. The Speyers—they're frauds." Ivy began to scoff, but Roux said emphatically, "Mark my words, no one in that family is honest. I've seen con artists more honest than they are. Gideon looks like he's about to have a hernia anytime anyone asks him a personal question. And Ted and Poppy? They're always so peppy and *nervous* . . . No, it's not *charm*, Ivy, it's some kind of perverse cover-up. They're hiding something."

"And Sylvia? What's she hiding?"

"Sylvia was the worst of them. She never lifted a finger for anything. She expected me to pay for all her vacations, her plane tickets, book her hotels and villas. As if getting things handed to her was her birthright. She's gotten by her entire life on this *charm* you worship— oh, she was charming when she wanted to be—but she was also spoiled and crazy." He withdrew one arm to pick up the flask. "Why do women do that?"

"Do what?"

"That push-and-pull thing. It's mad. One day she's hurt that I didn't tell her about my childhood in Romania, the next day she's telling me that I need to assimilate into America. That I had a chip on my shoulder." He shuddered. "I always thought she was cheating on me, but I couldn't prove it."

"Did you see her . . . ?"

"No, it was just a hunch. All those musicians and actors and writers—I couldn't tell if they were actually her friends or people she'd picked up on the street. Sometimes I thought Sylvia was conning *me*."

"For what?"

Roux shrugged. "I don't know. Money. It's always about money in the end."

"But say Gideon did forgive me," Ivy repeated, shivering with the wind. "What would you do?"

"We don't live in that kind of world," he said coldly. He handed her the flask but she shook her head. "If we did," he continued, "I wouldn't have had to corner you like this. We'd be together already. Instead of on this frozen mountain, we'd be in my bed. Soaking in the tub. You'd be redecorating my apartment."

Ivy saw it just as he described. The bed. The tub. The fresh start. Children. Asia. The ease she'd felt with him their first night together, on Poppy's four-poster bed in Cattahasset, returned to her now, singing its haunting, irresistible tune.

"Tell me the truth," he said, guiding her chin up to meet his eyes. "Have you told him yet? Because if you haven't, this grandiose gesture isn't going to change my mind."

"I told him about us," she said. "We broke up."

He flinched. "I don't believe you."

"I love you." She smiled gently, the gentleness of a mother.

Roux lowered his head. He kissed the hollow of her neck where the skin jumped with her heartbeat. She understood by the aching pain in her throat and her dry, hot eyes that her words were not a lie. He was Roux, and she was Ivy. Who else in the entire world would ever understand what that meant?

She thought he, too, might be overcome by emotion, but when he looked up, she realized the slight tremors she felt from his body were laughter. His eyes were the clear glittering gray of a frozen lake in which drops of dew hung in eternal suspended beauty; she felt she could see down the depths of a subterranean world, just by peering at those hard, gray eyes.

"Let's get going," he said, jumping to his feet.

She didn't move. Something like grief was clawing at her temples. "Are we sure we want to go on? The temperature's dropping. And it's supposed to snow soon."

"What are you talking about? We came all this way."

"Let's just go back, Roux. I don't want to do this anymore."

"You lazy cat." He pulled her up. "I'm getting my second wind. Come on, I'll carry the bag." He began to whistle as he brushed snow off his pants.

"Please let's go back!"

He broke off in astonishment. Staring at her stiff, frightened face, he said gently, "It was so important to you earlier that we see your special spot. I've never believed in omens, but I think we were meant to be here today. I can't explain it. I want to be here with *you*. So we'll always remember today. Do you understand?"

She could only nod, exhausted by her outbreak to the point of dumbness. He squeezed her hand.

Ivy slowly shook out their picnic blanket and folded everything back in her backpack. It was just as Roux said, she told herself. They were only going to see her special spot. Reality was how you framed it. Gideon had taught her that. "We're going to be climbing down," she said, leading him to the edge of the rock. "Watch your step."

ALL HER LIFE, she had sought something she couldn't name. Love? Wealth? Beauty? But none of those things were exactly right. What she sought was peace. The peace of having something no one could take away from you. Had she ever been at peace for a single minute in her life? She was tired of the struggle to achieve that innocent simplicity she admired in old-fashioned people like the Speyers, or the effortless, entitled elegance of Sunrin, traits that appeared so natural in others but which she could only emulate through cunning calculation. She was tired of trying. More than anything, she longed to rest.

"Rest how?" said Roux.

They wove their way down the narrow path between the boulders, gripping their shoes in the slim crevices where the snow was frozen.

"Rest knowing I've reached the top," said Ivy. She could feel the heat of Roux's irritation warming her back as his sharp voice echoed between the large stones.

"Ivy. There. Is. No. Top. We're all in this hellhole together. What you're looking for—that peace?—it doesn't exist."

They dropped onto the two-foot-wide ledge on the side of the mountain, the cliffside boulders blocking out the sky. The temperature here was even colder than the open expanse above. In identical gestures—a step forward, necks stretching outward—they stared down at the narrow gulf. The motion made Ivy so dizzy that she quickly leaned back against the wall to steady her quaking legs. She had a fear of heights. How absurd, considering. Her arms shook beside her body.

"It looks man-made, doesn't it?"

"Divine nature," said Roux. "What is it?"

"Frozen sediment, I guess. The overhang from where we had lunch protects it from the weather. It's sort of this secret hole I discovered once."

"How'd you find it?"

"An ex-boyfriend—he fancied himself a woodsman. He slipped on the rock above us and luckily there was this platform here."

Roux whistled. "Lucky dude. If you fell down from here, there's no way to climb back up."

"And no one would ever find you either," Ivy whispered. "This isn't close to any of the other hiking trails." She looked at the thin sliver of dirt two hundred meters down at the bottom of the conical valley. The walls were smooth and silver and covered in ice. Sharp spires made intricate shapes, like frozen snowflakes, their jagged points rising toward a sky they would never reach.

"I don't understand," she cried suddenly, spinning to face Roux with anguished eyes, "why you love me. We'd be miserable together. We'd fight constantly. You'd cheat on me. I'd steal from you. We'd be horrible parents. We'd die some horrible, pointless death. You said people don't change. That's who we are together." If he had painted one version of their future, she was painting its underbelly. She was begging him to see, to agree with her, because she could think of no other way to save them both. Yet even through her anguish, a tiny voice continued to jeer at her own theatrics: you know you don't mean a single word, you're just trying to get out of a tight spot, same as always, you feel nothing, you're a selfish monster . . .

"You're just scared," Roux said hoarsely. "When I was a kid, I thought I could control my destiny. Do whatever I wanted once I had some money. But now I think our lives were decided for us a long time ago. Everything that's happened so far, the way we met again—doesn't it feel inevitable?"

"Oh, I don't know, I don't know anything anymore!" Ivy shook her head violently and began to cry, a hiccupping, choking cry, but for once there was no shame in it. The vastness of the mountain, the oppressive silence, the whistling of the wind made everything feel as though it were happening from very far away, as if she were watching herself from an airplane window, thousands of feet off the ground. She was simultaneously in the airplane and on that ledge, both the participant and the observer of her small life.

But she did know! It was *her* life! Who cared if it was small or insignificant, it was *hers*!

Roux was petting the back of her head, which was resting on his chest, murmuring words of comfort. She could feel the vibrations from his voice going straight into her bones; the sensation calmed her. As quickly as they came, her tears receded; her mind went to that quiet place. *Lives are like rivers. Eventually they go where they must.*

She looked up. He cupped her face with one hand. Wiped her eyes with his thumb. Roux—!

"If you stand at the edge," she said, "close your eyes, and shout your wish—maybe it'll come true."

"I doubt it," he said.

"Here, I'll go first." She inched out steadily.

"Careful."

She took another step forward . . . her toes had reached the edge of the ledge. One step farther and she'd fall.

Ivy opened her mouth. She shouted the first thing that came to mind. "*I wish I was an angel!*" Her voice bounced off the walls, boomeranging back toward her: *annnggelll-ggelll-lll.*

She heard Roux's laughter behind her, mixing with the echo. "That one's going to take a miracle," he said.

"Your turn." She stepped back and pressed her back against the safe surface of the cliff. Her heart was pounding so hard she felt she was being swallowed by its rushing beat. But her mind was absolutely clear.

Roux stepped forward. He looked down at the gulf. Time slowed.

"Wait—Roux."

He turned around. "What?"

"I never thanked you."

"For what?"

"For loving me."

She would remember his smile in that second for the rest of her life. There was a loud rushing in her ears—Roux turned away to face the divide, his eyes fluttered closed (how she would miss those gray-blue eyes!), his body teetered on the ledge—

"*I wish—*"

With all her might, she reached out her hands and pushed.

PART FIVE

21

HE DIDN'T MAKE A SOUND. HE DIDN'T SHOUT. THE ARMS AND LEGS bicycled in the air for a fraction of a second, and then Roux was rolling down the side of the valley, bouncing with surprising sprightliness for such a tall, lanky frame. She could make out the faint thuds each time his body hit the rocks. Three-quarters of the way down, his fleece got caught on a particularly jagged edge and the body stopped rolling. She saw the odd angles of the limbs, contorted like a Chinese circus acrobat; the head was dangling in a position that was too close to the shoulder. She could make out the blood on the side of the cliff, a faint red smear like the trail marker that'd led Roux to his end here in this frozen valley in which no creature stirred.

She waited five minutes to make sure the body didn't move. If the heart hadn't stopped yet, it would most definitely stop by morning from hypothermia. Hikers died all the time on unmarked trails. It was an accident. A tragic accident. Tragic. Tragedy. An accidental tragedy. With difficulty, Ivy roused her limbs and climbed her way back up to the flat expanse where only moments ago, she and Roux had drunk the Dalmore and whispered their lovers' talk, a memory that was transforming by the second into a hazy dream from which she would wake and think that the man whose steely arms had embraced her were the arms of a stranger.

Why am I here, she asked herself, tripping over a branch and cutting her palm open, two drops of blood staining the snow in the shape of a spiky flower, a brilliant red spiky flower whose name she could not recall but had seen once—at the Crosses' wedding, perhaps. *A tragic accident.* Without knowing it, she'd begun to run, slipping and stumbling through the snow like a wounded animal whose only remaining instinct is to seek repose in the safety of its own dark den. *A tragic accident.* She repeated this phrase all the way to the main highway.

Snow was falling in thick tufts at the bottom of the valley. Every one of her footsteps was promptly filled with fresh powder. She reached the gravel road where she'd parked just as the sun dipped behind the top of a mountain. The windows of the car were frosted over with ice, the roof covered with an inch of snow. She blasted the heat inside the car. Without waiting for the air to warm, she stripped down to her underwear and changed into the outfit she'd packed that morning: gray sweatpants, a flannel shirt, an old college sweatshirt, fresh socks, shearling boots, a heavy goose-down parka that fell to her knees. As the temperature rose, her jaw finally loosened and her teeth began to chatter uncontrollably. Peeling off her socks revealed feet that were grotesquely devoid of color and shape, just white blocks of flesh so bloodless they gave the impression of being made of rubber. There were various bruises along her limbs, as if she'd taken a fall, and the skin around her ankles was stretched thin over the swollen joints and ached when she tightened the laces of her boots. With her fresh suede gloves, she wiped the steering wheel, the gearshift, the buttons. She examined every crevice for stray hairs, the bleached strands now easy to spot against the black leather. The inspection complete, she locked the car, hoisted her backpack over one shoulder, and walked.

STOCKSFIELD WAS AN eighty-five-minute walk away. Other than Red Wingz, the only other attraction for visitors was a bus stop where the 5:20 p.m. Concord Coach bus made its daily run to South Station. According to her plan, she would make it there with an hour to spare.

The sun had long disappeared but light was still clinging to the edges of the sky, which gradually became infused with color, wispy pinks and mauves and azure blues, the farther she pulled away from the mountains. She'd been afraid that cars would see her walking along the highway and pull over to ask where she was going, but there were few cars, only the odd SUV or truck, and no one stopped or even seemed to notice her. Twenty minutes later, when she'd walked herself into a trancelike rhythm, the cold didn't reach her anymore. Occasionally, she was seized by the sensation that something was missing, like the time she'd left her purse behind at a restaurant. She would stop and rack her brain, going over all the details again. Wallet. Phone. Car. Clothes. Body. Snow. Only when she felt certain that no detail had escaped her would she begin to walk again. She felt empty and alone and numb. She imagined that this was what it would be like to be back in her mother's womb, surrounded by amniotic fluid, the outside world a strange and foreign place that did not touch her.

Soon she began to see signs of civilization. There were more cars, the two-lane highway became a local road called Crest Lane. Ivy took notice of the cars she passed, the pedestrians waiting by the cross-walk. She used to be afraid of the crossing guard when she was young. What a silly girl she'd been. She was so tired. She was down to her last cigarette.

When she finally reached town—a dirty, graffitied sign wearily announced itself: WELCOME TO STOCKSFIELD, HOME OF THE FIRST TAVERN—she turned onto the main road and saw a Dunkin' Donuts. She checked her phone. It was twenty past four, exactly an hour before the bus arrived. She marveled at her own punctuality. She went inside, ordered a half dozen donuts and a large coffee, and wolfed everything down at a booth overlooking the deserted parking lot. The donuts were delicious.

A police officer walked into the store. Ivy ducked her head so violently she knocked over the coffee. Scalding liquid spread through the thick fibers of her sweatpants, lighting her thighs on fire. She grabbed her backpack and fled to the bathroom. She immediately heaved into the toilet, bringing up the colorful mush of undigested pink frosting and rainbow sprinkles, and then a thin yellow liquid near the end. She sat on the cold floor, head between her knees. Seconds, maybe minutes passed, she didn't know. The sound of wailing startled her. It was coming from her throat.

When she stopped heaving, it was 5:02. She peeked out the door. The policeman had left. She rinsed her mouth and came out from the restroom. At the commercial-sized dumpster behind the store, she unzipped her backpack and took out the plastic bag containing her hiking boots, thermal underwear, fleece jacket, gloves, wool socks, the keys to the Audi, and Roux's phone, pounded to a pulp by a large piece of scrap metal she'd picked up somewhere along the highway—and dumped the entire load in the black bin.

She made it to the bus stop with five minutes to spare. She slept the entire ride back to Boston.

WHEN ANDREA KNOCKED on the bedroom door holding an extra-large beef noodle soup in a Le's takeout bag, Ivy was so weak and feverish that Andrea insisted they go to urgent care. The overwhelmed night nurse, knee-deep in bronchitis cases, took one look at Ivy and promptly instructed Andrea to take her to the emergency room.

After hours of blood tests and urine samples by white coats prodding her swollen stomach, pressing their cold stethoscopes against her chest and back, all of them wearing the same mask of distracted confusion and concern, it was finally a baby-faced nurse who asked Ivy about her diet. "Have you had any fruits or vegetables in the last six months?" Ivy said she couldn't remember. "You're the roommate," the nurse said to Andrea. "What does she eat?" Luckily, Andrea, like all chronic dieters obsessed with food, could rattle off every single bite she'd ever seen Ivy put into her skinny mouth. Instant ramen, canned spam, canned soup, dried crackers, bread, peanut butter, marshmallow fluff, the occasional pastry and chocolate, boiled noodles, alcohol,

more alcohol, soda, coffee. All in minuscule quantities,
alcohol. "Let me guess," said the nurse, "she smokes as
nodded eagerly. "Constantly. It keeps the appetite down. ....
married in two months."

An hour later, a large crowd of doctors had assembled inside Ivy's
room and gathered around her bed, the atmosphere one of suppressed
hilarity and amazement, to see the crazy lady who had gone and given
herself scurvy, the sailor's disease, in the modern age.

ANDREA CAME BACK to the hospital with a bag of fruit from the vendor
on the corner: five oranges, three apples, a bag of muscat grapes, and
a pomegranate she hacked open with a paring knife. "I called Gideon
and told him what happened," she said. "He wants me to tell you he's
taking an earlier flight back."

After Ivy finished eating, her belly was stretched out like a pregnant
lady in her second trimester. She was on the toilet all night long, her
body no longer used to fiber. But the next morning, the swelling in her
belly and ankles went down, the cut in her hand began to clot, and she
was discharged with vitamin C: a hundred milligrams every day for
the next three months.

That first night home, she couldn't recognize her face in the bathroom mirror. It was a frightening face, the face of a deranged mental
patient she'd once seen in a Japanese horror film. There was a long
scratch down her throat as if someone had clawed her. She picked at
the thin scab until it started bleeding.

Gideon came to the house the next morning. "You dyed your hair!"
he said, depositing a grocery bag full of fruit juices onto the bedside
table.

"Isn't it gorgeous?" Andrea prompted.

"She's always gorgeous," said Gideon, his light tone veiling the
flicker of concern as he kissed one sunken cheek.

He came every night thereafter to deliver Poppy's home-cooked

meals: roasted cauliflower, pork chops, hoisin-flavored stir-fries—
"She's bought a Chinese cookbook," said Gideon. And always fruit:
grapefruit, plums, unripened kiwis as hard as apples.

"You don't have to come every day," said Ivy. "I'm perfectly fine." Indeed, she did feel better, terrific actually, in terms of mental clarity. Her
muscles were still weak and atrophied but the sluggishness had receded;
she felt pleasantly alert, like the steady buzz you get after a second cup
of coffee. With nothing to do but eat and regain her strength until the
wedding, she began to knit a scarf for Gideon. Her disorderly thoughts
gathered around this project like cotton around a spool, giving purpose
to otherwise formless impulses. After the scarf, she purchased a camera
and began to take photos. She liked to photograph corners—windows,
doorframes, book spines. But mostly she took photos of herself. She'd
always been vain, unable to resist any mirror or reflective surface, but
now her preoccupation with her looks reached truly narcissistic lev-
els; she couldn't stop examining herself, thirty times a day, in the bathroom, the camera, her laptop screen. She no longer derived pleasure
from her looks because she no longer thought herself beautiful, and
yet this new ugliness fascinated her. It was the ugliness of a woman
stripped bare, without the armor of makeup or contrived cynicism, as
if the white translucent skin stretched over the high cheekbones were
the only thing separating the soul from the flesh. The masklike eyes
gazing through the Polaroids were not her own.

Her birthday came. She was twenty-eight, peering into the prec-
ipice of thirty, that frightening decade where frivolity went to die.
She had never before longed for frivolous things as she did now; she
wanted to go to Disney World, wear her old Grove uniform, suck on
lollipops, clap her hands over prettily wrapped presents with bows.
Gideon made her a stack of blueberry and chocolate chip pancakes for
breakfast. He'd stuck a single pink-and-white-striped candle on top:
"Make a wish." She blew the candle out without wishing for anything.

After breakfast, they went around his old stomping grounds in
Cambridge. Gideon got a double scoop of mint chocolate chip at J.P.

Licks and then they went up to the Lowell House bell and rang it, sharing nostalgic stories of their college years. The view from the tower looked out onto a snow-covered courtyard and steepled rooftops of brick buildings where bundled students hurried in and out of revolving doors. It seemed to Ivy a world in miniature, but the cold, the wind, the height gave her a sickening sensation that she'd been here before. She quickly descended. Over dinner, Gideon handed her a book wrapped in tissue paper. "It's not much . . ." It was a journal, not a book, bound in calfskin leather so buttery Ivy's bare fingers scuffed the brown cover just holding it. Her name was engraved on the lower right corner. "You're figuring a lot of things out now," said Gideon, "and I thought it would help to write down your thoughts."

Ivy took his hand over the table.

"Today's been . . ." She started again. "I'm so lucky to have you."

"We'll be married soon."

"Yes."

"How are you feeling?"

"Wonderful. Amazing. I can't wait to be married to you."

He seemed on the verge of saying something, but then a look of resolve came over his face.

"What about you?" she asked quickly.

"I feel the same way," he replied, squeezing her fingers. Again that flicker of hesitation. "It's just I want you to be sure," he said. "It's been a whirlwind and I think this is a good time to catch our breath. Check in with each other."

Ivy's acutely tuned ear heard the doubt in his voice—it was he, not she, who wanted to be sure—and responded to it by clinging to him even more tenaciously: staying over at his house, cooking him breakfast, greeting him after work with bottles of wine and elaborately plated cheese boards. She was desperate, she'd lost the ability for subtlety. She felt her sins must be leaking out of her and causing Gideon to have these second thoughts.

One night, she woke up as if someone had screamed in her ear. Her breath came in shallow gasps. A small reading lamp was on; Gideon was working on his laptop beside her.

"Did I wake you?" he asked apologetically.

"No." Her trembling hands clenched into fists underneath the linen sheets.

"You were talking in your sleep."

Ivy stilled. "What'd I say?"

"Something about cats. It was cute."

She made a meowing noise, nerves coloring her cheeks a pretty pink. They laughed easily and he went back to his laptop.

The next day, Ivy went to a sleep specialist.

"I have nightmare disorder," she said, rattling off the symptoms she'd looked up on the Internet. The doctor prescribed her two hundred milligrams of trazodone. Ivy doubled the dose, just to be safe. She stopped dreaming entirely, but the downside was that time now passed by at the speed of molasses dripping down a windowpane. She no longer liked to leave the house. She had the newspaper and groceries delivered to Gideon's apartment, and subscribed to a wine-of-the-week club in his name.

THREE WEEKS LATER, she saw an article about it in the *Boston Globe*. "Missing Hiker Fell to Tragic Death." Panting, she scanned the pages.

It was all there, the details she'd planted and some she hadn't considered: Roux Roman, a thirty-one-year-old restaurateur, went hiking in the southern end of the White Mountains, where he fell to his death in a hidden ditch. They'd discovered a frozen-over car parked by the side of the road. The highway snow patrol phoned the police when the driver failed to come back after two days. When they went to the address listed on file, no one was home. The obvious conclusion was that he was still in the mountains somewhere and had never made it back to his car. They sent out a search team to cover the vicinity of the mountain. Nothing was found. The snow had covered all the tracks.

It wasn't until the snow melted that another hiker stumbled upon Roux's location. A fifty-year-old native of New Hampshire explained that his dog kept barking at this one ledge, and, curious, the man had walked over and seen an empty bottle of Dalmore and a man's wallet on the edge of a cliff. He reported it to the park rangers, who matched the driver's license to the man who owned the car. That was how they were able to use a rope to lower down the side of the mountain and spot the frozen body of Roux Roman, exactly where Ivy had left him.

"DID YOU HEAR about Roux?" Sylvia asked. Her honeycomb eyes were glistening with tears, the skin pink and swollen, casting her peaky face with a girlish innocence. "I can't believe it—I can't believe it."

"Sib—breathe. Tell me what happened."

Sylvia thrust the paper into her brother's concerned face. They scanned it. Ivy allowed her expression to sink. "Oh no," she said. "This is awful."

Gideon went to his sister, who cried on his chest, her hands curled into two little fists tucked under her chin.

"I don't understand. What was he doing *hiking*? He hates hiking. He hates leaving his house. I just can't believe it."

Gideon soothed Sylvia, motioning for Ivy to hand him the box of tissues on the side table. From the sharp pressure in her chest, Ivy knew she was suffering. But unlike the suffering of before whenever she witnessed the bond between the Speyer siblings, now her pain seemed beside the point. It was a matter of contrast. People could almost always adapt to chronic pain.

"You said you saw him a few weeks ago?" Gideon asked his sister.

Ivy dropped the tissues.

"We ran into each other at Frederich's exhibition." Sylvia sobbed. "And I *ignored* him. He l-l-looked *horrible* . . . there was some woman with him . . ."

Gideon looked at Ivy. She couldn't breathe. Gideon *knew*. His eyes were full of accusation . . . of hate!

Gideon tilted his head, still staring at her. His mouth moved but no sound came out of it. It took a second before Ivy realized he was mouthing *tissues* as his eyes flicked toward the fallen box of Kleenex on Sylvia's carpet.

Covered in cold sweat, Ivy reached down with trembling fingers . . .

"How are *you* feeling?" he asked, thirty minutes later on their drive back.

"A little sleepy," she said. "Too much wine."

"I meant about Roux. You must be upset."

"Oh, I know. It's such a tragic accident."

"You guys were close"—Ivy recoiled—"when you were young," Gideon finished. His eyes gleamed red in the reflection of a stoplight.

ROUX'S MEMORIAL WAS on a Wednesday. It was drizzling, the leaves just beginning to bud, the wet earth and grass and worms drenching the graveyard with smells of spring. The ceremony was already under way when Ivy arrived. There was a small group of people, no more than twenty, most of them Italian, and two pasty-skinned men conversing in what sounded like Polish. There were only three other women there besides Ivy, all over the age of fifty and wearing identical outfits of wool, knee-length skirts with black stockings, and turtleneck sweaters with silver brooches on the left breast.

Ivy knew it was stupid of her to come. But since the article announcing Roux's death, the floodgate had opened and she could think of nothing else but Roux. Roux, naked in his apartment, drinking orange juice. Roux at Finn Oaks, his feet propped up on the deck of the boat, one arm thrown over his eye. Roux in the tub with skin like pink pebbles. Roux's dark locks flicking over one eye, dimples flashing, as he bent down to light a cigarette. The body she'd left behind on that mountain—she placed no more significance on it than on the roadkill she passed on the freeway. That wasn't Roux. At least not her memories of him. But over the last month, time had slowly thawed her frozen emotions and now she awoke to the reality that Roux was really gone. It felt like a bad dream. It was as if he really *had* died in a hiking accident, an event that had nothing to do with her, and she was only here at his funeral to mourn their friendship, the same as any other bereaved guest.

They'd cremated his body and the ashes were held in a silver urn. When they lowered the urn to the ground, a flock of crows took off from a nearby power line; their wings flapping, their desolate cries sounded to Ivy like an accusation. She thought she was relatively hidden under the awning of a giant oak, its dark branches brushing the ground like knuckles, but one man kept glancing toward her. When he took off his sunglasses, Ivy recognized Ernesto Moretti, now a bulky man of thirty, with a long hooked nose, deep-set eyes, and floppy black hair. She stepped farther back into the tree's shadows.

The officiant said a few words, then the mourners went up and dropped handfuls of dirt onto the mound. The workers began to fill the hole. By the time the ground was level, the light drizzle had turned into a downpour.

"Excuse me? Are you Ivy?" Ernesto's surly face was suddenly before her. She'd been too focused on the workers.

Blood rushed to Ivy's face. "I—no—" She backed away.

"Would you like to get a cup of coffee?"

Before she could decline, Ernesto was steering her into a black Benz parked around the corner. Ivy's heel caught on a sewer hole. Ernesto said, "Be careful now," and gripped her tighter with one meaty fist.

He knows everything, Ivy thought. And then the fear left her. She could finally surrender; there was no need for futile pretenses in the presence of an all-knowing being.

The driver went around the corner to a Starbucks.

In a dimly lit booth, Ivy and Ernesto sat facing each other, waiting for the other to speak. The barista called out Ivy's name. She went and fetched their drinks, carefully placing the espresso in front of Ernesto with two hands.

"Roux's spoke of you to me," Ernesto said finally.

"Yes."

"So you know?"

"Yes."

He reached down and pulled out from his briefcase a small package wrapped in brown paper.

"Open it when you get home," he said. "If you ever need anything, my number's on the inside. Just call."

"What is it?" Ivy asked.

"Open it at home."

They stared at each other—she in confusion, he with an air of expectancy.

"Thank you," she said at last.

"You were the little girl from Fox Hill, weren't you?"

"Excuse me?"

"I never forget a face. You and Roux were always hanging around back in the old neighborhood." All the lines on Ernesto's face smiled with him.

Ivy said, "I guess." Her throat closed in sorrow. She waited.

"Do you know how he died?" he asked.

"I—I read about it in the papers."

"Do you believe it?"

She whispered, "Do you?"

Ernesto sighed, a deep rattling sound from the depths of his protruding stomach. "This shit's fucked up. Poor fucker." He stood up, then scanned the Starbucks with the aggression of checking for bombs.

It dawned on Ivy he was leaving. Astonishment made her feet tap violently against the floor, the rubber heels of her sneakers squeaking against the linoleum tiles.

"Wait," she said.

Ernesto turned.

She had the wild idea of blurting out the truth—that it was her, it was *her*.

"Roux spoke of you, too," she said instead. "He said your family helped him out all those years ago. He talked about his mom and your dad . . ."

Ernesto's shoulders rose up. "The old man's dead," he said curtly. Then the door opened and the sound of rain drowned out his next words. She could see his mouth moving—the wide lips, the nicotine-stained teeth—but she couldn't make out his voice over the rush of tires, the howling of the wind. The door closed with a sharp bang.

IVY WENT HOME and opened the package. It was a book. The glossy front cover was a photograph of some business tycoon smiling with all his teeth showing. She opened it and made a noise of surprise. The center of the pages had been cut out. There was a pristine stack of hundred-dollar bills, almost two inches thick, and a note scribbled in a childish handwriting in permanent marker: *Call me when you run out.* It was the same handwriting as the person who'd left her the keys to the Audi in her mailbox. She hurried to the window and drew the blinds closed.

She lay facedown on her pillow. She didn't bother counting the money. Was he watching her, even now? No. I'm alone. The anguish came all at once, hot and suffocating. She hit the side of her head, once, twice. I'm alone, Roux.

WHENEVER SHE CAUGHT Gideon's eyes without meaning to—looking up from cutting her steak, coming out of the bathroom, when he glanced up from his laptop without warning—Ivy would feel a jerking sensation, like when your chair leans too far back. Fear would prick her temples, her heart would wrench as if trying to leap out of her rib cage. She could see the flicker of doubt and uncertainty as he sensed in her the presence of some furtive secret.

Then she woke one morning and discovered it was May. The sun was out and the dripping of snow melting outside her windowsill sounded like hope. Gideon came over with a sesame chicken salad and a huge carton of strawberries. "First of the season," he said. Ivy noticed that he'd cut off the stems of the strawberries, including the little brown knobs that she'd once told him she didn't like.

"I d-don't know why I'm crying," she said as Gideon held her. "Look, I've ruined your nice s-s-sweater . . . I'm so s-sorry—"

"We don't have to rush things, you know," he said, smoothing her hair. "If you feel any doubts whatsoever . . ."

She practically had to beg him to marry her all over again, blubbering that it wasn't the wedding, she loved him and she wanted to marry him, she was just being sentimental, her grandmother was getting old, there was so much *pressure*—

"But that's what I'm saying," Gideon said, gripping her tightly by the shoulders, his own lips pale, his eyes insistent with some unutterable message he wished her to understand. "There shouldn't *be* any pressure. We can push things back, take our time to make sure this is what we really want, what *you* really want. I don't want you to regret anything—"

"You don't love me anymore?" she whispered. He knew. *He knew.*

I love you, he said, of course I love you. But he wanted her to be sure, he felt guilty sometimes because—

She kissed him to stop him from talking about guilt and other laughable things he couldn't possibly understand.

After that, no more was said about delaying the wedding.

From time to time, when Gideon didn't know she was watching him, she would see on his face the same conflicted, unhappy expression that told her she wasn't doing a good enough job of hiding her restless paranoia. She was on constant vigil against herself, observing her face each morning with the suspicion one feels for an enemy spy masquerading as a friend. She felt she was capable of anything—her arms might jerk the steering wheel and send her body careening into the Charles, her hands might choke her to death in her sleep. If only she could make it to the wedding, she would be able to breathe again. All her old hopeful vibrancy would be restored to those early days of her and Gideon's courtship, when the city air seemed perfumed with wine and sweet blossoms, and the indestructible certainty of her life was as present as her own heartbeat.

22

THE WOMEN'S DRESSING ROOM AT ST. STEPHEN'S WAS A CONVERTED music room. The instruments had been taken away and replaced with a love seat and armchairs; an enormous antique mirror was propped up next to an open window, displaying on a beveled edge Ivy's wedding gown in all its iridescent, billowing glory. At half past eleven, the Lins crowded inside. The mirror gave the impression there were a dozen Chinese people in the room, all clamoring for the bride's attention.

Nan insisted Ivy try on the dress one more time. "Your tailor's no good," she said about the expert seamstress from New York who'd done the alterations. "In the picture you sent me, the dress looked like it was falling off your chest." She scrutinized Ivy's breasts, then shook her head. "You'll have a hard time breastfeeding, like me."

Ivy changed into her wedding dress, mostly to stop Nan from nagging. There was so much fabric: layers upon layers of tulle and silk and lace embroidery. Having failed to regain most of the weight she'd lost, her shoulder blades poked out of her back, like stunted wings. Her arms were white bones, her face a sharp triangle. She'd dyed her hair back to black, for the photographs, and the heavy strands weighing her head back were the only voluptuous part about her, and even that was fake, buoyed up by forty hair extensions.

She stepped out from behind the dressing curtain.

"Put on the shoes, too," said Meifeng.

After much prodding and pinching, both Nan and Meifeng agreed that the waist needed to be taken in another centimeter.

"Does a centimeter really matter?" Ivy asked.

"Don't sulk," said Meifeng.

"I will do it," Nan decided.

"*Laura* will do it," said Ivy. "She's brought her sewing machine today, don't worry."

Nan wiped the edge of Ivy's lip with a handkerchief she conjured from nowhere. She asked Ivy if she wanted water, then immediately forgot her offer while fixing a loose thread on the hem of the dress.

Shen and Austin returned to the room. "Wow. So beautiful," said Shen. Austin said, "You look nice," and handed her a daisy he'd probably plucked from the bushes outside the church. Ivy impulsively stuck it behind her ear. Nan plucked it back out and tossed it on the table. "Did you take your medicine yet?" she said sternly. Austin said, "No, I forgot," and went to find a bottle of water to wash down his "happy pills," as Shen took to calling the Cymbalta.

"Try on the other dress," Meifeng told Ivy. She was talking about the gown Ivy would change into for the reception, a high-collared red-and-gold silk *qipao* Meifeng had custom-made for Ivy in China. The box it arrived in was as large as a funeral casket. It was actually Poppy's suggestion that Ivy wear a Chinese-style dress for the reception. It was a compromise they'd reached because Ivy had decided there would be no show or Chinese ceremony. Nan had only looked at her blankly when Ivy asked what rituals their ancestors had performed when they got married. "They signed papers and went out to a restaurant," said Nan. "So no dragon dances or tea ceremonies?" asked Ivy. Nan hooted with laughter.

When Meifeng saw Ivy step out in the *qipao*, she suddenly had to sit down. "Look at me getting all excited, too," she said ruefully, "like a fool. It makes me remember when your grandpa and I got married. We could only afford to take our families out to eat noodles. But it *felt* just like this."

Outside, Ivy heard the voice of her wedding planner directing the vendors this way and that.

"We have to go," said Shen, checking his watch. The Lins were having lunch with Ted and Poppy at the famous restaurant inside the Millennium Hotel. Ivy had heard her parents plotting earlier on how best to snatch the check, as if they expected resistance from the Speyers, who Ivy knew wouldn't lift a finger of protest. She'd learned long ago from Sunrin that not all forms of wealth were equal, and the form of wealth Ted and Poppy manifested was much like their breeding—omnipresent yet invisible. No one could touch it or see it or prove its existence, yet who was to say that they *weren't* wealthy, as Meifeng often grumbled, just because they didn't own their town house and couldn't afford repairs for an old summer cottage?

"Tell her now," Nan said to Shen.

"Later," said Shen.

"There won't be time later," Nan said impatiently. "Just tell her. It'll make her happy."

"Tell me what?" said Ivy.

"Your mama and I want to help you and Gideon buy your first house," said Shen. "It's our wedding present to you."

"You already paid for the wedding," Ivy said quickly. "It's enough."

"Not enough. When you're ready, just come to us." Shen patted her on the shoulder, then hurried out the door, the back of his neck a ruddy pink over the crisp white collar of his dress shirt.

Nan checked her reflection in the mirror one last time. "How do I look?" she asked shyly.

"Very well," said Ivy. "You look very pretty."

"Who looks younger, me or Gideon's mother?"

"*You* do."

Nan chuckled and called after Shen, "You hear our daughter? She says—"

Austin gave Ivy a long, clenching embrace on his way out. "I used to hate Gideon," he said. "I thought he was so stuck-up."

"And now?" said Ivy.

"He's not so bad."

Meifeng was last. She took Ivy's hand between her own.

"Remember you can always come home."

Home ... home ... home! Ivy's mouth trembled into a confused smile.

"You're a good girl," said Meifeng. "Grandma can die happy now, seeing you like this."

Finally, the exhausting procession was over and Ivy was blessedly alone again. She sat back down in her chair and waited for the next thing. She didn't know what it was but she was sure someone would materialize and direct her toward it. This was how her life would be now. The thought gave her great relief. When no one came for ten minutes, however, the lull suddenly became unbearable and she decided to slip outside for her last cigarette. She'd only had a handful since leaving the hospital. The idea of quitting now seemed no more difficult than abstaining from some poorly cooked dish she didn't much care for. Just like that—the last cigarette.

She idled over to the little garden some yards away from the chapel, wearing only her robe and hotel slippers, thinking she wouldn't run into anyone, when she heard familiar voices coming from underneath the weeping willow. Gideon and his groomsmen were supposed to be playing a round of golf before getting ready at the church by three o'clock. Instead, she saw Gideon and Tom deep in conversation, heads nearly touching.

"Hello," she called out.

They looked up in unison, blinking at her emerging figure silhouetted against the noonday sun. As she walked across the lawn, the stench of alcohol oxidizing on sun-baked skin grew presently stronger. She soon confirmed the source of the smell to be Tom, blotchy and pale, clutching a wineglass in one hand with a sheen of sweat covering his upper lip. Gideon wasn't holding a glass but he, too, was pale; he stood leaning against the tree with an alert stillness that struck Ivy as somehow unnatural.

She pretended to check her watch. "Christ, Tom, it's not even lunch yet."

Tom blinked woodenly.

"Where's Roland?" she asked.

"He's fetching the golf cart," said Gideon. "Someone took it out this morning without knowing we had a reservation."

"You're not supposed to see me yet," Ivy said suddenly, taking a step back as if to curb the damage. "It's bad luck."

"Should I cover my eyes?" said Gideon.

"Too late."

"Care to share?" said Tom. He was looking at the pack of Camels clutched in her other hand. Her robe didn't have pockets.

"They're not mine," said Ivy. They weren't. They were Roux's.

"Do you smoke often?" Gideon asked politely.

Ivy blinked in surprise. "No. Not often." She tossed Tom the entire pack. He barely managed to catch it.

"Go on," said Tom, flicking the lighter at her.

Ivy hesitated. She glanced at Gideon but he seemed mesmerized by the fountain across the lawn. What the hell. She took one. A breeze tickled the back of her neck. She listened to the faraway sound of a lawn mower, the chirping of birds, the gurgle from the two stone Cupids pouring weak streams of water out of fat Roman jugs. Polite, orderly sounds for the polite, orderly life awaiting her.

"That noise makes me want to piss," said Tom listlessly. No one bothered with a response.

Ivy shifted her weight from one foot to the other. The silence dragged on. She felt as if she were at the end of a sloppy party in which she, Tom, and Gideon were the only ones remaining, all of them dispirited and tired of one another yet unwilling to be the first one to leave.

"I really have to piss," Tom repeated. He stubbed out his half-smoked cigarette on the tree and flung it into the grass. He took a long while to pull himself upright. "Well—Giddy. It was a good run.

See you lovebirds on the other side." He gripped Gideon's upper arm in that forceful gesture macho men use in lieu of hugs.

Gideon said, "Wait, T-T-T-Tom." Tom turned around. "Sober up, pal," said Gideon.

Tom made a jaunty salute, his benevolent smile almost rendering his once-handsome face boyish again. Ivy watched him saunter into the chapel. She turned to Gideon with a sympathetic smile, as if they shared the same relief in being rid of a burdensome friend, but whatever words she'd been about to say died on her lips. Gideon's eyes were still on Tom's back. He was panting lightly, his mouth contorted, his brow so furrowed he appeared either in pain or in rage. She had never before seen such a look on Gideon's face.

When he realized she was watching him, his features artfully rearranged themselves, as if an invisible hand had smoothed over his face. "How are your parents liking Cattahasset?" He smiled with obvious effort.

She must have managed to formulate a response because he was nodding and smiling and she was smiling back—or else they were both so lost in their own charade they might as well have been two deaf-mute people miming to each other.

She kept hearing Gideon's infinitesimal pauses between the soft T's when he'd said Tom's name. She couldn't unsee the frightening look on Gideon's face as he watched Tom walk away, nor Tom's hands gripping Gideon's arm, the comic bravado of a tragic farewell. But why was there need for such a tragic farewell? Gideon was only getting married . . . yet he was in agony—the look on his face could only be called agony—because he didn't want Tom to leave. He wanted Tom to stay, because . . . because Gideon was in love with Tom.

And Tom . . . and Gideon—!

Her breath stopped. A million images filtered through her mind—there must have been clues. Yes, she remembered many instances now. Breadcrumbs become obvious when one sees through the eyes of a bird. But she hadn't known . . . she hadn't bothered to look! She'd believed in Gideon's integrity, in his noble character, his fine, dashing manners and courage, which had felt a little heartbreaking when it came to his impotence—but even that flaw had only served to reinforce his innocence, that he should lack the animal desire that'd led so many others astray.

She'd been wrong about everything. The shadowy figure she'd sensed between them hadn't been Roux but Tom. It'd always been Tom.

What to do. *What to do.*

"There's Roland," Gideon said, nodding toward the green golf cart slowly making its way up the hill.

"I'm going inside," Ivy heard herself say. She repeated Tom's goodbye: "See you on the other side." Gideon's lips were hot and dry on her cheek. She floated back to the church. She was still holding her cigarette. The remaining clump of ash fell on her arm. She didn't feel a thing.

IVY LAY ON the love seat watching the minute hand tick by. Why had Gideon asked her to marry him? What did he want from her? She could call off the wedding, she thought listlessly. She could take a taxi home. But she didn't move.

Andrea arrived at two o'clock in a torrent of shopping bags and overwhelming perfume. "Ivy, you're flattening your extensions!" she squealed, dropping her bags in front of the mirror. Ivy opened her eyes. She wondered if she'd fallen asleep.

"Have you eaten?" Andrea asked. She pulled a large platter of assorted sashimi and two bottles of green tea from a takeout bag. Since returning from Machu Picchu with an eight-carat diamond ring, Andrea had lost no time in starting her wedding diet. Only fish and seaweed. She ran five miles a day around the Common, fractured her tibia, and continued running.

Ivy obediently picked up her chopsticks. Her stomach turned at the taste of raw, oily flesh in her mouth. She spit the salmon in a napkin and turned to Andrea abruptly. "Do you think a gay man can love women?"

"Norman's *not* gay," said Andrea, her eyes watering from a large mound of wasabi. "I know everyone thinks he is because of the way he looks—he gets hit on *all the time* at gay bars—but trust me, he's practically homophobic." Andrea paused. "He's not homophobic—oh, you know what I mean."

Ivy went back to staring at the minute hand ticking by.

When Sylvia drifted through the door in cutoff shorts and studded ankle boots, she greeted Ivy with an air of bemused friendliness, as if she'd ended up here by accident. She flung herself down on an armchair.

"Mom wanted me to give you this." She took out a little silver tiara from her tote bag. "It's one of her last-minute whims. She cried for an entire hour by herself this morning looking at Gideon's baby photos."

Andrea made a gasp of pleasure and asked if the photos would be displayed at the entrance table.

"No, I don't think so," said Sylvia, smiling quizzically.

"We met at the Swingbox party," Andrea prompted. "You were there with Jeremy?"

"Remind me your name again?" said Sylvia.

Andrea told her.

"You're engaged to Norman Moorefield."

Andrea looked as if she might die of happiness.

Ivy said, "Andrea, can you see if you can find a cooler and some ice? There's a kitchen somewhere in this church."

"For what?"

"For the bucket of champagne over there."

After Andrea left, Ivy gestured toward the sushi.

"Thank you," said Sylvia. "I love this place."

"Did you know this entire time?" Ivy asked, deliberately waiting until Sylvia was fully immersed in her food.

"Know what?"

"About Gideon and Tom."

"What about them?"

Ivy was impressed. Sylvia hadn't even stopped chewing, so seamless was her transition from friendliness to battle. Or maybe battle was her normal mode of existence. Her impassive face revealed nothing but the cold-blooded hardness of someone used to calling other people's bluffs and winning.

"You did know," Ivy said with a soft sigh. She lay back down on the love seat and let her arm flop over her forehead. She saw herself from the bird's-eye view: *Fainting Woman on Chaise*. She told herself to focus. She'd come so far.

The room was silent except for the sound of her own shallow breathing. She could practically hear Sylvia's mind churning.

"Is that why you threw me at him?" Ivy asked, talking more to herself. "You sold your family to me so aggressively. You knew what I wanted to hear. I always wondered why you set me up with Gideon even though you hated me. All those talks about how *perfect* I am for him . . ." She drifted off, shocked by the pain in her chest. The blue-blooded visions of love and family she so admired were, for Tom and Gideon, also shackles that kept them marching in lockstep to the beat of a patriarchal master. For a brief moment she even felt a flash of pity. That Gideon loved Tom hurt less than the fact that Sylvia had made a fool of her. She wondered why that was.

"I don't know what you think you know," Sylvia said finally, putting down her chopsticks. "I don't hate you. I quite admire you, actually. The way you're able to draw Gideon out without smothering him—a fine line many others have failed to walk."

"Draw him out," Ivy repeated. "Why? Because he's keeping me at a distance *out of love*? *It's a fear mechanism?*" She hadn't realized until that moment how much she'd relied on Sylvia's explanations, provided so aptly at the beginning of her courtship with Gideon, to reassure herself that the lurking hesitations she'd sensed in him weren't real issues, because his sister said they were normal, and in fact, Gideon only behaved thus because Ivy was *special* to him.

"I need a drink," she said in panic.

Sylvia went to the corner, uncorked one of the bottles of champagne, and poured out a tall glass.

"Here—chug it. Try not to pass out on me. I don't know CPR."

Ivy drank and drank. It wasn't champagne but some kind of sweet brandy, rough and fiery, shooting straight through to her pelvis. "Did you find him all his past girlfriends, too?" she said hoarsely, wiping her mouth on the back of her hand.

Sylvia watched her with a vague air of disgust, the kind usually reserved for hysterical women like Andrea.

"Why me?" said Ivy.

"You and Gideon *are* perfect for each other," Sylvia said after a while. "He needs a woman like you to feel useful. He wants that kind of hero worship. And you want a hero." Ivy flinched. "And here's the thing," Sylvia pressed on perceptively, "he'll never let you down. What other man out there has that kind of consistency? Sure, they can be perfect for a month. A year. But a lifetime? *You've* been around the block. There's a reason you get bored with other men, yet Gideon keeps you infatuated. It's because you sense his ironclad resolve. You want to break him, but you can't."

Despite her pulsing anger, Ivy felt a twinge of admiration. She'd never thought selfish Sylvia was capable of putting up such a fight on behalf of another person. Had she ever done anything half as heroic for Austin?

"Did he really have other girlfriends?" she repeated. This seemed to be the most important point in the whole world.

"Of course. He wasn't a monk before he met you, no matter what Poppy thinks."

"And they were happy?"

"How should I know?"

"Should I leave him?"

Sylvia's gaze sprayed over her like a cold sea breeze. "Why? What is it you think he's done? Let's go find him right now and talk it over."

The horror was immediate and overwhelming. Ivy felt she could do anything, kill anyone, to avoid *that* conversation. This was Sylvia's final trump card, she realized. Gideon's sister knew Ivy couldn't do it. Couldn't say it. Sylvia understood the power of social conduct. That unimpeachable code of silence that had brushed generations of scandals under a linen-draped dinner table.

Also . . . Ivy hadn't *really* seen anything out of the ordinary . . . Sylvia was right, what *was* she accusing Gideon of? He'd only called out Tom's name. It'd led to her moment of blind terror out on the lawn, but her mind was under enormous stress from her meds, the drinking, the paranoia that Gideon would leave her . . . *perhaps her mind had concocted a reason to leave Gideon.* People sabotaged themselves all the time. And in the virginal afternoon light of the music room, with Sylvia idly applying lipstick in front of the mirror as if the situation were so inconsequential she couldn't be bothered to give it her full attention, Ivy felt her doubt grow like thorns, crushing the buds of her previous certainty.

Sylvia blotted her lips with the pad of her ring finger. "So you're planning to leave Giddy at the altar?"

"No!"

The response flew out of Ivy so vehemently it surprised both of them.

"There you have it then," said Sylvia, watching her from the mirror. The hard, amber eyes gleamed with triumph.

"I don't care about Gideon's past," Ivy said, picking Austin's daisy up off the table and rolling it between her fingers. "We all have our secrets. What's important is that we both love each other." It was true. She loved Gideon. He loved her. And there was the white billowing dress hanging on the mirror, the shimmering *qipao* that had brought Meifeng to tears, two hundred guests about to arrive in a few hours for a night of revelry, the tiara Poppy had bequeathed her, and years and years of vacations in Cattahasset waiting for her, the house Shen would buy for them when they were ready . . . *Remember you can always come home* . . . that's right, even if the world imploded, she could always return home . . .

A wonderful tranquillity washed into Ivy's heart. She finally understood the thing that no one could take away from you—it was family. That burdensome, unbreakable, everlasting, unsentimental backing of one's family. She would draw upon the new strength and power of the Lins to face her in-laws for the first time as an equal. She'd even glimpsed the real Gideon—what else was there to fear? And perhaps . . . perhaps he had always seen the real her . . . Either way, she'd never know, because he would never slip up again, so it needn't matter. There would be no strings attached to their marriage, only mutual acceptance and admiration, unmarred by petty things like expectations. She would never again lower herself under anyone else's thumb.

She placed one hand over her heart, as if to affirm her decision, her existence. How strong the heart beat on.

She walked over and circled her arm around Sylvia's waist. "I'm so pleased we had this chat," she murmured. "I admire you, too. You take what you want without asking for permission . . . did you know that Roux always said you were a crafty fraud"—their eyes met in the mirror; she tucked the limp daisy behind Sylvia's ear—"but I never believed him because you are just *so beautiful*. I hope we can keep this talk between us girls—I don't want Gideon to think I wavered . . . *dear* Sibbie . . . we'll be sisters now." She felt the startled tremble of Sylvia's rib cage under her damp palms.

AT LONG LAST, her future was here, unfurling before her like a sunlit path lined with flowers and green things. Ivy was unaware of the guests, the music, the lights, the flowers, all the things she'd so foolishly assumed made up the magic of a wedding. The magic came from inside her. She only saw Gideon . . . Gideon standing upright in front of the altar, Gideon smiling, Gideon with an expression she'd waited for all her life, the expression she knew was reflected on her own face . . .what was it . . . oh!

It was a look of peace, that elusive feeling she'd sought, that they'd sought together . . . she stepped on the altar and didn't look back.

ACKNOWLEDGMENTS

Thank you to my wonderful agent, Jenni Ferrari-Adler, for believing in me from the get-go. You made everything possible; to have met you was my luck and *yuánfèn*, to have you on this journey with me is my fortune.

I am so grateful for my editor, Marysue Rucci, for being the most meticulous of readers and passionate of champions. You said an author only gets a debut once, and thank god mine was with you. *White Ivy* wouldn't be the book it is today if not for your innumerable insights, patience, and conviction in this story. In addition, thank you to the entire S&S team, particularly Zack Knoll, Hana Park, Maggie Southard Gladstone, and Elizabeth Breeden. You guys made this process seamless and welcomed me with warmth and encouragement.

Thank you to my two boisterous, loving families: the Ye and Yang clans. To my parents for making me feel brilliant and supported; to my brother, Derek Ye, lifelong serf, favorite eating companion, ally to the last; my yéye, in whose lap I learned the magic of stories; my Chongqing family who spoiled me all those hot, magical summers; and to my mother-in-law, Helen Fan, the epitome of class, grace, and strength; I hope to be half the woman you were.

I wouldn't have made it here without the wise advice of Glen David Gold, the early encouragement and astute edits of Josh Ferris, or the terrific writing communities of Tin House, Sackett Street, 92nd Street Y, the Writers Grotto, Squaw Valley Writers Workshop, and Slice

Literary Writers' Conference. These institutions are an aspiring writer's lifelines, and make all the difference.

Thank you to Stephen Hogsten, Tiffany Jin, Michelle Yang, and Emily Yang, for your early readings and kind feedback. Thanks to Pablo Montoya for your beautiful designs and for always having my back. To the friends who've supported me from the beginning, letting me write in your homes and during our cross-continental visits: Aneesh Devi, Joosung Kim, Hayang Lee, Rich Lem, Angela Wu. I am forever grateful to Lucy Tan, fellow INFJ, kindredest of kindred spirits. I would never have found the grit to write this novel if it weren't for your trailblazing example, candid advice, and writerly commiserations—I'm in your corner, always.

Lastly, thank you to Alex Yang, best of friends, best of husbands, and best of champions. To try and list everything you've done for me and this book is an impossible task. But make no mistake—*I know*. You will always be the first reader, and the last. Home is where you are.

ABOUT THE AUTHOR

SUSIE YANG was born in Chongqing, China, and has since lived in fourteen cities across three continents. While in San Francisco, she launched a start-up to teach entrepreneurs how to code. She studied creative writing at Tin House, Sackett Street, and the 92nd Street Y. She has a doctorate in pharmacy from Rutgers University. *White Ivy* is her debut novel.